The Secret Cottage

by

Kate Ellington

The Secret Cottage

Cover Art by *Jennifer Greeff*

The Wild Rose Press, Inc.
PO Box 708
Adams Basin, NY 14410-0708
Visit us at www.thewildrosepress.com

Publishing History
First Edition, 2024
Trade Paperback ISBN 978-1-5092-5366-4
Digital ISBN 978-1-5092-5367-8

Published in the United States of America

Acknowledgments

The first person I want to thank for unwavering support is my husband, Tom. When I had the idea for *The Secret Cottage*, he suggested I write it down. I never dreamed I'd fill one page of a notebook, never mind an entire book. He encouraged me not to give up on it being published one day, and listened to me talk about the story all the time.

My sisters Peggy, Laura, and Pammy have been supportive throughout the entire process. Pammy and Laura read the original manuscript when it was twice as long and almost a whole other story.

My wonderful friend Nancy read every version and gave invaluable feedback.

I must also mention my friend dear Brian, who always believed in me.

I'd like to thank my beta readers: Laura, Pammy, Nancy, Tom, Cat, and Christina. With their input I was able to polish and improve the story.

A few other people whose support has meant the world are: my parents, grandparents, nieces, nephews, and my friends Heidi and Corrine.

I'm grateful to my children, who on more than one occasion waited patiently for me to finish writing so we could move on to other things. They were encouraging, supportive, and helpful.

Lastly, I'd like to thank my amazing editor Nan Swanson and the team at The Wild Rose Press for publishing *The Secret Cottage*.

Chapter One

The mullioned windows of Thornwood Manor glistened in the early morning sun as Robert Claremont strode across the grounds, seeing to final preparations for today's May Day celebration. The clouds had finally lifted, leaving a clear blue sky still touched with shades of pink.

Taking a deep breath of crisp air, he gazed over the rolling hills behind his home. The maypole's multicolored ribbons fluttered in the breeze, and behind it, close to the lake, bows stood ready for the archery contest. Musicians would perform throughout the day, and dancing would last well into the evening.

On his way back to the manor, Robert caught sight of his friend Simon struggling to lift a long wooden bench. "Here, let me," he said, taking hold of the other end.

Simon looked up, wiping his brow. "It's heavier than it looks."

Together they lifted the bench and placed it at the end of a long row of tables.

"Ample room for everyone at the feast," Simon said with a satisfied nod.

"For the village folk, at least." Robert wiped his hands on his jacket as they walked toward the house. "I admit, today I'd rather be outside than in the great hall."

Every year Robert's parents hosted a May Day

festival, and every year he started dreaming of it in midwinter. Spring was the best time of year, in his opinion. Lush grass, fragrant flowers, and the world coming to life after its long sleep. As children he, his brother William, and Simon had spent May Day capering about, eating sweets, and playing with the ribbons of the maypole. As young men their fancies shifted to pretty maidens, strong ale, and staying out until dawn.

Simon glanced at the sky. "It looks like a perfect May Day."

"Yes, and I think everything's finally ready."

"Almost. It's time we dressed. I need to change my clothes, and you look like you've been rolling in the dirt," Simon said, brushing Robert's shoulder.

"And it's time we get William out of his hiding place."

Simon shaded his eyes and scanned the grounds. "Where is he?"

"Last night he mentioned something about meeting up with Bess."

"She's sure to be in the kitchens."

Robert shook his head. "The kitchen's too crowded for what he has in mind."

Simon nodded in understanding. "Dower house?"

"No, it's full of guests."

Their eyes met and Simon said, "He must be at Edmund's."

They crossed the field and followed a path through the woods to Edmund's ivy-covered brick house. Robert knocked once and entered, followed by Simon.

William strolled out of the bedroom, buttoning his shirt. "What are you two doing here?"

"We came to find you," Robert said. Trying to see

into the bedroom, he whispered, "Are you alone?"

William ran a hand through his tousled blond hair. "Bess just left."

"The guests will be arriving soon," Simon said. "We need to get ready."

"They certainly don't need to see you like this," Robert said.

"I wouldn't be certain of that. Many of the maids would welcome a look, I'd wager." He grabbed his jacket off a hook beside the door and slung it over his arm.

Robert gave him a wry smile. "Yes, the ladies will be impatient to see you in all your glory."

"Ah, you wouldn't understand." William walked past him and out the door.

"Well, I—" Robert began, but stopped when he saw Edmund coming down the path, not looking the least bit surprised to see the three men coming out of his house.

"Good morning, Mr. Bailey," they said in unison, the same way they'd greeted him in the schoolroom every day when he'd been their tutor.

Edmund laughed. "Good morning." He peered at William. "Why do I get the sense you've been up to something?"

"Always suspicious," William said with a shake of his head. "Old habits die hard, do they, Edmund?"

Edmund's eyes sparkled with mirth. "In your case, yes."

"Bess," Robert said.

Edmund grinned. "Old habits die hard, do they, William?"

"This particular habit will never die. If you will excuse me, gentlemen, I must dress for the festivities." He strode on without a backward glance.

Robert looked at his pocket watch, still on the fine chain Edmund had given him when he'd turned sixteen. "We'd better go, too," he said to Simon.

"Do you have a moment, Robert?" Edmund asked.

"Oh, yes, of course," he said, though he was anxious to get back to the house.

"I'll see you later," Simon said, and ran to catch up to William.

Once he'd gone, Edmund said, "Your father wants to see you before the guests arrive."

Robert groaned inwardly. "Not Margery Penrose again."

"Very astute."

"It wasn't difficult to guess. He hasn't exactly been subtle." Every time their neighbor, Mr. Penrose, was mentioned, Robert's father made sure to praise his daughter Margery's beauty, wit, and charm. And fortune.

"I didn't want you to be caught off guard, but it seems that was unlikely."

"I'll speak to him as soon as I get back to the manor."

"Are you looking forward to the celebration?" Edmund asked, turning to accompany Robert out to the grounds.

He bobbed rather than nodded his head. "I am."

"But?" Edmund raised his brows.

Robert laughed. "Talking of astute." He paused and said, "I wouldn't want to be like William when it comes to ladies, but I wouldn't mind being more at ease with them. Father has dreams of me making a grand match, but I can hardly string two coherent sentences together when I'm faced with a pretty woman. Or *any* woman."

"You make it sound as though you're facing a

dragon," Edmund said, clapping a hand on his shoulder.

"Some of the women I've met seem like they could breathe fire once they realize I'm not so well spoken and handsome as my brother."

Edmund considered Robert for a few moments, and from his expression Robert could tell he was trying to think of something positive to say. Why was he having to try so hard?

Finally, Edmund said cheerily, "You're a good dancer. That could win over some hearts."

"If all they want from a husband is a man who can dance and excels at swordplay."

"You have fine penmanship..." Edmund raised his brows and grinned.

"I don't think they'll be impressed enough with my handwriting to want to marry me. Not that they would have a chance to see it, at any rate."

"There's your answer, Robert. Write dazzling love letters to them."

"If only I could dance and write letters at the same time." They laughed together, and Robert made for the manor while Edmund went back to his house.

****

Isabel Tate gazed out her bedroom window, watching the day come to life. A light breeze ruffled the branches of the cherry trees, sending delicate petals fluttering to the ground. In the distance, sunlight shimmered on the river at the edge of the woods. She'd just finished breakfast when Nell, her aunt's maid, knocked once and came in. "Your aunt has sent a gown for you."

Isabel met her halfway across the room and ran her fingers over the sumptuous pale blue fabric, smiling as she admired rosebuds and green leaves embroidered into the skirt. "Oh, help me put it on, Nell."

"There'll be no lack of partners for you today," Nell said as she added the final touch—a green sash around Isabel's waist. "Now I must go attend to your aunt."

After she left, Isabel added the linen fichu she'd embroidered especially for today. As she brushed her wavy auburn hair, she wondered what her mother and baby half-sister were doing back home in Salisbury. She'd hoped they might come down for May Day, but perhaps her mother didn't want to travel until Victoria was a bit older. Or perhaps her new husband had forbidden it.

Isabel hadn't seen her mother for six months. After Victoria's birth, Isabel had spent every day with her mother in the nursery until her stepfather decided her presence was no longer needed. Her mother had been in no state to protest, as the birth had exhausted her and she'd confided to Isabel that she wasn't sure she could go through it again. Mr. Branwick would demand she try, though, as he wanted a son.

She'd just pinned her straw hat into place when her young cousin burst into the room.

"Good morning, John."

"It's time to go. Mother's ordered the carriage." He looked into her face as if to be sure he was addressing the right person and added, "You don't look like yourself."

"It *is* me, only not covered in mud from chasing you through the gardens." She bent to tickle him, and he ran out of the room, giggling. Isabel followed him down the corridor, but he'd soon left her behind.

She made her way to the parlor, where her aunt was

waiting.

"Isabel," Verity said, "That dress is lovely on you."

"Oh, thank you, it's perfect for today."

They walked outside to the carriage, where Isabel's uncle Francis handed her inside. John scrambled up beside her, and once they were all seated the carriage pulled away from Kerensly Hall.

Uncle Francis looked at her with twinkling eyes, as if about to give her a delectable treat. "Now you'll meet the Claremonts and see Thornwood Manor."

Isabel had heard much about Thornwood since she'd arrived in Holton two weeks ago, and her curiosity was beyond piqued. "What's the family like? Do you socialize with them often?"

"From time to time," Verity said. "Geoffrey and Eleanor have two sons, Robert and William."

"How old are the boys?" Isabel wondered if John would be included in their games.

Uncle Francis chuckled. "Men, now."

Her aunt raised her eyebrows at Isabel and grinned. "Handsome ones. And unmarried."

"Verity," Uncle Francis chastised, "they will be no concern of Isabel's."

"Why not? She'll dance, won't she?"

Isabel nodded. "Indeed, but I hadn't thought about partners. I don't know anybody in Holton."

"By tonight you most certainly will," Verity said.

John tugged at Isabel's sleeve and pointed out various landmarks, but she spent most of the ride wondering what the celebration would be like. Before her father's death two years ago, her parents had hosted many a ball, but nothing on the grand scale she'd heard the Claremonts provided. She was an accomplished dancer and would welcome a turn on the floor. But most of all, she wanted to see the archery competition, as she'd practiced the sport for years. Isabel hoped to meet some women her own age today and make a friend or two, if only for the summer. Aunt Verity was one of her dearest friends and practically a sister, but she was often busy. Verity's hints about handsome men made Isabel wonder if she was going to attempt some matchmaking. It wouldn't be the first time. She'd introduced her to a few young men before they left Salisbury and they were all charming enough, but nothing resembling a beau. Based on Uncle Francis's reaction, he wasn't keen on the idea of Verity trying to find her a husband. After watching what had happened to her mother, Isabel wasn't that keen on the idea herself. She put it out of her mind as John began a detailed description of the cakes, drinks, and entertainment that had been at last year's May Day celebration.

Chapter Two

When Robert reached the manor, he crossed the echoing great hall and mounted the curved staircase to the second floor. He strolled through the long gallery under the painted eyes of the many Claremonts who had lived here before him. Thornwood Manor had been home to Robert's family for generations. Originally a mere fortress, it had undergone countless changes over the centuries. At the end of the gallery, Robert pushed aside a tapestry and followed the corridor leading to his father's rooms in the most ancient wing of the house. The dark stone walls and perpetual chill suited his father well.

Mr. Claremont didn't look up when Robert entered the room. Sitting at his desk, he continued to read the letter in his hands.

"You wanted to see me, Father?" Robert prompted after some minutes.

His father tucked the letter into a drawer and removed his spectacles, fixing his gray eyes on Robert. With his dark hair, tall stature, and rugged features, there was no mistaking who Robert took after. William had inherited the fair hair and almost unearthly beauty of their mother.

"I've engaged an artist to paint portraits of you and William. He writes that he'll arrive next week."

Robert nodded. "I presume that's not all you summoned me here to tell me?"

Mr. Claremont stood and walked to the fireplace, hands clasped behind his back. After gazing into the flames for a moment, he turned to Robert. "Margery Penrose will be here today. I want you to win her."

"Win her? Surely she'll have some say in the matter."

"Convince her that you're the right man for her. Woo her. Charm her."

"I highly doubt Margery will be convinced of that. My chance of charming her most likely ended when I pushed her into the fish pond when we were thirteen."

Mr. Claremont ignored this. "She comes with a substantial dowry, and her father's lands adjoin ours. It's a fine match for you."

"There must be other women to choose from." Robert walked to the window and stared at the forest.

His father's voice took on a sharp edge. "You know my thoughts on this matter, Robert."

"I'd rather not wed myself to a woman I have no feeling for," he muttered. He'd always known his father would one day find a bride for him, but he'd hoped it would be someone who could be, if not a great love, at least a friend.

"You'll grow accustomed to each other. What does it matter? Get some heirs, and then you needn't bother with her."

"I want a companion."

"You have Simon for that. Women aren't real companions for men. They're ignorant in most things, and some don't even hunt."

"I'm not looking for another hunting partner." He turned to face his father. "I don't want to be miserable because I'm in a loveless marriage."

"Miserable? Loveless! Who puts these ideas into your head? Marry Margery and find another woman to warm your bed, if you will."

"I'm not William, bedding women high and low."

"No, you're not William. You are the one I depend on. You're the obvious choice to inherit after I'm gone, but having both my sons born on the same day complicates matters." Years of frustration came across in his barely controlled rising voice.

"William's just as responsible as I am. He has a talent for running things and a good head for sums. Let him marry Margery. Perhaps it will settle him." And perhaps it would leave Robert free to choose his own bride.

"No, it must be you," his father insisted.

"Why does it matter? Either one of us could make the match with Margery."

"Yes, Father," William interjected, walking into the room, "we're virtually the same man, so it hardly matters which one Margery weds and beds."

Robert winced and put a hand to his forehead. Leave it to William to walk in at exactly the wrong moment.

"William!" Mr. Claremont exclaimed. "How long have you been listening at the door like a maid?"

"Long enough to hear that you believe I'm not to be trusted with the simple matter of securing your heiress or running the estate," William fumed.

"Until you show me otherwise, what else can I believe?" his father asked coldly, returning to his desk.

"Perhaps if you gave me the same opportunities you throw at Robert, you'd see me differently."

Mr. Claremont gave William a skeptical look, turned away, and began rifling through papers.

"William, Father knows you're capable, he just meant—" Robert began, but William cut him off.

"I'm quite aware of what Father thinks of me, Robert, and I'll thank you to keep out of it." He turned on his heel and stalked out of the room.

Robert started for the door.

"Oh, let him be," Mr. Claremont said, shrugging. "Having one of his pouts."

"I'll speak to him, I'll explain."

As he was leaving, Mr. Claremont called, "Remember—Margery!"

Robert hurried to catch up to William, but he was already gone. Robert sighed. As twins with no other siblings, they had an even stronger bond than most brothers. But as they'd aged, William had begun to drift. He spent more and more time courting women and frequenting taverns, while Robert was left helping their father on the estate. In that case, could William really blame Mr. Claremont for assuming he was irresponsible? Robert knew he was just as devoted to Thornwood as he was. After all, one of them would inherit it one day.

Robert went to his room to dress, and as he was changing, someone knocked on the door. He crossed the room and opened it, thinking it might be William, but Simon stood there, his eyes full of questions.

"Come in," Robert said.

Simon walked in, closing the door behind him. "What happened to William? He looked like thunder when I saw him in the hall just now, and he didn't answer when I hailed him."

Robert explained what William had overheard.

Simon sat on the edge of the bed. "He believes you and your father think him incapable of taking any responsibility for the estate?"

"Yes, well, Father, at any rate," Robert said, buttoning his plum waistcoat and pulling on a light blue jacket. "And the same for making a satisfactory marriage. But that's not what I meant, and William should know that."

"Should he?"

Robert drew his head back. "When have I ever said William can't run Thornwood?"

"You don't need to say it. It's the way your father turns to you first, the way you deal with the tenant's issues before even asking William's opinion. He feels second to you. He always has."

"That's ridiculous." The way William strutted around Thornwood and the village, it was clear that if he felt second to anyone, it was more of a tie for first. But where their father was concerned, Simon could be right. Hadn't William said the same thing that very morning? But Robert couldn't help thinking he wasn't their father's favorite, only the one turned to more often simply because he could be found.

Simon shrugged. "William thinks nobody takes him seriously. He needs to be given a chance to prove himself."

"I'll speak to Father about it. Come," Robert said, "I want to find William before the feast."

****

Before long, the carriage transporting Isabel and her family turned down a winding, tree-lined drive and Thornwood came into view. The sand-colored stone manor was built in the shape of a letter E, and off to the left was another, decidedly older, wing. With its lone turret and dark gray stones, it looked like a miniature

13

castle shadowing the main house.

They finally reached the house, where two small courtyards flanked a staircase leading to the front doors. After exchanging the usual pleasantries with Mr. and Mrs. Claremont, who were greeting guests at the foot of the stairs, Isabel and her family made their way inside.

Uncle Francis immediately drifted off, saying something about the gaming tables, while Verity continued on to the great hall. Isabel and John strolled outside to the back of the manor, where a joyous atmosphere prevailed. From all sides came the sound of talk and laughter, and couples danced to the musicians' jaunty tunes. Booths served beer, lemonade, sandwiches, delicacies of all sorts, and the small cakes John had raved about. The delectable scent of roasting meat and fresh bread wafted from the manor. A young woman wandering through the crowd with garlands of flowers handed one each to Isabel and John.

Isabel slipped one over her neck and gave the other to John, who wrapped it around his arm.

He tugged her hand. "I want to see the maypole."

They reached the maypole just as children were gathering around.

"Go on," Isabel said, lightly nudging John forward. He skipped over and grabbed a ribbon, beaming as a minstrel struck up a brisk song.

A sweet morning breeze kissed Isabel's face as she tapped her feet to the melody. Soon nothing could be seen of the pole itself, only braids of colorful ribbons. When he was finished, John ran to Isabel and took her hand, laughing.

After they'd stepped into a booth for a glass of lemonade, she said, "Come, let's find your mother."

They entered the great hall, admiring its decorations of ivy and yew leaves. Daffodils adorned each table, and garlands of colorful wildflowers hung in the windows. Isabel spotted her aunt and uncle, only one table away from the dais where Mr. and Mrs. Claremont sat. She and John made their way through the crowd.

John flopped onto the bench beside his mother. "I skipped around the maypole, and we had lemonade, and there are minstrels here, and I saw a huge gray horse, and there are cakes."

"That sounds lovely." Verity untangled the flower garland from his arm and draped it around his neck, then turned to Isabel. "Did you enjoy yourself?"

"Oh, yes. There are so many people here, and the musicians are wonderful. I saw the archery range." She gave her aunt a sideways glance and smiled. "If I entered that contest, I know I'd win."

"It's not a very ladylike hobby."

"Hobby! I've been practicing since I was five years old. My father thought it was important for me to have skills besides dancing and sewing." Her eyes softened as she remembered him beaming with pride the first time she'd hit a target. She let out a sigh. "It still pains me to think of him."

"All that is in the past," Verity said kindly, covering Isabel's hand with hers. "You must try not to dwell on those sad times."

"My mother said coming here would help me forget. But how can I forget Father?"

"She doesn't expect you to forget your own father, Isabel. But she knows it's difficult for you to be—" Verity paused and pursed her lips.

Isabel glanced around before whispering, "With Mr.

Branwick. I know you don't like him, either."

Verity reddened. "It isn't a matter of my liking him."

Last year Isabel's mother had married Mr. Branwick, and to say he looked down on her family was an understatement. He'd bought a house far from the one Isabel had spent her childhood in, and rarely allowed her mother to visit Verity. The close-knit community Isabel had grown up with was lost to her now.

Isabel scowled. "I do my best to be amenable to him, but it's as though he doesn't *want* to like me." She couldn't get a true sense of her stepfather, and she couldn't explain why he made her uneasy. Sometimes she caught a strange glint in his eye when he looked at her, but then he'd smile and she'd wonder if she had imagined it. He ignored her whenever her mother wasn't with them, which she didn't mind in the least but found odd. Thankfully, she hadn't seen him for months and most likely wouldn't for some time.

A veil came down over Verity's face, as it often did when they spoke of Mr. Branwick. Isabel felt certain she knew some secret about him, but she would never divulge it.

As expected, Verity changed the subject. "You've been so looking forward to today. Do your best to enjoy it."

Isabel squared her shoulders. "I'll try. It's what my father would want for me."

Verity took on a tone Isabel had heard her use when trying to convince John how enjoyable going to sleep could be. "After the feast there will be more dancing, and the maypole. You can watch the archers."

Isabel laughed. "I'll decide who I would have bested."

"Oh, Isabel," her aunt said with an indulgent smile.

"On a day such as this, how can I not enjoy myself?"

Isabel glanced around the hall, curious about the townsfolk who would be her neighbors for the summer. As she looked around the room, she was startled to see a man staring intently at her. Their eyes met, and she had the sense he'd been watching her for some time.

She looked away before he did and leaned over to whisper in her aunt's ear. "Who is that man?"

Verity followed her gaze. "That's one of the sons of the house. Robert Claremont."

"Indeed?" Isabel stole another glance at him.

"Yes, and the man beside him is Mr. Kensington. He's lived with the Claremonts since he was a boy. He's a friend of your uncle's."

"Did you not say there was another brother?"

"Yes, and there he is. William Claremont, Robert's twin."

"Twin?" asked Isabel, taken aback. "They look nothing alike."

"It sometimes happens that way."

Isabel watched the Claremont brothers and their friend cross the hall to the high table. Once they were seated, Isabel was able to study the brothers more closely. They were both tall and had blue eyes. William was blond and exceptionally handsome. He looked confident, even arrogant, and Isabel knew at once he would be popular with the ladies. From the way he surveyed the women in the room, William knew it, too.

The other brother, Robert, was striking in his own way, with wavy black hair and high cheekbones. His angular face suggested haughtiness, but there was a lightness underneath—as if he was thinking of a jest but

17

trying not to laugh.

"Verity, will the Claremont brothers join in the dancing?"

Her aunt cast her a knowing look. "I think so. Why?"

"Oh, I just wondered about the customs of the area," Isabel said, attempting an air of nonchalance. She couldn't say why, but something about Robert Claremont drew her eye to him over and over during the course of the feast. It was almost as though he was a friend she used to have but couldn't quite remember, or someone she'd once seen in a dream.

****

Robert was on his way to the high table with Simon when he saw her. He knew they'd never met before. He wouldn't have forgotten that lustrous auburn hair, those delicate features. She was engrossed in conversation with a woman, then drew away, laughing. Suddenly she turned and saw Robert staring. He was too distracted by her beauty to bow or even nod. She turned back to her companion and whispered something in her ear.

"Who is she, Simon?" Robert asked, not taking his eyes off her.

"Miss Tate. She resides in Salisbury, but is currently staying at Kerensly Hall with the Collisons."

"Who has caught your eye, brother?" asked a deep voice from behind him. Robert turned to see William, who was now appraising Miss Tate.

"Nobody." Robert didn't want to draw William's attention to Miss Tate. If he approached her first, Robert wouldn't get a chance to speak to her at all. It was like that with William and women.

"You needn't concern yourself with that woman, though she is fair. Father expects you to pay court to

Margery. You're apparently the only one of us worthy to win her favor."

"William, please forget what you overheard. Father didn't mean it. I'm not interested in his scheme with Margery, and I'm certain you'd do a better job at winning her hand than I would. But if Father demands it of me, I must at least try."

"I know how it is, Robert. I know how it's always been. Somehow you outshine me in everything we do."

"That's not true," Robert insisted.

William met Robert's gaze, a hint of a smile on his lips. "I know you have faith in me, even if Father doesn't. If only there were a way I could prove it to him. I'm just as much his son as you are."

"He knows that. Don't take his comments to heart."

William shrugged and turned away. Robert followed him to the dais, where he and William took their places beside their parents while Simon joined Edmund at the end of the table.

Robert piled his plate with venison and pheasant, then filled his goblet with red wine and drank deeply. As he ate, his eyes kept flickering over to Miss Tate's table. She was smiling, choosing food for herself and chatting with her companions. Robert was admiring her when he felt an elbow dig into his ribs.

"Ouch!" He rubbed his side and scowled at William, who looked pointedly at Margery, seated on Robert's other side.

Shifting in his chair, Robert said, "Good afternoon, Margery."

She turned to him and inclined her head as her full, red lips turned up in a disinterested smile. It was easy to see why she was considered beautiful. Every feature was perfect, from her shiny black hair to her luminous skin to her pale green eyes that wouldn't hold Robert's. She was well educated and came from a family of good standing. But something about her had always made Robert uncomfortable, even when they were children. He had the feeling he was a joke to her.

He cleared his throat and set his fork down. "Are you enjoying the feast?"

She lifted a shoulder. "It's fair enough."

"Oh, good. Are your parents well?"

She looked to her right, where her parents were sitting. "They are." Her eyes wandered over to the windows.

"Good," Robert said lamely. "Will you dance today?"

She took a long drink of wine before answering. "No."

"You will watch, perhaps?"

"Perhaps," she replied in a voice that told Robert she would most assuredly not watch.

"Do you still like to hunt?" Robert asked, trying to think of any topic that might interest her.

She half turned away. "When I must."

Out of the corner of his eye Robert saw Miss Tate rise and walk outside.

William gave Robert an exasperated look and leaned over him. "Margery."

She turned to look at William, brows raised. "Yes?"

"You look stunning today. You're putting all the other maidens to shame. I hope you'll honor me with a dance later."

"Perhaps." Her cheeks took on a rosy hue, and Robert sensed that this "perhaps" was more of a "Yes, by all means."

"I couldn't help overhearing your conversation with Robert."

"Oh, about my parents' good health?" It looked like she didn't even try to refrain from rolling her eyes.

Robert leaned back in his chair, wishing he could switch seats with his brother instead of being spoken over like he was five years old.

"No," William said. "About hunting. I'd think a spirited woman like you would love to hunt. Perhaps you haven't yet found the right mount. You need one that is robust, tireless, eager to please." He held her eyes with his.

Margery gave him an appraising look. "That could be. I've yet to find one that fits me perfectly. He—I only ride stallions—must be strong and fast. But I wouldn't want one that is wayward. I must be in control."

"It's more enjoyable to be carried away when riding, though, don't you think? You must allow me to help in your quest."

"And what makes you think you could satisfy me in this matter?"

"I have years of experience. You may have heard of some of my exploits. On the hunt."

"Indeed I have and will gladly accept your help."

"I'm certain you won't regret it," William said, smiling.

She nodded and turned back to her meal. She didn't speak to Robert again, but he saw her smile when she looked at William out of the corner of her eye.

Once they'd finished eating, Robert and William rose from the table and strode across the hall.

"Clearly Father's chosen the wrong brother for this

task," Robert said.

"You're like an old fishwife. A woman like Margery has spirit, and needs it in return."

"I thought her cold."

"She was to you. Perhaps she hasn't forgotten the fish pond."

"My attempts to, as Father says, 'Charm her,' fail miserably." He paused and said, "Perhaps my reputation precedes me."

William snorted. "You *have* no reputation."

"It's well known that you're the…the experienced one," Robert muttered, his face growing warm. "And that I'm the—what did you call me?—the old fishwife."

"How would she hear of that?"

"From the servants?" he asked with a shrug. "I don't know."

"Would you take some advice? About being with a woman?"

"I've *been* with women." Robert looked around to be sure that nobody was listening to their conversation.

"Perhaps. But you're not so refined in the art of flirtation."

Robert wanted nothing more than to end the discussion. "I'll handle Margery."

"You'll have more chances to speak with her today. Try to be a *bit* more diverting," William said before leaving the hall.

Simon caught up with Robert, and they followed William outside. White fluffy clouds drifted across a vibrant blue sky, and a light breeze carried the fragrance of flowers.

Robert searched the crowds for Miss Tate and finally spotted her down by the lake, observing the archery competition.

"Come," he said to Simon. He didn't want William observing his attempts at getting acquainted with Miss Tate. As they made their way to the lake he asked, "Have you met Miss Tate? Can you introduce me?"

"I don't know her, but I know her guardian, Mr. Collison." He pointed to a group of people strolling toward Miss Tate.

"Do you know anything about her?" Robert asked as they skirted a throng of people gathered around the maypole. All he really wanted to know was if she was married or engaged, but he thought it best to keep that to himself for the moment.

"Her parents are Edward and Jayne Tate. Edward died under scandalous circumstances. He was thrown from a horse while fleeing with gold that wasn't his. The family denies it, of course."

"Is it true?" Robert asked, watching Miss Tate in the distance. She was shielding her eyes against the sun to better view the archers.

"I hear there's some doubt, but the man who accused him is very powerful. You may have heard of him—Giles Branwick. He has now wed Miss Tate's mother."

"I've heard of him but have never had dealings with him."

"You're better off not to. He has a reputation of being most unpleasant."

When they reached the lake, Simon approached Mr. Collison, who was standing with his family.

"Mr. Collison," Simon said, extending his hand.

"Mr. Kensington. I haven't seen you since last year in Salisbury." He shook Simon's hand vigorously.

"You're looking well."

"Thank you. You remember my wife, Verity? And this is our son, John."

Verity inclined her head and John smiled.

Miss Tate walked over and Mr. Collison presented her to Simon and Robert. "This is my niece, Miss Isabel Tate." He turned to her and said, "Mr. Simon Kensington and Mr. Robert Claremont."

"A pleasure," Robert said. She was only a little shorter than he and had a delightfully curvaceous figure.

"Mr. Kensington," she said to Simon, inclining her head. Isabel turned to Robert. "Thank you for the hospitality, Mr. Claremont. Your home is magnificent."

"Thank you. Would you like to watch the archers? The view— It's a better view from the other side of the lake."

She glanced at her uncle, who nodded. "That would be welcome," she said.

He offered his arm, and they strolled in the direction of the archery range, Simon following a few paces behind.

They walked in silence for what felt like too long, so Robert cleared his throat and asked, "How do you find Holton?"

"I like it very much." She turned to him with a smile.

He lapsed into silence for a few minutes before asking, "How long are you here? In town?"

"I'm here through the summer, or for as long as my aunt and uncle stay. It's so refreshing to see another part of the country."

"Yes." He scrambled for an engaging conversation topic. "The weather has been so nice for today, hasn't it?" He cringed inside. *The weather.*

"Yes, I worried it might rain."

Her attention was caught by the archers, and she stood on her toes as she watched an arrow soar through the air, only to land far short of its target. She turned the other way to watch the next archer. He might be in danger of losing her attention entirely if he couldn't come up with something remotely interesting to say. "There's—oh, music. Thomas plays it. Will you like the dance?"

She looked at him as though he'd spoken another language, and he couldn't blame her.

Willing his face not to flush, he amended, "Do you like to dance? There will be dancing, and if you'd like to, perhaps we could. Together. Later."

Her brow furrowed slightly. "Who is Thomas?"

Robert blinked. Why would she be interested in who *plays* the music? "Oh, nobody. That is, somebody. One of the minstrels. He's an old friend."

Isabel looked away, and he braced himself for an excuse—she's otherwise engaged, she turned her heel in the last dance, she suddenly remembered her aunt wants to speak to her.

But she met his gaze with her brown eyes. "When will the dancing begin?"

Robert had no chance to answer. From the tail of his eye he saw William striding across the lawn toward them.

Chapter Three

Robert did his best to sound civil when introducing William to Miss Tate. "My brother, Mr. William Claremont."

She inclined her head. "A pleasure to meet you."

"Miss Isabel Tate," Robert said.

"Delighted," William said, looking far from it. "Robert, Father would like to speak to you."

He wanted nothing more than to stay with Miss Tate, but there was no way to argue with William in front of her without looking like a fool. William probably found her attractive and meant to separate them for the sole purpose of having her all to himself. Over the course of the years, Robert had lost the favor of more than one lady this way. Well, William wouldn't manage his old trick today.

Robert turned to Isabel. "Mr. Kensington will see you back to your uncle."

"Oh…thank you." She pressed her lips together and looked toward the archery range.

He called to Simon, "Please escort Miss Tate back to her family, or on to the archers if she desires."

"It would be my pleasure."

Robert gritted his teeth as Miss Tate took Simon's arm.

He stalked across the grounds with William and when they were out of earshot demanded, "What was that about? Your subtle interference?"

"You're wasting your meager talents. You're to court Margery, not whoever that woman is."

"Stay out of my affairs, William." Robert stormed up the hill, where his father was standing with Margery and her parents.

****

Isabel watched Mr. Claremont walk away. It was clear he hadn't wanted to leave her. They'd barely become acquainted when his brother interrupted. In the distance, he reached a group of people including a woman Isabel had seen at the high table. She had dark hair like his. Perhaps she was a relative? After a few minutes, Mr. Claremont offered the woman his arm and they walked away together.

Perhaps it was presumptuous to ask, but her curiosity got the better of her. She turned to Mr. Kensington. "Is that woman with Mr. Claremont his sister?"

"He doesn't have a sister." He looked up the hill, then hesitated before speaking. "That's Miss Penrose, soon to be his betrothed."

"His betrothed?" She hoped the shock wasn't written all over her face. Mr. Claremont had certainly not acted like an engaged man.

"Yes, if accounts I hear are true," Simon said as they approached Verity and Uncle Francis.

"Back so soon? Enjoy yourself?" Uncle Francis asked.

Isabel tried to mask the disappointment in her voice. "Yes."

She stood by as Mr. Kensington and her aunt and uncle chatted about Salisbury and discussed people she'd never met. After a time Verity turned to her. "The maidens' dance is beginning soon at the maypole. Do you wish to join in?"

"Yes, let's go." Isabel nodded to Mr. Kensington and Uncle Francis, then followed Verity and John to the maypole.

As Isabel grasped a yellow ribbon, she noticed Mr. Claremont chatting with one of the minstrels. He smiled, and she felt his eyes on her but didn't look at him again, having no desire to spend the afternoon flirting with someone else's fiancé.

She forgot all about him as she and the other dancers weaved in and out of each other's paths, singing and laughing as they braided the pole with ribbons. When it was over, the musicians struck up a new song and couples began dancing.

Isabel rejoined Verity and John. "What a delight!" she said breathlessly. "I think I'll get some lemonade. I'm parched." She put a hand to her cheek, warm from her exertions.

Verity nudged her arm and gestured for her to turn around. Robert Claremont was making his way through the crowd, his eyes on Isabel.

"He may want a dance," Verity said.

"I heard he's betrothed."

"I've heard that, too. Still, you must dance if he asks, Isabel. It would be an honor to be singled out."

Isabel was uncertain about dancing with an engaged man, but before she could decide what to do, he was beside her.

Mr. Claremont put his hands behind his back and gave her a half-smile. "Hello, Miss Tate."

She looked into his eyes, which seemed to pull their

color from the lake and clear afternoon sky. "Hello."

"A dance?" He seemed to hold his breath as he awaited her answer.

She looked to Verity, who nodded her approval.

"Yes, thank you," Isabel said, still wondering if she was making the right choice.

****

Robert led Miss Tate to their place among the dancers, and as they moved through the steps he caught a whiff of her perfume—honeysuckle, he thought, or a similar sweet scent.

"You looked like you enjoyed the maypole. The dance, that is," he said.

"And you. You seemed quite interested."

"I was. I am. I couldn't take my eyes off the dancers. One in particular."

She lowered her eyes. "I assume you mean Miss Penrose?"

"She wasn't among the dancers." He'd meant to compliment Miss Tate, but it didn't seem to be working.

Miss Tate said flatly, "There were a dozen others. I cannot think who captivated you so."

Around them, other couples laughed and chatted, none of them as stiff as Robert and Isabel, who looked like two people who'd never danced before in their lives. He seemed to have offended her, but how? The song would soon end, and he hadn't really spoken to her, never mind *charmed* her.

"Do you ride?" he blurted out.

She looked slightly puzzled. "Yes, I go out daily."

"Perhaps you would allow me to accompany you one day?"

The puzzled expression shifted to something like

disapproval. "Do you think it appropriate, under the circumstances?"

Before he could ask what she meant, the music ended and couples separated.

Across the lawn Simon stood at one of the wooden tables, holding two glasses of beer. He motioned for Robert to join him.

Robert waved, then turned back to Miss Tate. "I'll speak to your uncle. About riding. With you."

She nodded but said nothing as he escorted her back to her aunt. The musicians struck up a new tune as Robert wove his way through the crowd and joined Simon, who handed him a glass.

Robert took a long drink, then gestured over his shoulder toward Miss Tate. "I'm going to ask Mr. Collison for permission to go riding with her."

"Miss Tate? But you're courting Margery." Simon finished his beer and placed the glass on the table.

"I only want to get to know her. It won't interfere with my father's plans."

"I saw you with her. You like her."

"She's enchanting. Have you heard her voice? It's like angels singing."

Simon raised a brow. "I've never heard an angel sing."

"Nor have I," William said. Neither of them had seen him approach.

"I wasn't talking to you, William," Robert snapped. "And would you cease springing upon me in the middle of private conversations?"

"How is it you ignore the luscious Margery but pine for this girl?" William snatched Robert's beer and took a gulp, then set the glass beside Simon's.

"I'm not *pining*." Robert scowled at William and retrieved his glass to get the last sip.

"She's practically betrothed," Simon said.

"I don't think so. She didn't mention it." Robert had checked her left hand for a ring and seen none.

"She doesn't know."

"How could she be oblivious to her own betrothal?" William asked skeptically, leaning against the table.

"I spoke to Mr. Collison about her. He told me Miss Tate's stepfather plans to wed her to his nephew."

Robert looked at the ground. "Is it a good match for her?"

"For her, yes. I told you about her father."

"Not in detail."

"What have you heard, Simon?" William prodded.

"Supposedly her father was fleeing with gold that belonged to Giles Branwick. Tate's horse stumbled and threw him, breaking his neck. Branwick says the gold was his, owed him by Mr. Tate for a gambling debt. With Miss Tate coming from such a family, not many would welcome her as a daughter."

"Betrothed," Robert muttered under his breath.

"Bad luck, brother," William said, clapping Robert on the back. "But there are plenty more. Margery for a start. Come, we'll go speak with her now. She's in the garden."

"I'll find her on my own." Robert strode across the lawn, but the brightness had gone out of the day. He could hardly blame Miss Tate for his premature thoughts of courtship. What did it matter anyway if she was almost betrothed? He was in the same situation. Destined for Margery. William was right—he needed to secure her if it was at all possible. When he reached the garden, she

31

was there with her parents and Robert's also. Mr. Claremont looked pointedly at Margery, and Robert knew his efforts would have to begin.

"Have you toured the maze today, Margery?" Robert asked.

"I have not."

"It's blooming at this time of year. Would you care to see it?" Robert offered her his arm and led her through the garden to the maze entrance.

"After you," he said and they strolled down the path. In a bitter twist of irony, Margery Penrose was one of the only women with whom he could hold a conversation. Not through ease, but from years of familiarity.

"Lovely plants," she said after a few minutes, clearly bored.

"Did you ever install a maze at your estate?"

"I'd expect you to know the answer to that. You and William have been there dozens of times."

"I haven't been to visit of late." Robert ran his fingers down the chain of his pocket watch but resisted checking the time.

"Yes, it's been some time since I've seen you at Penhollow." She picked the head off a rose and sniffed it, then tossed it on the ground.

They walked deeper into the maze and Margery gasped in appreciation when they reached the fountain in the center. Water flowed from two marble fishes' mouths, splashing into a pool at the fountain's base. Two curved benches wrapped around the pool, and a myriad of flowers filled the clearing with their heady scent.

"How charming," she exclaimed.

"My mother designed this maze and had it planted when William and I were infants. We spent hours playing here when we were boys. Haven't you seen it before?"

She circled the fountain, hands behind her back. "Not in some time."

"I'm glad you could see it today." He was about to suggest leaving when Margery spoke.

Tilting her head, she looked at Robert with slightly lowered lids. "We are quite alone."

"The house is just the other side of the hedges," Robert said, a lump forming in his throat.

She took a step closer. Much closer. She licked her lips and her green eyes sparkled. Sparkled with what Robert couldn't tell. Desire? Mischief? He couldn't say, but had an inkling about her intentions. He swallowed, a creeping nervousness filling his chest. As she closed the distance between them Robert stepped back, stumbled over the bench, and fell to the ground. She laughed derisively and whatever warmth that had been in her eyes vanished.

Robert stood, brushing the dirt off his breeches.

"It's as I thought," she whispered, almost to herself.

"Excuse me?" he asked loudly.

"You're not so like your brother as I would have supposed."

"I'm sorry to disappoint you." A flush crept up his cheeks.

She looked at the ground, adjusting her gloves. "No more than I expected."

So, Robert thought, she'd hoped for some of the flirtations, or more, that William was so adept at.

"This way." He led the way out of the maze, Margery following a few paces behind.

He walked in silence, stewing over what had just happened and knowing he'd missed a perfect opportunity to woo her. He knew what William would have done. Flirt, banter, even kiss her. Maybe more? But he was not William. This whole scheme was ridiculous, and today only proved what he'd already known. Perhaps he'd known Margery for too long, or perhaps he inherently knew she could never make him happy.

When they returned to the garden, Robert caught a glimpse of Miss Tate walking alone near the lake. Margery went to take his arm again, but he sidestepped and her hand grasped only air. A look of irritation distorted her flawless features, and her eyes narrowed as she followed his gaze to the lake.

"William," he called to his brother, who was standing nearby, "Please escort Margery into the hall."

William was beside her in the blink of an eye. "My pleasure. This way, Margery."

"I welcome a lively companion such as yourself." She shot Robert a disdainful look and took William's arm.

Robert breathed a sigh of relief as they walked away. William leaned down and said something to Margery, and her laughter rang out across the garden. William looked back at Robert and shook his head at him. Once they disappeared into the house, Robert hastened to the lake.

****

Gentle, sunlit waves rippled on the water as Isabel walked along the lake to the archery range. A discarded bow and quiver lay in the grass. She picked up the bow and notched an arrow on the string, then drew her arm back and let it fly. It met its mark easily. As she reached for another arrow, she heard clapping. She lowered the bow and spun to see Robert Claremont standing just a few feet away.

"One more," he said.

Isabel hesitated.

"Just one?" he encouraged.

She sent an arrow singing through the air to land dead center.

Mr. Claremont followed when she went to retrieve the arrows. "Years of practice and I'm no match for you. Where did you learn to do that, to shoot like that?"

"From my father."

The sun disappeared behind the horizon, casting an orange glow over the sky. From a distance came the strains of a languid song played by a solitary lute.

What was Mr. Claremont doing here? She'd been waiting all day to try her hand with the bows, and now here he was trying to engage her in pointless conversation after she'd just seen him emerge from the maze with his fiancée. Trying to mask her irritation, she asked, "Won't Miss Penrose be looking for you?"

He looked genuinely puzzled. "Margery? Why?"

"Because she's your betrothed." Isabel set the bow against a tree and started walking away.

"Margery—betrothed? No. No, she isn't. Where did you hear such a thing?"

She turned to face him. "From Mr. Kensington. He told me you're marrying Miss Penrose."

His eyes widened. "Did he? Well, Mr. Kensington is wrong."

In the distance, carriages were lining up on the drive, and horses whinnied as they set off down the road. Her family would be waiting to leave.

"I really must be getting back," she said. Oh, why couldn't he have sought her out sooner? Now that she knew there were no complications with Miss Penrose, she welcomed the chance to get to know him better.

"A little longer?" he asked. "The—a turn around the garden?"

She agreed readily. "A small one. It's growing dark."

Isabel followed Mr. Claremont around the torchlit garden for much longer than she'd intended, listening more to his voice than to the occasional, halting words he spoke of herbs and flowers. After a time they wandered into the maze where the silence, coupled with the gathering darkness, made for a pleasant change after the busy day. It occurred to her that it wasn't entirely appropriate to be walking thus with a man she barely knew, but she felt so at ease with Mr. Claremont that the thought vanished almost as soon as it had come. When they reemerged from the maze, it was fully dark. The extra time with him was worth Verity's irritation, and she hoped he'd speak to her uncle about riding with her so she'd be able to see him again soon.

The crescent moon shone brightly, disappearing now and then behind fast-moving, mountainous clouds. A brisk wind carried the sweet scent of springtime over the grounds of Thornwood, and at the edge of the forest, fireflies flashed among the trees.

When they reached the drive, Mr. Kensington jogged over to Isabel. "I've been looking for you, Miss Tate. Your family is departing."

"I'll go to them directly." She turned to Robert. "Good night, Mr. Claremont, and thank you."

"Goodnight," he said, then cleared his throat. "And…would you—please, call me Robert?"

Isabel hesitated. So soon? But when she looked into his face as he awaited her answer, she again felt that inexplicable ease and simply said, "Very well, Robert. Then you must call me Isabel." Hurrying away before he could see her pink face, she glanced over her shoulder at him one more time. Her heart fluttered when he smiled at her. There was something about him that made her wish the moon and stars would step aside and let the sun come out for a few hours more.

"Isabel! There you are." Uncle Francis came over and offered his arm.

Verity looked past Isabel toward Robert, then eyed her shrewdly. "You look flushed. We'd better get you home. It's been such an exciting day."

"Yes. A perfect day."

"I want to stay," said a sleepy John, coming to stand beside Isabel.

"You want a bed." She took his hand and led him to the carriage. Once inside, John promptly fell asleep with his head on her shoulder. She absentmindedly stroked his hair as they rode home through the starry night and, though Isabel didn't sleep, she dreamed as much as John.

Chapter Four

Robert watched the carriage roll down the drive. It hadn't even reached the gates when William and Simon joined him.

"Robert," Simon said, "What's the meaning of all this?"

"The meaning of what?"

"Miss Tate. I told you she's as good as betrothed. Both of your absences were noticed this evening. Your father is not pleased."

"No, he's not," said William. "And neither am I."

"What does it matter to you?" Robert asked.

"You know how important the Penrose match is to Father. He explicitly told you to court Margery. Luckily I was on hand to entertain her."

"And that was a hardship for you? Entertaining a woman? That's all you do, William. What does it matter if it's Margery or a kitchen maid?"

"It matters if I'm stuck courting your would-be bride," he snapped.

"Bride? You're getting ahead of yourself. She hardly spoke to me all day."

Simon said nothing but shook his head and walked into the house as the brothers bickered.

"It's not Margery's fault if your conversation bores her," William said. "You've never been good at idle chatter."

"I'd rather have actual discussions with women instead of all the pointless babble you're so adept at."

"Once more, we disagree," retorted William, raising his hands. "Women enjoy idle conversation. They like to feel that you care about their nonsensical chatter. Just listen to them long enough and they'll be very agreeable to you."

"I want something beyond idle conversation."

William put a hand on his shoulder. "It would strengthen our estate to join it with Penrose's. Margery is a fine match for you. If you can find some common ground perhaps she'll warm to you. Leave Miss Tate alone."

"Perhaps you're right," Robert said, knowing he wouldn't give up on Isabel so easily.

A few days later, Robert and Simon were riding through the forest when they heard voices. One was clearly that of a child, the other a woman. Rounding a bend in the trail, Robert couldn't stop the grin that came to his face when he recognized Isabel.

She stood with her hands on her hips, looking up into a towering oak. "Come down, John! It's time to go home."

No answer.

"John," she pleaded, "We need to go."

"I am *Prince* John."

"Prince John," Isabel said in a sing-song voice, "Please accompany me to our castle, where tea and cake await you." She swept a low curtsey.

John's smiling face emerged from the greenery. "Princess Isabel, I have slain the dragon and will escort you to our keep." He started down the tree but lost his footing, clinging to a branch ten feet up. "Help!"

"Hold on!" Isabel attempted to climb the tree but slipped on her skirt, landing hard on the ground.

Robert jumped off his horse and ran to help her to her feet.

As she turned back to the tree, Simon said, "No need, Miss Tate." He'd guided his horse, Blaze, directly beneath John and easily pulled the struggling boy from the tree.

"Isabel, a knight rescued me," John said.

Simon laughed. "I am at your royal command." He tried to put John on the ground, but the boy clung to the reins. Simon shrugged and set him on the saddle in front of him.

"Which way are you going? May we accompany you?" Robert asked Isabel.

"That would be welcome."

Robert led his horse by the reins as they followed Simon and John down the sunny woodland trail. He searched for something to say. "So. So, the boy…John? He's your brother?"

She grinned. "My cousin."

Robert felt his cheeks growing warm. "That's right. I met him on May Day. Do you have a brother? Or a sister?"

"I have a half-sister, Victoria," she said, her face lighting up. "She's just a baby."

"And she's here, too?"

"No, she's in Salisbury with our mother."

A cloud passed over her face, and Robert had the sense something was amiss about the situation, but he doubted she'd want to discuss it with someone she barely knew.

They continued on in silence for a time before he

asked, "How are your aunt and uncle?"

"Very well, thank you."

"Have you been riding this morning?"

She raised her brows at him, a smile on her lips, and looked down at her feet.

"Of course. You don't have a horse." He tried to cover his embarrassment with a dry cough.

She laughed, but not unkindly, her brown eyes sparkling.

"Well, have you been out riding on any other days?" he asked, hoping his face had gone back to its regular color.

She cast her gaze to the ground. "Yes. Though most mornings I've stayed home in case anyone should call upon me or my uncle."

Robert hardly knew what to say. She'd been waiting for him to call, but he hadn't yet done so. Apologize? Make an excuse? Since he wasn't sure of the best course of action, he remained silent.

When they reached the edge of the trail, the road lay before them in opposite directions.

"Thank you for your assistance," Isabel said. "Our home is this way. Come, John."

John slid off Blaze and took Isabel's hand.

"Farewell, my lady, and Prince John," Robert said with a grin.

Isabel inclined her head and started down the road.

Robert mounted his horse, his eyes on Isabel as she walked away. Whatever he had to do to see her again, he would do it. And soon. He turned to Simon, who had a smug, knowing look on his face.

"Is she not beautiful, Simon?"

"Yes, she is. But what about Margery?"

"I've told my father a match between us is unlikely."

"He won't give up on it easily. Edmund says your father thinks your stability is what will win over Mr. Penrose. That's why he appointed this to you, not William. Everyone in the village knows William isn't likely to settle down, even when he marries."

Robert accepted that his father didn't care about his marital happiness, only for this alliance. He even agreed with him in some ways. But that was before he'd met Isabel. If only she knew how often he thought of her. By now she'd realized he hadn't keep his word about asking her uncle for permission to see her. She would think him faithless, and that he couldn't bear.

"I'm in a bit of a quandary," Robert said.

Simon leaned forward to stroke Blaze's neck. "What is it?"

"It's Isabel. I want to get to know her better."

Simon shook his head. "That would lead to nothing but trouble. You're obviously attracted to her."

"That doesn't mean she can't be my friend. On May Day I told her I'd ask for permission to take her out riding. I haven't done this because I don't believe Mr. Collison will allow me to court her if she's on the verge of becoming betrothed."

"Court her? You just said you only want to get to know her as a *friend*." Simon clicked to Blaze and started down the road, Robert keeping pace.

"Maybe I do want something more. My father would have me rush into marriage with Margery before I try to find someone on my own."

"What purpose could that serve? He wants the Penrose lands and Margery's dowry. Miss Tate can bring you neither of those things."

"Be that as it may, I'm determined to keep my word and take her riding. No harm can come of a simple ride through the forest."

Simon didn't look convinced, but gazed off into the trees for a few moments before speaking. "The answer is simple. You somehow contrive to meet her when she's out riding, and let her believe it was Mr. Collison's idea that you should go after her."

Robert rubbed his chin. "I don't feel right lying to her, but perhaps it's the only way."

"She won't question it. We'll go out riding together and see if we can find her. You'll need a chaperone."

"If you insist," Robert said as they urged their horses to a trot.

"Oh, that I do," Simon said and laughed.

****

A few days later, Isabel was riding through the forest after spending the morning with Verity, planning what they'd wear to the Penroses' upcoming ball. Isabel had chosen a sky-blue gown with a full skirt and rather scandalously low bodice. Isabel's mother had always said her neck and shoulders gave her a graceful air.

She shivered as she recalled Marcus once being so bold as to say the same thing. As if she wanted his opinion on *anything*. Marcus was her stepfather's nephew, on whom he doted. He stayed at their house often, and Isabel knew he was being groomed to inherit should her mother fail to give Mr. Branwick an heir. He had a way of appearing whenever Isabel was alone. In the library, walking in the garden, heading out for a ride. Difficult as it had been to part from her mother and Victoria when she'd come to Holton, she'd been more than glad to leave Marcus behind.

She turned her horse into the woods and directed him to a gurgling stream under a canopy of trees. The forest was quiet but for the splashing of the water, bird songs, and the rustle of branches. They hadn't been there long when Isabel heard a new sound. Hoofbeats and muffled voices. She urged her horse closer to the road and easily heard the riders' conversation.

"What makes you think she came this way?" a man asked.

A deeper voice said, "Merely a guess. It seemed as good a place as any to look. It seems I'm thwarted again."

"Let's turn back, we can look again tomorrow."

"I'm sitting for the portrait tomorrow."

Isabel's pulse quickened as she recognized the deep voice. Robert Claremont. So he'd been looking for her. Why hadn't he come to the house? She started back toward the stream, but suddenly her reason left her and she guided her horse through the trees, emerging just as Robert and his companion rounded the bend going in the opposite direction.

They hadn't seen her. Isabel paused for a moment, thinking what to do. Go back home and hope he came to the house soon? Or seek him out for herself? Her reckless side won. She spurred her horse to a gallop and chased after them. Robert turned in his saddle, and Isabel was delighted with the look of shock on his face as she sped past him and his companion, who she could now see was Mr. Kensington.

"Isabel!" Robert cried.

She heard Robert's horse charging up behind her and pushed her own mount faster. The road widened and Robert gained her right side. Soon they would be level.

How would he react to her little game? Would he be cross? But no, he was laughing.

They reached an open field and she gave her horse his head. He flew over the grass, but Robert's horse easily overtook her. He pulled up ahead and motioned for her to do the same. She reined in, her horse rearing slightly as he came to a halt.

"Good boy!" she said, patting his neck. Isabel dismounted just as Robert was coming to assist her. His horse, a dapple-gray stallion, followed close behind him. Her chestnut gelding was not quite as fast, but she knew he'd held his own.

Robert smiled warmly when he reached her side. "What a merry chase you've led me on."

"You barely overtook me," Isabel said, returning his smile.

"Apollo had your horse beaten without even trying."

"This is Dion, and you must see he's older than your Apollo. He's still fast, though. You nearly caught me," she said playfully.

"Nearly? I beat you by five lengths."

They laughed together easily.

"Where are we?" Isabel asked. "I don't know my way around very well yet. I was following my usual route before I saw you, but I've never come so far in this direction before."

"We're on the border of my estate, close to the waterfall. Have you seen the falls yet?"

Isabel shook her head.

"Would you like to see them?"

She hesitated. Nothing would please her more than to spend more time with him, but she couldn't really traipse about the woods with him unchaperoned. A tiny voice urged her to do it anyway, no matter how inappropriate. She considered for a few moments, then looked up and noticed him waiting for an answer. "Alone?"

"We're not alone. Mr. Kensington is right over there." He pointed to the trees, where Mr. Kensington was just visible.

"In that case, I'd love to see the waterfall. Is it far?"

"Not very." They mounted their horses and Robert turned into the woods, Mr. Kensington following. "We'll take the woodland trail instead of the main road."

Isabel and Robert chatted easily as they rode, and she was pleased that he seemed to have gotten over his shyness. He hadn't paused, stuttered, or blushed once the whole time they'd been talking. Not that she minded when he did—it was somehow endearing.

Before long, flashes of blue broke through the trees and they entered a clearing.

"We walk from here," Robert said. They wrapped their horses' reins around a tree branch, and Isabel followed him down a winding path.

Emerging from the forest, Isabel was greeted by the sight of a broad, deep river. Boulders stood on the bank, surrounded by thousands of multicolored pebbles. Sunlight glistened on the surging water.

"It's beautiful," she said.

"This has always been one of my favorite places. As children, William, Simon, and I spent countless days playing in the water or fishing. We'd hide from our tutor, Edmund, here. I should say we *tried*—somehow he always found us." He guided her along the riverbank to a flat, stony cliff that jutted out over the side of the waterfall. "Here's a good spot."

The cliff was so wide they could have brought their horses with them, not that Dion would have willingly come. Isabel leaned forward to watch the water cascading down to the river eighty feet below, where rainbows shimmered in the mist. She lost track of time as they sat on the sun-warmed stone, talking about nothing in particular.

When it was time to leave, Isabel followed Robert back to the woods, though she wished she could sit with him beside the river all day. Mr. Kensington, who'd been discreetly waiting beneath the trees, now led their horses over and handed her Dion's reins.

She mounted and turned to the forest.

Robert turned Apollo in the opposite direction. "This way."

"But the trail…"

"We know of another trail," Mr. Kensington said.

"It's seldom used and doesn't take much longer than the path we took to get here. Are you up for more adventure?"

"Yes, please." Anything to prolong their time together. He seemed much more comfortable with her today. Perhaps he felt more sure of himself now that he had Uncle Francis's permission to accompany her on her rides.

Instead of going into the forest, they rode up a steep trail to the cliffs. The view from the top took her breath away. In the distance a mountain range stood out against the sky, the world awash in spring colors. Far below, the river jumped and splashed like a living thing. From her perspective high above, Isabel saw where the water slowed and became a wide, meandering stream that disappeared into the woods.

After riding for a time, Robert turned onto a narrow path that led back into the cool forest. Isabel's eyes took a few moments to adjust to the darkness, and just as she was about to ask Robert where they were going, he guided his horse through a glade of trees and disappeared from sight.

"Robert?"

"I'm here."

She followed his voice and emerged in a vast ocean of wildflowers—orange, purple, yellow, blue, and white. The grass reached Dion's belly and over Isabel's boots.

"What a charming meadow," she said. "I've never seen it during my rides."

Robert brought Apollo closer to Dion. "It's not so far from the village, but we've come the long way around. It's off the main trail and quite secluded. I myself come here only rarely. I thought you'd enjoy seeing it."

"I do, thank you for bringing me."

Isabel looked behind her as Mr. Kensington approached. He hadn't spoken to her very much, addressing most of his comments to Robert. She wondered if he was shy or merely giving them privacy. He had a quiet, stable presence, and she had the feeling he was a kind man.

"Home now, Robert?" he asked.

"Yes, it will be nearing supper time."

"Is this meadow easy to find? I must come back one day," Isabel said.

"Not difficult at all. With the right guide," Robert said. She raised her eyes to his, and her heart picked up its pace as a glimmer of understanding passed between them.

"And where might I find such a guide?" she asked,

eyes twinkling.

Robert grinned. "I think I know of someone who could help you."

Mr. Kensington tipped his hat. "Always happy to be of service."

"I think not!" Robert laughed as he urged Apollo after Mr. Kensington, who'd shot off like an arrow.

Isabel raced after them, but slowed to a trot when something on the edge of the woods caught her eye. A glint of metal. She guided Dion to it and dismounted. Among the brambles and overgrown vines was a rusted, wrought iron gate. Crumbling stone walls disappeared into the forest on either side.

"Isabel," Robert called, "This way."

She waved him over.

When he reached her, he slid off Apollo. "Is something wrong with Dion? Did he throw a shoe?" He glanced at the horse's hooves.

"He's fine. What's this gate?" She tugged at the vines. "Where does it lead?"

His brows furrowed as he looked closer. "I don't know. I've never noticed it before."

"We'll find out then," she said, a mischievous gleam in her eyes. She pushed on the gate fruitlessly. "The latch is stuck."

"Here, let me." Robert tried pushing it, even kicking it, but it wouldn't budge. Finally he climbed over.

"Well, if this is the only way." She lifted her skirt up to her knees and scrambled over. Robert's eyes widened, his mouth agape. He looked away, turning his back on her.

On the other side she paused to adjust her skirts, then gave him a grin. "Let's go."

"After you." Robert moved aside for her to walk past him.

They started down the twisting, overgrown path—so narrow Isabel doubted a horse would fit through it. The trees came together in a thick canopy overhead, blocking out the sky.

"Perhaps it's an old trail back to the river," she said.

"I don't think so. I feel sure I would have seen it before."

"Even the stone wall was hidden, which would explain—" Isabel stopped abruptly.

At the end of the trail the forest revealed its secret. An old stone cottage stood on the other side of a grassy clearing. It had clearly been abandoned for some time. The cottage had two windows; one bare, the other half covered by a broken green shutter. A brick well stood in the courtyard, and a stone building peeked from behind the cottage.

"What is this place?" Robert whispered.

"It's perfect." She hurried down a flagstone path to the arched wooden door and flashed Robert a smile before turning to open it.

"Wait!" He reached her just as she put her hand on the door. "Let me go first. It could be unsafe."

She took a step back as Robert reached for the latch. The door easily swung open, though with some creaking. They stood shoulder to shoulder, peering inside. Sunlight poured in from holes in the roof, illuminating the interior. A table and three overturned chairs sat in the center of the room, while on the right hand wall was a smoke-blackened stone hearth. Over to the left stood a bed and a wooden trunk. Isabel could just make out the outline of a doorway beyond the bed. Another bedroom?

She took a step inside, but Robert put an arm out to bar her path. "I'll go first."

Isabel nodded and watched as he crept across the room, his feet stirring up years' worth of dust. He looked through the back doorway.

"You'd better come see for yourself," he called over his shoulder. "It's quite safe to come in. The building is sound, if old."

Isabel crossed the room and looked over his shoulder into the other room. Only it wasn't a room. It was a short hall leading to a walled garden. The flowers were wild, tangled, and unkempt. Isabel much preferred it to the manicured gardens at Kerensly Hall. Here was a garden one could lose oneself in.

Isabel stepped outside, brushing her hand along the waist-high grass. "Who lived here?" she wondered aloud.

"I have no idea," Robert said, coming to her side. "It's well hidden to begin with, and now that the gate is so overgrown, it's a wonder we found it at all."

"Had you never seen the gate in the meadow?"

"No. I'll ask Edmund if he knows anything about it."

She took his hand. "Oh, please don't. I—" Their eyes met and she lost whatever words she'd been about to say. Isabel was suddenly aware of how quiet it was, how alone they were, and how handsome he was. After a moment she pulled her hand away and tucked a lock of hair behind her ear, not that it needed it.

Robert cleared his throat. "Aren't you curious about this place?"

"Yes, but I like the idea of a mystery. If you ask Edmund, he might come here. I'd rather keep it secret."

Robert smiled indulgently. "Very well. Our secret. Now it really is getting late. We'd best get you home."

"Oh, yes. In fact, I didn't tell anyone I was leaving. They'll be wondering where I am, although I daresay my uncle knows I'm with you."

Robert's brow furrowed for a fraction of a second, but then his expression cleared. "Leaving without permission, you say?" he asked teasingly as they walked through the cottage to the courtyard.

"Not exactly."

Robert looked at her, eyebrows raised in question.

"Yes. I did," she admitted.

"Why?"

Isabel didn't answer as they crossed the yard. She stopped for one more look at the cottage, then turned down the overgrown path.

She finally replied, "I like to get away by myself. I love riding, but when I bring a groom with me I can't choose my own path and speed."

Robert nodded. "I can understand that."

"It's different for you. As a man, you go where and when you please without a groom."

"True, in a way. I usually have Simon with me, though, or my brother."

"That isn't really the same. They're your companions. The groom is like my guard. If I stop to look at a pretty view, he's there. If I want to gallop across the fields, he's there. My favorite thing about riding is enjoying nature and letting my mind wander where it will. It's not easy to do when from the tail of my eye I see the groom, who is clearly as dissatisfied with his duty as I am."

Robert picked a leaf off a tree and starting picking it

apart with his fingers. "Don't you have a chaperone in Salisbury?"

"Yes, but it's different somehow. In town I'm limited to riding slowly through the lanes, surrounded by other people. But here, once I'm beyond the Kerensly grounds, the fields and trails call to me. They seem endless and full of possibility." She blushed, wondering if she was talking too much or sounded foolish.

"I understand. You want to be free to do what you want."

"Yes. And I *am* twenty, so it doesn't seem unreasonable that I should go out alone in a small village like Holton. What could happen?"

"Not much," he said and laughed. "I suppose I've never thought about what it would be like to be shadowed all the time. Like you said, it's different for me. I enjoy Simon's company and occasionally William's, as well."

"You don't always like being with your brother?" She wondered if it was too personal a question, but he smiled.

"Not always. But that must be the way it is with all siblings. Or anyone, really. As you said, everyone likes to be alone sometimes."

"Perhaps it's time I spoke to my aunt about riding out on my own more. In any case, I'm glad I can ride with you now. You're much more—" She stopped and pressed her lips together.

He looked into her eyes. "More?"

"Oh, nothing," she said, certain she was red as a strawberry. There was no need to tell him he was much more handsome, agreeable, and amusing than a groom. Based on his pleased expression, she didn't need to tell him. Oh, she was acting like a foolish schoolgirl! "We'd better hurry if I'm to be home before dark."

Isabel stayed a step or two ahead of him as they walked down the trail, as she had the feeling that if she tried talking to him again, *she* would be the one stuttering and blushing.

When they reached the gate, Robert climbed over first and then offered his hand to help her.

"There you are," Mr. Kensington called from across the meadow as he led their horses over. "I thought perhaps you'd walked home or gone back to the falls."

Isabel gave Robert the tiniest glance to remind him that the cottage was a secret. Her heart skipped. *Their* secret.

"We followed an overgrown trail. It doesn't lead anywhere," Robert said.

"Many of those around here," Mr. Kensington replied. "It must be part of an abandoned farm."

Isabel and Robert mounted their horses and followed him through the meadow. A gap in the trees led to the main road, much farther away from where they'd crossed paths hours ago.

"I'll have to make haste if I'm to be in time for supper," Isabel said. She spurred Dion and cantered down the road, the men close behind. She slowed when they reached the fork in the road which led to Kerensly Hall. "Thank you for an interesting afternoon. Will you come to the house?"

Robert brought Apollo closer to Dion. "No, my mother expects me to dine with her tonight, and she doesn't abide tardiness. I'm having my portrait painted tomorrow. Would you come talk to me while I sit?"

"Would that not be a distraction?"

He grinned. "Yes, a welcome one."

"When shall I call?" she asked, glad he wanted to see her again so soon.

"We start right after breakfast. Meet Simon in the back garden and he'll bring you up to the solarium."

She tilted her head. Had she heard him right? "Why not the front door?"

Robert gave her a sheepish look. "I'm not sure my mother would approve of me having female company during the sitting."

She tried to keep the disappointment out of her voice. "I wouldn't wish to displease your mother. Let's meet another day."

"Please come," Robert implored. He'd brought Apollo close enough that his boot was brushing the hem of her skirt.

"I don't want to offend anyone, least of all your mother." This was most unusual. Why on earth would he keep her visit a secret? Was it only from his mother, or his whole family? She knew what Verity would say. And her own mother. And her own conscience. Under no circumstances should she try to sneak into Thornwood without Mrs. Claremont's permission. But was Robert trying to advance their friendship? It would be soon for that, and yet, looking at him, she realized there was nothing she'd like more. Of course, this could be wishful thinking on her part. Perhaps his mother simply didn't want him to be distracted during his sitting. But he certainly did. She could tell by the look in his eyes how much he wanted her to say yes.

"Adventure...?" Robert prompted, with a smile that finally broke through her resolve.

She nodded, though she knew she should be shaking

her head. "I'll come."

He kissed her hand, and a single butterfly in her stomach stretched its wings.

She thought of nothing but him all the way home.

Chapter Five

Robert went over every moment of their time together as he rode home silently beside Simon, smiling when he recalled getting through entire conversations without faltering. He liked to think he'd managed to actually flirt with Isabel without sounding like a fool. For him, being this comfortable with a woman was unprecedented.

When he and Simon arrived at Thornwood, they led their horses to the stable and handed them off to a groom.

Simon broke into his pleasant thoughts. "I have some things to attend to. I'll see you later."

Robert just nodded and walked into the house, where he found William waiting for him at the foot of the stairs.

"Where have you been all day?" William asked.

"Riding," Robert said, climbing the staircase.

"All day?"

"All day."

When Robert went into his room, William followed and sat in a chair beside the window. Robert went to the wash basin and splashed his face with water. He smiled, recalling Isabel's joy at their discovery of the cottage.

"What has you so distracted?" William asked, picking Robert's journal up from the desk and leafing through it.

Robert dried his face with a towel and turned to face

him. "Miss Tate. Isabel."

"Of course. Your riding companion. Did you enjoy yourself?"

"It was pleasant." He couldn't begin to explain how Isabel made him feel, what it was like to be in her company.

William scoffed. "You spend all day with a woman you consider merely 'pleasant'? My hunting dog is pleasant."

"More than that. She's sweet and smart and intriguing." He snatched the journal out of William's hands and stashed it in a bureau drawer. "There's something about her. I want to see her as often as I can."

"Then you shall, in your spare time. She can be your mistress after you're married."

"It's not like that with Isabel and me," Robert said hotly. Then his tone softened. "It couldn't be like that."

"I feel sorry for you, Robert. I do." William stood and put a hand on his shoulder. "I can see you like this woman, but you have a duty. As Mother is going to remind you at supper."

"It's time to go," Robert said shortly and left the room.

They made their way to the dining room and found their mother already at the table.

"Good evening, Mother," said Robert, kissing her hand. William followed suit, and they took their seats on either side of her.

Mrs. Claremont rang a bell and servers appeared with dishes of roast duck, pigeon pie, wild rice and pears.

"What did you do today, Mother?" Robert asked, and took a bite of the tender duck.

"My usual pursuits. Needlework, reading. I took a

walk in the afternoon."

"That must be why you look so refreshed," William said, carving up his pigeon pie.

"And you?" she asked Robert. "I hear you went riding with Simon."

He sipped his wine. "I did." He looked up to see William smiling smugly at him.

"Simon and...?" Mrs. Claremont continued, folding her hands on the table.

"And Miss Tate," Robert muttered, putting his fork down. How could she possibly know he'd been with someone besides Simon? Only one person could have told her.

"Who did you say you were with?" William asked.

"Miss Tate," he stated loudly, glaring at William, who raised his glass in a mock toast.

"Did your father not make himself clear about Margery Penrose?" Mrs. Claremont asked in a soft yet steely voice.

Robert wiped the corners of his mouth with a napkin and pushed the plate away. "He did."

"So?" Mrs. Claremont asked.

Robert tried to insert some disappointment into his tone. "I tried wooing her. She's not interested. She's cold and—"

"Cold? You only need to learn how to warm her," William cut in.

"No need for that talk, William," Mrs. Claremont reprimanded.

"I beg your pardon, Mother. But I don't believe Robert has sincerely tried with Margery."

"She appears to like you, William," Robert said. "Perhaps Father would allow you to court her." He sipped his wine.

"Your father wants her for you, Robert."

He banged his glass down on the table. "And what of what I want?"

"What you want," Mrs. Claremont said, enunciating every syllable, "is to serve your father and your house."

"I consistently put the family's needs before my own wishes. Usually they coincide. But this is my future, my life. I would choose my own bride." He finished in a rush, as though pressing himself to speak the words aloud.

"You do not have that liberty," his mother said.

"You have the chance to bring much wealth to the family," William said, leaning back in his chair.

Mrs. Claremont nodded. "The match will ensure that our estate flourishes for generations."

"It already will," Robert argued. "We don't need the Penrose fortunes for that."

Mrs. Claremont and William exchanged a significant look.

Robert's stomach sank. "What is it that you aren't telling me?"

"Thornwood isn't as stable as you believe, Robert," William said soberly. "We have enough. For now. But Father has been—"

"Been?" Robert prompted, impatient now.

"Gambling!" Mrs. Claremont cried, "Gambling with our future!"

Robert scoffed. "He cannot have lost that much."

"You would be surprised," William said.

"How do we stand?" Robert asked.

His mother looked him in the eyes. "We're not in danger of losing everything right now. But unless something is done, your grandsons will not run this estate. Thornwood will be in someone else's hands."

"Impossible! How did this happen?" Robert demanded.

"You recall that your father went to stay for a time with Giles Branwick at his country house last year?"

"I do. He was gone for some weeks. William and I managed the estate while he was away."

"Apparently most of the entertainment was gaming tables. Your father doesn't know when to stop. We're not destitute, to be sure. But we're not as wealthy as we were even a year ago." She crumpled the napkin in her lap.

"Why didn't Father tell me about this?" Robert asked, his supper long forgotten.

"He's ashamed," William said. "As he should be," he added, earning him a cold look from his mother.

"If we act quickly, nobody need know. We can secure Margery's fortune and forget this ever happened," Mrs. Claremont said.

"Is there no other way? Miss Tate is Mr. Branwick's stepdaughter, wouldn't a match with her help our cause?" Robert suggested hopefully.

"Align ourselves with that snake?" Mrs. Claremont cried. "I'll never be connected with that family, and neither will you. I'm not convinced he played honestly, but you cannot accuse a man like him. We're stuck. You must marry Margery."

"Why not William?"

"You know why," William said, before his mother could answer. "Father explained it all to you. You're the golden boy, I'm the disappointment."

"You're not a disappointment," Mrs. Claremont said, "but your focus isn't what it should be. You would not deny that you have the well-earned reputation of a rake. What father wants to turn his daughter over to someone who has his hands up every skirt he can reach?"

William flushed, but didn't argue.

"That's all to be said for now," Mrs. Claremont said. "You know your reason, Robert. Now do your duty."

"Yes, Mother." He didn't agree with her but was tired of arguing.

Mrs. Claremont rang the bell again, and servants returned with more wine, fruit, and cakes with honey and almonds.

Robert immediately picked up the cakes and offered one to his mother. She waved it away, but William was happy to have one.

"How are the portraits coming?" Mrs. Claremont asked.

"Well enough," Robert said, "William's is done. He wouldn't sit still, so the artist is making the painting from a sketch. Mine's almost finished. Tomorrow may be the last sitting."

"We have the ball to think of now," Mrs. Claremont said.

William and Robert both look at her in surprise.

"Ball?" they said together.

"Of course. To unveil your portraits. And Robert, we'll expect an announcement from you that night," Mrs. Claremont said, looking him in the eye.

"Yes, Mother."

"When is the ball to be?" William asked.

"Oh, not for some weeks. The paintings must be finished, then framed. Then, of course, I need to make all the arrangements and send invitations."

"Just make sure Cook makes more of these cakes,"

Robert said as he and William both reached for the last one. Robert got it first, but broke off half and shared it with William.

Mrs. Claremont rose from the table. "I will retire now."

"Good night, Mother," said Robert.

"Good night," William said.

She kissed them both on the cheek and left the room.

"I'm going up to the library. Care to join me in a game of chess?" Robert asked William as they walked out into the hall.

"No. I'm off to bed."

"That's not the way to your room," Robert said as William headed for the front door.

"No, it isn't, but I know a bed awaits me," William said cheerily, running a hand through his hair and straightening his cravat.

"Bess?"

"Does it matter? It will be warm." William gave Robert a wicked grin and strode out the door, whistling.

When Robert got back to his room a fire crackled in the grate. He changed into his nightshirt, crawled into bed, and put his arms behind his head, thinking about Isabel and the afternoon they'd shared. Smiling at the thought that he would see her again tomorrow, he drifted off to sleep.

Robert was the first one down for breakfast the next day and was just finishing his meal when Simon entered the dining room.

"Is she here?" Robert shot out of his chair.

"I'm going to meet her shortly. You told her to meet me after breakfast, remember?"

"Oh, yes," he said, taking his seat. "But don't tarry

long. She'll be waiting."

"There's more than enough time."

Robert tapped his foot under the table as Simon sat to a leisurely meal.

Simon looked up. "Will you eat?"

"I did, before you came in. I want to get started on the portrait early. If it doesn't take too long, I'm going to show Isabel the grounds."

"How will you manage that without being seen?"

"Nobody will see us. William and my father won't be here, and Mother is unlikely to be gazing out her window at the precise moment I escort Miss Tate to the rose arbor."

Simon glanced at the grandfather clock, then rose. "I'd better go."

"Bring her straight to me when she arrives. And you'll need to stable her horse if she rode."

"Leave everything to me," Simon said and left the room.

Robert made his way upstairs to the solarium where the artist, Laurence, was already organizing his materials.

"Sit." Laurence picked up his brush and set to work.

Robert shifted in the chair, crossing and uncrossing his legs. Isabel could be here at any moment. He sat for another quarter of an hour before a sound came from the stairwell. He sat up straighter, straining to hear. Footsteps.

"Are we expecting someone?" Laurence asked, eyes on the canvas.

Robert didn't answer, but stared at the door. It opened, and there she was, stunning in a moss green gown.

Laurence let out an exasperated sigh, setting his brush down as Robert rose.

"Good morning." Robert took Isabel's hand and drew her into the room. Over her shoulder he caught Simon's eye, who shook his head at him before settling himself in a chair at the head of the stairs.

She smiled. "Good morning."

"Who is this?" Laurence asked.

Robert hesitated, not wanting to divulge her name.

Laurence picked up his brush. "No matter. Sit."

Robert helped Isabel into a chair directly in front of him, then took his seat. Red highlights in her hair shone in the sunlight streaming through the windows, and her cheeks were delicately flushed, perhaps from the ride over.

"How was it, getting out this morning?" Robert asked. The restlessness he'd felt all morning had disappeared the moment he'd seen her face. What was it about her that set him so at ease? Perhaps her warmth, or her sense of humor, or the way she always met his eyes and seemed genuinely interested in what he had to say. The awkwardness around women that had dogged him for his entire life was simply gone.

She smoothed down her skirt. "The walk over was invigorating."

"You walked? It's quite far, isn't it?"

She smiled. "Not for me, I enjoy long walks."

"I do, too. Perhaps we could take one together." It crossed his mind that he was being too forward, but she took to the idea at once.

"I'd like that. It would be interesting to see more of Holton, especially with the *right guide*." She grinned, arching a brow.

Robert laughed and after a moment said, "I've been wondering about that cottage we found."

Her eyes brightened. "As have I! I wonder what it was? How did it come to be there?"

"We'll try to find out. We could go back and look for clues about who once lived there."

"What a wonderful idea." She leaned forward in her chair. "When?"

"Today? When I'm through here?"

"I'd love to."

"Mouth closed," Laurence said, reminding Robert that they weren't alone.

Robert shrugged and tried to assume the usual thoughtful-yet-slightly-amused expression he wore for his sittings. Isabel smiled and held his eyes for a moment before sitting back in her chair and glancing around the room.

Thirty minutes later Laurence said, "Done," and rose from his chair.

"You're finished?" Robert reluctantly turned away from Isabel.

"Yes. I have only small details to finish, and I can do those without you here." He took a step back to admire his work.

Just then Simon came in. "It's been almost an hour. Shall I escort Isabel home?"

"We're going to see the garden," Robert said, not divulging their true destination: the cottage. A thought suddenly struck him. "Simon, would you take Isabel outside while I speak to Laurence?"

"I'd be happy to."

Isabel threw Robert a puzzled look but followed Simon from the room.

Robert approached Laurence. "Could you paint her? From memory?"

"I don't need to do it from memory." Laurence held up an accurate sketch of Isabel.

"When did you do that?" Robert asked incredulously.

"Just now, as you were speaking to her."

"Could you make a miniature of her? And one of me?"

"Ah, a set, is it?" Laurence said with a knowing look. "Alas, I was only commissioned for the portraits of you and your brother."

"I'll pay you myself. I'd like to keep this between us."

Laurence looked at Robert for a long moment, considering. At last he said, "Yes. I'll paint your miniatures."

"When can they be finished?"

"In time for the ball, but I'll need to send them to you. I'm leaving here as soon as your portrait is completed, which will be a matter of days."

"Send them to my care only, so nobody else sees them. And thank you."

Laurence nodded and turned back to his work.

Robert left the room and flew downstairs, where his spirits plummeted at what greeted him in the garden.

Chapter Six

William stood with his arms crossed, smiling at Simon and Isabel, who looked as if they'd been caught trying to steal a horse.

"Look who's here, Robert," William said, a gleam in his eye. "It's Miss Tate. With Simon, of all people."

"Oh. Good morning, Miss Tate." Robert covered his face with his hand but quickly brushed aside a nonexistent hair to cover the movement. He had to act surprised to see Isabel, and at the same time pretend her being here was of no consequence. Inside, he was seething. Isabel's jaw was set and he could tell that, though mortified, she was trying to seem unruffled. It was Robert's fault she was in this position, and he'd be lucky if she ever spoke to him again after today.

She looked at the ground. "Good morning."

"Miss Tate's here on an errand for her aunt. Something about…what was it?" William asked, clearly enjoying himself.

"A gown," Simon provided.

"A gown?" William asked.

"Yes." Isabel nodded, casting Simon a grateful look. "Yes. My aunt admired the gown your mother wore on May Day and would like to know what seamstress made it for her."

"She needn't have sent you all the way over here for that," William said. "She could easily have sent a message."

"Yes, I suppose that's true," Isabel agreed, clasping her hands in front of her.

Robert moved to her side. "Well, you're here now. Would you like to see the garden?"

"Unchaperoned!" William said, feigning shock.

Robert glared at him. "Simon will be with us."

"No. I must get home," cut in Isabel.

"To the stables then." William offered her his arm.

She hesitated. "I walked over."

"Did you? A fine day for it," William said.

"Yes. A fine day. Good day to you all," Isabel said, her narrowed eyes on Robert. She turned and marched away.

As soon as she was out of earshot Robert turned on William, eyes flashing. "How could you be so rude?"

"Me?" William shot back. "What's she doing here? That lie about an errand for her aunt! Come to see Simon, more like."

"Simon?"

"Me?" Simon exclaimed.

"Yes. She looked positively delighted ambling about the garden with you." He turned to Robert. "See? Not worth your time. She's happy with any handsome man who comes her way."

"That's not true," Robert said, fuming.

"Well, then?" William asked.

Robert was about to reply but stopped when he noticed the glint in William's eyes—he was clearly goading him to discover what he was doing with Isabel. But he wouldn't play along. She might be in trouble with her aunt and uncle if they knew she'd called on him without their approval. Of course, Isabel thought she *did* have their approval. His stomach twisted. But the main thing now was to get William off the scent.

"Maybe she does like Simon. It's nothing to me. I'm going riding." Robert went to the stable, saddled Apollo, and raced down the road. Isabel had a good head start, but he soon saw her up ahead.

She turned as she heard him approach. When she saw who it was she put her hands on her hips. "Never again! I don't like this skulking around. If your parents disapprove of me, I won't see you."

Robert jumped off Apollo and hurried to her side. "I apologize for putting you in that position."

Her brows furrowed as she wagged a finger in his face. "I'm only coming to your house again with a written invitation. From your mother."

He took a step back. She looked so angry he wondered if she'd ever come back at all. "It won't happen again."

"No, it won't," she snapped.

"I didn't want to wait another day to see you," he said, shifting from foot to foot, "so I concocted this foolish plan. I'm sorry."

She gave him a small smile and sighed. "It's all right. I wanted to see you, too."

Robert's heart leapt to his throat. She'd wanted to see him, too. They stood looking at each other for a moment, eyes locked.

"Would you like to take a walk with me?" he asked.

"Oh, yes. Could we go to the cottage?"

"It's a bit of a walk from here. We'd better ride."

"Perhaps another day." The disappointment on her face made him all the more determined *not* to wait for another day.

"Apollo can carry us both." Robert could almost read her thoughts. It was one thing to be out walking with a man alone, but riding together? "You can sit sideways in front of me, there's plenty of room."

"I think it's the only way," Isabel replied at last. "But I hope we're not seen."

Robert helped her mount and climbed up behind her. He picked his way carefully through the trees, and before long they came to the meadow.

He pointed toward the edge of the woods. "From here you can't see the gate, even knowing it's there."

Isabel craned her neck to search. "Do you think it's meant to be hidden, or is it merely overgrown?"

"It's hard to say."

Halfway across the meadow Robert said, "Hold on!" and spurred Apollo to a gallop. Isabel gasped and grabbed Apollo's mane as Robert's arm tightened around her. He pulled up just before the gate and Isabel slid off Apollo, laughing.

She gave Apollo's nose a rub, then turned to Robert. "You're quite a rider."

"It's but one of my many accomplishments," he joked.

"One?" Isabel asked, grinning.

"You'd be surprised. I'm a man of hidden talents. Over time you will see…" He trailed off, not wanting to appear presumptuous.

"I look forward to discovering your secrets," she said in a way that set his pulse racing.

Flustered, Robert turned to secure Apollo's reins to a tree, somehow needing three tries to make a proper knot. He turned back just as Isabel was heading down the path.

Kate Ellington

"Shall we?" she called over her shoulder.

He leapt over the gate and caught up to her, and before long they reached the clearing. The sun shining down on the cottage gave it an enchanted look.

"Inside or out?" Robert asked.

"Let's go to the garden."

The garden was even prettier than Robert remembered it. They waded through the tall flowers until they found a grassy area that was not quite so wild.

"Here's a good spot," Robert said, and they sat down across from each other.

Isabel picked a flower and twirled it in her fingers. It was hard to imagine her delicate hands stringing the bow, as he'd seen her do the other day. It pleased him to see how relaxed, even happy, she seemed in his company. Considering how uneasy he usually felt around women, his contentment with her was nothing short of miraculous. He looked up and caught Isabel staring at him. He smiled, and instead of looking away she held him with her warm gaze.

Robert's hands began to sweat, his stomach a tight knot beneath his galloping heart.

"What occupies you when you're in Salisbury?" he asked to break the tension.

"I pay calls, ride, practice my archery, go to the theater with my friends. I'm kept busy most days. I especially enjoy playing with my baby sister. And what do you do? I know you dance tolerably well," she teased.

"Tolerably? You seemed to enjoy my dancing on May Day."

"So I did. And what else of you, Robert?" she asked. The sound of his name on her lips set his heart racing again.

"Oh, the usual pursuits. Riding, hunting, swordplay, taking advantage of our library. The estate takes up most of my time. My father's been teaching me all aspects of managing it since I'll share responsibilities with William."

"You'll both manage the estate?" she asked, clearly surprised.

"Until the time comes for one of us to inherit. Eventually William or I will be master at Thornwood and the other will move away. Or perhaps we'll both stay on at Thornwood and manage it together. It's not entirely settled yet. When the time comes, our father will decide what's to be done."

"Would you enjoy working with your brother?"

Robert could not hold back a grimace. "I think so."

"But?" she asked, raising her brows.

"William isn't always the easiest to get along with. And even when we work together my father expects more of me than of him. I don't mind the work, but I'm who he looks to if something goes wrong, and the first one he seeks out if there's a problem on the estate. It's as if he thinks I automatically know what to do, simply because I'm his son. But I don't, not always, and—" He stopped. Why was he telling her this? He'd never told anyone else of the pressure he felt being, as William called him, the golden boy. He cleared his throat and tapped his riding crop on his boot. "I don't want to bore you."

She leaned in. "I'm not bored."

"I'm boring myself," he said with a dry laugh.

Isabel looked down at the grass. "I know what it's like to have expectations cast on you. When my father died, my mother depended on me for everything. I was all she had left. She didn't pay social calls or leave the house, and wanted me with her all the time. I didn't mind, not really." She looked up at him. "I love her and was glad to help. But I think, perhaps, she forgot that though she lost a husband, *I* had lost a father. I probably sound ridiculous." She rubbed her temple.

"No, you don't." He reached for her hand, but pulled back at the last moment.

Isabel's shoulders slumped. "I was lonely. My father was just…just everything to me. We had so much in common. When I was young, he and my mother and I traveled and rode together, and they both tutored me at home. It was always the three of us. Perhaps that's why, when he'd gone, my mother needed me to support her and forgot that I also needed support. So, in a sense, I lost a mother, too." She looked away and pulled her knees up to her chest. "Oh, I sound so selfish."

"Not at all. Sometimes I think my father forgets I'm his son first, and his heir second. All he cares about is preserving Thornwood. You have no idea how vexed he is that he has twins. You'd think any man would be glad to have two sons, but he has to prepare both of us to inherit, not knowing who will. I don't understand why he hasn't decided already. It's for him to choose. And there will be no more children, so he has to choose between William, who I won't shock you by saying is a bit wild, and me, who is steadfast but ultimately—"

She nudged his foot with hers. "What?"

"Ultimately I want to make my own decisions about my life."

She looked into his eyes. "We all do."

"I love Thornwood, and it's an honor to do all I can for it. But if I knew what position I hold I'd have an idea of what direction my life will take. Am I the heir, and will spend my life here on my beloved estate, or am I the second son who must make other plans? Perhaps I might travel or go to school or move across the sea. William thinks I have it so easy. He says it must nice to be our parents' favorite. But I'm nobody's favorite, and he doesn't understand what it's like to have the weight of the entire family on my shoulders. We should be splitting responsibilities equally. Now who sounds selfish?" he said, pulling up blades of grass.

"Neither of us is selfish," she said. "But I have another confession that might make me sound like I *am*. I adore Victoria, but sometimes I wish my mother would remember that she has two daughters. After the initial shock of my father's death, we settled back into our old routine of spending all our time together, and in a way we felt more like friends than parent and child. But once Mr. Branwick started courting her, she barely had any time for me. She put everything aside for him, even her old friends. The weeks after Victoria was born were wonderful because we grew close again and the three of us were together every day. But then, for no reason, my stepfather sent me away. I think he might be jealous of how close my mother and I were, and I suspect he tries to keep us apart. Since I moved away she sometimes goes weeks without writing to me, and I think he has a hand in that. I'm glad I have Aunt Verity."

They sat in silence for a few moments before Robert said, "I'm glad you have your aunt, too, because otherwise we wouldn't have met."

She smiled. "So one good thing has come of my stepfather's sending me away."

He returned her smile but would rather have taken

her in his arms and kissed her. What would she do if he did? His mouth went suddenly dry. He stared at her profile as she looked at the trees. "Would you like to come out again tomorrow? We could go back to the falls."

"I won't be able to. My aunt does allow me my freedoms, but I can't leave so often without telling her, not unless I want her to assign a guard to me until we go back to Salisbury," she said and laughed.

"And when will that be?"

"The end of the summer."

He picked a buttercup. "That's months away. I'm glad."

"Are you?" A pink hue appeared on her cheeks.

"Yes." He handed her the flower. "We'll be able to see more of each other. If I may be so bold, that is."

Isabel tucked the flower into her bodice and said softly, "You may."

Robert's heart thundered as he met her eyes. He'd felt such a strong connection to her since that first moment he'd seen her in the great hall. Should he tell her how he felt? Was it even possible she didn't know? He took a deep breath and his heart ceased its wild beating as a calm settled over him. Now was the time to tell her. He opened his mouth to speak.

"Oh!" Isabel exclaimed. Clouds had rolled in while they'd been talking, and now plump rain drops spattered down on them.

"Quick—inside!" Robert said.

Isabel dashed into the cottage, and he ran in behind her just as the rain began in earnest.

"Now what?" Isabel said with a laugh.

"We wait."

Robert looked around the cottage, deeply conscious of the fact that they were utterly alone. Isabel walked to the window and watched the rain. He'd never known a woman more beautiful and agreeable in every way. She was everything Robert could have wanted, only he hadn't known it until he met her. Isabel turned to him as if she'd heard his thoughts. Suddenly the cottage shrank. He took a hesitant step toward her. She didn't move, but faced him with an almost determined look on her face as he walked across the room, not stopping until he was close enough to see the raindrops clinging to her lashes. Robert took her hands in his, knowing without a doubt that he was looking into the face of his future. Her lips parted.

Just then a voice pierced the air, and they leapt apart.

"Robert!" someone shouted.

He recognized the voice at once as Simon's.

Robert saw his own disappointment mirrored on Isabel's face. On their way out of the cottage she took a deep breath and put a hand on her chest as though to steady herself. The rain had slowed to a light drizzle, the drops looking like tiny diamonds glittering in the sunshine. Robert had expected to see Simon in the courtyard, but there was no sign of him. They heard him call again, louder.

"This way," Robert said. They walked down the shady path in silence. Was Isabel as thoughtful as he was? To think what had almost just happened! One look at her face showed Robert that she was indeed distracted.

Simon, sitting astride Blaze, was waiting for them in the meadow holding Apollo's reins.

"Robert, what were—" Simon stopped when he caught sight of Isabel, unable to mask the shock on his face.

Robert glanced at Isabel. She wouldn't meet his or Simon's eyes but looked at the ground.

"I was bringing Isabel home. We meant to see the river, but the rain caught us," Robert lied. "What are you doing here?"

"I was just passing and found Apollo wandering the meadow without you."

"I must have tied him too loosely." Robert gave Apollo a pat, inwardly cursing himself for his lackluster knot tying earlier. If Apollo hadn't run off, he and Isabel might have come to an understanding, might even now be wrapped in the embrace he longed for.

"I'll escort you home," Robert said to Isabel.

She still wouldn't look at him. "Thank you."

"Take Blaze," Simon said to Isabel. "I'll walk home."

"It's not too far?"

"Not at all," he assured her, dismounting. "I'll take the short cut back to Thornwood, on the other side of the river."

"I'll have Blaze seen to when I get back," Robert said.

Simon nodded and cast Robert a disapproving look before striding off in the direction of the river.

Robert helped Isabel to mount. Clearly she'd had experience riding without a woman's saddle, as she rode well enough perched sideways in Simon's. They guided the horses back through the meadow and onto the main road.

"I'm going to make that cottage habitable again," Robert said.

She broke into a grin. "What a splendid idea."

They chatted about what kinds of repairs the cottage needed and before long reached the fork in the road where it was time to part.

"I'll walk from here," Isabel said, dismounting.

He had to know when he'd see her again, but he couldn't call at Kerensly, and after this morning's debacle at Thornwood he wouldn't try sneaking her in again.

"Are you attending the Penroses' ball?" Robert asked as he dismounted and moved to her side.

"Yes, my family will attend." She handed him Blaze's reins.

He took a deep breath and asked, "Will you dance with me there?"

She lit up. "I'd love to."

He took Isabel's hand and kissed it tenderly, then held it for a moment as he looked into her eyes. "Until the ball."

"The ball," she said breathlessly.

****

Isabel entered the hall just as Nell reached the bottom of the stairs.

After one glance at her, Nell put her hands on her hips. "Where have you been? Tramping about, from the state of your skirts!"

"I went walking." She *had* walked, so it wasn't exactly a lie.

"I've been looking for you. Your aunt wants to talk to you about your ball gown. It seems there was a misunderstanding with the seamstress."

"I'll go up directly."

When Isabel entered Verity's suite of rooms, the first thing she saw was the gown hanging in the open wardrobe. It was absolutely perfect. Sky blue, with tiny silver and gold stars embroidered into the hem and cuffs. The neckline, trimmed with delicate lace, scooped well below her collar bone. She couldn't take her eyes off the dress, and it was some minutes before she recalled herself and turned to face her aunt.

"Have you ever seen such a marvelous gown?" she asked, beaming.

Verity set her book aside. "Isabel, did you order alterations to this gown? I thought we had it settled."

"We did. I just wanted it to be…" She flourished her hands, searching for words.

"To be what?"

"Magical. And it is. Oh, it is!" She ran her hands over the fabric and touched the stars, imagining how the gown would shimmer as she danced.

Verity gave the dress a disapproving look. "Is it not a bit revealing?"

"No more than gowns I see on other women. I went to balls in Salisbury, and the gowns there would make you blush. This is just enough."

"Enough what?" Verity asked, smiling now.

"Enough to look special. To stand out."

"If you're looking to be noticed, you will be."

"I hope so." Isabel envisioned herself dancing with Robert in this dress, his strong arms holding her as they glided around the ballroom.

"Where did you go today?" Verity asked.

"Oh, out walking. I'm acquainting myself with the neighborhood." Isabel joined her aunt on the couch.

"Your skirts!" Verity exclaimed.

"It was muddy."

"I'm about to take some refreshment. Will you join

me?"

"Yes, but first let me change."

Upstairs in her room, Isabel went out to the small balcony overlooking the forest. If only she could see the cottage from here. Or better yet, Thornwood. Her bedroom was good sized, yet snug. A four-poster bed draped with green curtains stood beside the window, its coverlet matching the delicate pink roses painted on the cream-colored walls. A wardrobe, vanity, bedside table, and writing desk completed the furnishings.

After changing into a mauve dress and taming her windblown hair, she returned to Verity's room. A table set up in front of the sofa held a tray of sandwiches and fresh fruit.

Verity was sitting at her desk. "Help yourself, Isabel. I'm just finishing a letter to your mother."

As Isabel ate, she recalled her day with Robert. He was most intriguing, and such a gentleman. What would have happened if Mr. Kensington hadn't come to the meadow? She'd been sure Robert was about to say something important. What would she have said in return? Surely it was much too soon to talk of love. But she'd told him things she'd never told anyone else, and felt like she'd known him for years, not days. It made no sense—they'd just met. Yet her heart skipped when she saw him, he was ever in her thoughts, and she wished she could spend every moment with him. Was this what it was like to fall in love? Or did she simply enjoy his company?

"Isabel!"

"Yes?" Isabel said, startled out of her reverie.

"I called you multiple times. You look as though you're dreaming."

Isabel shifted uncomfortably in her seat.

Verity moved to the sofa and sat beside her. "You're hiding something."

Isabel played with the sleeve of her dress, not meeting her aunt's eyes. "Verity, what's it like to fall in love?"

She clasped her hands in front of her, green eyes shining. "Love! Who is he?"

Isabel didn't reply. Must she turn red at every inopportune moment?

"What young man has inspired this talk of love? Someone you met in town?"

"Not in town…no."

"Is it someone you know from Salisbury? Oh! Who is it?"

"Robert. Robert Claremont," Isabel admitted in a sighing voice.

Verity couldn't mask her surprise. "Robert Claremont? But you've only met him once."

"More than that. He asked Uncle Francis if he could ride with me, and he gave consent."

"I'm surprised your uncle didn't mention it to me. He's been so busy of late, it must have slipped his mind. Why hasn't Robert called at the house?"

"We've had chance meetings out and about." Isabel didn't mention today, which had definitely been planned.

Verity's eyes widened. "Alone?"

"Mr. Kensington has been with us."

She nodded her approval and smiled. "Well, Robert is a fine young man. I never hear gossip about him, unlike his brother."

Isabel leaned back on the sofa and hugged a pillow to her chest. "Oh he *is* fine. He's kind, considerate, amusing, and so handsome. He was quite shy at first, but not anymore."

Verity put a hand on her arm. "But love, Isabel? You haven't known him long."

"This is what confuses me. I've never loved a man before, and I'm not sure how to know that it *is* love." If love was determined solely by how she felt giddy when he said her name and how she wanted to kiss him every time she saw him, then it *was* love.

"Does he love you?" Verity poured herself a glass of sherry and took a sip.

"I know he likes me. He's sought me out two times, and asked to dance with me at the Penroses' ball."

"He would be a fine match for you."

Isabel sat up straighter, casting the pillow aside. "I hardly think it's time to speak of matches yet."

"Never too soon. I knew your uncle for only three weeks before he proposed. And your parents. Your mother told me she knew during their first dance. Edward made her an offer the next day, and she didn't hesitate to accept him. Our parents were happy to support both of our matches, and as you know, we had a double wedding not one month later," Verity said dreamily.

Isabel frowned. "It's not always like that. Look at Mother now."

"She's not in love with Mr. Branwick, but she has security. You'll see how important that is when you're older." She took another sip of sherry. "I've heard of a match between Robert and Margery Penrose. What's come of that?"

"He tells me there's nothing to it."

Verity pressed her lips together. "Hm."

"What?" Isabel asked, shifting in her seat to face her.

"Forgive me, but could he be merely amusing himself before his wedding?"

"Robert wouldn't do that. And there's no wedding set or even a betrothal."

"Be wary, Isabel. He has a fine reputation, but his brother doesn't. It would be unfortunate to discover too late that he's not as different from William as we believe. My only counsel is to guard your feelings for now. Be truly sure of him before you let your own feelings be known."

"I'll be careful. Oh, how will I go without seeing him for a fortnight?" She flopped back into the sofa cushions.

"John will keep you busy. He's been asking for you all morning. Go to him now, if you're finished eating."

"I will. I promised to watch him ride his pony today."

Verity returned to her desk. "Before I seal this letter to your mother, may I tell her how things stand between you and Mr. Claremont?"

"I'm sure she'd like to hear of it. But don't imply that anything is settled. I'll know more after the ball."

Verity resumed her writing, and Isabel made her way to the paddock to find John.

****

After leaving Isabel, Robert rode home. When he'd mentioned repairing the cottage it had been on a whim, but the more he thought of it the more he liked the idea. He was considering exactly what the cottage needed when Simon stepped out of the forest up ahead. Robert released the reins and let Blaze trot to his owner.

"At the cottage today?" Simon asked as he grabbed Blaze's bridle.

Robert paled. "What?"

"The cottage. You were there with Miss Tate?" He climbed into the saddle.

So it was not as secret as they'd hoped. "You know about the cottage? How?"

"I found it years ago when I was lost. I must have been eight or nine. I was playing in the woods one day and couldn't find my way home. I wandered around for hours before I stumbled across the place and spent a very damp, cold night there."

Robert nodded. "I remember that. You were missing all night and half the household was out looking for you."

"In the morning I made my way to the meadow and a groom found me."

Robert nudged Apollo, who started walking down the road. "Why didn't you ever tell me about it?"

Simon shrugged. "There weren't many places I could call my own when we were children. I haven't been back there in years."

"Does anyone else know about it?"

Simon looked off into the distance as if searching his mind. "I've never heard anyone mention it, but I suppose it's possible."

"How did you know we were there today?"

He smirked. "I saw you climb over the gate, but you were so focused on each other you didn't see me. It was obvious you'd come from that direction."

Reddening, Robert looked down at Apollo's mane. "Why didn't you say anything?"

Simon laughed. "Miss Tate looked mortified enough as it was. I didn't want to embarrass her."

"Thank you for that. The cottage is so secluded I'm

surprised William doesn't use it for his trysts."

"He's never been there, as far as I know. If he brought women there, he'd have boasted about it. You know how he is."

"Yes I do, and at least the bed would be clean. When we went in everything was covered in dust and half the furniture was broken. You must be the only person to go inside for decades. It's surprising William and I never found it when we were children."

"Not really. It's so deep in the woods, and I only found it by accident."

"True. I must have been through the meadow hundreds of times and never noticed that gate. I'm going to repair the cottage."

"I'd be happy to help."

"Only let's keep this to ourselves. Isabel very much likes the idea of it being our secret place."

Simon turned to him, brows knitted. "Be careful. You know your family doesn't approve of her."

"I do know." Tired of everyone trying to dissuade him from pursuing Isabel, he let Simon think the subject was dropped and urged Apollo to a canter.

Chapter Seven

By midsummer, Robert was spending a few days a week at the cottage, doing repairs. His only obstacle to spending every day there was his father's attempts at matchmaking. Mr. Claremont had taken to sending him on random errands to Margery's house, inviting the Penroses for supper, organizing hunting parties, and doing anything else he could think of to throw them together. It wasn't working. Robert could tell by Margery's demeanor that she wasn't remotely interested in him, no matter how advantageous the match. He had, however, seen William walking with her one day when he was supposed to be in the village. This gave Robert hope, for if William could win her affections, the alliance could go forward, leaving Robert free to pursue Isabel.

He was mulling this over as he rode home from the cottage one day. The roof had been replaced, and he was now working on the chimney. It would be time to start on the interior soon, cleaning it out and making it a home. He and Simon had discovered some clues about the previous owner. They'd found an old monk's habit stuffed into a cupboard, and a small wooden cross had been hidden in a secret compartment in the bricks of the fireplace. This led them to believe the cottage had belonged to one of the monks from the nearby abbey that had been closed for at least two hundred years.

Robert had neither seen nor heard from Isabel for

almost a fortnight. It felt like much longer, and every day he longed to ride to Kerensly. He'd hoped he might see her riding in the woods, but this hadn't happened. Just one more day and he would see her, for tonight was the Penroses' ball.

He spent an idle afternoon meandering about Thornwood, unable to settle to anything as the hours crawled by. When it was finally time to get ready, he donned his white shirt, brown waistcoat, forest green coat, and breeches.

When he arrived at Penhollow, Robert craned his neck to see above the crowd waiting to get inside, but there was no sign of Isabel. The Claremonts mounted the stairs to the front doors, where Margery and her parents were greeting guests. Margery nodded at Robert and was about to greet the next person in line when Mr. Penrose spoke. "Robert, will you do Margery the honor of opening the ball with her?"

Robert balked. Of course he didn't want to open the ball. He would seem aligned with Margery, and what if Isabel saw? And more importantly, what if it caused him to miss Isabel altogether? But there was nothing for it. It was an honor to be asked, and his mother was glaring at him, waiting for an answer.

"Yes, I'd be delighted." He looked back at Margery, who gave him a frosty look. His hesitation had apparently not gone unnoticed by her.

"I'll seek you out when the time comes," he said.

She turned away with no reply.

Robert proceeded into the house and walked through the ballroom, the supper room, the parlor, and the garden, but there was no sign of Isabel. He'd just decided to check the drawing room when a bell rang, indicating the ball was about to begin. Time to find Margery. After opening the ball with her, he'd seek out Isabel and secure at least two dances with her, though he wished decorum would allow him to stay by her side all night.

The first strains of music began as he entered the great hall, and there was Isabel. Apparently she'd just arrived, for she was still wearing her cloak while scanning the room—looking, he knew, for him. When she found Robert in the crowd her face lit up with a radiant smile. He caught his breath. Either he'd never fully appreciated how beautiful she was, or she'd grown more lovely in the past two weeks. He hurried across the hall, but just as he was about to reach her, Margery swooped down upon him.

"The dance!" she hissed.

He pasted an eager expression on his face. "Yes, I was just coming to find you."

"Indeed." Margery looked from him to Isabel, whose smile had evaporated.

Robert took Margery's arm and led her into the ballroom. He looked over his shoulder at Isabel, hoping to wordlessly express that he would rather be with her. She had turned her back on him.

The ball began, and Robert took Margery stiffly into his arms. They moved gracefully through the dance despite Robert's preoccupation. She didn't say a word to him, and wouldn't meet his eyes. Robert remembered William's advice about trying to draw her out and thought he'd have an easier time drawing sunlight from the moon. As the music played, more couples joined in, and soon the ballroom teemed with dancers. Robert was disheartened to see Isabel in the arms of a handsome man.

Almost before the music ended, Margery disentangled herself from his arms and stalked away, leaving Robert free to go in search of Isabel. The next song started as he searched the crowd. She was wearing a blue dress, he remembered. He at last found her partnering Simon. Robert paced the edge of the ballroom waiting for them to finish. The musicians ended with a flourish and Robert pressed through the crowd, but before he could reach Isabel she was in the arms of yet another man. After the song ended, an older gentleman immediately stepped in and claimed her for the next dance.

As he stood watching her, his mother approached with a young lady in tow. "Robert, you remember Rosamond, Margery's sister."

Rosamond was a few years younger than her sister, and Robert didn't know her very well. He suspected this was her first ball, so he would do his best to make it memorable for her, though he'd rather be with Isabel.

"Would you care to dance, Miss Penrose?" he asked, offering his arm. She beamed as Robert led her onto the dance floor. Based on the number of times Rosamond stepped on his feet, it *was* her first ball. Shy at first, she soon blossomed under Robert's attentions and began a lively discussion about her spaniel, Olive, as well as Olive's parents, puppies, and littermates.

Robert stayed with Rosamond for the next song, listening as she chattered away about her horse, Mini. She did ask Robert enough questions about Simon that he felt he must alert him that he had a fervent admirer.

After the tune ended, he escorted Rosamond back to her mother and, finally, saw what he'd been looking for all night; Isabel not in someone else's arms. He smiled, but she met his eyes briefly and hurried away. Robert made to follow her, but a hand came down on his shoulder.

"Robert." It was Edmund, wearing an expression similar to the one he'd made when Robert filled his ink bottle with milk when he was ten years old.

"Let me go. I must find her," he said, twisting away. If he wasn't quick, she'd have ten men lined up to dance with her as soon as the music began.

Edmund barred his way. "Listen to me."

He clicked his tongue. "What is it?"

"It's been noticed that you're tracking Miss Tate all night."

"Tracking?"

"Staring at her while she dances, following her around. Many other ladies go partnerless while you chase after her."

Robert crossed his arms. "I danced with Rosamond."

"Yes, I saw that. One dance where you actually paid attention to your partner."

"Two dances. What does it matter? Who even notices what I do?"

"Your parents. Margery's parents. Most of the guests." Edmund leaned in closer and whispered, "You look like a fool."

Robert knew he was right. It wasn't polite to hound someone who clearly didn't want his company. They went back to the ballroom, and Robert didn't catch even a glimpse of Isabel, but the ball was so crowded that didn't surprise him. He danced with seven ladies before deciding he'd performed his duty. On his way out of the ballroom, he noticed Simon dancing with Rosamond, who looked enchanted.

Robert was making his way to the gaming room when he glanced out the window. The moon was a luminous orb, low in the sky. It was the kind of night that begs to be enjoyed.

He strolled through the gardens, enjoying the clear night and shining stars. As Robert walked, a woman came from the opposite direction. A woman in a blue gown. His heart skipped a beat. Isabel paused, recognizing him in the same instant he saw her. She hesitated, then continued forward without looking at him, though her posture told him she was acutely aware of him. She made to walk past, but he called out to her.

"Isabel, wait. Please."

She walked a few steps, then stopped, and Robert caught up to her. She stared straight ahead, hands clasped tightly in front of her.

"Please accept my most humble apologies," Robert said. "I didn't expect to be asked to open the ball with Margery, but when pressed I felt obliged. I came to find you as soon as the dance was over, but you were engaged."

She looked at him, her brown eyes hard as granite. There was no warmth there for him tonight.

"Yes, I was engaged. I'll not simply sit and wait while you determine who you want. You claim you're not interested in Margery Penrose, but your actions say otherwise."

"You must understand, I have a duty as my father's son. Certain things are expected of me, like opening the ball tonight."

Isabel didn't reply.

"Please believe that the entire time I was dancing

with her, I thought of you." Robert paused, then caught her gaze. "I've been so looking forward to tonight. I've barely been able to stand not seeing you these last two weeks."

The light came back into her eyes. "Truly?"

"Truly." Robert stepped forward and took her hand.

"I want to believe you," she said at last. "But I don't like these games."

"They're not games of my choosing, I assure you. My father still deludes himself that there could be a match with Margery. I've told him outright it's fruitless, but he persists."

They started back toward the house, and Robert was pleased that she didn't remove her hand from his.

"I think she likes William," Isabel said, surprising him.

"Do you? I had the same thought. Oh, that would ease my burden."

"Would it? If given the choice between you and William, why should she choose him? You're clearly more…" Her voice trailed off.

He stood up straighter and gave her a sideways look. "More what?"

"I will not say. You already look too pleased with yourself."

They reached a gazebo and, still holding Isabel's hand, Robert mounted the steps. They stood in the center and gazed at each other as music floated to them from the open ballroom windows. He opened his arms, and she went to him at once. They moved to the music, making up the steps for this, their own dance. It was thrilling to be so close to Isabel, to hold her in his arms. He felt perfectly relaxed with her but was filled with a burning excitement at the same time. They went round and round the gazebo, fitting each other's steps perfectly. When the music ended, Robert started to release her, but Isabel held him fast.

She held his eyes. "One more."

"Hundreds more."

He swept her into his arms and spun her around. Isabel laughed gaily, her eyes sparkling. They danced to the next song, and the next, and the next.

Finally, Isabel led him to the gazebo steps. They sat in silence, holding hands and admiring the summer sky.

"I wonder what time it is?" Isabel asked.

"I don't know," Robert said, "Or care."

Isabel laughed. "You should. We've been out here for so long, I'm surprised my aunt hasn't sent my uncle to find me."

"I'm sure everyone assumes we're among the dancers. Nobody even knows we're together."

Isabel stood. "I must go back inside."

"So soon?"

She laughed. "I've been with you half the night."

"Not long enough." Robert rose. "But if you wish to return, of course we will."

They strolled through the gardens and back to the house. Before they went in, Robert reached for her hand.

"Isabel, wait."

She turned to him expectantly.

"Will you meet me tomorrow at the cottage? I want to show you something."

"Oh, yes. I've longed to go back."

"Will you be able to get away?"

"Easily. My aunt goes to visit my mother in Salisbury tomorrow. I was going to spend the day with

Nell, doing needlework. I much prefer a ride in the woods."

He kissed her hand. "I'll see you in the morning."

She led the way inside and they shared one more private glance before going in opposite directions and disappearing into the crowd.

****

Isabel lay in bed as the sun rose, basking in sweet memories of last night. After Robert had chosen Margery Penrose for his partner at the beginning of the ball, she'd spent most of the following dances believing all was over between them. But now she knew better. A soft smile came to her lips as she remembered his sincere apology and the dances they'd shared in the gazebo. She had no doubt he genuinely cared for her.

She dressed in her teal riding habit, then went downstairs. After a quick breakfast, she went to the stable and saddled Dion. As she spurred him to a canter, day was truly dawning. Preoccupied with thoughts of last night, the ride sped by, and soon she was guiding Dion into the meadow, where dew sparkled on the grass and birds sang their sweet morning songs. She'd planned on leaving Dion in the meadow but, seeing the gate had been left open, walked him through it. There was now enough room to ride through the lane, but the entrance was still hidden to keep others from stumbling upon it accidentally.

When she reached the end of the lane, she stopped short. The dilapidated old cottage was gone. In its place stood a welcoming, cozy home. The walls had been washed, the roof repaired, and the shutters mended. Flowerboxes full of colorful blooms perched on the windowsills.

Isabel had just dismounted when Robert came out from behind the cottage and called, "Bring him to the stable."

She started walking Dion toward him but then dropped the reins and broke into a run. Robert hesitated for a only a moment before running to meet her beside the well, where they stopped inches from each other; chests heaving, eyes locked. Isabel reached out tentatively and he pulled her into his arms, holding her as if he would never let her go.

And she never wanted him to.

She buried her face in his shoulder and inhaled deeply, memorizing his scent—wood fire, dewy grass and warm sunshine. As they stood entwined in each other's arms, Isabel lifted her face to his. Her heart pounded and she felt near to fainting with joy as he bent to kiss her. Nothing had ever been so soft, so searching as his kisses. Isabel's lips knew what to do of their own accord, as though they'd been only waiting for his. A warm tingling began in her belly and spread through her; a lush, molten sensation unlike anything she'd ever known.

"Oh, Isabel," he said, "I love you."

"I love you, Robert."

They stood gazing at each other, their declarations of love hanging sweetly in the air.

Isabel feared that if she spoke she'd break this magical spell, but felt she'd burst if she didn't tell Robert of her feelings. "I feel as though I've loved you my entire life."

"As soon as I saw you on May Day I felt as though I already knew you," Robert whispered.

"How has this happened?" she asked wonderingly.

He kissed her tenderly. "How does love ever happen? Who can say how the stars destined us for each other?"

She stepped back and took his hands. "Even if I spoke all day I couldn't tell you what you mean to me."

"Perhaps we need no words." His lips met hers and she twined her arms around his neck, opening her mouth to his, enchanted by the sweet taste and smell of him. She smiled—she couldn't help it—breaking their kiss. He laughed and put an arm around her waist.

They strolled through the yard, basking in the newfound knowledge of their love. After a time she said, "I can hardly believe what you've done here. It's unrecognizable."

"I needed a distraction. I couldn't stop thinking about you, and this gave me something to do, to keep me from riding to your house every day."

"I love the cottage, but I would have loved to see you more." It was wonderful to finally be able to share her heart with him. She brought his hand to her lips and kissed it.

"So...the stable," Robert said, looking flustered. "I think it was only intended for one animal, but it's so large I added another stall." Apollo was already there, munching on some hay. Robert gave a whistle, and Dion trotted over. After settling him in the second stall, Robert took Isabel's hand and led her to the cottage.

As soon as she walked in, Isabel was home. The freshly painted room looked like new, and a fire crackled in the repaired grate. Shiny copper pots hung from a ceiling rack, and the broken table and chairs had been replaced. An open wooden trunk at the foot of the new bed held blankets and towels. As a final welcoming touch, a vase full of pink roses sat on the bedside table, their delicate scent adding to the homey feel of the room.

"It's wonderful," Isabel said, clasping her hands together.

"I'm glad you like it. You were on my mind the whole time I worked here. And now for the best part." He took Isabel's hand and walked through the back door.

The yard had been transformed. The overgrown weeds had been removed and other plants trimmed, leaving an enchanted garden full of wild flowers, hyacinths, roses, and two lilac bushes. Apple trees cast dappled shade over one side of the yard. Isabel led Robert to a wooden bench under the tallest tree and rested her head on his shoulder.

"It's perfect," she said.

"It is now that you're here." He kissed her hair and rested his cheek on the top of her head. "There's a small stream behind the stable for fresh water. And I've made a discovery about the previous owner."

He told her about the monk's habit and the secret compartment in the fireplace.

"It must have been some time ago," Isabel said.

"Yes, that's what I thought, too. Whoever it was, they're long gone."

"I hope they were as happy here as I am." Isabel took his hand. She could hardly believe he really loved her. The last years had been lonely without her father, and there had been so many changes—a relocation, her mother's marriage, and now her sweet baby sister. It had seemed life would never be peaceful again. Now, with Robert, she felt...solid. Safe. As if she'd found something she hadn't known was missing.

The feel of Robert against her, the scent of the

flowers, the buzzing of lazy bees, and the warm sun upon her made Isabel feel as though she'd fallen into a dream. She brought Robert's hand to her lips.

He kissed her, then pulled away just enough to look into her eyes. "I've wanted to kiss you for so long. Every time we met, it was all I could do not to take you into my arms."

"I've wanted that, too. I used to wonder—" She looked away, color flooding her cheeks.

Robert put his finger under her chin and gently raised her face to his. "What did you wonder?"

A tiny laugh escaped her. "I used to wonder what your lips would feel like."

"Like this." He brushed his lips against hers, and a shiver went through her as everything disappeared but the gentle demand of his kisses that she was more than happy to meet.

They sat on the bench together all afternoon, holding hands, talking about this wonderful thing that had happened to them.

Sooner than they would have liked, it was time to leave. As they rode out of the yard, Isabel looked back. The sun cast a rosy glow on the cottage, and she knew that for as long as she lived she would remember this day.

Chapter Eight

Over the next few weeks, Isabel saw Robert as often as possible. She'd persuaded Verity she was old enough to take solitary rides, though Isabel felt a twinge of remorse every time her aunt waved her goodbye with a smile. If she only knew that Isabel was *not* alone in the woods. But there was no way to explain she was meeting a man, and in any case, the lie was worth it. To be able to spend entire days with Robert in the forest made them the happiest days she'd ever known. She talked to him for hours about anything and everything, but liked it best when he spoke of himself. She couldn't hear enough about his thoughts and dreams.

They usually met at the cottage but sometimes rode or walked in the woods. The summer sun shone bright and warm, as if determined to make their days even more perfect.

The only blight on Isabel's happiness was the fact that Robert still hadn't called at Kerensly Hall. She wanted him to get to know her family, but every time she asked about it he eluded the question or changed the subject.

One day she confronted him about it again as they sat on the cliff over the waterfall, a favorite spot of theirs. "Why do you never come to my uncle's house? You find excuse after excuse. Are you afraid of your father finding out?"

"Does it matter? Let's go for a walk." He reached for her hand, but she would not be distracted.

"Robert, what's going on?" She crossed her arms over her chest. "I have the feeling you're keeping something from me, and I don't like it."

"It's nothing, really." He picked up a stone and threw it over the falls.

"You must know you can trust me. What is it?"

Robert's shoulders slumped, and he let out a long, slow breath. "The truth is, Isabel, I never did speak to your uncle."

Isabel gasped. "What?"

He turned and grasped her hands. "I couldn't talk to him. I'd heard you were engaged, and I knew your uncle wouldn't give me permission to court you if I asked. But I had to see you, Isabel. I had to!"

Isabel scrambled to her feet. "Engaged? What nonsense!"

"I heard it from Simon."

"It hardly matters where you heard it. I must return home at once." She turned to go.

Robert reached out to her but she backed away.

"Please, Isabel. It matters not to us," he said urgently.

"No matter? No matter that I've spent countless hours in your company, alone? I thought we were bending the rules a little, but I didn't know it was an outright lie. My uncle will be furious when he hears of this."

"But how would he ever find out? We're always at the cottage or in the woods," Robert said, following Isabel to Dion.

"This is a small village and you're well known. It's

possible someone has seen us together." She looked around the woods furtively, realizing for the first time that the shelter she enjoyed could also enable someone to watch them unawares. "And furthermore, I haven't kept our meetings a secret."

Robert looked surprised. "Who did you tell?"

"I thought it didn't matter," she said spitefully.

"I regret saying that. It matters, of course it does. Who knows about us?"

"Aunt Verity."

Robert laughed. "Your aunt? She won't tell anyone."

"No?" she asked, arching a brow. "My uncle? My mother? My *stepfather*?"

Robert blanched. "Forgive me. I didn't intend to compromise you. It wasn't honorable of me."

"No, it wasn't." She mounted Dion. Robert leapt onto Apollo and they turned down the trail.

"Forgive me?" he pleaded again.

"I can't continue disobeying my uncle now that I know the truth," she said, trying to keep her voice firm.

Robert pulled Apollo to a stop. "You mean to say you'll stop seeing me?"

She turned Dion to face him. "If you want to court me, you must speak to my uncle. As you told me *you already had*."

"I do want to court you. I want more than that. I wish I could be with you every minute of the day. The hours away from you are meaningless."

Isabel knew he meant what he said. But how could she believe he respected her after he'd been so dishonest for weeks? Did he consider her a woman of loose morals, one he could trick into intimacies with no thought of a future together?

When she met his eyes they were somber—full of shame and uncertainty. She didn't want him to doubt her love for him, even for a moment. Her mind told her to be wary, but her heart said his love was true.

Her face softened. "It's like that for me as well, and I don't want to part from you. But we can't go on like this. When will you speak to my uncle?"

"As soon as I can. Is he home today?"

"Unfortunately, no."

"When will he be back?"

"He's gone for the next five days."

"Five days! Isabel, I can't bear to part with you for so long."

"It would be an eternity. But what else can we do?"

"I have an idea," Robert said, his voice hopeful. "May I call on you and your aunt?"

Isabel brightened. "Yes. If you call and see both of us, that would be acceptable. But you mustn't act so familiar with me. My aunt does know that I've seen you, but she would be shocked at the depth of our…friendship."

"I'll try, but it will be difficult, as all I want to do when we meet is this." Robert nudged Apollo forward until the horses stood side by side, then leaned in close and kissed her until Dion started walking away and they broke apart, laughing.

****

When Robert arrived home, he was immediately summoned to the gallery, where he found his mother and William admiring the portraits Laurence had sent over.

"Robert, here you are," Mrs. Claremont said. "The portraits look wonderful."

"You're pleased with them?" Robert stood beside

her and looked at the paintings, which were propped against the wall while workmen mounted hooks to hang them.

"Oh, yes. Now you two will have your rightful place in the gallery."

"As usual, you look more handsome than me," Robert said to William.

"Can I help it if I got the good looks?"

"You are both handsome," Mrs. Claremont said.

"When is the ball to be, Mother?" William asked.

"On your birthday next week. You'll be twenty-one, and that seems an age to celebrate."

"It seems an age to be married," their father said from behind them. He took his wife's arm. "We were married much younger than this, weren't we, Eleanor?"

"I was not yet seventeen," she said reminiscently.

Mr. Claremont bestowed one of his rare smiles on her. He stood for a moment looking at the portraits and said, "Yes, they came out quite well."

"Almost worth all the time spent locked up in the solarium," Robert said.

"How are you getting on with Margery, son?" Mr. Claremont asked.

"Fine," Robert and William answered together. They looked at each other, Robert wide-eyed, William cringing.

Their father scowled at both of them. "What is the meaning of this?" he shouted.

"I said fine. It's going fine," Robert said.

Mr. Claremont turned on William. "What have you to do with it? Are you chasing after Margery?"

William, for once, looked flustered. "No. No, of course not. I was telling you how I thought Robert was doing."

Mr. Claremont looked skeptical but apparently decided to drop the matter for now. He turned to Robert. "Will we have a proposal to announce at the ball?"

"Don't count on that, Father. Margery doesn't like me."

"Well, then, make her like you!" Mr. Claremont growled and marched away.

Mrs. Claremont cast her sons an exasperated look and chased after him.

William and Robert watched as workmen mounted the portraits on the wall side by side.

"I suppose this means we aren't boys any longer. Men, now," said Robert, putting his hands in his jacket pockets.

"We haven't been boys for years." William smirked. "At least I haven't."

"You know what I mean. Time to settle down."

"According to our parents," William replied as they left the gallery and walked down the corridor.

"Talking of settling down, what's going on with you and Margery?"

"*That* is none of your business."

"You have plenty of other conquests. Why bother with her?"

"You wouldn't understand," William said smugly. "What's it to you? You're not courting her."

"No, but at least I'm supposed to be. Is there an understanding between you?" Robert asked hopefully.

"No."

Robert detected an unexpected note of disappointment in William's voice. "If you're fond of her, why not speak to Father about it? It would help us both."

William looked down at his feet. "I've tried."

"William—" Robert put a hand on William's shoulder, but he shrugged it off.

"Spare me your pity, Robert. Father wouldn't even listen to me, and Mr. Penrose told me in no uncertain terms that he won't give his daughter away to a roving philanderer who has no guaranteed inheritance."

"But you might inherit. Father could choose you."

"I highly doubt that. It's clear he's going to make you his heir."

"Then why hasn't he?"

"I don't know, but I suspect it's because of Mother. She wants us both to inherit."

Robert's eyes widened. "Does she? How do you know?"

"She mentioned it when she told me about Father's gambling debts."

"If we both inherited, there's no reason for Mr. Penrose to oppose the match."

"But Father's young yet, and who knows if he'll go along with Mother's scheme? As far as Mr. Penrose knows, I could end up virtually penniless. So, as before, it's up to you."

"Does Margery love you? Would she elope with you?"

"I somehow doubt she'd give up her fortune and position for me, no matter how much I amuse or satisfy her. At any rate, I'm willing to sacrifice my own wishes for the good of the family. As you should."

"At this point I could never let go of Isabel."

"I still mean to contrive the match between you and Margery. Then perhaps Father will see me as something more than useless."

"So that's why you're hounding me endlessly about her?"

"It is indeed."

When they reached Robert's bedroom, he stopped and leaned against the door.

"You may as well stop trying. I need to make Father understand the match will never happen, and tell him about Isabel."

"You'll need to tell him, and soon. I don't envy you that. He's bound to hear rumors of the two of you, if he hasn't already. Even I know you're with her almost every day. "

"How can you possibly know that?"

"I have eyes. Don't worry, nobody else knows. Well, Simon, of course. And Edmund."

"How?" He'd thought they were being so careful.

"Do you think you two are invisible, walking in the woods? Just because you don't see us, that doesn't mean we don't see you."

Robert straightened and took a step toward William. "You've been following me?"

William snorted. "I have neither time nor interest to follow you. I've caught glimpses of you when I'm out riding."

Robert said nothing but ran a hand over his furrowed brow. Isabel had been right. They needed to be more careful.

"Give her up, Robert," William said in a surprisingly gentle tone. "I can tell how much you like her. I haven't seen you so relaxed around a woman…ever. But this has gone too far already. You know you can never have her."

"I don't see why not," Robert said stubbornly.

"You ever were the dreamer." William started toward his own room.

"Don't tell Father," Robert called after him. "I'll tell him myself when the time is right."

William turned back to him. "I won't. And I won't tell him what's in the package the artist left for you, either."

"What? Where?"

"Here." William drew a package from inside his jacket, tossed it to Robert, and continued down the hall.

Robert went into his room and sat on the bed. The package had been opened and clumsily resealed. He untied the loose strings holding it together and the miniatures fell into his hands. First his—almost identical to the one now hanging in the gallery. He set it aside and picked up the one of Isabel. Laurence had done a wonderful job capturing her. Her expression was peaceful and happy, her brown eyes leapt off the canvas as if looking right at him. Robert could hardly bear to part with hers, but if his plans came to fruition, the miniatures would hang side by side forever.

****

The next day Isabel went about in a state of great anticipation. Knowing Robert would keep his word and call on her today, she took extra care with her dress. He usually saw her in riding habits, so today she chose a delicate white muslin gown.

She restlessly wandered the house all morning and jumped at every sound, thinking it was someone at the door. When she finally heard the knock, she was sitting in the library's deep window seat, watching foals frolic in the meadow. She didn't move, but a smile came to her face. Within moments a footman opened the door and showed Robert into the room. He wore a handsomely cut navy riding jacket that brought out his eyes.

He kissed her hand, taking in every detail of her dress. "Miss Tate. How beautiful you look this morning."

"Mr. Claremont."

A discreet cough from the doorway told them that Verity had entered the room. Robert dropped Isabel's hand, but gave her a secret smile before turning to her aunt.

"Good morning, Mrs. Collison."

She inclined her head. "Please, sit down."

He sat in a chair across the room from Isabel.

"Would you care for refreshment?" Verity asked.

"No, thank you. I've only stopped by for a quick but pleasant errand."

"I'm afraid you've missed my husband."

"That's unfortunate, but how lucky I am to find the charming ladies at home. I've come to invite you to a ball we're having to celebrate my and my brother's birthday. My mother will send a written invitation, but I wanted to ask you in person."

"Oh, how delightful," Isabel said, giving him a broad smile.

"When will the ball take place?" asked Verity.

"Next week. My mother's invitation will have all the details."

"Thank you for the invitation. You may count upon us being there," Verity said.

Robert met Isabel's eyes and said, "I look forward to it." He rose to go. "It's time I took my leave."

It was a disappointingly short call, but Isabel could hardly protest in her aunt's company.

"Thank you for stopping by," Verity said.

"Goodbye, Mr. Claremont," Isabel said as she walked Robert to the door. He caught her hand and gave it a light squeeze. Once he was out of sight she went to the couch and collapsed onto it, beaming.

"Oh, Verity," she said with a dreamy sigh.

"You've been seeing more of him, I presume. What do you think of him now?"

"He's perfect."

Verity laughed. "He's indeed handsome, and does seem smitten with you."

Isabel sat up, eyes shining. "Oh, do you think so?"

"It's very obvious, Isabel, even in the few minutes he was here."

Her aunt would be even more sure of it—and shocked—if she'd seen them together at the cottage a few weeks ago. Now came a moment she'd been dreading, but could put off no longer. "There's one problem, Verity."

"What is it?"

"Don't think too harshly of Robert, I beg you. I was going to keep this a secret, but I feel I can trust you. Can I?"

Verity's forehead creased. "Yes, yes, of course. What is it?"

Isabel sank into the couch cushions, cringing as she spoke. "Robert never asked Uncle Francis's permission to go riding with me."

Verity's expression hardened. "How dare he! He lied to you? This is underhanded indeed."

"No, no, it isn't like that. He was afraid permission would be denied, so he didn't ask. Oh, please don't tell Uncle Francis." She sat up straight, clasping her hands together.

"I did wonder why your uncle never mentioned the conversation. Because it never happened," she said, glowering. "I thought Mr. Claremont was a trustworthy young man. This changes my entire view of him."

Isabel's shoulders slumped. She'd counted on her aunt as an ally.

"Verity, if only you could get to know him better. He wanted to court me but heard it was impossible. I don't condone his lying, but please know it wasn't done in spite. When he told me the truth, I came home at once, after telling him I'd only see him when supervised. He agreed readily, which is why he called today. He's a good man, truly he is."

Verity sighed. "I don't approve of this. Not at all. But I do believe you when you say his heart was in the right place. He's young, and goodness knows we all make mistakes when we're young."

"You won't tell Uncle Francis?" Isabel asked hopefully.

Verity deliberated for a few moments. "No. But if Mr. Claremont intends to court you, he must speak with your uncle or your father without delay. Stepfather, that is," she amended.

Isabel took her hand. "Oh, he will, as soon as he can."

"There's one other small problem," Verity said gravely.

"What is it?"

"I've already written to your mother, telling her that Mr. Claremont had asked to call on you."

"You sent the letter?"

"Yes. It was some weeks ago now, but I haven't heard back from her. Perhaps she won't mention it to your stepfather until you write to her about Mr. Claremont yourself."

The blood drained from her face. "My stepfather…"

"He would be most displeased to find out you took up with someone without permission."

Isabel didn't even want to imagine what Mr. Branwick would say if he discovered Robert had lied. He would need to be informed of their courtship at some point, but she'd put it off as long as possible.

"Robert and I have been keeping our meetings secret, so I don't see how he'll hear unless Mother tells him. As you said, she might keep it from him, at least for a little while."

Verity gave her an affectionate yet exasperated look. "Oh, Isabel, you've been most unwise meeting this man so often. I can see by the way you look at each other that it's been more than one or two times. But the horse is out of the stable now. We can only hope no rumors reach your stepfather. You seem overexcited, my dear. Why not go to your room and rest?"

"Yes, I will."

Isabel strode from the room but didn't go to her bedroom. After retrieving her bow and quiver, she made for a rolling, open field behind the stables. At the edge of the forest she stood with legs firmly planted, back straight. She notched an arrow, aiming for a knot in an oak tree fifty feet away. The seam at her shoulder ripped as she drew her arm back. Eyes on the target, she let out a slow breath and let her arrow fly; it made its mark. Two more followed, each obeying her command. Isabel was about to send one more to join them when a twig snapped behind her. She spun, bow ready.

Robert stood behind her, arms raised in mock

surrender. Isabel put her bow on the ground.

"Robert! What are you still doing here?" Her dress was torn and probably dirty, but she didn't care. "I thought you left long ago."

"I would have, but Apollo threw a shoe and your smithy was accommodating enough to fit a new one. I'm glad, for now I've had the privilege of watching you shoot. You're very talented with your bow."

"Thank you."

He approached her with a mischievous grin. "Now that I'm here, will you show me your secrets?"

"I have no secrets. Not from you." She resisted the urge to throw herself into his arms, but he must have read her mind, for the next moment she was caught up in his embrace. Isabel pulled away to look at him and saw that his eyes were closed. She stood on tiptoes to kiss him lightly on the lips. He smiled and opened his eyes.

"You're wonderful," he said.

She reluctantly stepped out of his arms. "We're too visible here."

"You're right," Robert agreed, taking her hand. "Come into the woods."

Isabel laughed and pushed him away playfully. "I have other things to keep you occupied."

"I doubt anything will distract me from you," he said, looking her up and down.

She picked her bow up from the ground and handed it to him. "Show me what you can do."

"Not much. I'm better at swordplay."

He notched the arrow and sent it flying—well short of the mark, and too far over. Isabel covered her mouth to hide a smile as Robert tried again. This time he did get it to the tree, but it landed at the base.

"So, swords?" she asked.

"I did warn you," he said, and they laughed.

Isabel suddenly remembered her conversation with her aunt and recounted it to Robert.

"You explained the reason?" Robert asked, eyes full of concern and not a little embarrassment.

"I did. She agreed not to tell my uncle, provided you speak to him as soon as possible. The bigger concern is that she told my mother. Once she finds out you didn't ask permission, she'll be furious."

"Will she be angry with you?"

"Not me. You. The fact that you lied to me won't place you high in her esteem."

"Do you think your aunt will tell her that I lied?"

"Yes, otherwise my mother will think *I* did. I'm less worried about my mother than my stepfather. He's not the forgiving type, and there will be real trouble if he gets word of this ruse."

Isabel's head drooped, eyes swimming with tears as she looked at the ground.

"Come here," Robert said, gathering her into his arms. "Whatever happens, we'll face it together. I'll apologize to your mother and explain to your stepfather if need be."

"If you're with me, I'll be all right. But now you should go. We've lingered here too long already." She glanced up at the house. A number of windows overlooked the field, and anybody could be watching.

"May I call tomorrow?" Robert asked as they started walking toward the stables, Apollo trailing behind.

Isabel hesitated. "Oh, Robert, I long to see you again, but…"

"But?"

She lifted her hands in a helpless gesture. "I need to wait until you've spoken to my uncle."

Isabel hated to disappoint him, but what else could she say? She was facing enough trouble already.

"But your uncle won't be home until the night of the ball."

She took his hand. "I'll long for you the entire time."

He gave her fingers a gentle squeeze. "Could you meet me the morning of the ball? At the cottage?"

Her stomach squirmed. "You won't have spoken to my uncle yet."

"I know, but it's important. I'll speak to him as soon as I can after the ball. The very same evening, if I can manage it."

"All right. It will need to be early. I need time in the afternoon to dress."

"Very early." He smiled. "I'll be waiting for you."

As they started up the hill, Isabel paused. "I left my bow down by the trees. I need to fetch it," she said, looking to the sky. "It looks like rain."

"I'll get it for you."

"No. Much as I hate to part, you should go."

"I understand," he said, unable to mask a frown. "In a week or so, we'll be able to spend time together without all this hiding."

"It's only a few days, but it will feel like a hundred."

He kissed her hand, mounted Apollo, and trotted away.

Isabel found her bow and slung the quiver over her shoulder, then shot three arrows in fast succession. She smiled when she noticed the ones left over from Robert's earlier attempts. As she went to retrieve them, William Claremont stepped out of the woods.

115

"Impressive," he said.

Isabel jumped and her hand flew to her chest. "Mr. Claremont! What are you doing here?"

"Watching. Though I don't seem to be as welcome as my brother."

"Are you looking for Robert? He just left." She pointed up the hill.

"I'm not looking for Robert. I'm looking for you." He crossed his ankles and leaned casually against a tree.

"You came to see me? Whatever for?"

"Oh, I think it's time we knew each other better."

"I think we know each other quite well enough. I must get back to the house. Excuse me." She turned to go.

"I don't agree. All I really know is your name," William said. "There must be something about you that draws my brother to you."

She turned back to him but said nothing.

As he walked toward her he stooped and picked up a discarded arrow. Handing it to her, he said, "Tell me, Isabel. Are you so talented with all…shafts?"

Isabel's eyes hardened as she dropped the arrow and spun on her heel. Before she could get away he grabbed her arm, all pretense of friendliness gone.

"Unhand me at once!" she cried, wrenching out of his powerful grip.

He didn't attempt to hold her again, but said coldly, "You will stop seeing Robert. You'll make an excuse and disappear from his life."

"I don't know what you mean," Isabel stammered.

"Do you not?" William started walking in a circle around her. "Rides through the woods…walks by the river…his portrait sitting…today's lovely tête-à-tête."

Isabel's face betrayed both her guilt and her surprise. How did he know so much?

William continued, "If you wish to see him fall out of favor, to lose everything, then by all means continue to chase after him. If not, it's time you said goodbye to my brother."

"It's not for you to say," Isabel said, cursing her voice for shaking.

"Robert already has an intended bride. It would be a shame if our parents have to hear from me that he's going behind their backs with a harlot. Or perhaps your stepfather would be interested to hear what you've been doing alone with Robert in the woods."

Isabel gasped and took a step back.

"Is it his money you're after?" William asked as he stopped his pacing. "Sadly, that will be gone if he doesn't marry Miss Penrose."

Speechless with fury, she turned to go.

He planted himself in front of her, holding her with those blue eyes that bewitched most women. "Have I made myself clear?"

"Leave me alone!" Isabel cried, lifting her skirts and running away.

Halfway to the stables she turned back to see William watching her, shaking with laughter. Her fingers tightened around her bow. "Let him laugh," she muttered to herself, "I should have skewered him!"

Chapter Nine

The next day Isabel went in search of Robert. He must be warned of his brother's threats. She rode as close to Thornwood as she dared, avoiding the house lest she encounter William. After guiding Dion into a sheltered glade of trees close to the road, she dismounted and settled in to wait. After nearly two hours, Robert came into view riding Apollo, fortunately alone. Isabel stepped out into the road and called his name.

He started when he saw her, then smiled. "What are you doing here?"

"I had to see you. Come with me." She took Apollo's bridle and led him into the woods, where Robert dismounted at once.

"Here? Why?"

"I didn't want to be disturbed," she said soberly as she took his hand and walked through the trees.

"What's troubling you?" Robert asked, bringing her hand to his lips.

"William."

"William?" he asked, surprised.

"He came to my house yesterday, right after you left. He must have been watching us the whole time."

Robert's face grew stormier by the minute as she described their conversation.

"How dare he! I'm sorry he insulted you."

She entwined her fingers with his. "I'm afraid,

Robert. What does he mean by it all?"

"William thinks that if he can push me into Margery's arms he'll earn our father's trust."

"Margery!"

"I don't believe for a moment that he'd betray us to my parents. I'll be telling them about us myself soon enough."

She put a hand to her chest. "He says I'll ruin you if I don't give you up."

"The only thing that could hurt me would be losing you."

Robert sat on a leaf-strewn boulder and pulled her onto his lap. Though Isabel knew she should stand at once, she did no such thing.

"But what about his threats to tell my stepfather?" she asked, wringing her hands.

He met her eyes. "Trust me. It was an empty threat. He won't go to your stepfather."

She shuddered. "How can you be so sure? I didn't doubt him for a second."

"This is just the type of thing he would do to amuse himself at our expense."

"It's not amusing to me."

"Nor me. I'll speak to him and make it clear that he's not to approach you again."

Isabel leaned against him, her head tucked under his chin. It was easy, here in his arms, to believe she had nothing to fear from William or anyone else.

"I'm glad I found you today." She looked into his eyes. "I'm glad I found you every day."

Isabel put a hand behind his head and drew him in, holding her lips a breath away from his.

"Isabel," he said in a reverent voice.

Her heart pounded as she closed the tiny gap, relishing the feel of his mouth on hers, somehow hot and cool at the same time. Sooner than she would have liked, they broke apart.

Isabel stood and smoothed her skirt. "I must get home. My aunt doesn't know I'm gone."

"So soon?" He rose and took her hand.

"Yes. I shouldn't have left the house at all."

"Ride to the falls with me?" Robert asked as they walked back to the horses.

"You know it's in the opposite direction," she said with a laugh. "You must be patient and see me at the ball."

Robert helped her mount Dion. "I have no patience when it comes to seeing you."

"You'll speak to William?" Isabel asked, serious again.

"I will. Put it out of your mind."

"I'll try. It will be much more difficult to put *you* out of my mind."

"Don't," Robert said, holding her hand as he looked up at her. "Let me stay in your mind, day in and day out, as you are in mine. Let us meet together in our dreams."

"Tonight and every night," Isabel whispered before riding away.

****

On his birthday, Robert woke before the sun. Tonight was the ball, and this morning he'd propose to Isabel. There would be difficulties with their families, but she was the only woman for him. Once they were betrothed, nothing could stand in the way of his happiness, not even his father's ire.

After dressing, he retrieved the miniatures from his

trunk and placed them in his jacket pocket, then went to his desk to get his grandmother's ring—a single round diamond set in a gold band etched with vines and flowers. It wasn't elaborate, but it was enough for a promise. He slipped it into his waistcoat pocket and headed downstairs. Robert passed through the kitchens and packed fresh bread, strawberries, goat cheese, and a flagon of ale in a sack, then went out to the stables, where he saddled Apollo himself.

When he reached the cottage, there was no sign of Isabel, so he took Apollo to the stable, then went inside to set the food on the table and build a fire. The first flames were springing to life when the clatter of hooves came from the yard. He reached the door just as Isabel dismounted, and he crossed the yard to take her in his arms, relishing the feel of her body and the sweet scent of her hair.

"Good morning." He kissed her lightly.

The beauty of her smile rivaled the sun. "Good morning."

After taking Dion to the stable, they entered the cottage hand in hand.

"You've been busy." Isabel removed her cloak and hung it over a hook next to the door.

He pulled a chair out for her. "I knew we'd be hungry."

As they sat side by side eating breakfast, Robert glanced sideways at Isabel and bubbly warmth filled his chest. He wiped his palms on his breeches. He'd been with women before, so why was he so nervous? Been with women, but never loved one. No other woman had mattered this much, no other conversation would mean so much.

After their meal, they meandered out to the back garden, where the flowers were past their first bloom but still colorful and fragrant. Birds serenaded them with a morning song.

As Robert looked into her eyes, his nervousness disappeared and he knew the moment had come.

"Isabel, come with me." He took her hand and led her to the bench under the apple tree, then sat beside her. He pulled the package from his pocket and placed it on her lap. "Open it."

Isabel grinned and opened the package. The first miniature she saw was his.

"Oh, Robert, it's perfect! It looks exactly like you. The artist did a splendid job."

"He did. Especially with the next one."

"The next one?"

He took his miniature out of her hand, leaving only hers.

She looked at it, a puzzled look on her face. "But how?"

"I commissioned these the day you came to the sitting. I had to have a picture of you, and I want you to have mine."

She smiled, her eyes glistening with tears. "Oh, Robert."

"These last weeks have been the happiest of my life. I know love now, in a way I never thought possible. I want to see you more often—every day."

"That would be wonderful," Isabel said. "You'll speak to my uncle tonight?"

"Yes. Well, perhaps your stepfather first. I must speak to my own father without delay. It wouldn't do for him to hear of this through anyone but me."

"Hear of what?"

Robert's heart hammered as he knelt on the ground before her and took her hand. "I love you, Isabel, and I don't want to live a single day without you by my side. Will you marry me?"

"Can this be?" she asked wonderingly. "My heart has been yours from the day we met."

Joy flooded through him. "You'll marry me?"

"Yes. Oh, yes!" She sank to the ground and wrapped her arms around him.

Robert lost himself in her. Nothing else mattered but her breath on his cheek, her voice in his ear, her soft mouth on his.

"I have something else for you." He wiped a tear from his eye and held out the gold ring.

She extended her trembling hand, and Robert slid the ring onto her finger. A perfect fit. They would never be separated now. There must be a wedding, of course, but from this day on, they belonged to each other.

Something of his thoughts must have shown on his face, for Isabel said, "I'm truly yours now."

He beamed. "And I am yours."

"When will we marry?"

"I'll speak to my father tonight, after the ball."

She held up her hand to look at the ring. "I would that we could marry today."

"Soon, my dearest," Robert said. "I don't want to lose one moment by your side, but I must return home to prepare for tonight."

After gathering their things from inside the cottage, they saddled the horses and walked them out into the sunny yard. Robert would have liked to skip the ball altogether and spend the entire day with Isabel. He took her hand and drew her in for a soft, lingering kiss.

Isabel took the ring off. "I'll never remove this again once we're married, but for now you must hold it for me. If I wear it home, it will bring questions that I cannot answer."

"I'll keep it close to my heart." Robert took it from her and placed it back in his pocket.

"And the miniatures. Though I hate to part with them, I can hardly bring those into my uncle's house, either."

Robert took those from her as well, secretly glad to have her image with him for another day. They mounted their horses and trotted back to the road, savoring each moment together. When they came to the fork in the road, they kissed goodbye and Isabel went on her way.

****

By night fall, Thornwood had been transformed. Moonlight streamed through the tall, arched windows of the long gallery, and a myriad of candles and lamps illuminated the room. Mrs. Claremont had decided the gallery was the perfect place for the birthday toast, followed by supper and dancing in the more spacious rooms downstairs. The ballroom windows had been draped with gold and blue curtains, while potted plants and fragrant flowers gave it an exotic air. The hefty wooden tables in the great hall had been replaced with smaller ones, and several previously empty alcoves now held tables for two.

After dressing, Robert went to the gallery, where he found William overseeing the footmen as they draped the portraits in preparation of the unveiling.

"What time do the guests arrive?" William asked him after the footmen finished and left the room.

Robert glanced at his pocket watch. "Eight o'clock, Mother said."

"I think I hear someone in the drive."

They looked out the windows facing the front lawns, and sure enough, carriages had arrived and people were making their way inside.

"It's our night," William said, rubbing his hands together.

"Happy birthday, William."

"And a happy birthday to you, Robert. I still wonder which of us came first. Strange that nobody knows."

"We've heard the story often enough. They were afraid for Mother's life and everyone was focused on her. Once they'd ascertained that we were boys, we were handed off to the wet nurse. Nobody took the time to notice who was who."

"And from all accounts, we were identical at birth."

"What does it matter? Besides, I'm quite certain it is I who was born first," Robert joked.

He turned back to the window, and his heart leapt as Isabel's carriage came up the drive. He leaned out the window and waved, just as she looked up. A bright smile lit her face.

Simon joined Robert at the window. "Looking for someone?"

He shrugged.

"Remember your manners tonight," William said.

"I don't know what you two are talking about," Robert said, heading for the stairway.

"You're a guest of honor and many of the ladies will want a dance with you," Simon called after him.

"Yes, yes." Robert waved him off impatiently and walked downstairs.

William followed him, and they entered the hall together. As they wove in and out of the crowd of distinguished men and bejeweled women, Robert kept an eye out for Isabel, but she was nowhere to be seen. He and William took their places beside their parents, who were receiving guests at the door.

Finally Robert caught sight of Isabel mounting the steps with her aunt and uncle. She greeted his parents warmly but ignored William altogether.

At last she stood before him, trying to hold back a smile. "Mr. Claremont."

"Isabel." He held her hand, and when their eyes met, nobody watching could have missed the sparks flying between them. The line outside began to back up until William cleared his throat, reminding Robert where he was.

As Isabel passed, Robert said, "Save the first dance for me."

She smiled and nodded, then accompanied her aunt and uncle into the house. Robert followed her with his eyes, trying to keep track of her in the throng.

William nudged him to bring his attention back to the receiving line, and Robert looked up to see Margery in front of him, more remote than ever.

"Good evening, Margery."

"Mr. Claremont," she replied, and passed on without a second glance.

Robert turned to William. "You see?" he whispered. "She won't even speak to me."

"Why should she? You scarcely looked at her."

"Are we finished here?" Robert asked when the line of guests finally seemed to be at an end.

"Yes," his mother said. "Now we'll go up to the

gallery and unveil your portraits. Afterward, you and William will open the ball with your partners. Have you both secured a lady to dance with?"

"Easily," William said, straightening his cravat.

"Yes, Mother," Robert said, hoping he could find Isabel in time.

A gong sounded and the guests were directed upstairs, where champagne was served to the assembled company. Mrs. Claremont pulled a velvet cord hanging between the two portraits, and the curtains covering them fell to the ground. While people moved forward to get a better look at the paintings, William and Robert walked around the room, accepting handshakes and birthday wishes.

"Who will you open the ball with?" Robert asked.

"I haven't decided yet. I'm still considering my choices." William looked a nearby woman up and down. She smiled encouragingly. "Do I need to ask who you're looking for?" he asked as Robert peered over the crowd.

"Isabel."

William took hold of Robert's arm and led him to an alcove where they wouldn't be overheard. "Ask Margery to partner you."

"No. Why even ask me to? That farce has been over for weeks. She and I aren't pretending, even if the rest of you are." Robert pulled his arm out of William's grasp and adjusted his cuffs.

William leaned in closer. "You know this rests on you."

Robert looked him in the eyes. "I love Isabel, William. Do you know what it means? I *love* her and I won't give her up. Mother and Father will have to understand. I depend on you, my brother, to support me."

"That's a pretty speech, Robert. But love? It cannot be so grand as that. I do support you, but not in this. By disobeying father, you will ruin us all." He paused and said in a lighter tone, "If you detest Margery so much, we'll find you another heiress. You and I can leave tonight, go to Salisbury, and woo some other maid. Come with me—it will be another adventure for us." His eyes gleamed in that roguish way Robert knew so well.

He just shook his head. "That's not for me, William, and you know it. You know me better than that."

"I do know you," William said, all playfulness gone. "You're Robert Claremont, heir of the house, and you always do your duty. Do it now."

Robert drew himself up to his full height. "We are *both* heirs. You have just as much responsibility as me. You claim you want to be taken seriously? Find yourself an heiress, if that's the answer. I'll have no part of it."

Before William could answer, the first strains of music began. Without looking at each other, they marched out of the alcove.

Robert stalked through the ballroom in search of Isabel. How dare William try to tell him how to live his life! Couldn't his own brother be happy for him instead of putting the weight of their family's troubles on his shoulders? He unclenched his fists and took a deep breath through his nose, then let it out slowly as he searched for Isabel. The moment she came into view he forgot everything else. He held her eyes as he crossed the empty dance floor to join her.

They shared a smile as he took her hand. "Will you open the ball with me?"

Isabel hesitated. "Are you sure it's all right?"

Robert followed her worried gaze to his parents,

who watched them intently. They were both smiling, but only someone who wasn't their son would believe they were anything but livid.

"It's my ball, and I say yes." He led her onto the dance floor.

William appeared with none other than Margery, who looked Isabel up and down and smiled derisively. When the music began, Robert took Isabel into his arms and swept her around the room. Other couples joined in, and after a time they were surrounded by a sea of dancers, including a delighted-looking Rosamond Penrose in Simon's arms.

"Good evening," Robert whispered in Isabel's ear.

Her smile made his heart soar. "Happy birthday, Robert."

He bent his head slightly as if to kiss her.

Isabel leaned away. "Robert...remember where we are."

She was right—too many eyes were upon them here. Difficult as it was, he must act as if they were merely dance partners. When the music stopped, another man stepped forward to claim Isabel for the next dance, but Robert held his hand out and she slipped hers into it. A new song started and once again Robert's world shrank to the face in front of him. He delighted in every look and touch the dance afforded them. There was no time for speaking, but they needed no words.

At the end of their fifth dance, a bell sounded, indicating it was time for supper. Robert gave Isabel his arm, ignoring the disapproving looks from people in the crowd. He escorted her to a small table and left her there while he went to choose food from the buffet. On his way back to her, his mother waved from across the room but he pretended not to see.

"What have you brought?" Isabel asked when he returned.

"Everything." He sat down and handed her a plate of thinly sliced beef, swan in creamy sauce, nuts, and his favorite, pheasant. "Even I couldn't eat this much."

"I think I could, I'm famished. The last time I ate was this morning at the cottage. What a lot has changed since then." She reached for his hand under the table.

"The world has changed since then."

He was about to kiss her, not caring who saw, but caught a movement out of the corner of his eye and saw Edmund gesturing to him from beside the window.

"Excuse me, Isabel." Robert gave her hand a squeeze and went to meet him.

"Enjoying yourself, Edmund?"

He sighed. "Not particularly."

"And why is that? Soon the dancing will begin again, and I see many ladies who would partner you."

"Be serious, Robert," he said urgently. "I'm sent by your father to remind you of your responsibilities as a guest of honor. You shouldn't be cloistering yourself with Miss Tate. You were supposed to eat supper at the high table with your family. Your mother says she has a surprise, and she wants you to be present for it."

"I'll be there when the time comes." He turned and walked away, leaving Edmund standing there.

"Robert!" Edmund hissed, but he ignored him.

He went back to Isabel and took his place beside her.

"What's wrong?" she asked.

"Nothing's wrong. A misunderstanding. How do you like your supper?"

Isabel looked skeptical. "Nothing?"

"Edmund informed me that I'm expected at the high table. Apparently my mother has something planned. It is no matter."

"You must go to her. I'll sit with my aunt," Isabel said, rising.

"Absolutely not." Robert took her hand. "I'm going to speak with my father after the ball. He'll see how it is between us and will understand why I chose to sit with you. It will all be made clear tonight."

"You're speaking to him so soon?" Her voice hovered between elation and concern.

"Yes. I don't want to waste a single day. I want to marry you as soon as possible, so we'll put up the banns tomorrow if I have my way."

"Oh, Robert, you've made me unbelievably happy," she said. But then a cloud passed over her face.

"What is it, my love?"

She looked into his eyes. "My stepfather. Your parents. William. They all oppose the match. What if they try to stop us? I could never go back to life without you."

"They'll come around. I've spoken to William, and he'll give us no more trouble. We *will* be married. I love you. You love me. It's as simple as that. Everything else will fall into place."

"I hope you're right."

Robert raised his glass. "To us."

"To us."

"So here you are, Robert," said William from behind them. "And with the lovely and talented Miss Tate."

Isabel stiffened and turned away.

"Did you want something, William?" Robert ground out.

He swept his arm toward the high table. "Our mother awaits us."

"Very well," Robert said and turned to Isabel. "I'll return as soon as I can. Stay here and wait for me."

She gave him a soft smile. "I will."

As they made their way to the high table, William said, "Sometime you must enlighten me to the nature of her charms. She seems quite plain to me."

"You wouldn't understand."

"I might. I do have a certain understanding of women."

"But not of love," Robert said and picked up his pace.

When Robert reached his mother, her usually warm eyes were steely. He'd apologize later and explain everything to her. She'd be pleased that he'd found someone to love, once she got over her disappointment. Guests on the other side of the room clapped as four servants carried in the biggest cake Robert had ever seen. His mother beamed at him and William, her displeasure apparently forgotten for the moment. She led the crowd in a birthday cheer, and the cake was served. Afterward, Robert stood and kissed his mother on the cheek. He shook his father's hand and made to return to Isabel.

Mr. Claremont caught his arm. "There is more than one lady here," he said through clenched teeth, glancing around as if to be sure nobody was listening. The forced smile he wore would fool no one. "You will stop embarrassing yourself with that girl."

That girl would soon be his daughter, but Robert doubted this was the time to tell him.

"I left Miss Tate unattended. Allow me to escort her back to her family."

"And then see to the other ladies."

Robert nodded. Let his father think he was getting his way. Anything to return to Isabel sooner.

When he reached her, he offered her his arm. "Would you care to walk in the garden?"

"I'd love to." She rose and tucked her hand into the crook of his arm.

Bright moonlight drenched the garden as Robert and Isabel strolled to the fish pond and sat on a bench overlooking the water. Sighing contentedly, he wrapped an arm around her and she rested her head on his shoulder as they sat gazing at the full moon.

"Where will we live?" Isabel asked dreamily, interrupting the silence.

He smiled. "Anywhere you like."

"Our cottage," she said at once.

"Our cottage would barely fit the two of us, never mind when a baby comes along."

Their eyes met. *A baby.*

"We'll start there," Isabel said, "and move when we need more space."

"There's a dower house on the estate that could suit. It's mainly used for guests. Many rooms, a good stable. I'll ask my father about it when I speak to him tonight."

"It sounds ideal. But to me the cottage will always be our true home. That's where you first told me you love me."

"Oh, Isabel." Heart racing, he placed a hand on her shoulder as she raised her face to his, waiting for his kiss. Robert started at the hollow of her throat, her pulse quickening with each brush of his lips as he made his way to her mouth. When he kissed her, she responded with reckless passion that made him forget the rest of the world. Every one of her delicious curves molded to him as they clung together. After a few perfect moments, they stood and faced each other, hands entwined.

Robert touched a loose strand that hung over her shoulder. "Your hair has come loose."

"Oh, no! Help me pin it up."

"I know nothing of dressing women's hair," he said, laughing. "I am no maid."

"You must pretend, then. Here, take this pin and secure it in the back."

Robert did as instructed. "You look so beautiful, nobody will even notice your hair. Am I presentable?"

Isabel looked him up and down, then smoothed his jacket and ran her fingers through his hair.

"Anything else?" he asked.

"Just this." She kissed him once more, then took his hand.

As they approached the house, another song began, and they slipped inside unnoticed. Robert took her into his arms and danced her across the room. Isabel looked at him with such love that Robert felt his heart would burst. His world was now complete. True, there were obstacles to overcome. But that was for later. For now, there were only these precious moments. When the music stopped, they stood in front of each other, neither wanting the dance to end.

When a new song began, he reached for her hand. "Another?"

"As always, yes."

They danced around the ballroom, laughing together as they tried to keep up with the fast, light steps. Robert put an arm about her waist and lifted her, spinning in a circle. Her eyes shone with mirth, and he started to lift her again but stopped when he saw her ashen face.

"What is it?" he asked. "Too fast for you? Would you like to sit down?"

She didn't answer but stared across the room, her eyes wide, her hand in his suddenly moist and shaking.

"Isabel?" Robert asked, alarmed now.

She looked into his face, her eyes brimming with tears, and after one long, mournful gaze, her fingers slipped out of his hand and she walked away.

Chapter Ten

Robert watched in disbelief as she strode away. "Isabel?"

She looked over her shoulder, not meeting his eyes. "No, Robert," she said, softly but firmly, and continued walking.

As Robert trailed behind her, he understood what had frightened her. A grim-faced man stood by the door, glaring at Isabel. A younger man standing beside him watched her greedily as she approached. The music stopped and the eyes of everyone in the ballroom followed Robert and Isabel. She slowed as she approached the older man.

Robert called out again, "Isabel!"

She did not look back.

Just as he was about to rush to her, Robert felt two strong hands on his shoulders. Simon and William were on either side of him, holding him back.

"You'll only make it worse for her," Simon whispered urgently.

"He's right," William said. "Let her go."

Robert didn't take his eyes off Isabel. "I can't!"

"That's Giles Branwick, her stepfather," Simon said.

William lowered his voice. "She will pay the price if you confront him."

When Isabel reached Mr. Branwick, he bent to say something in her ear. Whatever it was, she stiffened. She squared her shoulders and left the room without a backward glance. Branwick gave Robert a triumphant look, and the young man beside him smirked as they followed Isabel out. Silence echoed through the ballroom until William signaled for the musicians to start, and soon everyone was dancing again.

But not Robert. He stood as a pillar amongst the dancers, staring at the door.

William took his arm, and Robert allowed himself to be led from the room, still reeling from the last ten minutes.

His stomach felt like a cannonball had landed in it. What just happened? "I must get to the stables," he said when they reached the foyer.

"You can't go after her," said Simon.

"And why not, pray?" Robert demanded.

"Because you are a guest of honor, and—" William began.

"What do I care for that? I won't lose her." Robert pushed past him, striding toward the door, but Simon barred his way.

"Simon, move at once!" Robert barked.

William joined Simon in blocking his exit. Robert clenched his fists.

"Do you know who that was?" William asked, pointing over his shoulder to the drive. "Her stepfather. Her very powerful stepfather. And his nephew, Mr. Abbot—her intended. Do you hear me, Robert? She is to marry him."

"Never! *We* are getting married. It's all arranged."

"Be that as it may, you cannot simply ride to her home, demand the wench, and be gone," William said.

"I know you want to go after her," Simon said,

trying to reason with Robert, "but not tonight. Tomorrow. Tomorrow we'll decide what to do. For tonight, let her be. Her stepfather will surely punish her more harshly if he sees the extent of your feelings for each other."

Robert went cold at the very idea of anyone hurting Isabel. But if they were right—if Branwick was as cruel as his reputation implied—going to Kerensly Hall would be as good as striking the blow himself.

"Very well," he said in a brittle voice. "Tomorrow."

"Come, let's go back to the ball," William said.

Robert ignored him and walked outside just in time to see Isabel's carriage disappear into the darkness. When he could no longer hear the sounds of the carriage, he went upstairs, bypassing the ball.

He went to his room and collapsed into a chair beside the window, gazing outside. Was it really the same moon he and Isabel had watched together no more than an hour ago? He retrieved the jacket he'd worn earlier that day and took Isabel's ring out of his pocket. He placed it on his smallest finger, which it barely fit. He smiled wistfully. She'd been so happy when he'd given it to her. He pulled out the miniatures, then lay down on his bed, staring at the depiction of Isabel's face. He clutched the portrait to his chest and closed his eyes.

****

Robert didn't sleep until almost dawn, and the morning was gone by the time he woke. He jumped out of bed and ran to the stables, still in his clothes from the night before. What Mr. Branwick had done was atrocious, and Robert wouldn't stand for it.

"My horse!" he bellowed as he burst into the stables. The groom dropped his pitchfork and scurried off to Apollo's stall.

"Going somewhere?" William asked. In his haste, Robert hadn't noticed him standing beside the stable door.

"I'm going to Isabel. She needs me."

William walked toward him. "Does she? I've heard otherwise."

"I have no times for your games, William," Robert said through gritted teeth.

"Perhaps you have time for this."

"What is it?" Robert asked impatiently as he waited for Apollo to be brought to him.

"Only this." William held out a paper. "A message Branwick sent to Father early this morning."

Robert snatched the note from William. His hand shook as he read it.

"This is impossible. I don't believe a word of it!" Robert cried, flinging the paper to the ground.

The groom approached with Robert's mount, but William shook his head slightly and he led Apollo back inside.

William picked the note up from the ground and smoothed it out. He read aloud:

"Dear Mr. Claremont,

My stepdaughter is marrying Mr. Abbot within the month. Isabel is pleased with the betrothal and is delighted to be reunited with her fiancé. I don't know what transpired between Isabel and your son, but she is spoken for. Keep him away from her.

—Mr. Giles Branwick."

"It's clearly a lie," Robert said, throwing his hands up.

"Is it? To what end? Why would Branwick lie about such a thing?"

"He desires this match, though Isabel certainly doesn't. I'm going to speak to her."

As Robert looked around anxiously for Apollo, he saw Simon jogging across the yard. What next? Why must he have such meddlesome friends?

"He's determined to see that woman," William told Simon when he reached them.

"No, Robert," Simon implored.

"I'll do as I please. Both of you leave me alone."

He turned to go into the stables and saddle Apollo himself, but Simon spoke.

"Didn't you see the note from Mr. Branwick?"

"I saw it. It proves nothing."

"She's betrothed. I told you that on May Day."

"*Practically* betrothed, you said."

"It doesn't change the fact that she's marrying someone else," William said.

"But she loves me," Robert insisted. "We're going to be married."

William opened his mouth to speak, but Simon put up a hand to stop him.

"She may have loved you," Simon said. "I've seen you together, and it's clear she favored you. But she's marrying Mr. Abbot. You know she cannot marry you if her stepfather has promised her to someone else."

"But she has promised to be my wife."

"It is not her promise to make," William said.

Simon looked at Robert sadly. "William's right."

"But—" Robert began. He couldn't explain his feelings to them, or how, no matter what anyone else said, Isabel was meant to be his wife. As certain as he was of the ground under his feet, he was certain he and Isabel belonged together.

"Why not send a message to Isabel?" Simon suggested.

"Yes," William agreed. "Ask her to explain herself."

"How could I do that? I'd look faithless."

"She is the faithless one," William said. "I saw her mooning after you, playing you false. She's been enjoying your attentions enough, but now that Mr. Abbot is here she willingly goes to him."

"You saw her last night. She was shocked to see him," Robert said.

"How could she not be shocked?" William said with a harsh laugh. "Caught in the arms of her lover when her betrothed arrives unexpectedly?"

"Robert," Simon interrupted, "we all saw her last night. Yes, she was caught off guard by Mr. Abbot. But she didn't even glance back at you. She went willingly to him. She even told you not to follow her."

Robert shook his head. "I won't believe it of her."

"Believe it or not, Robert, she's going to marry her intended. Branwick's message says so," William said.

Just then a messenger arrived from Kerensly Hall. "I have a message for Mr. Robert Claremont. The butler told me I could find him out here."

Robert grabbed the note from his hand. His face paled as he read it.

"What does it say?" Simon asked.

Robert turned and walked away, the note fluttering to the ground.

Simon picked it up and read it aloud:

"Dear Mr. Claremont,

Mr. Abbot has come for me and I'm happy to say we will soon be married. I'm sorry if I misled you. Please, leave me alone.

—Miss I. Tate"

"Is there a reply?" the messenger asked.

"No," William said, tossing him a coin.

The messenger bowed and left them.

"I cannot but think she is being coerced. I must see her," Robert said again, though less urgently. He tried to banish the doubt creeping into his heart and mind.

"Robert, stop. It's done," William said. "You see it now in her own hand."

Robert wheeled. "She could have been forced to write that. She wouldn't turn me over so abruptly."

"Who's going to force her? Her aunt and uncle? Her mother?" William asked.

"Her mother is there?"

"Yes," Simon confirmed. "She arrived with Branwick last night."

Robert put a hand to his forehead as this last bit of proof clicked into place. He couldn't imagine Isabel's own mother standing by and allowing her to be married against her will. William was right. Nobody but Branwick would even think of forcing her to write a letter, and furthermore, Isabel was not a weak woman. They couldn't *make* her write it. He'd never seen her handwriting, so there was nothing to compare the note to. Their dream was over. His dream, anyway. She'd move on, marry Branwick's nephew. Bear his children. He shuddered and looked up to find William and Simon staring at him. Simon looked concerned, William impatient.

Robert whispered, almost to himself, "She must have written it. That must be how she truly feels." Something cracked inside. How had he been so wrong about her?

"Be glad, Robert," William said. "Be thankful she's shown her true colors now, and not after you wed. She was hoping to snag a fine inheritance but has settled for this other man in order to appease her stepfather. A woman so fickle is not to be trusted."

"But I did trust her. Foolishly, it seems." He left without another word and walked aimlessly through the grounds until, some time later, Simon caught up to him at the edge of the woods.

"Do you need anything? Can I get you anything at all?" Simon asked.

"Isabel," Robert muttered.

Simon looked at his feet. "Robert, you saw her message."

"I did. William's right. I was a fool."

"No."

"Yes, I was. But no matter. I worried she'd think me faithless if I questioned her love, but it's *she* who is faithless," he said flatly. He added under his breath, "I was going to marry her. I was going to tell my father last night."

"I'm sorry, Robert."

"I should have listened to you and William and stayed clear of her."

"I can see why you didn't. It was clear she cared for you."

Robert raised his tortured eyes to Simon's. "If you could have seen how she acted with me when we were alone, could have heard her promises—"

Simon squeezed his shoulder. "Try to forget her."

"I doubt I can. But in future I'll be more guarded with my feelings."

"You've given up on trying to see her?"

"What for? I woke up intending to storm Kerensly Hall and demanding to speak with her. But now there's no point. She's made it clear she doesn't wish to see me again." Robert took a deep, shuddering breath.

"It will be for the best, you'll see," Simon said comfortingly.

"Not for the best. But it's done. She's chosen another life. I'd like to hear it from her own lips, if I could."

"Perhaps in a few days we could ride there together."

"Perhaps we'll be invited to the wedding," Robert murmured bitterly.

"Robert…"

He put a hand on Simon's shoulder. "Don't pay me any mind. Now leave me, please." His throat would allow no more words.

Simon turned reluctantly and walked back to the manor.

He didn't see Robert move into the trees. He didn't see him sink to the ground. Robert sat for hours, reliving his time with Isabel. He remembered the dreams they'd shared, the laughter, the kisses, the feel of her body and the sound of her voice. She'd been full of tenderness. Just yesterday he'd held her in his arms.

"She loves me!" he cried, slamming his fists into the ground.

Perhaps she once did, but she'd chosen duty and her stepfather's wishes over their love. If she had truly loved him at all. Robert laughed mirthlessly, thinking of all he'd planned to give up for her sake. There was no need now.

Tomorrow he would call on Margery. If he couldn't make himself happy, at least he could please his family.

****

Isabel lay on her bed, trying in vain to stifle her sobs. With bitterness she recalled the ride home from the ball the previous night. She'd sat stoney-faced in the carriage while her stepfather berated her about Robert.

"What are you playing at, girl?" he'd asked, face red with rage. "We sent you here to visit your aunt, not to fall in with the first pretty face you met."

Isabel hadn't answered.

"How did you come to be with this boy?" her stepfather pushed.

"We met on May Day."

"Met? And what more? You looked more than a little friendly with him."

Marcus, who'd been looking bored until now, tried to meet her eyes. "Just how far has this gone, Isabel? What kind of arrangement do you have with Claremont?"

Isabel stared out the window. She was not about to discuss her feelings for Robert with Branwick and his wretched nephew.

"I saw what Verity wrote to your mother," Branwick said. " '*Isabel has been getting along quite well with Robert Claremont. I would not be surprised if he makes an offer for her hand*,' " he mimicked. "That's why I dropped everything in Salisbury and came here as fast as I could. Whatever plans or romantic fancies you may have had, forget them. You're marrying Marcus."

Isabel whipped around to face Branwick. "You surely jest!"

"Don't go hurting your betrothed's feelings, now. He may think you don't like him."

"I'll never marry him. Never!" Isabel spat.

Marcus glared at her, but addressed his uncle. "Giles, you said it was all arranged. You said she would be my wife."

"So she shall…if she ever wants to see her mother and sister again."

"What are you talking about?" Isabel asked tremulously.

"Only that Jayne will not defy me. If I take her and Victoria away, there's no reason for you to join us, or even to know where we are."

"You can't take her away. She's my mother!"

Branwick assumed a shocked yet mocking face. "Is that bond really as strong as the one between man and wife?" Then he added, almost to himself, "And besides, mothers don't always stay." His eyes took on a strange, glazed look that Isabel didn't understand. Or want to. Her blood went cold. What was he implying? What would he do to her mother?

She leaned forward. "You can't seriously believe my mother would stand for you keeping us apart."

He shook his head as if clearing it, then said harshly, "Jayne will stand for whatever I *tell* her to stand for. I'm not the most patient of men. Or gentle. Your mother has learned this during our time together."

A chill crept up Isabel's spine. "You would not dare hurt her."

Branwick reached across the carriage and grabbed her wrist. She tried to free herself but was trapped in his iron grip. He squeezed until she winced in pain, but she kept her eyes on his, refusing to give him the satisfaction of seeing her cry or beg to be released.

"It wouldn't be the first time," he said, throwing her arm aside. Isabel massaged her aching wrist, where a bruise was already forming.

"You are a brute!"

"Perhaps, but I'm your father now. And you will do as I say," he said menacingly.

Isabel glared at him, but didn't speak.

"That's settled, then," Marcus said, chuckling. He crossed to the other side of the carriage and sat beside Isabel, moving his hand toward her knee.

"Don't touch me," she hissed with a scorching look.

"Oh, let her be, Marcus. You have your whole life to enjoy her charms." They both laughed coarsely as Isabel stared out the window, refusing to let her tears escape.

It was not until she reached the sanctity of her bedroom that she gave vent to her feelings, crying until there were no tears left. Nell had come in to light the candles, but Isabel sent her away and locked the door. She undressed slowly, preparing for bed. Mere hours ago she'd been in Robert's arms. Holding her gown against her, she inhaled deeply and caught a whiff of his cologne. The memory of their enchanted last night together brought tears to her eyes. She would never see him again.

"Robert...Robert," she whispered into the darkness before falling into broken and dreamless sleep.

The next morning, as she sat gazing out her bedroom window, Nell came in. She gave Isabel a pitying look. "You're wanted downstairs."

Isabel sighed. She'd known it wouldn't take her stepfather long to summon her. She sent Nell to the kitchens for food, then sat in her room and ate at her leisure. Let him wait. Though she had no appetite, she ate a crusty roll with fresh butter and drank some coffee.

At length, she rose from her chair, resigned. On her way out of the room, she caught a glimpse of herself in the mirror. Her restless night showed on her face, but her brown eyes were defiant. In her heart she would hold to her knowledge of Robert's love, for nothing gave her more strength than that.

In the drawing room, Mr. Branwick was waiting. To Isabel's surprise, her mother stood beside him.

"Mother!" Echoes of Branwick's threats to keep them apart flooded her mind as she rushed to her side. She'd already lost her father—she couldn't lose her mother, too.

Mrs. Branwick stopped Isabel from embracing her, but gave her a dry peck on each cheek.

Isabel looked around for her sister. "Where's Victoria?"

"With her nurse."

"Sit down," her stepfather said.

Isabel did so, and her mother joined her on the sofa.

Mr. Branwick held her eyes for a moment. "You haven't had enough supervision here. We've come to take you home."

"But I was to stay until the end of summer."

"That was before you started sneaking around with that scoundrel Robert Claremont. Your uncle told me he never asked permission to court you but tricked you into believing he had."

"It wasn't like that," Isabel began. "Please, allow me to explain—"

"Silence!" he yelled.

Isabel looked imploringly at her mother, who was unmoved.

He continued, "Now that we've seen how undisciplined you are, we've decided it would be best if you wed Marcus without delay."

"I will never marry Marcus."

Her stepfather said in a low voice, "You will. You're lucky to make such a match."

Isabel stood. "I won't! You can't tell me what to do!"

Branwick took a step toward her, his hand raised high. Isabel sidestepped out of his reach and sat down again, clutching her mother's arm.

"You will not speak that way to me," he said in a deadly tone.

"Mother, please," Isabel said, her voice quaking.

Finally, Mrs. Branwick looked at her. "This is for the best, Isabel. Marcus is a suitable partner for you."

"There," said Branwick, as if that settled the matter. "Remember what I told you last night, Isabel. You'll do this, or suffer for it."

Isabel was about to speak, but her mother looked her in the eye and gave a small shake of her head.

Branwick went on, "You'll be pleased to hear that you're marrying Marcus in three days."

Isabel started to object, but he interrupted her.

"You *will* appear at the church with a smile on your ungrateful face. I will not have Marcus made a fool."

"Marcus needs no help from me on that account. Why is my intended not here on bended knee? Where is my sweet proposal?"

"Don't be flippant, Isabel," her mother snapped.

"What does my aunt say of this?" Isabel asked. "Where is she? And Uncle Francis?"

"This is no business of theirs," Branwick said. "I sent them away this morning. It's your aunt's fault you're in this scandalous situation. Guardians, indeed."

"You sent them away from their own house? Where? Is John with them?"

"Calm yourself, Isabel," her mother said. "Naturally John is with them. They've gone to their house in Salisbury for the rest of the summer."

"May I be excused?" Isabel asked. The anger she'd felt earlier had been replaced with hopelessness. So much for fighting, or compromising, or having her say. They'd already made up their minds about Robert and planned her future without a thought to what she wanted. She couldn't stand her mother's indifference or her stepfather's cruelty another second.

"You're excused. For the time being," Mr. Branwick said.

"I'll be up later to show you what I've chosen for your wedding dress," her mother said, as if this would cheer Isabel.

She walked out of the room, head held high. Across the hall, a door opened and Marcus stood there. "Psst...Isabel." He gestured for her to come in, but she ignored him.

As soon as she was out of sight of the door she sped to her room, threw herself on her bed, and wept. After giving way to her sorrow, Isabel spent the afternoon pacing her room, trying to devise a plan. Escape was the only choice, but impossible. Her stepfather had placed guards outside her room and below her second-story window.

In the evening, her mother and the seamstress arrived to discuss the wedding dress.

"The wedding is so soon I'm afraid you won't be able to have a new gown," her mother said. "I would have liked to see you in white muslin, but yours is torn, so something else from your wardrobe will have to do."

"It matters not what I wear," she told her mother

despondently.

"Really, Isabel," her mother said, clicking her tongue. "You're not going to the gallows. Marcus will have a large income and you'll be mistress of your own home. Many women would be grateful for such a position."

"Let many women have him. He disgusts me."

"Love isn't all that matters in a marriage."

"You loved my father," Isabel said softly.

Her mother's face reddened, and her eyes lost their warmth. "Yes, I did. And see what it's gotten me. Heartache and an early widowhood. Now that he's gone, I'm in a new marriage. Not based on love but on practicality. I'm comfortable and have secured a future for you and Victoria."

"I'll make my own way," Isabel muttered, looking down at her feet.

"How? As an archer? Or a governess?" her mother scoffed. "Enough of this talk, Isabel. Try the gown on."

The seamstress came over with the sky-blue dress in her arms.

"No! I won't marry that lout wearing this gown." It was her special dress, her dress for Robert.

Her mother looked startled by her reaction. "Isabel, it's your best and newest gown. Of course you'll wear it."

"No, Mother. You can force me to do many things, but I will go naked to the wedding before I wear that."

"It's of no consequence," she said tiredly with a wave of her hand. She turned to the seamstress. "Find the next best gown and bring it in."

Isabel stood still while the seamstress helped her into a green-and-gold-striped gown.

Her mother smiled and clasped her hands against her chest. "Perfect."

Isabel turned away. "Take it off."

Her mother motioned for the seamstress to assist her in disrobing. She took the gown away, and Isabel put on a pink dress decorated with sprigs of purple flowers.

Isabel went to the window, her back to her mother. "Please, leave me."

A moment later the door clicked shut.

Alone in her room, Isabel realized there was only one course of action. Robert. She would have to get word to him somehow. He could send help, or come himself. She went to her desk and wrote a short note:

"My dearest Robert,

I'm being held captive at Kerensly and will be forced to marry Marcus in three days. Please, come at once.

All my love, Isabel."

As soon as Nell came in to assist her in preparing for bed, Isabel went into action.

"Nell, I need your help."

Her brow creased as she peered into Isabel's face. "What is it, are you ill?"

Isabel held up the note. "I need you to get this to Robert Claremont."

Nell took a step back. "Oh, I dare not! What would Mr. Branwick say? I cannot, Isabel."

"I wouldn't ask if it were not of the utmost urgency. Please, Nell. You know what he has planned for me. I can't get out of here on my own."

"There must be some way," Nell said, glancing over her shoulder as if frightened of being overheard.

"Will you help me? Please?" Isabel begged.

"I can't risk it, Isabel." Nell wrung her hands. "I do

wish your aunt was here! She would know what to do."

"I doubt she could do much either." She collapsed onto the bed.

Nell walked over to the fireplace. Neither of them spoke for some time before Nell turned back to her and took a deep breath. "I know your aunt would want me to help you."

"Oh, Nell!" Isabel leapt off the bed and hugged her.

"I'm only saying I'll try my best. I can promise nothing. Mr. Branwick has men lurking around every corner."

"Thank you, Nell, oh, thank you!"

Nell took the note and hid it in the folds of her skirt. At the door, she looked back and said, "I can only try."

Isabel climbed into bed, more hopeful than she'd been since she left Robert at the ball. The emotional toll of the day caught up with her and she fell into a deep, untroubled sleep.

****

Isabel rose late the next morning. Knowing she'd taken some action to free herself had guaranteed a sound sleep. She got up and dressed, then looked outside. Men paced the yard, one standing sentinel right beneath her window. When Isabel went to her door and opened it, a bulky guard stepped in front of her, barring her way.

"Am I not allowed out to break my fast?" Isabel demanded.

"I'll send for food."

"Where's my mother? I want to see her."

"She isn't allowed in, and you aren't allowed out."

She slammed the door in his face.

Not long after, the doorknob turned. Isabel opened it at once, expecting breakfast. Marcus stood there, arms crossed. He was probably considered handsome by some. His green silk suit and chestnut hair were immaculate, as always, and his eyes held some secret amusement. She went to close the door but he braced it with his arms.

"I want to talk to you," he said. "We can do it here, or I can come in."

Isabel stepped into the doorway, blocking him from the room. "Well?"

"I hear you're putting up a fuss about marrying me, but I don't see why. We got along just fine in Salisbury."

Her forehead wrinkled. "We barely even talked in Salisbury."

He shrugged. "So?"

"So we aren't even friends."

"Yes, we are. We're more than that. We live in the same house. We've even gone to the theater together."

"Not *together*. We just happened to be there on the same night." Was he really going to stand here and act like they had some kind of relationship?

"I can give you jewels, gowns, a home. Giles says he'll give me—us—a small fortune if we marry. We could live in Salisbury, near your mother."

"But I'm not looking for any of those things." She didn't want to come right out and admit she couldn't marry him because she was in love with Robert. It was nobody's business but theirs. She doubted it would change anything anyway.

He let out a heavy sigh. "Why are you being so stubborn? Why won't you marry me?"

Almost at a loss for words, she finally managed, "I don't love you."

"I don't love you, either. But what does that matter?

I'll be good to you, as long as you're good to me. In some ways I'm much like my uncle." He touched her cheek lightly, a shadow of a threat in his dark brown eyes.

She jerked back and half closed the door. He grabbed the knob and took a step closer, bringing with him the scent of heavy-handed, musky cologne.

"Please leave, Marcus."

"Hear me out. Giles wants us together. We'll be *together* until you're with child, and then I'll go on my way until it's time for the next one."

She couldn't stop the grimace that came to her face. Bed Marcus? "Absolutely not."

He cocked a brow. "You don't have much choice, do you?"

"I—I...I'm going to—" To what? What could she possibly threaten him with? She was going to scream? Run away? Step on his foot?

He smiled. "At a loss for words?"

"No, I'm not. You sicken me, and I'll jump out that window before I marry you!"

He rolled his eyes. "Stop your hysterics. Look, Isabel, I don't want you any more than you want me. I have a woman, but Giles insists I also take *you* as a wife. We'll both benefit from it. Maybe more than you think." Marcus grabbed her chin but she turned her face just in time for his kiss to land on her cheek, not her lips. Isabel used all her strength to pull out of his grip and drive her shoulder into his chest. As he reeled backward, she slammed and locked the door. She heard him coughing, trying to catch his breath just outside the room.

"You *will* marry me. I'll be back tomorrow morning," he growled and stomped down the hall.

Isabel collapsed into the chair beside the window,

wiping her cheek with her sleeve. Marcus was even worse than she'd thought. He was telling her he didn't want to marry her—but he would do so to please Giles and get paid for it? He'd have his mistress and keep Isabel perpetually with child? Oh, and he may or may not beat her, depending on how she behaved? She laughed to herself. Had he thought that would be an irresistible proposal? He clearly thought she had no choice, but he didn't know she'd written to Robert. *Oh, Robert,* she thought, *Hurry.*

****

An hour later, breakfast arrived and, ravenous, she ate every morsel. Then it was time to prepare for her escape. Robert would arrive later today, no doubt. She must be ready. How would he get in? Would he barge in and demand her release? Arrive with a force of men? Perhaps he'd sneak in and they would run away together. She tied a small velvet pouch full of coins into her skirt. If nothing else, she would have money.

The sky was a golden russet color when a servant arrived with supper, hours later. He set the tray on the table. "With Mr. Branwick's compliments," he said, and left.

There were two covered dishes, bread, and a glass of ale. In the first dish she found a delicious hearty stew. When she finished, she opened the second dish.

Her heart sank like a stone.

Sitting on the plate was a small piece of paper. She knew what it was even before unfolding it with trembling fingers. Her note to Robert. He'd never seen it. Isabel threw herself on her bed and wept with frustration. After releasing a torrent of tears she rose, wiping her eyes.

"No!" she said out loud. Her father had not taught

her to give up at the first sign of trouble. He'd taught her to be strong, to care for herself. He'd want her to fight—and fight she would. She'd find a way out herself. She would escape somehow, retrieve her bow, and then let anyone try to stop her!

Chapter Eleven

After changing into her brown wool riding habit, Isabel sat on the edge of the bed, waiting impatiently for nightfall. Once the house was quiet, she'd make her way out.

As she sat in the dark, her mind dwelt on Robert. Where was he? Even without the note she'd tried to send, it was surprising he hadn't come to see her. Would he abandon her completely after that scene at the ball? No. He must not realize she was in trouble, or nothing would have kept him from her. She knew this to be true.

When a knock came on her door, she didn't answer but got into bed and pulled up the covers. Her heart hammered as a key turned in the lock. Who would dare enter? Marcus? Would he visit her tonight, not even waiting until after their bogus wedding? She kept her eyes closed, feigning sleep, and tried to think of anything in the room she could use as a weapon.

The door slowly creaked open. "Isabel?"

"Mother!" she cried, sitting up. "What are you doing here?"

"Quiet," her mother said in a hushed tone as she came into the room, locking the door behind her. She sat on the bed. "I'm here to help you."

"But you agreed with Mr. Branwick. You want me to marry Marcus," Isabel said bitterly.

"I don't wish that on you, my daughter." Her mother

reached for her and they embraced, then Mrs. Branwick stood.

Isabel looked up at her mother, puzzled. "But yesterday, downstairs—"

"Yesterday I let Giles think he's in charge."

"But if you'd stood up for me, perhaps I would be married to Robert right now."

Her mother shook her head. "There's no way he'd agree to that. I did speak to him about it, when we first heard Mr. Claremont was courting you. He became almost…unhinged. He said—"

"What?"

"He said no daughter of Edward Tate's would disobey him, and if you're unhappy in a marriage with Marcus you deserve to be because it would be *your* fault."

"It isn't my fault if he's marrying me to his toad of a nephew."

"That's what I told him. He said terrible things about your father, and he mentioned the day his mother died and spoke of revenge. He made no sense. I think he must have been drunk."

"But Father was his best friend."

"As I said, he was speaking nonsense. But one thing was clear. He'll do anything to make you marry Marcus. If Giles's only idea was to secure a good match for you, I wouldn't worry so much. But Marcus isn't the right man for you. And there's something about the way Giles looks at you, talks about you, that makes me believe you aren't safe unless you're far from him. I can't explain it. Mother's intuition, perhaps."

"I've had the same feeling. I don't know what I could have done to offend him. I've thought perhaps he's jealous of how close you and I were."

"That could be. One day, when you're married and have a family of your own, we'll be that close again." She paused. "So, Robert Claremont. You love him? He'll make you happy?"

"Happier than I ever thought possible. We're already betrothed."

Mrs. Branwick smiled softly, then glanced at the clock. "There isn't much time. I'm going to help you escape. That note was a foolish idea. Of course Nell was caught."

"Oh! Is she hurt? Did he harm her?" Isabel asked, cringing as she climbed out of bed.

"Giles struck her, of course. He delights in bullying those who cannot defend themselves. I've seen to her, and aside from some bruising she'll be fine."

A horrible pang of guilt pierced Isabel. She'd make it up to Nell somehow. But right now there were more pressing matters.

"What can we do? How can I escape without Robert's help?"

"I'm not as meek as you think me, Isabel."

"But you married that monster!"

"You must remember that Giles was not always thus. Or at any rate, he hid his true nature well. Though many people don't trust him, even fear him, he played the kind friend to your father when he was alive. After he died, Giles was a most attentive suitor. Do you think I would have associated with the man suspected of killing your father, had I known? Let alone marry him? Bed him?" She shivered.

Cold fury coursed through Isabel. "You believe he killed Father?"

"I've heard rumors, whispers. Too many to ignore. Your father was an excellent rider. There's no way he would have been thrown."

"But why would Mr. Branwick do such a thing?"

"I have no idea. I hope, as time goes by, I'll be able to discover the truth about what happened. If I find proof, I will report him to the magistrate."

"But how can you stay with him now?"

"I have little choice. I won't divorce him, and I can't strike out on my own with your sister. And besides, I have my own plans for Giles. I married him for the security he can provide for us. He won't live forever. He wants an heir. I shall give him one." She placed a hand on her stomach.

"Oh, Mother! Indeed?"

"I am two months gone."

"What if you have another girl? You aren't strong enough to endure many births. Your doctor told you so after Victoria was born." Isabel didn't think it polite to mention that her mother was no longer young. She must be nearly forty.

"I'll keep trying until I have a son by that man. My son will be his true and rightful heir, even before Marcus. Then all Giles has will be ours when he finally dies. He took your father from us. The best man, the best father and husband anyone could ask for. We shall take Giles's fortune. It will never compensate, but we'll be free."

"What you have gone through—" Isabel began, but her mother cut her off.

"We'll get you out of here tonight. You will marry for love, as I did when I married your dear father."

"How do you stand it?" Isabel asked, shaking her head.

"There's more than one kind of strength. Remember that. I know what I do now will benefit you and your sister. But first we're getting you out of here."

"Mother, how can I ever thank you?"

"You can be happy. You can give me grandchildren. And someday, when Giles dies, you and Robert will never want for anything."

Isabel was stunned. Here was a clear path, an answer. But she still didn't see how they would escape unnoticed.

"What's your plan, Mother?"

"I've sent the guards away on a fool's errand. By the time they return, you will have fled."

"But will Branwick suspect you?"

"Me? I'm a harmless and stupid woman," her mother said in a simpering voice.

"He truly believes that of you?" He was even more ignorant than she'd thought.

"Oh, yes. He has no idea what I'm capable of. I'm going to Giles tonight to tell him I'm expecting. He'll be overjoyed and will be swimming in wine and drunk within the hour."

Isabel embraced her mother. "When will I see you again? Mr. Branwick said that if I don't marry Marcus, he won't even tell me where you are. I couldn't bear that."

Her mother put a hand to Isabel's cheek. "We must bear it, at least for a little while. I'll get word to you, somehow. Once you are Mrs. Claremont, I doubt Giles will make good on his threats. When you're out of his reach I'll finally sleep better."

"But will you be safe?"

"Yes. He will not seriously harm me."

"Seriously? But that means…"

"Isabel, enough! It's time for you to go. I'll take care of myself."

She wanted to argue but knew it would be pointless. She would find a way to see her mother again soon, regardless of what her stepfather said. But now for the task at hand. Escape. "What will we do?"

"We'll leave here together, and I'll lock the door after we've gone. Your absence hopefully won't be noticed until morning. There's much merrymaking in the great hall, so I doubt anyone will even see you leave the house. You'll go through the back gardens to the stable and saddle your own horse. And then ride, Isabel. Ride as fast as you can to your Robert."

They crept downstairs without seeing anyone. Isabel peeked into the great hall, where many people were celebrating her upcoming wedding. A buxom woman sat on Marcus's lap, running her hand through his hair as he bit into a huge leg of meat.

Isabel and her mother at last reached the garden.

"Go now, Isabel."

"I'll get word to you once Robert and I are settled, after we're married," she promised.

Her mother kissed her cheek. "Go—and be careful!"

Isabel ran through the gardens. She turned back once and her mother waved, then entered the house.

Night closed around her, darker and quieter now that she was alone. She raced to the stables, found her uncle's fastest horse, Jacinth, and saddled her. She retrieved her bow and quiver and slung them over her shoulder. The familiar weight gave her much-needed confidence and new courage. After mounting, she guided Jacinth over the lawn. Isabel turned to look at the house. Would she ever see it again? She cared not. The future was ahead of her now. Robert was waiting. With that thought to lift her spirits, she galloped into the night.

The moon came out from behind the clouds just as Isabel reached the lake where she'd first met Robert. In the distance, the lights of Thornwood Manor beckoned. She wondered which window was his. If only she could get inside and find his chamber. Since she had no idea where he was, the best course of action was to find a spot in the forest and wait until daybreak. He rode every day, so if she hid near the stables she was bound to see him. If not him, then Mr. Kensington. If Robert trusted him, she could, too.

Isabel skirted the woods until she reached the stables. Suddenly she heard a sound that stopped her heart. Singing. Someone was coming out of the stable, carrying a torch in one hand, a bottle in the other.

William.

He sauntered toward her, his steps unsure. "Who goes there?" he called out, laughing and slurring his words. When he recognized her, he stopped short.

"So it's you," he said icily. "What are you doing here? Come to break my brother's heart again?"

Isabel saw at once that he was drunk. "What do you mean?"

William paced back and forth in front of Jacinth. "Left the ball without even looking back, going to the arms of your other lover. You never loved Robert." He looked up at her through narrowed eyes and took a gulp from the bottle, then wiped his face with his sleeve.

"I've been a prisoner!"

"A prisoner?" William waved the torch around wildly in front of him. "A prisoner in your doting uncle's home? The servants talk of little but the grand preparations at Kerensly Hall. We've heard guests are arriving for a wedding. Your wedding. To Mr. Abbot. My brother's been beside himself. He thought there was a mistake at first. But then you sent that note. He knows now you were only using him. He knows now you never loved him. Simon and I have finally convinced him you're nothing more than a lying *whore!*" he said, hurling the last word at her.

"That's a lie! You know it is!"

"Do I?" He stroked Jacinth's neck.

"Why are you out at this hour?" she asked, hoping to distract him. If he would move away, she could get past him and ride into the woods.

"I'm out after an evening with Bess. She's asleep in the dower house. Well satisfied, I might add." He took another swig from the bottle and offered it to Isabel.

"No." She turned her head away.

He sneered. "I thought not."

"I have to go. I'll return tomorrow."

"I'm afraid that won't be possible." William grabbed Jacinth's bridle.

"Let go!" Isabel reached for her bow.

William saw the action and grabbed her hand. Jacinth started and reared and, caught off guard, Isabel landed on the ground with a thud.

William loomed over her; his eyes hard, out of focus. He threw his bottle away and it landed at her feet. "It's time you disappeared, Miss Tate. Robert was getting on quite well before you arrived in Holton. I'm taking you back to Kerensly Hall where you will no doubt be married to Mr. Abbot without delay. Once you return to Salisbury as a blushing bride, Robert will finally be rid of you and get back to courting his true intended."

Isabel stood and scanned the horizon, her heart pounding. She and William were utterly alone on the dark grounds.

William saw her looking and laughed. "Robert's fast asleep in his bed. He cannot help you."

He took a step closer and gave her a mocking bow. "Now, if you will allow me to escort you to the carriage, we'll reunite you with your betrothed, who must be missing you."

She licked her dry lips and said in a voice much smaller than she'd intended, "Robert will discover what you've done, and never forgive you."

"I don't think so. I'll go back to bed, still warm with my sweet Bess. She will attest that I've been with her all night."

Isabel knew he was right. If he did as he threatened, there was no hope for her. She started to run. William wasn't expecting it, so it bought her a few precious seconds. He tripped over the bottle and dropped his torch on the ground. Jacinth startled and bolted. As William got to his feet, Isabel grabbed an arrow and set it to her bowstring. She walked backward, facing him as she inched away. "Don't come any closer!"

William paused. "You will shoot me in the dark?" he asked, laughing.

The dying torchlight on the ground gave her just enough light. "I warn you," she said, "My aim is true."

William advanced on her. "Robert will not thank you for attacking his only brother."

"And he will not thank you for threatening me!"

"He'll never hear about that, though, will he? You'll be married and away, and he'll never hear from you again!"

William lunged at her, and Isabel let her arrow fly. He cursed in the dark. She'd only grazed his arm, but it was enough to tear his shirt and draw blood. He came at her with a murderous look in his eyes, but she was already running to the trees, her bow clutched in her hand. Isabel could have wept with relief when she saw Jacinth standing nearby. Just as she mounted, William grabbed her skirt and tried to pull her down. She kicked him in the face, and he grunted as her boot struck his nose. Blood gushed from it and he collapsed, his face in his hands.

Isabel spurred Jacinth and galloped away. When she looked back, William was still writhing on the ground, but she knew he'd be up and after her as soon as he was able. Once out of sight of the manor she pulled up Jacinth and dismounted. She slapped her on the rump and the horse galloped down the road toward Kerensly Hall. Isabel picked up her skirts and ran into the trees. There was only one safe place now. The cottage. She couldn't let herself be captured by Branwick or William.

Her only hope was Robert.

Isabel knew he'd find her at the cottage. She hoped he would. She bit her lip, thinking about what William had said. Could Robert honestly doubt her love for him? If he knew her at all, he knew she loved him. Isabel picked up her pace, trusting the darkness to conceal her. She had a long way to go before she reached the safety of the cottage, and she must arrive before dawn.

****

In the hazy morning sunshine, Robert practiced swordplay with Simon. This was something he normally excelled at, but today he'd already been disarmed twice.

Isabel filled his mind. Rumors abounded that she was to marry Marcus Abbot this very day. His heart froze at the thought, but after that note she'd sent he was forced to accept she no longer wanted him. She'd had ample opportunity to contact him again, but hadn't. If she still loved him, why hadn't she come to him? And why ask him to stay away?

"Robert, I could have slain you just now. Again." Simon's voice jostled him out of his thoughts.

He shook his head to clear it, then paced around Simon, looking for a weak spot. Simon got some fierce thrusts in before Robert finally managed to disarm him.

"Pathetic," William said, walking over from the house. His face was covered in bruises.

Simon peered at him. "Talking of pathetic."

"What happened to you?" Robert asked. "You look terrible. Another brawl over someone's wife?"

This seemed to amuse William, who laughed as he spoke. "You're very close to the mark." His nose was swollen and both eyes were black.

"Who was it?" Robert asked. "I thought I heard someone leaving the stables late last night. Did someone's husband pay you a visit?"

"Not her husband, no."

He sat on the ground to watch them and would say no more. Simon and Robert exchanged a look. They were used to William's scuffles over women, but he usually boasted about it.

Robert circled Simon, then jabbed at his side. Simon pushed back, knocking Robert off balance.

"Robert, you're leaving your left side wide open," William said. "You might as well stab yourself now and save Simon the trouble. Don't stand still for so long.

168

Keep moving."

"He's doing fine without your help, William," Simon said, losing his balance and nearly falling over as Robert barreled toward him.

They were about to start again when the pounding of hooves rent the air. William rose and went to Robert's side as ten horsemen thundered into the yard, Branwick at their head. He dismounted, throwing his reins to another man.

"Where is she?" he boomed at Robert, shoving him to the ground.

Robert sprang to his feet. "You'll pay for that!" His sword was steady as he pointed it at Branwick. Simon and William closed in around Robert, ready for a fight.

"She's here, she must be here! Search the grounds!" Mr. Branwick bellowed, ignoring Robert's sword. His men dismounted and gathered behind him.

"What the blazes are you talking about?" William demanded, not leaving his place by Robert's side.

"Isabel. She has flown, and I know to what nest," he cried, pointing wildly to the manor.

"Isabel isn't here," Robert said, his sword dropping to his side. "Where has she gone?"

"You know," Branwick said, jabbing him in the chest. "You must know. We have a wedding today and are missing our bride. I believe she came here for one last tryst with you. Bring the little slut to me at once."

Robert moved to strike Branwick, but Simon held him back.

"How dare you insult her!" Robert spat. "I don't know where she is, but I'm glad she's gone if it means she's away from you."

Branwick turned to his men. "Search the house, and

leave no stone unturned. I want her found. She weds Marcus this afternoon."

Steel flashed as William drew his sword. "Mount your horses and go. Isabel isn't here. Do you honestly think my brother would be out here with us if his mistress was lurking somewhere inside?"

"There's one way to find out," Branwick said, pushing past William. He motioned to his men, who streamed past William, Simon, and Robert despite their protests.

"Stop!" Robert yelled. He, William, and Simon advanced with swords aloft, ready to defend their home, when another voice boomed through the courtyard.

"Cease this at once and get off my land!" Mr. Claremont, surrounded by a swarm of armed men, strode to Robert's side.

"We'll leave when we have the girl," Branwick said.

"She's not here," Robert insisted. How he dearly wished she were.

"Girl? My son told you there's no girl here. That's as good as my own word. You'll be sorry if you don't leave. Now."

"I'll leave once I've searched your estate."

"Now." Mr. Claremont advanced on him, sword drawn.

Mr. Branwick looked around. His party was far outnumbered. "If you give me your word Isabel isn't here, I'll go," he said reluctantly.

"My word."

Branwick nodded and mounted his horse, then spoke to the crowd of Claremont men assembled in the courtyard.

"All of you; hear me," he cried. "There is a

handsome reward to whoever delivers Isabel to me. Unharmed and unsullied."

Robert didn't like the gleam of greed in some of the listening men's eyes as Branwick and his men rode away.

Mr. Claremont dismissed his men, then turned to Robert. "She's not here? For certain?"

Robert shook his head. "I haven't seen her since the ball."

"Good. She's nothing but trouble."

"Father," Robert said, pulling Mr. Claremont aside.

His father sheathed his sword, looking at Robert with thinly veiled impatience. "What?"

"I must find Isabel. I want to—" He swallowed, hard. It was now or never. "I want to marry her."

Mr. Claremont's face turned a vivid shade of red. "Out of the question!"

"I didn't succeed with Margery. I could never be with her now that I've met Isabel. I love her."

For a moment Robert thought his father would strike him.

When Mr. Claremont spoke, his voice trembled with suppressed rage. "If that's your choice, so be it. But you can expect nothing from me, Robert. Nothing, if you marry that girl! I thought that in you I had the one son I could depend on. It seems I'm quite mistaken."

Over his father's shoulder Robert saw William put a hand over his eyes and shake his head.

"Father, I—" Robert began, but his father's icy glare silenced him.

Mr. Claremont turned on his heel and marched back inside.

Well, it was done. Let his father be angry. All that mattered now was finding Isabel. Robert ran to the stable. "My horse! Saddle my horse!"

A groom rushed away to do his bidding.

"Robert, wait!" Simon said, following him.

Robert spoke over his shoulder., "If she has indeed run away from Mr. Branwick, she must have been on the way to me. She may have been waylaid or hurt. I need to find her."

"No, Father's right," William said. "That wench is nothing but trouble."

Robert spun on his heel. "Don't speak of her that way!" He drew his sword, holding Simon and William at bay.

"Has it come to this, Robert?" William asked tiredly. "You would fight us over her? She is nothing. We're your brothers."

Robert let his sword drop. "I won't fight you. But if you keep me from Isabel, my life might as well be over now."

William rolled his eyes, while Simon looked pityingly at Robert.

Simon shook his head. "This is not the way."

"There is no other way," Robert said.

"Robert, see reason," William implored. "You heard Father. He'll disinherit you if you disobey him in this. Would you watch your Isabel starve? How will you keep her? Look at the trouble she's caused you already."

"I'll do whatever it takes to keep her safe and happy. Now I must find her before Branwick does. Don't follow me."

He turned his back on them and ran into the stable. Moments later, they jumped out of his way as he thundered past on Apollo. He knew exactly where to find

Isabel. The cottage. He could not ride fast enough, for she was waiting for him.

Chapter Twelve

Robert went cautiously—the last thing he wanted was to lead Branwick to the cottage. He kept to the road for a while, then turned into the forest and in time arrived at the meadow. The trees had become overgrown during the summer, the gate more hidden than ever. He dismounted and opened it, leading Apollo by the reins. When he entered the yard, there was no sign of Isabel or Dion. Could he have been wrong? Was Isabel lying injured somewhere, needing him? Robert's chest burned as panic rose within him. Where was she?

He ran to the cottage and threw open the door. Relief flooded through him, for there she was, fast asleep on the bed, her face stained with tears. Robert rushed to her side.

"Isabel," he said softly, stroking her hair.

She stirred in her sleep, opened her eyes blearily, and sat up. "Oh, Robert!"

He sat on the bed and pulled her into his arms, holding her close as she sobbed.

"William said you hated me," she said, wiping her eyes. "He told me you believed I abandoned you, but I'd never do that, Robert, never."

"William!" exclaimed Robert, jumping to his feet.

"I escaped and came to Thornwood last night to find you, but I encountered William. Oh, he was terrible! He threatened to hand me over to my stepfather." She

174

relayed the whole encounter.

Robert was momentarily at a loss for words. When he finally spoke, his voice shook. "He will pay dearly for this."

"He's already paid. I grazed him with an arrow, and kicked him in the face."

Robert's jaw dropped and he fought to keep a smile from his face. "You did that? We thought he was in a brawl."

Her chin went up a notch. "He merely crossed the wrong woman."

"Did he hurt you?"

"Not much." She rubbed her still raw wrist.

Robert held her hand, scowling as he examined the abrasions. He gently kissed Isabel's wounds, then sat beside her on the bed. "Where have you been all these days? Why didn't you come back to me?"

"My stepfather held me prisoner. I tried to send you a message, but he intercepted it. He was going to force me to marry Marcus. In the end, my mother helped me escape. I went straight to Thornwood, but I didn't make it past William." She looked into Robert's eyes. "You must know I've always been true to you."

"I do now. I was afraid you'd left me, that you'd somehow been coerced into marrying Marcus. I should have come and asked you myself. I'm sorry I didn't. Once I read your note, I thought all hope was lost."

"What note?"

"The note telling me to leave you alone, that you wanted to marry Marcus."

"There is no end to Branwick's treachery! He must have written it himself, and it caused you to doubt me."

"That message was all that stopped me from riding

to Kerensly Hall."

Robert reached into his pocket and drew out her ring. She gasped with delight as he slipped it onto her finger.

She brought her hand to her heart. "It will never leave me again."

"And you will never leave *me* again," Robert said, embracing her. "We'll be married tonight, and nobody will be able to separate us."

"How?" Isabel asked, her face alight with joy.

"I know a vicar who will do this for us. We need a witness. I daresay Edmund would be willing to come. We need someone my father trusts, else he won't believe it even if I show him the documents." Robert didn't mention that he was disowned if he married her.

"When will we go?"

"We'll wait here until nightfall. Your stepfather is still searching for you. He came to Thornwood."

"Will he find our cottage?"

"Only Simon knows about it, and he doesn't know we're here. I told him and William I was riding out to search the roads for you."

"Then we're safe." Her shoulders relaxed as she let out a deep breath.

"For the time being."

"I knew you'd find me." She slid down onto the bed and reached for him, her eyes half shy, half surprised at her own boldness. Heart galloping, Robert stretched out beside her and took her into his arms. Their eyes held for an eternity before he kissed her softly.

"I love you, Isabel."

"I love you. Hold me. I don't want to let go of you today."

Robert tightened his grip on her and she smiled contentedly before drifting to sleep in his arms. He watched her for quite some time, then fell asleep himself, confident in their future, in their love. Nothing would ever separate them again.

When Robert awoke, it was dusk. He looked over at Isabel, who was already awake.

"It's time to leave soon," he said.

"I'm glad. I don't like this waiting."

Robert climbed out of bed and stretched, reaching his arms above his head. Isabel stood and wrapped her arms around him.

"Tonight, after we wed," Robert said, "we'll stay at an inn. A fine inn with a good table."

"Could we not come back here?"

He shook his head. "We need to get right away as soon as we're married. Branwick is searching for you, and I still have William to contend with. If he knew what I was doing, he'd try to stop me."

Robert wouldn't take any risks. Once they were married, she was under his protection. Even Mr. Branwick couldn't take her away when she was his wife. But he doubted they'd be able to persuade Branwick or his father to listen to them in their current moods. After the wedding they'd go away for a time, then come back and speak to them.

"I'd hoped to be here for our wedding night," Isabel said.

"We'll come back when all this is over. After we're married tonight, we'll stay at an inn for a few days, then go to the coast. In a month or so we'll come home."

"So long? I must write to my mother and tell her I'm safe."

"You will. Once we truly *are* safe."

Robert looked out the window. Sunset was upon them. They walked to the stable and Isabel stood by while Robert saddled Apollo, attaching her bow to the saddle.

"Only one horse," Robert said with a grin. "You'll have to ride with me."

"With pleasure."

He helped Isabel mount, then climbed up behind her. Instead of taking the road, Robert went through the forest. As they reached the border of Claremont land, they saw torchlight flickering in the dark and heard men's raised voices coming from the road just over the ridge. Robert pulled Apollo to a stop, glad of his decision to stay in the trees.

A man said, "They're not here. I told Mr. Branwick so, but he's convinced they're in the area."

"Not likely," said another voice. "Claremont has her holed up somewhere."

"I told Mr. Branwick he should search Salisbury. That's what I'd do," said the first man.

"Claremont might not have found her. He could be back at home right now, for all we know," a third man said.

"We would've heard. The manor's being watched."

"Mr. Branwick said we're to patrol constantly until they're found. I don't want to be the ones to let them slip through the net," said the first man.

The horsemen moved on. At least three. And all armed, Robert would wager. He tightened his grip on Isabel and spurred Apollo on.

"We'll travel along the river," he said. "There's a trail that leads to Edmund's from there. Branwick won't know of it."

"If I met him, I'd shoot an arrow straight through his heart," Isabel said vehemently. "My mother believes he's behind my father's death. But there's no way to prove it."

"That's for later. For now, we must escape. Once we're married, even he can't separate us."

"Can he not? He has his fingers in many pies. Men as ruthless as he is, willing to do his bidding. As we heard."

"Edmund will aid us. By morning, we'll be far from here."

Ever alert to sounds of pursuit, and with only the waning moon to light their way, they eventually came to the path leading to Edmund's. After dismounting, they walked up the steep hill, stopping at the forest's edge. In the distance, the house stood shrouded in darkness. Robert took Isabel's hand and they sprinted across the field with no trouble, but he would only feel safe when they were inside.

He knocked softly on the door. No answer.

"Is he here?" Isabel whispered.

Robert knocked again, louder this time.

Sounds of movement came from within. "Who is it?" Edmund called.

"Robert. Let me in!"

A candle flickering in his hand, Edmund swung the door open wide, his face a mask of astonishment.

They leapt across the threshold and Edmund slammed the door. Before Robert could speak, he snapped, "Why would you come back here?"

This was not the reception he'd been expecting. "We need—"

"If you're seeking help from your father, you won't

get it. I've never seen him so furious. He has Simon and William out scouring the countryside for you two. He's planning to deliver Isabel to her stepfather."

Isabel shrank into Robert's side, and he put a protective arm around her as fury swept through him. "I know he doesn't approve, but that's despicable. Why would he do such a thing?"

"You know why. He wants her married and out of the way. He thinks you'll settle back down and attend to your duties once she's gone."

"He couldn't be more wrong," Robert said, holding her closer.

"All this trouble..." Isabel muttered.

"It's no trouble. You're worth whatever it takes for us to be together," Robert said, looking into her eyes.

"Is she? Is she worth what you're doing to your family?" Edmund asked coldly. "She's betrothed. You were set to court Margery Penrose before you met Miss Tate. You should part ways now, then go to your father and beg forgiveness."

"Beg forgiveness? Edmund, do you know me at all? I've never shirked my responsibilities before. I do everything for the family. But this is one thing I cannot do. I love Isabel, and I won't give her up."

"This will pass," Edmund said. "These things do."

"This will *not* pass. I came here for help. I was sure I could depend on you."

Edmund put a hand on his sleeve. "Be reasonable, Robert."

"I'm beyond reasoning. Help us, or let us go without hindrance. For years you've been my friend and confidant. Now it's for you to choose. Are you my loyal friend, as I hope, or are you my father's lackey?"

"I am no man's lackey. Not your father's, and not yours!" Edmund marched across the room and paced back and forth in front of the fireplace. From time to time he glanced at Robert and shook his head. At last he spoke. "You're making a terrible choice. But I'll help you for the sake of our years together. What do you need?"

"We need to get to the church and find the vicar so he can marry us. Now, tonight."

Edmund blanched. "You asked for help, not for the impossible."

"It's not impossible. And we need to get there without being seen."

"Impossible," Edmund said again, crossing his arms over his chest.

"You said you'd help. Please," Robert said.

Edmund sighed. "Sit down, Miss Tate. You look dead on your feet."

Robert helped Isabel into a chair at the table and sat beside her.

"What's your plan?" Edmund asked.

Robert took Isabel's hand, and she entwined her fingers with his. "We marry tonight, then make for the coast. Nobody will look for us there."

"Some people might," Edmund said, rubbing his chin. "William, for one. And your father."

"You'll tell them you saw me alone. I couldn't find Isabel but am determined to keep looking. I've gone to Salisbury. Tell them that. They'll trust you and believe all you say."

"Yes, they will," Edmund said. "I don't like lying."

"I wouldn't ask if it weren't so important. They'll only stop looking if they think they know where I've gone."

Edmund sat at the table. "And what of Isabel? Is she supposed to have disappeared into the mist?"

"Branwick will keep looking, I'm sure of it. But if he believes she's not with me, he won't follow me. She'll be safe."

"I could be seen somewhere along the way," Isabel suggested, "or I could get a message to my mother, and she could tell my stepfather I've gone to Salisbury. I only know that if he finds me I'm doomed. He'll marry me to Marcus and my life will be over."

"We won't let that happen." Robert put an arm around her shoulders, more worried now than before they'd come to Edmund's. He was beyond disappointed in his father, whose plan to betray Isabel was unbelievable. How could his father think that after handing Isabel over to Branwick he could still convince Robert to marry Margery?

Edmund watched them for a moment, then rose. "No, we won't. Branwick will never find you. Come, we must gather some things for your journey." He filled saddlebags with food and blankets, then dug through a trunk and brought out two cloaks. "Wear these over your clothes. You'll be indistinguishable at night unless someone gets a good look at your faces. Keep your hoods drawn."

"We'll need a horse for Isabel," Robert said, fastening his cloak.

Edmund nodded. "I'll go to the stables. It's safer if you wait for me here. I'll be back soon." He hurried out the door.

"I need my bow," Isabel said. "It's still on Apollo."

"No matter. He'll be coming with us."

182

"I wish I'd brought the miniatures. I'd hate to lose them."

"We won't lose them. I've hidden them at the cottage."

"Oh, I'm so glad. But when? Where?"

"While you were at Kerensly. They're hidden in the compartment beside the fireplace." He didn't mention that he'd hidden them away because it hurt too much to see her face when he thought she'd cast him off for Marcus.

Waiting inside Edmund's house would have been peaceful but for the fact that a score of men were searching the grounds for them. Every noise was an enemy about to pounce. Just as Robert began to worry that Edmund had been waylaid, he appeared at the door.

"I have the horses," he said breathlessly.

Robert peered into the darkness. "You weren't seen?"

"No, the grooms are among the folk searching for you. We must make haste!"

Robert realized coming back here was the smartest choice he could have made. Nobody would expect it of him.

Just outside the house stood three horses. Edmund handed Isabel the reins of a white mare with a sidesaddle. "This is Willow. She's one of the fastest horses in the stable."

"Thank you," Isabel said as Robert helped her to mount.

They rode through the trees, Robert leading while Isabel followed and Edmund took up the rear. They made their way back to the river, then rode along the banks under the moonlight. Robert was glad of the light while they were so well hidden in the forest, but wouldn't welcome it when they were out in the open again. They could keep to the trees for much of their journey, but the church was quite exposed in the village. After riding for some time, they reached the road.

"I'll go ahead to determine if anyone is close by," Edmund said.

"Be careful," Robert whispered.

"I'll signal if all is clear," Edmund said, and was gone.

Chapter Thirteen

Robert and Isabel turned their horses to face each other as the minutes ticked by. How long ago had Edmund left? Ten minutes? Twenty?

Isabel frowned, her brows low as she looked furtively around them.

"It will be all right," Robert whispered and tried to smile.

She gave a tight nod just as the sound Robert had been waiting for came at last. A soft whistle.

He sighed with relief. "There's the signal. The way is clear, but we must be cautious."

On a rise just down the road, Edmund waited for them. Robert and Isabel spurred their horses to catch up and soon the church steeple came into view. They made their way into the churchyard, dismounted, and led the horses alongside the stone church, trusting the shadows to conceal them.

"Go inside and summon Mr. Bartholomew," Edmund said. "I'll tie up the horses."

The silent stillness of the church felt like an embrace after the flight through the forest.

"Wait here," Robert said, directing Isabel to one of the pews.

He walked down the aisle to the back of the church, where he knocked on a door and waited.

There was no answer. "Vicar!" he called.

Muffled words came from inside, and the sound of furniture falling over. Robert smiled when the vicar cursed loudly.

When the door finally opened, Mr. Bartholomew stood there in his night clothes, running a hand through his gray hair. "Who calls at this hour?" he asked sleepily.

"Robert Claremont."

"Mr. Claremont!" he exclaimed, all signs of tiredness gone. "What are you doing here? Have you come to seek sanctuary? I've heard men are searching for you tonight."

"I'm not here for sanctuary. I'm here to be wed."

"Wed?" Mr. Bartholomew blinked rapidly. "Do you jest? Come back tomorrow and we will speak then." He started to close the door.

Robert blocked it with his foot. "I do not jest." He called into the darkness, "Isabel."

When she reached his side, Robert took her hand. "This is Isabel Tate. We'd like to be married tonight."

Mr. Bartholomew's forehead scrunched up, and he tilted his head to the side. "In the middle of the night?"

"If you know I'm being hunted, then you know for what reason. Isabel's stepfather means to marry her against her will. I'll marry her tonight so she's out of his reach."

"She will never be out of his reach," Mr. Bartholomew said. "I know this man. Don't cross him. If you need to hide Miss Tate, protect her, I can do that. You don't need to wed her to keep her safe."

Robert's voice softened as he turned to look at Isabel. "I want to wed her because I love her."

"I see," Mr. Bartholomew said kindly. "Still, I cannot marry you. You haven't read the banns, and we have no witnesses."

"We do have a witness. Edmund is just outside, tying up our horses," Robert said, pointing over his shoulder.

Mr. Bartholomew stroked his chin, apparently deliberating.

"Robert," Isabel said, placing a hand on his arm, "he can't help us. We must run again while we still can."

Robert was silent for a moment, but could think of no more to ask of Mr. Bartholomew. "We'll ride on to the next town. They may have a vicar willing to marry us."

Robert and Isabel started down the aisle of the church.

"Wait!" Mr. Bartholomew called. "I've known you since you were a babe. I christened you here, in my arms. I will perform your ceremony."

Robert shook his hand. "We are grateful."

"Let me dress. I'll be out in a moment." He stepped back into his room.

Robert glanced at Isabel as they walked to the front of the church. He could hardly believe he was about to get married. He'd been so distracted with rescuing Isabel and evading her stepfather that he hadn't really let it sink in until this moment. Robert had never thought much about marriage. He'd known that when he was of age his father would find him a suitable bride, and he would marry her. A bride like Margery. And that's what would have happened, if he hadn't seen Isabel on that May Day morning. They would live together, have a family, grow old at each other's sides. He looked at her, overwhelmed with joy. She met his gaze, and he took her into his arms. They released each other only when Mr. Bartholomew approached the altar, followed by Edmund, who took his place beside Robert.

Mr. Bartholomew carried a Bible and a candle, which he placed on the pulpit. Isabel and Robert turned to face him, and he began. It was a short, simple exchange of vows, and when it was over Mr. Bartholomew took their hands and joined them together.

"You are bound eternally, and have made sacred vows to each other before a witness. You are now man and wife."

Robert took a step back, Isabel's hands in his, and looked into her shining, beloved face. They beamed at each other for a moment before their lips met in a soft kiss.

"The registry now," Mr. Bartholomew said. They followed him into the sitting room behind the altar and signed the book that stated they had been married. Edmund signed as witness.

"I wasn't prepared for a wedding, but I do have wine," Mr. Bartholomew said genially. He poured a goblet of wine for each of them and, after a toast, walked them out of the church.

Just outside the doors Robert turned to Mr. Bartholomew. "We cannot stay here for sanctuary, but I do ask you to keep our secret. If anyone asks, I beg you not to divulge that you've seen us. In time the registry will tell the truth. I only ask that you don't speak of this to anyone tonight. We're leaving at once and our only chance of avoiding capture is secrecy."

"I will keep your secret for as long as I'm able," he said. "I'll evade any questions that come my way, and avoid Mr. Branwick if I can. He can't question me if he can't find me. But the book is public, and if anyone asks for it, I can't hide it from them."

"I understand. Thank you for helping us. It means more than you know."

Isabel stepped forward. "We appreciate it so much. Thank you."

"Good luck. I wish you both well," Mr. Bartholomew said and went back inside.

Robert turned to Edmund. "Here is where we part, my dear friend."

"I could come with you."

"No. You must stay here and throw my father and Branwick off the scent. I'll return some day, and we'll celebrate my wedding properly."

"I'll hide your whereabouts for as long as I can. Be careful."

"We will." Robert gave Edmund a quick, heartfelt embrace.

"Oh, and congratulations," Edmund said as he started away.

"Thank you, Edmund," Isabel said.

Edmund said nothing but gave her hand a pat. Then he was gone.

Robert and Isabel walked out into the night, mounted their horses, and galloped away, wanting nothing more than to put many miles between themselves and those who hunted them.

After riding fast for a few hours, Robert decided they were far enough away from Holton to stop without fear of capture. They entered a small clearing surrounded on all sides by thick trees. A wide, deep river flowed through the forest on the far side of the clearing. They walked Apollo and Willow to the river, unsaddled them, and tethered them close to a glade of grass.

"Are we safe here?" Isabel asked, peering into the

trees.

"Yes. We're far from the road, and everybody searching for us thinks we're still in Holton or on our way to Salisbury, which is in the opposite direction. Furthermore, the inn we're going to is still a few hours away. Nobody would chance upon us here."

Isabel looked more relaxed than Robert had seen her since the ball. "You heard the vicar," he said, "Bound eternally. You are mine forever." He knew they needed to get to the inn, but right now all he could see was Isabel.

"I've been yours from the moment I saw you." She lifted her face to his.

He kissed her tenderly, and a dainty moan escaped her. It was enough. His lips never leaving hers, he fumbled with his cloak, untied it, and spread it on the ground. Isabel broke away from him, her eyes bold, her chest heaving. Robert reached for her, but she took a step back and smiled a coy smile that went right to his core.

They would not reach the inn tonight.

Isabel slowly removed her riding habit, leaving only a blessedly thin cotton shift between her perfect form and Robert's searching eyes. She lifted it over her head and unbound her hair, letting it cascade over her breasts and shoulders, brushing her round hips. Robert couldn't speak, swallow, or even breathe as she reached for his sword belt, unbuckled it, and let it fall. He ripped his shirt off and threw it to the ground, his heart hammering madly. Desire coursed through him as she ran her hands over his stomach, his chest, his shoulders.

He took her hand and put it over his heart. "I am yours now."

"And I am yours," she said, bringing his hand to her breast. They stood in silence, their pounding heartbeats the only sound in the moonlit glade. The heat of her body and the perfect, sweet scent of her made his knees weak. All at once Robert could stand it no longer. He took her in his arms and kissed her like he'd never kissed her before. Their hands upon each other were curious, sensual, desperate. His breath came fast and hard as he sighed her name. Robert unfastened his breeches and let them slide off his hips as he and Isabel sank to the ground. Entwined together on the cloak, she opened herself to him like a flower blooming for the first time, and he filled her completely, body and soul.

Later, as they lay satiated in each other's arms, Robert looked into her eyes and saw tears glistening there.

"What's this?" he asked.

"I'm happy. I never thought to be so happy."

He smiled, taking in every detail of her face. "I always want to remember how you look at this moment. I want to carry this with me every day."

She smiled. "You'll remember, for I'll be here to remind you."

Their lips met in a soft, tender kiss, and she nestled into his shoulder. After a few minutes her breathing steadied, and he knew she slept. He lay looking at the clear sky and limitless stars, Isabel warm against his side, and before long he, too, fell asleep.

****

The moment Robert woke up, he glanced at Isabel, who was watching him with a soft smile.

"Good morning," she said.

"Good morning." He kissed her and held her close, then rolled with her so that she was on top of him.

Isabel laughed. "What are you doing?"

"I'm getting a better view of my beautiful wife." Robert grasped her hips, delighting in their fullness as his eyes roved over her.

Isabel grinned. "I've learned enough to know *that* look, Robert."

"What look?" he asked in mock innocence, caressing her thighs.

She laughed. "There's no time for that now."

"There is always time for that." His hands inched higher.

"We'll have ample opportunity tonight, safe at the inn. And we shall have a bed. Now come—find me some breakfast."

"How you order me about already." He shook his head, grinning.

She stretched herself out on top of him and kissed him lightly. "But you don't mind, do you?"

Robert could not even begin to answer, as his voice had stopped working.

"I'd like to stay here forever." She rested her head on his chest.

He cleared his throat. "So would I, my love, but we must go." Nothing other than her safety could have induced him to move from this spot. A brilliant morning, the waking forest, and the love of his life naked on top of him... Leave? He must be mad. After savoring the feel of her skin on his for a few moments longer, he regretfully said, "I'm going into the river. Will you come?"

"Oh yes, that sounds lovely."

Robert took her hand, and they jumped into the water. The current was slow and cool, and after rinsing off they clambered back onto the riverbank. The sky promised a clear, dry day.

After they dressed, Robert rummaged through the saddle bags for the food he and Edmund had packed the night before—a bag full of hard brown bread, nuts, two flasks of wine, and a bundle of dried meat. He carried it over to Isabel, who was wringing out her hair. They sat on the riverbank to eat, and when they were finished Robert saddled the horses and picked his cloak up off the ground. Isabel took his hand, and they looked around at the little clearing where they'd spent their first night together. They shared a sweet kiss before mounting their horses and riding away.

After following the woodland trail for a while, Robert turned to Isabel. "We'll risk the road, to reach the inn faster. I tire of branches in my face every ten feet."

"If you believe it to be safe, I'm glad to leave the woods behind."

"We'll wear our cloaks and hoods in case we come upon anyone unexpectedly."

The road was deserted as far as the eye could see, and they rode for some time before encountering any other travelers, none of whom gave them the slightest notice but for a cursory glance. Soon Robert began to relax and to think of the hot meal they would eat when they reached the inn. And the soft bed they would share.

Suddenly a horse galloped down the road. This rider was clearly not a weary farmer on his way home, or part of a traveling family, as others they'd seen today. They moved aside to let him pass.

But he didn't pass. His horse reared as he reined in sharply in front of them. He gave no greeting, and after glancing at Isabel, addressed Robert. "I seek a lost girl. She has brown hair and would be traveling alone, possibly on foot."

Robert didn't recognize him from Holton but guessed he was one of Mr. Branwick's ruffians. "A girl? A child?" he asked, speaking gruffly to disguise his voice. He gripped the sword hilt under his cloak.

"No, a young woman."

"My wife and I haven't seen her."

The man didn't reply but spurred his horse and raced away without looking back.

Robert was surprised Branwick's men were searching so far from home. The man had been alone and Robert hoped he was the only one in this area. If so, they were safe. Robert and Isabel continued on the road, as he thought it would seem suspicious if the rider came back this way and they'd stopped outright or gone into the woods. Robert turned to Isabel, who was pale and clearly shaken.

"He didn't know you," Robert said. "You were wearing your hood."

"My stepfather won't rest until he finds me." Her voice trembled, and Robert wanted to hold her in his arms until she stopped shaking.

"Do you want to rest for a while? We could go back to the river."

She shook her head. "I want to keep moving. I'll only feel safe once we're at the inn."

They reached The Cat And Frog by midafternoon. It was a three-storied brick-and-timber building with a dirt courtyard and attached stable. Multiple gables adorned the top floor.

"Here we are," Robert said, turning to smile at Isabel.

They left their horses in the yard, and a man came

hurrying out. "Good afternoon. I'm Mr. Croft."

"Good afternoon. We need a room," Robert said. "See to our horses."

Robert took Isabel's arm as they walked through the front door, which entered into a noisy common room. A fire roared in the grate and the welcome aroma of baking bread and roasting meat wafted out from the kitchen. Around the room were tables of various sizes, filled with other travelers.

A woman approached them, wiping her hands on her apron. "I'm Mrs. Croft, the keep's wife. You'll be wanting a room?"

"Yes. And hot water to wash, and a meal," Robert said.

"Mutton today, with good bread and strong ale to wash it down. Follow me." She led them to a comfortable room on the second floor.

"Traveled long?" Mrs. Croft asked as Isabel sank into a chair beside the glowing hearth.

"Far enough to need a rest. We're bound for the coast in the morning," Robert said.

"A fine time to visit the sea. Will you eat in the common room?"

"In this room would be preferable. My wife is tired."

"Helena will be up with hot water," Mrs. Croft said and bustled out.

Robert crossed the room to Isabel. "Tired?" he asked, rubbing her shoulders.

"Yes, but better now that we're here."

There was a knock on the door, and Helena entered with a large jug of hot water. "I'll be back up with your food," she said and left the room.

Robert went to the basin and filled it with steaming

water, picked up a towel, and brought both over to Isabel. Saying nothing, he sat at her feet and removed her boots and stockings. He wet the towel and wrung it out, then gently took her foot in his hand and wiped it clean. Once he'd done the same with her other foot, he dried them with the towel. He washed her hands with fresh water and kissed them both lightly on the palm. Isabel sighed, leaning back in her chair, her hair loose about her shoulders. Robert fetched clean water, this time using it to clean her face and neck.

She watched him with warm eyes. "You are good to me."

"I intend to be, every day from now on."

As they gazed into each other's eyes, Robert suspected he was not the only one wondering how long they had alone before Helena returned with their meal.

When a knock came on the door, they both chuckled, having easily read each other's thoughts. But no matter. A whole night alone awaited them and, after that, thousands more nights.

"Would you like to go downstairs?" Robert asked after they finished eating. "I hear a minstrel playing. Perhaps there will be dancing."

"I'm too tired for dancing, but let's go down and have a drink."

Mr. Croft greeted them when they entered the common room. "A table?"

"Yes. And ale," Robert said.

Mr. Croft led them to a secluded table in the corner and went to fetch their drinks.

A minstrel in the next room strummed a lute while his companion played a small drum. Isabel smiled gaily and clapped in time to the music. She looked happy and carefree, and Robert vowed to himself to do all he could to spare her the anxiety and danger they'd faced in the past few weeks. They lingered in the common room, talking until the music had stopped and most other patrons had gone upstairs.

****

Sighing with contentment, Isabel stared into the fire. Here, beside Robert in this cozy inn, she had a glimpse of what the years ahead of them would be like. There would be hundreds of such nights, just like this. Sitting together, talking, laughing, holding hands. She turned to look at her husband and wanted to laugh with joy. Her *husband*. He was the handsomest man in the room. When they'd first met she'd liked his looks, but now that she knew him so much better, she found him perfect. The full lips, always ready to smile and wonderful to kiss, the birthmark in the hollow of his throat, and the way his blue eyes sparkled when he looked at her.

He turned to her suddenly and smiled. "Let's go upstairs."

Robert threw some coins on the table, and they made their way across the common room. As they mounted the stairs, she grinned at Mr. Croft, who met her eyes only briefly before frowning and turning away. She wondered if they'd lingered too long in the common room and he'd been waiting for them to leave so he could clean up.

Their bedroom felt like a cozy home after their time in the forest. She sat on the edge of the bed and removed her boots, then went to stand in front of the fire.

"Did you enjoy yourself?" Robert asked as he propped his sword within arm's reach beside the bed.

"Oh, yes! Perhaps tomorrow night we can join in the dancing. If we're still here."

Robert sat down and began unlacing his boots. "I thought we'd stay for at least a few days, if you like the inn."

"I do." She toyed with the cuff of her riding habit. "Only…"

"What?" Robert crossed the room and took her into his arms.

"I wonder if we should continue on, to get farther away from Holton." She glanced furtively out the window, then shook her head at her foolishness. Her stepfather wasn't likely to be standing outside in the dark just outside their room.

"There's no need for that. We're safe here. Try not to worry." He kissed her in a way that made it difficult to think, let alone worry.

She took his hand. "Let's go to bed."

They both undressed and slipped under the covers.

"I love you," Robert said, and kissed her.

"I love you, too. Are you tired?"

"Very." He stretched out on the deep feather mattress, an arm behind his head.

"Too tired?" she asked, eyes sultry and hands curious.

He turned to her with a hot look. "Never."

A sense of wonder overtook her as he gathered her into his arms and Isabel, naked, felt in the best way exposed. If anything, she wished she could bare more of herself to him. A sweet fullness, low in her belly, spread through every secret part of her as Robert's hands and lips roved over her body. Her hands wandered just as freely, feeling his strong, hard muscles beneath her fingertips, touching the broad, smooth lines of him. They made love sweetly, slowly, savoring each other in a way that had been impossible last night. The hours passed and still they lay entangled, discovering, giving, adoring. A hundred kisses, a thousand caresses, endless endearments before they fell into a deep sleep, wrapped in each other's arms.

Chapter Fourteen

Isabel woke to Robert shaking her shoulder. He was already out of bed, hastily pulling his clothes on. "Get dressed," he said urgently.

She jumped out of bed. "What's wrong?" She found her shift and pulled it over her head, followed by her habit, then went to the window to see what he was looking at.

"Stay back!" Robert whispered.

She ignored him and peeked outside. In the dim pre-dawn light, a host of men were gathering in the yard. Among them was her stepfather. Isabel fell against the wall, her face in her hands as fear flowed like icy water through her veins.

"We are caught," Robert said in a low voice as he yanked his boots on.

She shook her head to clear it of dizziness and stood up straight. "How did he find us?"

"We'll never know. Your boots—where are they?"

Isabel crawled over to where her riding boots lay on the floor and pulled them on with shaking hands. "What will we do?" she asked, her panic rising. "How will we ever escape?"

"I don't know. I only know we must try."

Isabel set her shoulders. If Branwick wanted her, she would not make it easy for him. She slung her bow and quiver over her shoulder, then crossed the room and kissed Robert hard on the mouth.

He embraced her and whispered, "They won't expect us to be awake yet, that explains them arriving before dawn. Our only chance is to get away before they realize we're gone."

Isabel nodded, then went to the door and opened it as quietly as she could. There was no sign of anyone in the hall. They crept from the room, careful not to make a sound. Isabel reached for Robert's hand as they tiptoed down the hall. She turned to the stairs leading down to the common room, but to her surprise Robert held her back. He pointed up and she nodded in understanding.

They passed the main staircase and went down the corridor. Isabel heard voices coming from outside now, among them her stepfather's, shouting orders. She'd recognize his voice anywhere.

At the end of the hall a narrow staircase led to the third floor. Robert turned to Isabel when they reached the top and put a finger to his lips. She stood by as he silently turned the doorknob of the nearest room but found it locked. He shook his head and moved on to the next. He didn't find what he sought until he reached the last room. After finding the door unlocked, he knocked softly. When there was no answer, they hurried inside, locking the door behind them.

The room was unoccupied, and the bedclothes of the large canopied bed were askew, as though someone had left in a hurry. Isabel spotted Mrs. Croft's apron hanging on a hook behind the door. Then she understood. This was the innkeeper's room. Mr. Croft was outside with Mr. Branwick, and his wife was probably somewhere downstairs. Robert crossed the room and pulled the curtains back slightly.

"Are we hiding here until they've gone?" Isabel whispered.

"No. We're above the stables, behind the main part of the inn. We'll jump down to the roof, and then to the ground. As soon as Branwick and his men come inside, we will escape."

"Is there no other way?" Isabel asked, terrified at the thought of jumping out of a third-story window.

"Not that I can think of. Can you?"

Isabel tried to remember if she'd seen any other ways out of the inn last night. There was nothing. She shook her head.

"We must bar the door," she said. A massive wooden chest beside the bed looked like it would suffice. She went to lift it, beckoning to Robert to help her. Together they heaved it across the room and propped it against the locked door.

"That might get us a few more moments if they try to get in," she said.

Robert nodded, then went to peek outside. "They're coming." He pried the window open. "Are you ready?"

Isabel looked down into the yard, which seemed miles away. She focused instead on the roof. It looked sturdy enough, and wasn't too far below their window. Just like jumping out of a tree, she told herself. Robert was still waiting for an answer, so she nodded.

"I'll go first," he whispered.

He climbed backward out of the window, then lowered himself so he was facing the wall, his fingers grasping the windowsill. He let go, landing on the stable roof with a thud. Isabel hoped the sounds of Mr. Branwick and his men would mask it. Robert stood and beckoned to her. She tossed her bow down—it would be impossible to climb out with it strapped to her back.

Heavy boots thundered up the stairs behind her. Heart hammering, she copied Robert's movements and let herself fall to the roof. A jolt ran through her when she landed hard on her knees. Robert grasped her hand and took a step toward the edge of the steeply sloped roof, but she held him back.

"It would be better to crawl," she whispered, and he nodded. She retrieved her bow, which had landed not far from her. The rough wooden shingles bit into her hands as she followed Robert on their slow and cautious way across the roof. When they reached the edge, Isabel was relieved to see a tall haystack leaning against the wall. Robert jumped into the hay and rolled down to the bottom of the heap. Isabel looked around the yard. There was no sign of anyone, but muffled voices came from inside. It sounded like the entire inn was being woken up. Isabel didn't waste another moment. She leapt into the hay, then crawled to the ground. Robert helped her to her feet, and they looked into the stables. Isabel's heart leaped to her throat. In the shadows, somebody stood waiting for them.

The cloaked man held their saddled horses by the reins. He put a finger to his lips.

"Who are you?" Robert demanded, putting an arm around Isabel's waist. She clung to him, eyeing the man warily. Was this some kind of trick?

The man removed his hood. "It's me, Thomas," he whispered.

Much to Isabel's surprise, Robert visibly relaxed.

"Thomas? How remarkable! What are you doing here?" He turned to Isabel and nodded, which she took to mean that this man was a friend to be trusted.

"I'm on my way to Salisbury. I saw you last night in the common room but didn't want to disturb you. I'm not surprised you didn't notice me." He looked pointedly at Isabel.

"This is my wife, Isabel." Robert couldn't contain his smile even under the circumstances. She loved him all the more for that.

"A pleasure to meet you," Thomas said, then glanced over his shoulder. "But there's no time to lose."

"What do you know of all this?" Isabel asked Thomas, motioning to the inn.

"Last night I overheard Mr. Croft telling his wife that one of Branwick's men passed you on the road yesterday. He followed you here to confirm your identity, then raced back to Holton. Mr. Croft told his wife they were to keep you here until Branwick arrived to capture you."

"How could they! They seemed so kind." Isabel recalled the night before, when Mr. Croft wouldn't meet her eyes. Of course he wouldn't. He was planning to betray them.

"It's fortunate indeed that you were here to help us," Robert said.

"I wanted to warn you last night, but by the time I knew what was happening, you'd already retired, and Mr. Croft refused to tell me which room was yours, even when I told him I'm an old friend. I was afraid that if I insisted he'd grow suspicious, so I planned to tell you as soon as you came down this morning. Now I regret not breaking down every door in the inn to find you. I never imagined Branwick would arrive so soon. He must have ridden all night to get here by dawn."

Robert put a hand on his shoulder. "You've already

done more than we would have expected."

Thomas handed Robert both sets of reins. "I recognized Apollo and assumed the horse sharing his stall to be your wife's."

"How can we ever thank you?" Robert asked.

"Tell nobody that I helped you. Branwick would seek revenge, I'm certain."

"We will tell no one."

Thomas handed Isabel a sword. "Take this."

She stepped back. "Oh, I wouldn't use it. I have my bow."

"With Branwick after you, you'd be a fool not to take it," Thomas insisted.

Isabel took the sword—cold, heavy, and unfamiliar in her hand—and secured it to her saddle.

"Will you come with us?" Robert asked Thomas.

"No, you'll travel faster without me. Now go. You haven't a moment to lose." He shook Robert's hand and dashed away.

From inside the inn came shouts and the crack of splintering wood. A door being broken in? Her stepfather would by now know that they'd fled. Isabel and Robert mounted and immediately guided their horses into the woods. From their sheltered spot Isabel could just see the yard, where Mr. Croft was pacing back and forth, wringing his hands.

A dozen men came streaming outside, followed by Mr. Branwick, his face red with anger.

"Find them! Find them!" he bellowed, and men scurried in all directions to do his bidding. Some went back inside, some to the stables. They would definitely have been caught if not for Thomas.

Branwick approached Mr. Croft and grabbed him

roughly by the arm.

Mr. Croft cowered before him, trying to pull away. "They must have left during the night. I didn't know. I swear it!"

"Liar! Someone must have seen them. Rouse the guests! Rouse them, I say!" Mr. Branwick yelled, shoving him to the ground.

Mrs. Croft scurried out into the yard and knelt beside her husband. "Rouse them?" she asked indignantly. "You've done that yourself, to be sure! You've searched the inn, now leave us in peace!"

Isabel winced as Branwick kicked out, missing Mrs. Croft by a hair. "Don't cross me, wench!" he spat and stormed back inside. The Crofts put their arms around each other and shuffled into the inn.

"Away now!" Robert said. "They must believe we're still inside, else they would be searching the woods and the road." They turned their horses into the trees.

"Which way?" Isabel asked, certain her stepfather's men would spring on them at any moment. "To the coast?"

Robert looked off into the distance and didn't speak for a moment. "No. No. We'll go back to Holton. I see now that it was a mistake to run. I must make my father see that we need his aid. You're his daughter now and as part of the family are entitled to his protection. If he still refuses, Edmund or Simon will help us. If nothing else, we could hide at Thornwood. Branwick couldn't possibly search the entire estate."

"We cannot hide forever," Isabel cried, eyes brimming with tears.

"We won't need to. Once we have my father's help, we'll go, with a force, and present your stepfather with the marriage lines."

"I doubt that will convince him. You've seen what he's like."

"We don't need to convince him of anything. There's nothing he can do about it. It's done."

"Perhaps you're right. We'll show my stepfather the proof and then be free of him."

"That's our plan," Robert said.

They made their way to the river, then rode along the bank, trusting the water to erase any sign of their horses' prints in the mud. Isabel was tired, but Branwick was far too close to even consider stopping.

After a time Robert turned to her. "There's a spot close by where we can rest."

"No, we must get as far away as we can."

He gave her a sympathetic yet firm look. "Our horses are tired. We need food. We'll stop for only a short time, I promise."

Reluctantly, Isabel agreed. They dismounted and tethered the horses in a shady copse where they could rest and graze.

Isabel sat on the riverbank and used her hands to cup the cold, fresh water. She drank deeply and splashed her face and neck, then rolled her shoulders, trying to release the tension that had been with her for days. The only moments of true happiness and calm had been those spent safe in Robert's arms. Once they reached Thornwood, she intended to spend a week locked alone with him in his room.

Robert came up behind her and massaged her shoulders.

"How did you know exactly what I needed?" she asked, lifting her face to kiss him.

He gave her a sweet smile and sat beside her. "I found more dried meat and nuts in the saddle bags. We can fill the flasks with water from the river."

Isabel leaned against him as they ate, enjoying the tranquil sounds of the river and the warmth of the sun shining upon them. Robert explained that Thomas was a minstrel he'd known since he was a boy. He often performed at Thornwood, and had been at this year's May Day celebration. Robert smiled often as he recounted some of his childhood escapades, and Isabel wished she could have known him when he was a youngster.

It would be a perfect moment if not for the fact her stepfather was still out there searching. They'd ridden far, but Isabel couldn't shake the feeling that he could be lurking around any corner, hiding behind any tree. She wouldn't feel safe until they reached Thornwood Manor.

She rose, brushing the dirt off her skirt, and Robert stood and took her into his arms. She breathed in his homey scent, allowing herself only a brief moment in his strong, loving embrace.

"Time to go," she said.

"After you," he said, and helped her onto Willow.

Robert mounted Apollo and they continued along the river.

Before long Isabel said, "I think we should try the road. This is too slow."

"Not the main road, but there's an old thoroughfare that begins a mile from here and leads to Holton. It's really more of a trail than a road now, it's so seldom used. My guess is Branwick and his men will keep to the main road. We have a good head start. He won't catch up."

"I hope you're right, but he'll do his utmost to

capture me."

"Even if he finds us, he can't take you away. We're married, so the marriage to Marcus can never take place. Once we show him the marriage registry, he'll be forced to leave you alone."

Isabel reined Willow in. Perhaps it was time to tell Robert the worry that had been growing in her mind over the last few days. After all, by marrying Robert she'd made Branwick his enemy, too. The least she could do was tell him the truth. "I don't think marrying me to Marcus is the only reason he wants me. He has designs on vengeance."

Robert pulled Apollo to a stop. "Vengeance? But you've done nothing to him."

"Not vengeance on me. Vengeance on my father. It all started years ago. He was my father's best friend when they were boys."

"What?" Robert asked incredulously.

"Branwick and my father were neighbors and played together as children. But something terrible happened when they were eight years old. There was a fire at Branwick's estate, in the stable. His mother ran in to save him and then went back for my father. While she was inside the roof collapsed. She somehow managed to get out, carrying my father. But she sustained injuries that could not be healed, and died a few days later. Branwick was left an orphan, as his father had died years earlier. Mr. Branwick never forgave my father for robbing him of his mother. I believe that's why he had him killed and made up the story about the theft to dishonor his name. I've often had the feeling he doesn't like me, even hates me. My stepfather would be glad to marry me to someone I loathe and watch me suffer. If I'd wed

Marcus, Branwick would have had me under his control for the rest of my life. He threatened to keep me and my mother apart. He's taking out his anger at my father on us. He told me himself that he hurts my mother, and he was none too gentle with me." Isabel rubbed the wrist he'd twisted so cruelly.

Robert's eyes widened. "He's mad! How can he possibly hold a grudge about a childhood tragedy?"

"He may well *be* mad. To him this is perfectly logical." She glanced behind her into the trees. They'd stayed still for too long.

"But it makes absolutely no sense. Even if he makes you and your mother suffer, it won't bring *his* mother back."

"I could never begin to explain how his mind works." She nudged Willow past Apollo and they continued through the trees.

"How long have you known about this?"

"My father told me the fire story years ago. The rest I've pieced together on my own recently."

"But your father must have known for years that Branwick was angry. Why didn't he stay away from him?"

"My stepfather hid it well. All part of his plan, I suspect. If he'd driven my father away, he would never have had a chance to take his revenge. He was kind to him, and kind enough to my mother that she took him as her second husband."

"But how can you be certain he wants revenge? Could it not be that he's simply a cruel man?"

"I didn't truly understand Branwick until he kept me captive at my aunt's house. What kind of person would do such a thing? I always thought, as you said, he's merely cruel to his enemies. But apparently *I* am his enemy. My mother told me he's been saying insulting things about my father, and ranting about the day his mother died. He even mentioned revenge, but since he was in a drunken stupor my mother didn't take him seriously. But now I believe he was serious. Deadly serious. I think my thwarting his wedding plans angered him so much he's let his friendly facade slip."

"I wouldn't have called him friendly to begin with. He's always been a man most people don't want to cross."

"Yes, but there are some who count him as a friend. Even your father joined him at his country house last year."

Robert scowled. "Yes, to our cost. Branwick is nothing more than a snake."

"A snake with power and men to do his bidding. I should have told you before the wedding, but once we reunited at the cottage I didn't spare time to think of much else. I'm sorry you've been dragged into all this."

"Don't apologize. You're my wife and your troubles are my troubles. I'm glad you told me. Now that I understand, I'll be able to protect you better. You must always share your problems with me."

She reached for his hand. "That means more to me than you could know. We shall have no secrets."

They rode on throughout the day, taking breaks only when necessary. The journey was taking far longer than Isabel would have liked, yet with each passing mile her fear lessened. Could they possibly have outrun her stepfather? If they reached Holton first, they would have no problem getting to Thornwood—their sanctuary.

Dusk was falling when Robert said, "If Branwick is

roaming these forests, he's bold indeed. We are now on Penrose land."

"We're safe?"

"Relatively. The Penroses are no friends of his. But we must still be wary, as we have some way to go before we reach Thornwood. My father won't deny us entry under the circumstances. Even if he wanted to, my mother wouldn't stand for it."

"And William?" Isabel asked bitterly. She hadn't forgiven him for the way he'd treated her that night at the stables.

"He was dreadful to you, I know. But when he sees how dire our need is, he'll help us. I must trust him. He's my brother."

"I lack your faith in him, though at this point I have no choice but to hope you're right."

They continued on, hearing only the wind in their ears and the beat of their horses' hooves upon the trail. Finally Robert turned to Isabel, beaming. "This is it. We've crossed the border. We are now on Claremont land."

Waves of relief swept over her. "Thank goodness."

"We should be home before full dark."

They continued on the trail for a time, then guided their horses out of the trees and onto the long, winding drive leading to the manor.

Isabel let out a sigh. They'd made it. In the distance, the lights of Thornwood stood out against the darkening sky. They hadn't gone far down the drive when she heard it.

A cold, triumphant laugh. She whirled around.

Branwick!

She reached for her bow, but froze at her stepfather's

words. "Leave it, Isabel. Unless you want your lover killed." He snapped his fingers and mounted men crept out of the darkness. They were surrounded.

Chapter Fifteen

Everywhere Isabel looked were armed men. They must have ridden hard and fast to arrive here first. Some had bows, others swords or spears—all pointed at Robert. A few held torches, illuminating the scene. Isabel let her bow hand fall. She couldn't use it. They would retaliate immediately. She remembered the sword from Thomas, strapped to her saddle. Also useless.

"What is the meaning of this?" she cried.

"Don't play the fool, Isabel. It doesn't suit you," Mr. Branwick said conversationally.

"You're trespassing on Claremont land and threatening myself and my wife," Robert said fiercely, never taking his eyes off Branwick. "You will leave immediately."

"You're wrong, Mr. Claremont. She is no wife of yours. She's my daughter. My dear daughter, taken against her will for your selfish purposes. Nobody will look twice when I run you through for kidnapping her."

"Liar!" Robert urged Apollo closer to Branwick. Men immediately closed the circle around him, and one held his sword tip inches from Robert's throat. Isabel saw Robert's hand wander to the hilt of his own sword.

"Oh, yes. I know of your little scheme," Branwick said, "You would take her away, bed her and leave her spoiled."

"That's not true! We're married," Isabel said.

"Oh, do you mean this?" he asked in a honeyed voice. He held up a paper that Isabel recognized at once. The registry from the church, proving they were married. So Branwick had gotten past the vicar. She hoped Mr. Bartholomew was not injured.

"How did you get that?" Robert demanded.

"I had some help." He motioned to one of his men, who brought forth a horse. Sitting in the saddle, his hands bound before him, was Edmund, his face bloodied and bruised.

"Edmund!" Robert cried, his face a mask of anguish.

"He had quite a story to tell, once I convinced him to talk," Branwick said, rubbing his bloody knuckles.

"Forgive me, Robert, forgive me! I didn't—" Edmund said in a shaking voice. Isabel winced as the man holding his horse's reins hit him hard across the face and his head slumped forward onto his chest.

"Release him!" Robert said through clenched teeth.

Branwick gave him a slow, mocking smile and shook his head.

Robert's fingers whitened on his sword hilt as, trembling, he stared at Edmund.

Isabel had to act fast before he lost control and attacked Branwick, which would surely bring all the armed men down upon him. She addressed her stepfather. "You're too late. We're married. Let us go and we'll forget this happened. I won't tell my mother."

"Your mother?" he said, his lip curling. "Do you think I fear your mother? Tell her what you will, it matters not. Come with me now, and I won't harm your lover. Marcus will still have you, though I wager you're no virgin now."

The men surrounding them laughed, and Isabel felt

her face go red. "He's not my lover, he's my husband. I will never marry Marcus."

"You will. You're coming with us. As for this? It is nothing." He ripped the wedding registry to shreds and threw the pieces to the wind.

"I'm married to Robert and you have no power over me!"

Branwick spurred his horse and was beside her in an instant. Her head snapped back with the force of his slap. He raised his hand again but she swung her leg over the saddle and jumped to the ground.

"Isabel!" Robert was off Apollo and at her side before Branwick's men could react. He put an arm around her, holding her to his side as she pressed a hand to her stinging cheek.

"I've warned you once, Branwick. You're trespassing. Now go!" Robert yelled, sword aloft.

"You are in no position to make threats. The marriage never happened. Isabel is my daughter, and I take custody of her. If you thwart me you'll be killed. Is she worth your life?" He snapped his fingers and his men dismounted.

Robert pushed Isabel behind him, but it was no use, they were far outnumbered. Isabel thought of her bow, useless now at this distance. The men inched forward, their swords held high. Robert turned in a slow circle as Isabel shadowed him, back to back. Willow was not far away. Isabel knew she could wield the extra sword stowed in the saddle. But how to get it? A sudden inspiration came to her. Sobbing uncontrollably, she put her face in her hands. "Oh, Mr. Branwick—Father—I'm sorry, so sorry. Don't hurt me, please, I beg you!"

She bent over as if overcome with grief, her hands

hiding the fact that no tears came. Robert tried to touch her, but she brushed him away.

Branwick eyed her suspiciously. "What is this?"

"I want to come home with you. I love Robert, I do. But—"

"But what, girl?" her stepfather snapped.

"But if we're not truly married, I've done something terrible. I will make it right. I'll marry Marcus. But don't hurt Robert, please!" Her shoulders shook as she renewed her dry sobs.

Mr. Branwick stood with both hands on his hips and shook his head. "Fickle girl. Never trust a woman, Claremont. They'll betray you as soon as bed you."

Robert looked at Isabel, and she could tell he knew she was acting.

He narrowed his eyes at her. "You say you love me? How could you if you leave me at the first sign of trouble?"

"I do love you. But I'm afraid. What will my mother say, what will Mr. Bartholomew say, when they hear what we did?"

"After all I gave up for you? I should have listened to my brother and stayed away from you." He turned away in disgust.

"Come, girl. We ride for home," Branwick said.

"And Robert?" Isabel asked in a small voice.

Branwick seemed to consider. "He won't follow us, not now that you've shown your true colors. Get on your horse."

"Yes, Father," Isabel said, noting how pleased he looked when she addressed him thus.

Mr. Branwick's men mounted their own horses while one of them assisted Isabel into her saddle. They took her bow and quiver from her, but that didn't matter. They couldn't see her hand wrapped tight around the sword hilt. She sat placidly on Willow as they brought her to her stepfather and he gripped her horse's reins. Isabel sniffled and kept her face lowered.

Mr. Branwick turned to Robert, gloating. "Don't fret over this girl. Find yourself a more worthy one. Isabel will wed Marcus before the day is through, and bed him before the night is old."

"Like hell I will!" Isabel yelled. She lifted the sword high over her head and brought it crashing down on his arm. Branwick screeched in agony and fell from his horse, blood gushing from the wound. He writhed in the crimson grass, the color in his face draining as fast as his blood.

"Robert!" Isabel called.

He ran over and swung himself up behind her, taking the reins. Willow reared and took off at a gallop. Isabel clung to the saddle as they plunged into the forest, branches striking them as they flew through the trees. She knew where he was taking them. The cottage.

There had been utter chaos when she attacked her stepfather, but Isabel knew his men would soon be in pursuit. They'd almost reached the meadow when shouts came from their left. Turning, Isabel saw four riders bearing down on them. Willow raced past the turn to the cottage.

"Where are we going?" Isabel cried.

"The river!" Robert shouted back. "The cottage is lost to us now, unless we want to lead them right to it."

"We'll be trapped!"

"Not if we reach the river first. We'll cross it and escape into the forest on the other side, then make for

Thornwood using the shortcut. They'll never find us."

Robert urged Willow on, Isabel's hair whipping behind them in the wind. Afraid of what she would see, she looked over her shoulder. Six riders pursued them.

At last they burst through the trees onto the riverbank. Willow whinnied, skidding to a halt as Robert yanked the reins. Torchlight blazed on the opposite bank. The rest of Branwick's men were blocking the shortcut. Their escape route was useless.

Robert dismounted and helped Isabel down. He took her in his arms and they clung together, breathless.

"Isabel," he said, his shaking voice full of despair.

She looked into his face, into his eyes that she loved so much. They were serious now, and scared.

"We must run while we still can!" She turned to go, but Robert pulled her to him, shaking his head.

"It's too late. They'll be upon us at any moment. We have one chance. The river."

"You mean to swim?" Isabel asked, confused.

Robert smiled gravely. "Not swim, no. We leap. Down the waterfall."

She drew in a sharp breath. "We will be killed!"

"We'll be killed if we stay here. You gravely injured or killed Branwick. His men want your blood. And I am nothing to them—nothing! If they capture us, we're certainly dead. If we leap, we have at least a chance." He stroked her hair gently, as if to comfort her from his own words.

"But they'll still chase us. We will never escape them!"

"We'll be swept away by the river in moments, but they'll need to find a route down the cliffs. It will take them hours. Beyond the rapids, the river slows and we can easily swim to shore. We'll escape into the woods and find our way up the hill to the cottage."

Dangerous as this plan was, Isabel knew he was right. If they were caught, she'd be sent straight back to Marcus, and she shuddered to think what Branwick, if he lived, would do to Robert. They were surrounded, alone. No help could reach them. If the choice was jump or be apprehended, they had to make at least one more desperate effort to escape.

"I'm afraid," Isabel said, unable to stop shaking. She could barely hear her words over the frantic drumming of her heart.

"I'm only afraid to lose you."

Looking into his eyes, Isabel saw her own soul reflected back at her.

"You will never lose me." She wrapped her arms around his neck and their lips met with fiery passion, their entire beings united in the promise never to be parted.

Torches closed in from all sides as men's shouts rang through the night.

Isabel and Robert skirted the riverbank, icy water sloshing over their boots. Just as men rode into the clearing, Robert stepped onto the overhanging cliff and helped Isabel climb up beside him.

"We must jump out as far as we can to avoid the rocks at the base of the falls," Robert said.

She nodded, looking over the side. Was it possible? Yes, it was. They would make it. They had to.

Men and horses swarmed the riverbank. There were too many to count.

"Get them!" came a harsh voice. Marcus. He urged his horse toward the cliff, accompanied by ten men, all with swords drawn.

Isabel and Robert stood for a moment, eyes locked. There was no other way. They could not be separated. She clung to him with all her might as they leaped, locked in each other's arms.

Every breath left her lungs as they plunged into the frigid water. The merciless current, stronger than she ever could have imagined, instantly trapped them. They struggled to the surface, gasping for air. Robert pulled her close, holding her head above water. With her heavy skirts threatening to pull her under again, she tried to swim, but it was no use. The river's iron grip held them fast. As they were swept away in the current, Isabel heard a thud, followed by a shuddering crack. They'd struck a boulder, and Robert had taken the brunt of it. He screamed out in pain, a cry that pierced her heart. His grasp on her loosened, but she held him fast.

The tumultuous waters pulled them this way and that, and it was all Isabel could do to keep hold of him. She spluttered and coughed as water streamed over her face. At last they were through the rapids and the river slowed, carrying them into slightly calmer waters.

That was when she saw the blood pooling around them.

Robert's blood.

"Robert? Robert!" She held him close, cradling his head in her arms as his legs floated before him. One of them stuck out at a sickening angle. When she kissed his lips his eyelids fluttered.

"Isabel..." he said weakly, his face chalky white against the cold, black water. His eyes half opened and tried to focus on hers.

She had to lean close to hear his hoarse whisper.

"Isabel…I…" He coughed and spluttered, then his eyes closed.

"Stay with me!" she cried, tears coursing down her cheeks.

He didn't answer.

She kissed him again, and tasted his blood on her lips. "Robert!"

He lay motionless in her arms as his hands fell away from her and floated on the surface. There was no flicker of a pulse in his throat. No rising and falling of his chest. She drifted with him there in the river for what felt like hours, praying he would open his eyes, or breathe, or move. But the only movement was the river tugging them this way and that, sometimes roughly, sometimes smoothly, but never gently.

"Robert," Isabel whispered through her tears. She knew before she spoke that he wouldn't answer. His face was still and cold, his blue, loving eyes closed to her. She bent and kissed his eyelids and then his lips as the river tried to rip him from her arms. Isabel looked frantically around her. The riverbank was just visible, but an impossible swim with her sodden skirts and lifeless legs. She would be lucky to make it to the shore herself, never mind pulling Robert. She tried to remove her clothes, but her fingers were too frozen to work properly.

As she struggled to keep Robert afloat, she caught a glimpse of lights moving on the hillside. Torches making their slow way down the cliffs.

There was only one thing to do, but Isabel was certain she lacked the strength. She would need to let Robert go.

Let him go?

And then swim to the opposite bank and hide in the

forest. He'd died to keep her from being caught. She must try to escape, for his sake. She gazed upon his beloved face, etching it into her memory. It was unfathomable that she would never look upon him again.

She kissed his cold, wet cheek and forced her arms to release him. The river embraced Robert at once. Isabel's heart shattered and she lunged out to take hold of him again, but his icy fingers slipped through her grasp. She tried swimming after him, but the river was too strong. Sobs shook her uncontrollably as the current stole Robert away. Caught up in the tumultuous waters, she struggled to keep from going under. It proved too much to fight her exhaustion, her anguish and the river. Wracked with grief, Isabel surrendered.

Hours later, Isabel woke to a hazy, empty dawn. She was face down on the riverbank, her numb legs and feet submerged in the river as water poured over her, tugging at her sodden skirts. Her head rested in her arms on a bed of cold, sharp pebbles. Every inch of her ached, but most of all her heart. She lay there bereft, lacking the strength even to open her eyes. How she wished she had never let Robert go. Even now she could be with him if she had only held on tighter.

Suddenly, over the roaring of the river, came a new sound—men's shouts. So her stepfather had found her. She didn't try to move, it no longer mattered what they did to her.

"Over here!" someone yelled, and then the sound of feet hurrying over loose stones.

A man knelt beside her and put a hand to her wrist, searching for a pulse.

"The cottage," he whispered in her ear, shifting her hair to cover her face. "Stay still."

His voice was familiar to her. Then she knew. It was Simon Kensington.

"She's dead!" he called out, and soon other men crowded around.

"It's what she deserves!"

Another voice asked, "You're certain?"

"No pulse beats in her," Simon replied coldly.

"Any sign of Robert?"

In a broken voice, Simon said, "None."

"Should we bring her back to town?" asked someone else.

"No. Marcus can come find her if he wants her."

A man muttered, "He'll not bother, not after what she did to his uncle."

"Should we bury her?" someone asked hesitantly, "Or throw her in the river?"

Isabel had lain in a fog during the conversation, but this got her attention and she wondered if it was time to give up the ruse. Bury her?

Someone pushed her shoulder with his foot. "No. Leave her to the wolves. I wouldn't lift a spade to bury her."

"She'll cause no more trouble. I rue the day Robert ever clapped eyes on her!" a man cried, and the rest of them chimed in with insults, crude names, and the punishments she'd deserve if she were alive. Isabel fought back the shiver threatening to overtake her, not allowing even a finger to twitch.

Stones crunched under their feet as they walked away, leaving her for dead. Isabel lay there for a long time. She had no will to move. Simon had told her to go to the cottage, but why? Robert was dead. There was nothing for her there. Nothing for her anywhere now. But the cottage was their special place, the place they had loved and laughed. It was their home.

Isabel struggled to get up. Her legs, numb with cold, would not obey her. Using only her arms, she dragged herself onto the riverbank and leaned against a large boulder. She pulled her torn skirt aside to take stock of her wounds. There were too many to count. Both legs were bruised, cut and raw. She rubbed them with her hands to bring them back to life—which she soon regretted. They tingled, stung, and began to bleed. Isabel looked at her arms. The sleeves of her riding habit had been ripped off so it was easy to see the cuts and bruises. Her shoulders were black-and-blue. When her head began to throb, she rested against the boulder and closed her sore eyes.

Some time later, she woke with a start. The sun, high in the sky, had dried her clothes and warmed her while she slept. She was parched but lacked the energy to crawl back to the river to drink. Somehow she had to get much farther than that. Isabel had to get to the cottage. Robert's miniature was there. The thought of seeing his face gave her the strength she needed to pull herself up. Holding onto the boulder for balance, she unsteadily stood to her full height. She would make for the cottage, and with luck would be there before nightfall. The remnants of her skirt clung to her aching legs as she staggered away, her face vacant of all emotion as she turned her back on the place that held the remains of her love.

A light rain began an hour after she started, making the way slippery. Isabel shivered with cold as she trudged through the woods, at times bent nearly double as she climbed the steep hill that led to the meadow. With no trail to follow, she went in what she only guessed was the right direction. Physically exhausted, sore all over, her heart in pieces, she had one goal: to reach the place where she'd spent so many hours with Robert.

Finally, Isabel looked up and saw the crest of the hill. Not long to go, then, before the terrain would even out. Perhaps she could find shelter among the trees and rest before going on.

Isabel made a last great effort, struggling to get over the ridge, and found herself on a narrow trail threading through the trees. As she walked, she thought of nothing, merely put one foot in front of the other. She followed the trail for a time before collapsing against a wide tree trunk.

All was silent and black when she woke. She slowly rose to her feet and shuffled along the trail with her arms out in front of her to keep from bumping into unseen trees. There was no way to know how many hours she'd been walking, but she thought she would have found the cottage or the meadow by now. She had no idea how far the river had carried her. It was possible she wasn't even in the right part of the forest. In the pitch dark, she stumbled over a tree root, and pain shot up her legs as she fell to the ground. It was all too much. She sat down in the middle of the trail to wait out the darkness of this endless night. Shivering with cold, she wrapped her arms around her knees. Her throat burned with thirst and her head throbbed with every beat of her heart.

Isabel was on the verge of sleep when a noise broke through her exhaustion. Snapping twigs. Muffled steps. An animal? Wolves? She raised her head. A flickering light was visible through the trees. She stayed completely still, willing whoever it was to pass by her. As the footsteps came closer, she lay down on the ground, thinking it would hide her better. Torchlight suddenly illuminated the trees around her.

"Isabel!" Simon knelt at her side. He looked as desperate and lost as she felt.

Isabel started to speak, but no words came. Instead, a guttural cry clawed its way out of her throat, the sound of deepest sorrow.

Simon said nothing but scooped her into his arms. Isabel clung to his jacket and let grief wash over her. She slipped into oblivion and knew no more.

Chapter Sixteen

Softness and warmth. A crackling fire. Someone moving about the room. Isabel tilted her aching head toward the sounds. She didn't want to open her eyes, didn't want to remember yesterday.

"Drink this." Simon put an arm around her shoulders and propped her up against the pillows. He held a warm cup of hearty broth to her lips.

Isabel just nodded and drank. When she finished, Simon took the cup away and she opened her eyes. She'd known where she was, of course. The cottage. She'd made it here after all, though she didn't remember how. Robert would have been glad. The thought of his smile reminded her of the miniatures. Tossing the covers aside, she gasped. She was nude.

She yanked the blankets up to her chin. "Where are my clothes?"

"I needed to wash and dress your wounds. They were plentiful. The worst are on your legs…" Simon trailed off when she cast him an angry look.

"I'm getting up. Fetch my clothes."

Simon put a hand on her shoulder. "You should stay in bed."

"I must get up. There's something I need to find."

"Your clothes are drying, though they're barely more than rags now." He held out his riding cloak. "Here, put this on."

"Turn around."

Simon complied. She knew he'd seen her last night, had undressed her and placed her in the bed. Still, now that she was awake she would retain her modesty.

Every muscle in her body protested when she stood on shaking legs. She slipped into the cloak, holding it tightly to keep it from falling open, and shuffled across the room. It seemed no part of her didn't ache. She found the loose brick in the mantel and pulled it out.

"What are you doing?" Simon asked, coming to stand beside her.

She didn't answer but put her hands into the compartment and found what she sought, then hobbled back to the bed, removed the cloak, and got under the covers.

Isabel lay down and held the bundle to her chest. The short walk had exhausted her, and she wanted to sleep again. But first she must see his face. She unwrapped the miniatures, and there he was, her Robert, smiling at her. Brushing away her tears, she touched the small face, stared at the perfect color of his blue eyes, his mouth. The mouth that would kiss her no more, never speak her name again. It was too much to bear. She curled up as small as she could make herself, holding his portrait close to her heart.

****

Simon stood over Isabel, her body wracked with sobs as she lay in the bed. She was but a shadow of herself. The last time he'd seen her she was vibrant, beautiful. More noticeable than the physical changes was that the light had left her eyes.

"Is Robert truly gone?" he stammered, dreading the confirmation.

Isabel wiped her eyes. "Did you not find him, Simon? On the riverbank? Downstream? Perhaps in the forest?"

The faint glimmer of hope in her voice broke his heart. "No."

"I knew he was gone, but I hoped…" She took a shuddering breath before continuing. "He would never leave me if he was not…dead." She faltered over the last word.

"You're quite certain he's dead?"

Isabel lifted her bloodshot eyes to his. "He wasn't moving. He was cold…so cold. He wouldn't open his eyes. His heartbeat stopped."

"What happened?" Simon asked gently, his eyes glistening with unshed tears.

"We jumped into the falls."

"Jumped? But why?"

"My stepfather's men chased us to the waterfall. Robert thought jumping was our only chance of escape. He feared they would take me, or kill us both on the spot after what happened to Mr. Branwick."

"What do you mean?"

"I think I killed him," Isabel said with no trace of regret.

"Branwick lives."

"With such a wound!"

"He lost much blood, and it's doubtful he'll use the arm again, from what I heard. He's very ill but expected to survive."

"I'm sorry he's not dead," Isabel muttered, as if to herself.

"You should not be sorry. It's a grave thing, to kill a man."

"For what he did to Robert and me I'll never forgive him."

"You loved Robert," Simon stated. Until this morning he'd worried that Robert had thrown his love—and his life—away on the wrong woman. But looking at Isabel now, there was no question that his loss had broken her in more ways than one.

"I do love him," Isabel said fervently as the tears began anew. "I'll always love him."

"I loved him, too." His voice quavered as he spoke. "I was only a boy when I met Robert and William. Did you know that? I was so small, I had nobody when I came to Thornwood. My father was Mr. Claremont's second cousin through marriage. It's a distant connection, but they took me in and treated me as one of their own. Robert and William became brothers to me. Especially Robert. I love William, too, but Robert and I were closer from the start. We liked to walk and ride together. We'd talk for hours about everything under the sun. He was my dearest friend." He looked away. It hurt too much to speak of him.

"How did you find out what happened to us?"

"Edmund came to Thornwood with a tale too horrible to believe—of himself being captured and beaten. He said your stepfather's men chased you and Robert away after Branwick was injured." He paused and looked at her. "He said you were married."

Isabel caressed the ring upon her finger. "Four days ago."

Simon paused. He hated to cause her more pain, but needed to hear from her own lips what had happened. Perhaps there was a chance, somehow, that Robert could still be saved. Or at the very least, buried. He shuddered.

That the words "Robert" and "buried" should exist in the same sentence made him sick to his stomach. He took a moment to compose himself. "I rode out with a group of men to find Robert. I couldn't believe Edmund's story. What…what exactly happened to him?"

Tears ran down Isabel's cheeks. "We were cornered, as I told you, and we leapt down the waterfall. We hit the water and I thought we were safe. But then we were swept away."

She stopped talking and put her head in her hands.

Simon touched her arm lightly.

"The current caught us," Isabel went on, staring at the miniature. "There were huge boulders in the water, hidden in the depths. We crashed into one of them. The river was so strong, so fast. Robert was holding me, trying to protect me. But he hit the rock…" She stopped again, her face ashen.

"He hit the rock? What then?"

"There was so much blood. He stopped moving. He wouldn't answer me," she said, breaking down again.

Simon could see it all. Of course that's what Robert would do. Sacrifice himself for the woman he loved. "Where's Robert now?" he whispered, as though trying not to startle a timid wild creature.

"I had to let him go," Isabel wailed, raising her anguished eyes to his. "The river took him from me. I should have held onto him! I should be beside him right now. But he's gone, gone!"

She turned to the wall again as her sobs overtook her.

Simon crossed the room and sat in a chair beside the fire, feeling heavier than he had in his entire life. He knew what Robert would want. He'd want him to protect

Isabel. She wouldn't be safe if Branwick knew she lived. He sat for a long time, thinking what to do. After a while he went outside. The morning was overcast, a light mist filled the yard. He didn't want to leave Isabel alone, but if he was to care for her, he'd need supplies. And he needed to know what was happening at Thornwood. He could ride there and be back before the end of the day.

When he went back inside, Isabel's crying had been replaced by slow, deep breathing. She'd fallen asleep. He placed a cup of wine and a steaming mug of broth at her bedside, then covered her bruised shoulders with a blanket before leaving the cottage.

Simon saddled Blaze and followed the path to the meadow. After passing through the gate, he dismounted and pulled some brush from nearby to hide it. It wouldn't do for anyone to stumble upon Isabel in her current state. He rode as fast as he could to Thornwood.

By the time Simon returned to the cottage, dusk had fallen. No smoke rose from the chimney, and he hoped Isabel wasn't too cold without a fire. Apollo whinnied, and Simon knew he was looking for Robert. He'd found the horse wandering aimlessly around the stables at Thornwood, unattended. He'd brushed him, fed him, and stabled him before deciding to ride him back to the cottage.

"He's not here, boy," Simon said sadly, patting his neck. He stabled Apollo and Blaze, who'd carried most of the supplies, and went into the cottage, taking two trips to carry everything he'd brought from the manor.

Isabel wasn't in bed, nor anywhere in the cottage.

"Hello?" he called.

Isabel's weary voice answered from the back garden. "Here."

Simon found her sitting on a bench, wearing her tattered riding habit, wrapped in a blanket from the bed. She was pale and wan, her eyes blank. Robert's miniature was clutched in her hand. She didn't look up when he sat next to her.

"I thought I heard Apollo. For a moment I hoped..." She trailed off.

"You did hear Apollo. But I rode him, not Robert."

"Where did you find him? In the woods?"

"He was at Thornwood. Somehow I couldn't leave him there."

Isabel nodded, her eyes on her lap.

"I brought you some clothes," Simon said. "They were among Mrs. Claremont's discarded gowns she gives to the women of the village, so she won't miss them."

Isabel said nothing.

"Are you hungry? I brought food."

She shook her head.

"Come inside."

Isabel didn't move.

Simon sighed and went inside for the blanket he'd taken from Robert's bed. "This is Robert's. I brought it from his room." He tucked it around her legs.

She touched the blanket lovingly and brought it to her nose. Tears came to her eyes as she hugged it to her.

Simon went inside to rebuild the fire. He then filled shelves and cupboards with everything he'd brought from Thornwood. He'd packed anything he thought would make Isabel comfortable, though he doubted anything could truly bring her comfort at the moment.

He prepared a meal and ate alone. There was no use trying to convince Isabel to come in before she was ready. It was full dark when she finally returned. She sat on the bed and ran her fingers over the dresses Simon had brought.

"Will you go so that I may change?"

"Of course. Here's a jug of water if you'd like to wash," he said, pointing out the water he'd gathered from the stream earlier.

Simon stepped outside, where twinkling stars flooded the clear night sky. He wondered how he could help Isabel, what was the best plan for her. She couldn't go back to Holton, at least not yet. Perhaps he could set her up somewhere else. He didn't mind leaving Thornwood for a time. He'd planned to return to Ridgefield, his own estate, shortly, but first he would see that Isabel was settled.

When Simon went back inside, Isabel was sitting on the bed, wearing a midnight-blue gown.

"Would you like to eat?" he asked.

"No."

"You must. You've only had broth since yesterday."

Carrying Robert's miniature, she walked over to the table and fell into a chair.

Simon placed bread, ale, and a leg of cold chicken in front of her. When she finished, Simon cleared the table while Isabel stared into the fire.

"What will you do now?" she asked. "Won't they miss you at Thornwood?"

"When I was there earlier, I told Edmund and Mr. Claremont I'm leaving Holton for a time."

"How was Edmund? He looked badly hurt when Robert and I…" Isabel swallowed. "When we saw him," she finished hoarsely.

"He's bruised but has no lasting wounds. Branwick

beat him to discover your whereabouts, but he refused to tell them where you'd gone. In the end, he told him you and Robert were married. Edmund thought that would convince him to call off the chase. Branwick went to the church and stole the registry."

"He ripped it up," Isabel said sadly. "Now there's no proof we were married."

"But you were. Edmund witnessed it. You truly were his wife. Mrs. Claremont," Simon said, to cheer her. But it had the opposite effect. Tears spilled out of her eyes, and she let them fall unchecked.

"Do you wish to go home?" he asked.

"Home? What home?" she cried. "Robert was my home, and Robert is gone. I can't return to Salisbury. My stepfather will be there, and I believe he'd kill me the moment he had the chance."

"You're safe from him for the moment. The men who were with me when I found you told everyone you're dead. It's assumed by most people that you were"—he paused and gave her an apologetic look—"That you were set upon by animals or carried away by the river."

She didn't even flinch when confronted with these ideas, but asked, "Why didn't you tell the men I was alive that day?"

He swallowed and looked away. "You would not have been safe from them."

She sighed heavily. "I see."

"I'm sorry I couldn't come back to help you right away. I had to return to Thornwood and tell the Claremonts that I didn't find Robert."

"How long were you waiting here for me?"

"A few hours. I set out at dusk to find you."

"I'm grateful you did. I wouldn't have made it through the night." She smiled wistfully. "Although, then I'd be with Robert right now…somewhere, wherever it is we all go—after."

His brow furrowed, and he said, an edge to his voice, "Please don't speak like that, Isabel. Don't wish you didn't survive."

She looked at him for a long moment before nodding. "Did you tell anyone the truth about me when you went to Thornwood?"

"No. You'd be in terrible danger from Branwick and Mr. Abbot, and I didn't want the news to reach them. But it's easy enough to tell everyone you're alive. I could even go back tonight, if you want me to. We could get a message to your mother, or I could bring her here."

She frowned. "My poor mother. But no. I won't tell her or anyone else."

"If that's the way you want it." He didn't think it was the right choice, but it wasn't his decision to make.

"Did you see anyone else today? Rosamond Penrose? I thought there was something between you two."

Simon shook his head. "No. We danced a few times at balls, but nothing more." He'd been on the verge of asking Mr. Penrose for permission to court Rosamond, but that would need to wait a few weeks now.

Isabel glanced around the room. "How did you know about this place?"

"I've known about it since we were boys. But don't worry. Nobody else ever comes here. You're safe."

She nodded. "As long as nobody finds out I'm alive."

"What will you do now?"

"Perhaps I'll go across the sea and start a new life under another name. Isabel Tate will cease to exist. You say everyone believes me dead. I'm dead, then. I died with Robert."

Simon didn't agree with this, but held his tongue.

She walked gingerly back to the bed, lay down, and covered herself with Robert's blanket, staring blankly at the ceiling.

Simon came over and sat on the edge of the bed. "You were badly wounded in the fall. It will take time, but you'll heal, Isabel. You'll stay here and rest, and I'll look after you."

"My body may heal, but I will never be whole again."

With that she turned over and was silent. Simon realized she wanted to be alone, so he went to the stables to feed the horses. Robert had supplied the stable with food before he left. This renewed Simon's grief, for it was clear Robert had planned to return here with Isabel. He'd planned on having a life with her.

After the horses were settled, he went back into the cottage and looked around for a place to sleep. He unrolled a rug he'd brought from Thornwood and laid it out beside the fireplace, covered himself with a blanket, and was asleep almost instantly.

****

When Isabel awoke, it was dark in the cottage but for the dying embers in the fireplace. Every time she shifted in bed, a new pain made itself known. Even her eyes were swollen and raw.

She sat up stiffly and limped across the room to stir the fire, carefully stepping around Simon, who was sound asleep on the floor. When it was hot enough, she hung a large pot of water to boil. After lighting two candles that stood on the table, she sliced the bread Simon had brought from Thornwood and ate it with hard cheese and wine. When the water was ready she brought it out to the garden and bathed in the pre-dawn light. Isabel scooped water into a pitcher and poured it over her head. The warm water flowing over her skin soothed some of the pain from the black and purple bruises covering most of her body. It took three pitchers before she felt truly clean. Afterward, she warmed herself in the bright morning sunshine, then put on a clean gown.

After dressing, she sat on the bench beside the apple tree. This was where she and Robert had pledged their love. She ran her fingers over the place he had sat. When she'd accepted his proposal, it had been the happiest day of her life. She'd never have imagined their marriage would last only a matter of days. And now her whole, empty life stretched out before her. What would she do? Where would she go? One thing was certain. As much as she loved the cottage, she couldn't stay here. She rose. It was time to talk to Simon.

On her way inside, she met him in the doorway. His hazel eyes looked tired, his light brown hair tousled.

"Have you just woken up?" Isabel asked.

"Yes," he said, rubbing his cheek. "It was the first sound sleep I've had in days."

"Come inside. I need to talk to you."

He followed her into the cottage and they sat at the table.

"I need to leave here as soon as possible," she said.

"But why?"

She looked around the cottage. "This place must be known to someone."

"Nobody ever comes here, and nobody's searching for you. They all think you're dead."

"I don't want to be found accidentally. It's better if I disappear. I'll make my way to the coast and find a ship to take me far away."

"Where would you go?"

She hadn't thought that far ahead. "It doesn't matter. There's nothing for me here now. Robert was my life."

Simon shifted in his chair. "Isabel…"

Isabel shook her head. "You don't understand. You can't."

"I do know that Robert wouldn't want you to waste your life in mourning for him."

"I'll go as soon as I'm well enough to travel," she said, her jaw set.

"Let me come with you."

"No. You hardly know me. And you have a life here." Why would he even *want* to help her? It was her fault Robert died.

"I owe it to Robert to see that you're cared for." Simon lowered his head. "I failed him. I let Robert be chased off his own land and killed. The least I can do is protect his widow."

"You didn't fail him. You couldn't have known the danger he was in. None of us knew."

He lifted his eyes to hers. "I'll help you. I'll make sure you have enough money, and a safe place where Branwick can never find you."

Looking into Simon's eyes, she knew how much this last act of loyalty to Robert meant to him. Loved him like a brother, he'd said. There was no doubt she needed assistance. How could she book passage on a ship, find a place to live, buy the necessary supplies without being recognized? She would need to remain in hiding at least until she was fit to travel, and she couldn't do this alone.

"I graciously accept your help."

He sighed and it looked like all the tension left his shoulders. "The first thing you need is rest. You're still wounded."

She went back to bed, propping Robert's miniature on the bedside table where she could see it every time she opened her eyes.

Simon covered her with Robert's blanket.

Before he walked away, Isabel grabbed his hand. "I'm grateful to you."

"And I to you, for allowing me to help you."

As the weeks passed, Isabel and Simon settled into a routine. They got along well and she enjoyed his easy company. She spent most of her days in bed or sitting in the garden. Simon did his best to keep her comfortable and nurse her back to health. Isabel hadn't tired of staying at the cottage but knew it would soon be time to make preparations for her departure.

Once her legs finally healed she took short walks around the yard to strengthen them and was delighted the first day she could mount Apollo unassisted. Simon had somehow procured a sidesaddle for her, and she rode around the yard and forest close to the cottage.

She went about with a sharp ache that went away only when she slept, and Robert was constantly in her thoughts. It had been weeks since she'd gone to sleep with dry eyes. She tried to hide it from Simon but suspected he knew. Isabel doubted she would ever pass a day not feeling wrenched in two.

But then something happened to give her a long-forgotten hope.

The summer flowers had faded when she first became suspicious of her condition. Sitting on the garden bench one evening, as she did most nights after supper, the full moon reminded her of Robert's ball, when they'd sat outside in the moonlight and talked of their future. She suddenly sat up straighter. Another full moon. She stood and paced around the garden, a quiet thrill running through her as she began counting backward on her fingers. How many days had passed since their wedding? Their wedding night? She gingerly lowered herself onto the bench, hands on her stomach. Could it be? Could she possibly have a part of Robert to hold onto forever? To see his eyes once more in a tiny, pink face? The very thought overwhelmed her. Heart racing, she hurried inside.

Simon jumped to his feet as soon as she walked in. "Isabel, what's wrong?"

She didn't answer, but sat on the edge of the bed. He sat beside her and put a hand to her forehead as though he suspected a fever.

Tears stood in her eyes.

"I miss him, too," he said.

"Oh, Simon!" Isabel said and burst into tears.

"What is it, pray?" He started to get up, but she took his hand.

"It's Robert. Robert's child. I'm going to have his child!" she said, crying into her hands.

Simon leapt to his feet. "You're certain?"

"Yes!" She clasped her hands together in her lap, laughing.

"When will the child be born?" He looked down at her stomach as if expecting it to be the size of a watermelon already.

"In the spring." Would that she could speed up time! "We'll need to leave sooner than we'd planned."

Simon looked surprised. "We can't leave here now."

"Why not? It's early yet, and I may travel. My mother rode until she was five months gone with Victoria."

"But where would we go? You aren't still thinking of going overseas?"

"No. I could move to the coast? Or Newton?" Isabel suggested. "I'd love Robert's child to be born here, in this cottage, but—"

"What?"

"It's too close. I wouldn't want to be found here and delivered to my stepfather. He wouldn't be lenient, whatever condition I'm in."

"I'd stay here and protect you. I could bring whatever you and the baby need. I know the land and the village."

She shook her head. "It's impossible to remain so close. It's still a wonder to me that more people haven't found this place."

"That's true," Simon agreed.

"There must be somewhere we'd be safe."

Simon stared out the window for so long she thought he hadn't heard her.

"Simon?"

He turned toward her, but kept his eyes on the floor. "There might be one place. My parents had an estate some days from here. I inherited it when they died. I came to Thornwood with the understanding that I'd one day return to Ridgefield and assume my place. My steward, Mr. Wentworth, has been there all these years, looking after it. I stay there for a few months every spring. I've always known I'd go back eventually, perhaps when I married. There's a small village close by that would have anything you need."

"I know what it is to lose a parent. I'm sorry for your loss," Isabel said softly.

He gave a one-sided shrug. "It was so long ago, I scarcely remember them. Only that my mother had yellow hair and sang me lullabies. My father loved to ride, and would take me out with him often. My brother was a year older than me. My sister was just a baby. They're all only vague memories now," he said sadly.

Isabel put a tentative hand over his. He took it and released it after only a moment.

"How far away is Ridgefield?"

"Six days' ride at a slow pace. We wouldn't rush, not in your condition. It's far enough away that you wouldn't need to worry about being seen by Mr. Branwick or his men."

"Do you think so? I worry that they'll find me." Her stomach tightened. The weeks in hiding hadn't erased her fear of discovery.

"You must put that out of your mind. Everyone in Holton believes you're dead. They aren't looking for you. I only meant you wouldn't meet them accidentally."

Isabel considered. Perhaps she could feel safe at Ridgefield and stop worrying every time she heard an unfamiliar sound in the woods. As hard as it was to leave the town where she and Robert had met, fallen in love, and shared their brief time together, she must think of their child now.

"It sounds ideal," she said.

"I'll send a message to Mr. Wentworth without delay. I suggest we leave in three or four days. Is that too soon?"

"No," Isabel said, looking around the cottage. "But I would stay here forever. Robert is here for me."

"Robert is always with you. You carry his child. He'll never leave you."

Isabel merely nodded, overcome with emotion, and placed a hand on her stomach.

Simon stood up. As he rose, Isabel took his hand again. She held it to her cheek for a moment, then let it drop. She lay down in bed and said no more.

Chapter Seventeen

Within the month Simon and Isabel were living at
Ridgefield—a three storied, gray stone manor house
situated in a lush valley. The simplest way to explain
Isabel's presence and condition had been to introduce her
as Simon's wife. She was now going by her middle
name, Dorothy. He still believed they were far enough
away to be safe, but if gossip somehow reached Holton
that Simon Kensington had returned to his family estate
with a woman named Isabel, that could raise suspicion.

After the first few weeks of settling in, Simon busied
himself with estate matters. Some of the older servants
remembered Simon's parents, and Simon himself from
when he was a child. He hadn't expected to enjoy having
his own home to run, but it suited him well.

Isabel's room on the second floor adjoined Simon's
own chambers. If their ruse of being married was to be
believed, they had to appear to be in love. He spent as
much time with her as he could, which was a pleasure,
as they had more than enough in common to spend a few
companionable hours together each day.

Simon knew everyone in the household believed
them to be truly married and were pleased to see them
happy together. More than once he'd considered asking
Isabel to marry him in truth. They could easily pretend
here at home, but sooner or later Isabel would venture
out into the world again. What name would her baby

have? Even if she moved away alone and took the child with her she could never use Robert's name. The Claremonts were well known, and if anyone ever heard the name they would ask questions.

He wouldn't expect wifely duties of her. They would wed only to protect her and give the child a name. What held him back from proposing was a certainty that she would say no. It was clear her heart was Robert's and she wanted to remain his wife forever. Perhaps later, after the baby was born, she'd be open to the idea. Simon knew he'd never marry anyone else—he was devoted to Robert's widow and child. He would take no chances with their safety, so a few months before the baby was due the best midwife he could find came to live at the house. By caring for Isabel and bringing his child safely into the world, he would have truly fulfilled his duty to Robert.

****

It wasn't long before Ridgefield felt like home to Isabel. The months passed, and the day Isabel first felt her child stirring within her was a wonder. She spent hours dreaming of the baby, picturing a boy with Robert's dark hair and blue eyes. Every day she and her maid, Maria, worked on the layette.

The world still felt all wrong without Robert. Isabel tried to hide her melancholy from Simon, who worked so hard to make her happy, but somehow he always knew. One morning as she sat picking at her breakfast he asked what was wrong. She shook her head, tears welling in her eyes.

He dismissed the servants and came to sit beside her. "Isabel?"

She looked into his warm eyes, full of concern. He'd

become such a dear friend during their long months together. He alone knew what she'd been through.

"Robert," she said simply.

Understanding dawned on his face. He was silent for a few moments before he spoke. "Did I ever tell you about the first time Robert saw you?"

She wiped her eyes. "No."

"We were walking through the great hall on May Day, and Robert suddenly stopped. I couldn't understand why until I saw that he was looking at a woman. You. He stared at you until you looked up and noticed him. I think, in that moment, when he saw your eyes, he lost his heart to you. I knew him almost his entire life, and I had never seen him so besotted with a woman before."

Isabel's heart swelled. "He was so handsome."

"Robert loved you dearly. I'm certain that when he married you it was the happiest day of his life."

"But I *shortened* his life," she said, sniffling. "He died because of me, protecting me."

"You mustn't blame yourself." He put an arm around her shoulders. "Think how happy he would be to know he saved you and the child. Don't dwell on the past. You must look forward now."

She leaned into him, grateful for the comfort and support he gave her. She had indeed come to rely on him. "I know you're right. But living without him is harder than I ever could have imagined."

Simon took her hand. "Come. There's something I want to show you."

"What is it?" Smiling, she wiped away her tears.

"Wait and see."

He helped Isabel to her feet and kept a hand on her back as they mounted the stairs. When they reached the second floor he led Isabel to a room she hadn't visited for some months.

"The nursery," she said.

"Yes. I've asked you to stay away for a reason. See for yourself." Simon opened the door and stepped aside so she could enter first.

A galaxy of tiny white stars adorned light blue walls, and a wooden cradle stood in the corner beside a yellow wingback chair.

Isabel turned to Simon, beaming. "It's perfect!"

"And I made this." Simon pointed to a wooden rocking horse, gray and white like Apollo, beside the bureau.

"I couldn't love it more." Just as Isabel turned to kiss Simon's cheek, the rustling of skirts alerted them that they were no longer alone.

The midwife, Peg, stood smiling in the doorway. "It's time you had your afternoon rest, Mrs. Kensington."

Isabel gave Simon's hand a squeeze and left the room.

Not long after the day she visited the nursery, Isabel began feeling what the midwife told her were signs of the impending birth. Simon insisted she rest, which she found impossible. Though tired, a mounting excitement made it difficult to settle to anything. She took to sitting beside the cradle in the nursery, dreaming of Robert and their child.

Her pains took her by surprise one day as she strolled outside in the garden, enjoying the warmest day since last summer. The pain was more than she'd expected, but not too much to bear. After waiting a lifetime for this day, she would finally hold Robert's child in her arms. She headed back to the house and summoned the midwife.

Peg came hurrying downstairs, grinning. "Mrs. Kensington, your babe will soon be here."

Isabel looked around the hall. "Where's Simon? Mr. Kensington?"

"You have hours to go before the baby is born. We'll send someone to fetch your husband."

"My husband…" She blinked back tears. She had no husband.

They went to Isabel's bedroom, and she eased herself into a chair as Peg arranged linens and prepared the bed, chatting about births she'd attended while assuring Isabel that having a baby was the easiest thing in the world. A housemaid carried the cradle in and set it beside Isabel's chair. All the waiting was about to end and a new reality would begin.

Maria came in and helped Isabel out of her gown so she was wearing her shift only. As time wore on, her pains came more frequently, and some were so strong she would have fallen down if Peg and Maria hadn't been there to support her. As day faded into evening, Isabel couldn't stand up anymore. She sat in the middle of her bed, riding out wave after wave, holding fast to Peg's and Maria's hands. Isabel vaguely wondered why Simon had not yet come, but then realized she wouldn't want him here. This was a woman's time, and a woman's room. Soon her pains intensified and she had no thought to spare for anything but her baby.

****

Simon had been fishing at the brook all day, with a pile of trout to show for it. A snap of spring permeated the crisp evening air as he tended his fire and prepared one fish for cooking, whistling under his breath. He'd wrap the rest up and bring them home for Isabel, who always enjoyed fresh fish. The brook was one of her favorite spots on the estate, and they'd discussed having a picnic here later in the summer. After eating, he lay down in the grass, hands behind his head, and watched the clouds go from white to dusky pink. Wanting to be home with Isabel by dark for their evening game of backgammon, he set about packing up the fish and saddling Apollo.

Just as he finished putting out the fire, a horse thundered down the trail. Recognizing a stable lad from his own home, Simon stood and hailed him.

The boy pulled up sharply, a cloud of dust coming off his horse's hooves. Before Simon could ask, he said, "It's Mrs. Kensington. The baby!"

Simon leapt onto Apollo and tore down the trail, cursing himself for not staying closer to home—he'd known Isabel's time was near. She'd needed him and he hadn't been there. He willed Apollo to go faster, asking him for every ounce of speed he possessed.

He finally arrived home just as darkness fell. Simon jumped off Apollo and sprinted into the house. As he strode toward the stairs, a scream rent the air, stopping him in his tracks.

"Isabel," he whispered, bolting up the stairs two at a time. When he reached her room, he threw open the door without knocking.

"Isabel!" he cried, forgetting their ruse of her false name.

Peg stood in front of him, fists planted on her hips. "What are you doing, storming in here?"

Brushing her aside, Simon ran in and stopped short, rooted to the floor by what he saw.

Isabel sat in the bed, face flushed, hair wet, wearing the happiest, most radiant smile Simon had ever seen. She held her hand out to him. "Oh, Simon!"

"The baby?"

"He's here," Isabel said, still reaching for him.

"He...?" Simon said wonderingly.

"Yes, Mr. Kensington, a son. You have a fine son!" Peg said and left the room.

He tiptoed over to the bed and sat on the edge. Cradled in Isabel's arms was the baby, smaller than Simon could have imagined. The baby's eyes were closed, his little mouth puckered, his dark hair damp. Simon reached out to touch his pink, velvety cheek.

Simon looked up and met Isabel's eyes. "He's perfect."

"Yes," Isabel said, "he is. He looks like Robert."

Simon touched the baby's hand, amazed by the small fingers. "What's his name?"

"Robert Henry for his father. But I'll call him Henry."

"Hello, Henry," Simon said softly.

"You will be his godfather?"

"I'd be honored." Simon smiled, unable to take his eyes off Henry.

She took his hand. "Simon, you helped me see I couldn't let go of life. Now I have my Henry, and Robert will live on in him. We both owe our lives to you. If you hadn't found me in the woods that night..."

"Don't speak of it. You're safe now. You have only to look to the future." He squeezed her fingers lightly.

Henry suddenly opened his eyes. Robert's eyes.

Peg entered the room with a tray of food. "You must be hungry, Mrs. Kensington."

"I am. I haven't thought of food for hours, but now I'm famished."

"I'll leave you to your meal," Simon said, sensing she wanted to be alone with Henry.

He leaned over and kissed Isabel lightly on the forehead before leaving the room, turning back once as he stood in the doorway. A look of intense devotion lit her face as she gazed at Henry, as if nothing existed but her child. Overwhelmed with a surge of love for both of them, Simon vowed to himself to stay with them and protect them always, as Robert would want him to.

****

After Isabel fed Henry, he fell into a deep sleep. She held him close, relishing his sweet warmth as she stared into his face. When she'd lost Robert, she'd thought nothing could ever fill her life again. She was now whole, as if she'd been waiting her entire life for Henry. With all her heart she wished Robert sat beside her, looking at their son. A tear slid down her cheek. It wasn't right that Henry would grow up without ever knowing his father.

She looked for Robert's features in the slumbering boy's face. Henry had his eyes and dark hair, though Peg had said this could change over time. Isabel hoped it wouldn't. She traced the outline of his round cheek. He was everything to her. Isabel, exhausted from the birth and the torrent of emotions it had unleashed within her, snuggled down into the blankets with her son.

Chapter Eighteen

Four years later

Isabel sat beside the open window, laughing as she watched Henry cartwheel across the lawn. When he stood up and brushed himself off she called, "Henry, come in now. Papa is home and it's almost time for supper."

"Yes, Mama," he said, with that smile so like his father's. He ran to Joan, his nurse, who would see that he was cleaned up.

It would be wonderful to have Simon home. Henry asked for him every single night when he was away. After the birth, Simon had taken on the role of father, and Isabel knew the only man who could have been better was Robert. Henry was too young to understand now, but one day she'd tell him the truth about his father. She still remembered the look of awe on Simon's face the first time he held newborn Henry in his arms. The day after Henry was born, Simon had asked Isabel to marry him. She'd hesitated, but Simon had been understanding and given her all the time she needed to decide.

One day not long after, as she held Henry in her arms, she'd realized nothing could be better for him than to be Simon's son. Her heart still ached for Robert; nothing would ever replace the love they'd shared. But over Isabel's long months of recovery and confinement she and Simon had become close, and she'd grown to love him as a friend. She couldn't ask for a better companion and, most importantly, she trusted him. He was a fine man and could offer the security she needed. She'd accepted Simon's proposal, with the understanding that she could never be a true wife to him and there would be no more children. They'd had a small ceremony in the Ridgefield chapel. The upper servants acted as witnesses—Isabel had told them she and Simon wanted to renew their vows after Henry's birth.

She grinned when she heard the familiar footsteps approaching and turned to see Simon in the doorway. He looked tired from his journey, but smiled as he crossed the room. Isabel stood to embrace him and kissed him lightly on the cheek. He held her close, then released her, keeping her hand in his.

He let out a contented sigh. "It's good to be home."

"Sit down, supper's on the way." She took his arm and led him to the table.

"Where's Henry?"

"He'll be along. He was outside playing just before you arrived. Joan's taken him to get cleaned up."

"I have some news that he'll be most interested in." Simon took his jacket off and draped it over the chair beside him.

"What is it?"

He grinned. "You'll find out when Henry does."

A footman arrived and set out creamy chicken served with rice and pears, then left the room, taking Simon's jacket with him.

"You enjoyed your journey?" Isabel asked, pouring them each a glass of wine.

"Yes, I'm glad I only go once a year, though. Four

weeks is too long to be away from home. I miss you and Henry when I'm gone."

"We miss you, too. Any news from Holton?"

He hesitated for a moment, then looked into her eyes. "I hear your mother had her baby five months ago. A boy."

Isabel took a deep breath. "They're both well?"

Simon nodded.

A tumult of emotions overtook her at the news. Joy that her mother and the baby were healthy, sorrow that she couldn't be at her side, and disgust that she was still with Branwick. But her mother finally had what she'd wanted, after years of trying. A son by that man.

Simon took her hand. "I know how difficult it is for you to hear about your mother."

She sighed. "I miss her and Victoria, and now I have a brother I'll never meet. What pains me more is that she stayed with Branwick after what he did."

"Your mother doesn't know his part in it. She believes the same story everyone else does—that Robert attacked Branwick and then you and Robert *fell* off the cliff."

"Some people know what really happened. Surely they would have told others."

"Only Branwick's men saw you attack him, and they'd never tell. As for the cliff…it was nighttime and so dark I don't think anyone knew you jumped rather than fell."

"Maybe one day I can tell her the truth."

"I could get a message to her. She wouldn't tell Branwick you're alive."

She shook her head. "It's too risky. Enough about that. How did you find the Claremonts?"

"They're well, for the most part." Simon sipped his wine. "William and Margery are still without an heir, but the Claremonts are hopeful there will be grandchildren in time."

Isabel had once considered taking Henry to meet his grandparents, but how could she appear with a young boy and declare him Robert's heir? The Claremonts wouldn't have her back, even if she wanted to go. They blamed her for Robert's death, and how could she forget the part they'd played in the tragedy? If they'd helped, Robert would be sitting beside her right now. Furthermore, much as she'd love her mother to meet Henry, she would never expose him to Mr. Branwick. No, that road was closed to her. "I'm certain they'll have a baby. A year isn't so long to be married."

"Speaking of which, Mrs. Claremont has been asking when I'll 'settle down.' "

"Has she?" She sipped her wine.

"Yes, and William has strongly suggested Rosamond might be the perfect bride," he said and laughed.

"Rosamond's liked you for quite some time, if I recall."

Simon shrugged. "She does call at Thornwood every day I'm there."

"You thought of courting her at one time, didn't you?" She was almost certain he had. One of the many things he'd given up in order to care for her after Robert died.

He shifted in his seat and looked away. "That was years ago."

"You enjoy her company?"

Simon grinned. "Oh, yes, she's charming. There's

almost always a ball while I'm in Holton, and we have a dance or two."

"I'm still surprised they haven't heard you took a wife."

"I suppose gossip from this part of the country is of little interest to Holton folk. And our wedding was such a quiet affair it would have been more surprising if the gossip reached farther than the Ridgefield gates."

They sat silently for a few minutes, eating supper, before Isabel turned to him. "Simon, do you ever regret not having a true wife? A family of your own?"

"I couldn't ask for more from any other woman, Isabel. You're my dearest friend and I look on Henry as my son."

"But did you never wish you'd fallen in love with a woman, wooed her, married her? Someone like Rosamond?"

He held her gaze for a long moment but said nothing.

"Simon, is everything well?"

He was fidgeting with his fork and had twice tried taking sips from his empty wine glass.

He cleared his throat. "I've been thinking."

"About what?"

Simon took her hand in both of his. They were warm and strong, enclosing hers in a comforting cocoon.

"Your talk of wives brings to mind something I've been wanting to speak to you about for some time."

Isabel tried to mask her surprise. Had Simon more than "visited" Rosamond? Would she come between them? A cold feeling settled in her stomach. "What is it?"

"It's something I need to tell you, for it concerns you more than anyone else—" Simon began, but at that moment Henry bounded into the room.

"You were gone a long time, Papa." He threw himself into Simon's arms.

Simon's face lit with joy as he caught Henry and held him. "I was. But now I'm home, and who do you think will come with me on my next journey?"

"Mama?" Henry guessed, standing and draping an arm around Simon's shoulder.

"Yes, Mama. And?"

"Me?"

"That's right. You're coming with us."

"Where are we going?" he asked.

"To a horse fair."

"Huzzah!"

"Wonderful! Where is it?" Isabel hadn't attended a fair in years, and Henry had never seen one.

"In Somerville. A day's ride."

"When will we leave?" Isabel asked.

"The fair starts in three weeks. There are some things around the estate I need to attend to before I leave again."

Henry poked Simon's shoulder. "What will be at the fair?"

"Horses and more. Jugglers, mummers, minstrels. Fine food, hundreds of people."

"I can hardly wait," Henry said.

Simon turned to Isabel and said in a staged whisper, "I'm going to look for a new pony for Henry."

"A pony? For me?" He began riding an imaginary steed across the room.

Simon and Isabel laughed, and Simon ran after Henry and picked him up, lifting him high into the air until he was crying with laughter.

Isabel couldn't help smiling as she watched them. Henry had inherited Robert's striking blue eyes, but had light brown hair. He really did look like Simon's son. Her life hadn't turned out as expected, and losing Robert had almost destroyed her. But the life she had here at Ridgefield was more than she could have hoped for. Simon looked up just then and caught her watching them. A warm feeling spread through her when their eyes met. She'd indeed found more than contentment with Simon.

Over the next few days, Isabel saw little of Simon, for he had much business to attend to now that he was home. He always made time to join her for breakfast, however, and after supper they would retire to the library to play backgammon or read together.

Whenever Simon had extra time, he took Henry riding around the yard—always on a lead, as Isabel insisted. He often watched Isabel practice her archery at the range she'd set up a year after Henry's birth. Recently, she'd begun teaching Henry the basic points. He had his own small bow and a target which he loved to aim for but seldom hit.

A week after Simon returned, they rode to the brook for a picnic. The cook had packed a basket of sandwiches, which they ate under the branches of a towering oak tree. Isabel sat in the shade, watching Simon and Henry explore the shoreline, and after a time Simon came and threw himself down on the grass beside her.

"He never tires," he said.

"No, he certainly doesn't," she agreed as Henry sprinted across the field.

"Have you thought of school for him, Isabel?"

"Not yet. Are you thinking of boarding school?" She

couldn't imagine Henry moving away.

"Certainly not. But perhaps we could engage a tutor."

"He's young yet."

"He'll always be young to you," Simon teased.

"That's the way with mothers, is it not? I would also say with fathers. At least, *certain* fathers."

"Yes, you're right. It would be difficult to part with him. Or you."

Isabel's heart skipped a beat. What was he saying? That parting with her was a possibility? Perhaps he really *had* become closer to Rosamond.

"You won't need to part with either of us. I like your idea of a tutor, when the time comes. Peg seems to think I'm too devoted to Henry. She says I should spend less time with him."

He scowled. "Why?"

Isabel was pleased that Simon found the idea as ludicrous as she did. "She says most women of my station allow the governess to take charge of the children."

"We do have Joan." Simon sat up.

"Yes, and Henry loves her. I feel that, after all we went through to have him, after…after losing Robert, I wouldn't want to give up even a minute with our son if I don't need to. Soon enough he'll be grown and this will all be over."

Simon took her hand. "Not all over. You'll always have me."

"Thank goodness for that," she said and smiled. *Would* she always have him? Whatever was on his mind, she hoped he'd tell her soon, because she didn't want to have to come right out and ask if he'd fallen in love with

Rosamond.

On the ride home, Isabel thought of Simon's words by the brook and wondered what they could mean. It had never occurred to her that he might leave. After all, they were married. But if he fell in love with someone, how could she stand in his way? Rosamond was young, pretty, and, from what she could tell, besotted with Simon. Isabel loved Simon enough to let him go if it came to that, but she dearly hoped it didn't. She'd have to start a whole new life somewhere with Henry, but Ridgefield was home to her now. And she'd come to rely on Simon. Not only for the home he provided, but for companionship, laughter, and a certain security she felt when he was near. It was hard to imagine life without Simon.

The next day, after breakfast, Isabel strolled through the garden, the fresh April morning a sweet reminder that summer would soon be here. She hadn't told Simon yet, but she'd thought of taking Henry on a trip to the seaside or the mountains. As she stooped to sniff a rose, she heard someone approaching from behind. Expecting Maria, she turned and was surprised to see Simon striding down the graveled path.

"Good morning," he said brightly.

She smiled. "I didn't expect to see you until tonight. Weren't you supposed to meet Mr. Gilbert in town today?"

"Yes," he said as he approached and offered her his arm, "but I postponed it. I haven't had much time with you since I returned from Holton."

"We did have our picnic yesterday."

"Yes, but there isn't much chance for talking when Henry's with us."

"What did you want to talk about?"

He went slightly pink and cleared his throat. "Oh, nothing in particular. I suppose even spending time together in silence is hard to come by when Henry's with us." He laughed and she couldn't help joining in.

"No, silence isn't something Henry is adept at."

They walked along, in silence, for a time, and Isabel wondered if he was preparing to tell her the news he'd wanted to impart the other day. He hadn't mentioned it since his first night home, but there'd hardly been time, with his busy schedule. A part of her dreaded hearing whatever it was, but it was better to know than to wonder. Perhaps it *wasn't* bad news, but simply something he'd had on his mind.

"Simon?"

He looked at her with a grin. "Hm?"

"What was it you wanted to tell me the other night? Something about wives?"

His grin faltered and he looked off toward the summerhouse. After a moment, he turned back. "Oh, I must have misspoken. I meant to say it was something about families. Just a thought I had about Henry's schooling."

Isabel felt herself relax. "You mean what we spoke about yesterday?"

"Yes," he said, smile back in place. "We don't need to discuss it anymore, for the time being."

"All right. What brings you out to the garden?" she asked as they passed through a hedged archway.

"You. You, and I wanted to show you something."

"Something in the garden?" She looked around but didn't see anything different.

"The summerhouse, actually."

As they walked over, Isabel had the sense Simon was either excited or nervous.

When they reached the summerhouse, he took her hand. "Close your eyes."

"Close my eyes?" she asked, a slow smile coming to her face. "We aren't playing hide-and-go-seek, are we?"

Simon laughed. "No, but I have a surprise."

She rolled her eyes good-naturedly. "Very well," she said, closing them. Shuffling along as Simon led her by the hand, she couldn't help giggling, scared to even lift her feet off the ground lest she trip and go sprawling into a flowerbed.

"Isabel, pick up your feet. I won't let you fall. Trust me," he said, and she could tell he was barely containing his own laughter.

She took a quick breath in through her nose and nodded. "All right. I trust you."

One arm slid around her waist and his other hand held hers tightly. After walking for a few more minutes, they stopped and he said, "Ready?"

Her smile deepened. "Yes."

"Open your eyes."

"A sundial!" she exclaimed, moving in for a closer look. The bronze dial sat atop a tree trunk-shaped pedestal, and a small plaque attached to the front was engraved with the phrase, *"I only count the happy hours,"* and beneath that, *"Simon, Isabel, and Henry Kensington."*

"Where did it come from?" she asked, walking around it.

"I commissioned it a few months ago, and it was delivered last night. Do you like it?" Simon looked like he could barely keep the smile off his face.

"I love it," she said, meeting his eyes. "Has Henry seen it yet?"

"No, I wanted to show you first."

"I'm sure he'll like seeing his name there."

"I thought so too. The whole family," he said proudly, running his fingers over the words.

Almost the whole family. Robert's name was not there. A sudden storm broke over her heart, but she kept a smile on her face to avoid ruining Simon's enjoyment of his surprise.

By that evening Isabel's mood was restored, and she sat with Simon in the drawing room long after Henry had gone to bed. Isabel told him her idea for a summer trip, and they spent an hour or so discussing where they would go, and when. Simon pulled out his maps and pointed out spots on the coast that he thought Henry would especially like. After a while, he folded them up, then walked to his desk and picked up an envelope.

He handed it to Isabel. "I've been meaning to tell you, we've been invited to a ball at the Darlingtons'."

Her stomach clenched. "A ball?"

"Yes. Peter's betrothed, and they're having a ball to celebrate."

"I haven't been to a ball in so long I'm not sure I even remember how to dance," she said with a dry laugh that didn't sound remotely amused. Images of the last ball she'd attended flooded her mind: Robert, laughing as they danced; their intimate supper; kissing in the garden; Mr. Branwick's arrival. She swallowed. "Perhaps we can go to their next ball. Or the wedding?" Reaching for her glass of sherry, she tipped it all back in one gulp.

Simon joined her on the sofa and took her hand. "We

need to get out sometimes. We've been invited to balls and parties over the years but have only gone to one. Old Mrs. Hamilton's birthday, and that was quite a small affair at the parsonage."

"I suppose it would be neighborly to go," she said with a resigned sigh.

"It would. And I do think you'd enjoy yourself. I seem to recall you being an accomplished dancer, back…back in Holton."

He almost winced, and she wondered if the same memories were crowding his thoughts, too. Isabel considered. It might be pleasant to see more of their neighbors. Perhaps she could get to know some of the women from town. She was happy in her somewhat solitary life with Simon and Henry, but if she was to spend the rest of her life as mistress of Ridgefield, it would be nice to have some other friends. Perhaps she'd meet someone who had children who could be playmates for Henry.

"Yes, I'll go. When's the ball?"

"As a matter of fact, it's the day after tomorrow," he said sheepishly.

"Two days? You expect me to be ready for my first ball in five years in *two days*? What will I wear?" She started mentally going through her wardrobe, wondering if she possibly had anything suitable for the occasion.

"Didn't you make a gown with that fabric I bought you for your birthday?"

"It isn't quite finished. Perhaps between me, the seamstress, and Maria, we could have it ready in time."

"If not that, you could wear your pink gown. The one with the white stripes."

"I'll see. Hopefully we can finish the green one. You

should wear your blue jacket with the waistcoat I embroidered for you last spring." Isabel glanced at the clock and stood up. "I think I'll go speak to Maria right now about that gown."

"Can't it wait until morning? I thought we might play backgammon. I want a rematch from last time."

She smiled and arched a brow. "We can't have a rematch every time you lose. And since I only have *two* days to prepare, I want to get started right away. Goodnight."

"Goodnight," Simon said and picked up his book from the side table.

****

Two days later, Isabel strolled into Simon's room without knocking. He turned to face her, his half-tied cravat collapsing onto his chest.

"What do you think?" she asked, holding her skirt out and spinning on the spot so he could see her new gown. "Do you think it will do? Maria just put the finishing touches on it an hour ago." She glided over to his mirror to look at herself, smoothing down the scooped bodice and adjusting her sleeves.

"It will do very nicely. I like the color."

She grinned. "Well, you did pick it out."

"I thought the dark green would look nice with your eyes. And it does."

She smiled. "Thank you. All I need is my wrap and we can be on our way. Are you ready?"

"Almost." He tied his cravat, then joined her in front of the mirror.

"You look very elegant," she said.

"And you look beautiful." He offered his arm and they made their way downstairs.

After retrieving Isabel's wrap, they went outside to the carriage for the short ride to the Darlingtons' ball.

"I don't want to stay very late," Isabel said as they bumped along the dirt road.

"Perhaps we could leave right after supper."

"Or earlier. I'd like to say goodnight to Henry."

"I don't think we'll be home quite that early," Simon said, glancing at his pocket watch.

"He said he'd wait up for us," she said with a soft smile. "But I think he'll fall asleep before we return."

"I don't doubt it. Are you looking forward to the ball?"

"I am. It will be a nice change."

"Will you dance?"

"At least once," she said. "With you."

He inclined his head. "There will be many partners lined up for you, so I'd better reserve the supper dance now."

She laughed. "It's been so long since I've danced, I may be tired after one song."

But Isabel was wrong on that count. The music swept her away the moment she stepped into the ballroom. Lighter on her feet than she'd expected after years without practice, she moved gracefully through the steps and was disappointed when the music ended.

"I'd better move along so other men can have a chance," Simon said, escorting her to the side of the room.

Within moments, a gentleman took her back out onto the dance floor. After that, her evening was a whirlwind of partners, music, and dances. From the corner of her mind she heard echoes of those two precious balls with Robert, but the memories only added to her enjoyment of tonight. Through the dancing crowd she caught glimpses of Simon, who had partners for every song. As interesting as her own partners were, she'd have preferred dancing with him. When it was time for the supper dance, Simon appeared at her side.

He offered her his arm. "Enjoying yourself?"

"Oh, yes!" She wrapped both hands around his elbow. "Very much. I'm glad you talked me into coming."

"Did I? I wasn't under the impression that I'm ever able to talk you into anything."

She laughed gaily and leaned into him. "You know you are."

He smiled. "Do you want to stay for supper or go home?"

"I don't mind staying a bit longer."

They went into the supper room, where they were seated at a table with a number of other guests. Throughout the meal Isabel chatted with their tablemates, and by the time the meal was over she'd made good progress in getting to know her neighbors, even promising to call on two of the women next month after she returned from the horse fair. There wasn't much chance of speaking to Simon, but she heard him among the rumble of men's voices at the table. When supper ended, he came and pulled her chair out for her.

"Perhaps one more dance?" he asked.

She smiled. "Yes, please. One more."

They took their places in the ballroom, and when the music started Simon took her into his arms, his eyes on hers. She couldn't remember the last time he'd been so relaxed and happy. Not that he was usually *un*happy, but there was a light in his eyes as if he hadn't a care in the world. The mood was infectious, and they laughed and talked through the dance.

On the ride home, Isabel sank into the cushions and gazed out the window. Stars glistened in a clear sky, and the moon shone bright as day. Before long they reached Ridgefield.

As they walked into the parlor, Isabel turned to Simon with a tired smile. "What an enjoyable evening."

"It was," he said, taking her hand, "I think Henry would have liked the music."

"We won't go to a ball again until he's old enough to come with us," she said, brown eyes sparkling.

"I see," he said with a grin. "You enjoyed yourself, yet are happy to wait another ten years for the next one?"

She laughed. "Maybe not ten. Five?" She sat in one of the chairs flanking the fireplace and removed her wrap while Simon poured out two glasses of brandy.

"I have a better idea." He handed her a glass. "We'll host a ball here."

"That's a perfect idea. Perhaps for Christmas next year."

"You'll have plenty of time to plan your gown, though I must say you looked ravishing tonight, even with only *two* days to prepare." He settled into the chair opposite hers and crossed his legs, then gave her a wide smile and raised his glass in a toast.

She clinked her glass on his. "Thank you, Simon."

They stayed up late discussing the ball and coming up with ideas for their own. Isabel eased back into her chair, sipping her brandy and gazing into the fire. This was the perfect way to finish her reentry into society. Wishing she could sleep right here in front of the hearth, she reluctantly rose some time later. "It's time I was in bed. I'm tired from all that dancing," she said through a barely stifled yawn.

"Yes, I am too." Simon stood and moved to her side. They looked into the fire for a moment, not speaking. Isabel gave Simon's fingers a squeeze and turned to leave.

But he didn't release her hand. Instead, he drew her to him. He stood before her for a heartbeat, eyes blazing. Then she was in his arms. Simon kissed her feverishly, hungrily, his whole body pressed against hers. Isabel responded. Without thinking, she responded. Her arms went around his neck, her kisses meeting his, and Simon let out a sigh of what could have been triumph. Isabel lost herself for a few moments—a part of her wanted to be lost.

But then reality crashed in on her. She pushed against Simon and took a step back. He stood before her, breathing heavily as he stared into her face. Isabel leaned on a chair to steady herself and wiped her mouth with the back of her shaking hand.

"Isabel…" Simon said, taking a step forward.

She put her hand up to ward him off. "Don't," she said firmly. "Do not come near me."

His hazel eyes seemed to drink her in as he spoke. "Isabel, I've loved you for so long. While I was in Holton I realized that I must tell you how I feel."

"Simon, you understood when we married—"

"Listen to me, please," he begged.

"Very well." She clasped her shaking hands in front of her.

"I know how you feel about Robert. That he's still your husband. But Isabel…" Simon looked as though he were steeling himself to speak. "Robert is dead. He's gone," he said almost apologetically.

"I am well aware Robert is gone," she said through tight lips.

"Is it not time you release him?"

Something melted inside. "Oh, Simon, I don't know if I ever can."

"Would you try? You've been happy here with me, and with Henry. Our son."

"He is Robert's son."

Simon stepped back as though Isabel had slapped him. He took a deep breath and continued, "But I'm all the father Henry knows. And I love you. I cherish you."

He went to Isabel and put his hands on her shoulders.

Isabel saw the love for her in his eyes. How had she never noticed it before? It was so obvious now that she knew it was there. She leaned into him, and he wrapped his arms around her. A most peculiar, long-dormant flutter in her chest almost stopped her breath. Oh, to be held! To be loved! Isabel surrendered herself to the beauty of it. When Simon bent to kiss her again, she lifted her face to his. This kiss was soft, sweet, and tender, like being enfolded in his love.

She allowed herself only moments before pulling away. "Simon, I do care about you—"

The light in his eyes dimmed. "But not like Robert."

"I will never love anyone the way I loved Robert."

He blanched and stumbled back.

"Simon, I—" She stopped when she heard how pitying her voice sounded. He must have noticed it too, for he straightened to his full height, cleared his throat, and gave her a short nod.

"Forgive me. I shouldn't have spoken." He half-ran

from the room.

She stared after him. Good God. What had he done? What had *she* done? Isabel sank into a chair, put her hands over her face, and wept. Before long a horse thundered out of the stables—Simon was going out alone into the night because of her. She rose and went upstairs.

In her bedroom, Isabel sat in the window seat, watching the night sky. Simon was out there somewhere, probably chastising himself. But how could he blame himself, when she had yielded? She hated to admit it, but yielded willingly. She was in truth more angry with herself than with him. She'd seen it in his eyes, in that split second before he kissed her. She'd had a chance to move away, to protest. But she hadn't. What did Simon mean to her? What could he come to mean to her? Isabel undressed and climbed into bed. She blew out the candles and lay for a long time, searching for answers in the dark.

Chapter Nineteen

The next morning, Isabel's first thought was Simon. She must speak to him, but first she needed to wake Henry up. She dressed and went to his room, where he greeted her with a happy, "Good morning, Mama."

When he was dressed she took him by the hand and listened to him chatter all the way to the dining room. Isabel wondered how Simon would react to her after what had happened last night.

She needn't have worried. He was nowhere to be seen.

"Where's Papa?" Henry asked, looking around the room.

"Perhaps he's gone for a ride."

"I'll get my pony," Henry said. "I'll ride fast and catch up to him."

"You'll do no such thing. You will eat your breakfast."

"Where's Mr. Kensington?" Isabel asked a footman as he placed platters of food on the table.

"I haven't seen him, ma'am."

"Please find out where he's gone."

The footman left the room, and was gone for what felt like hours before he returned.

"The groom tells me Mr. Kensington rode out late last night. He left no word of where he was going or when he would return."

She nodded, dismissing him.

Isabel pushed her plate away and sipped her coffee. Where had he gone? Had her rejection driven him away from her? It was a thought too painful to bear. She depended on him more than he knew. Perhaps even more than she herself had known until now.

Simon didn't return that day, or the next. It was four days later when he finally came home.

Isabel had kissed Henry goodnight and was sitting beside the library fire when the dogs began barking outside. A horse galloped toward the stables; at this hour it could only be Simon. She sat up a little straighter in her chair and put a hand to her hair to be sure it was in place.

Isabel shouldn't tell Simon how empty the house had been without him, how much she'd missed talking to him, being with him. She'd missed their games of backgammon, their frequent laughter, and simply knowing he was in the house or about the grounds. She definitely couldn't tell him how often her thoughts had strayed back to that kiss and to the embraces they'd shared. Such thoughts she must now keep locked up, lest they lead him to false hope.

But was it a false hope? His declaration had thrown her into a tumult of confused thoughts and conflicting emotions. She loved Simon. But was it the right kind of love? Enough to truly be his wife? The very thought felt like a betrayal of Robert. But wouldn't he want her to be happy? Would he expect her to mourn for the rest of her life, never seeking love again? She thought of him daily—he'd never really left her. But it had been five long years since they'd been together. She'd lived with Simon longer than she'd even known Robert, and they shared a deep and loving friendship. The question was, could it ever be more? Did she want more? She wasn't in love with Simon, but she trusted him, loved him and cherished him. It was more than many women could say about a second husband, or even a first. If she opened her heart, wasn't it possible they could grow into much more than friends? She must see him.

She rang a bell, and after a few minutes the butler appeared.

"Mr. Kensington has returned?"

"Yes, ma'am. He looked in on Henry, and just sent for a supper tray in his room."

"Thank you." So he'd avoided her, purposefully not coming to the library because he knew she was there. Isabel supposed that was his right, after the way she'd spoken to him. And he may be unsure if she even wanted his company. Isabel sat long by the fire, waiting in vain for him to come down, before eventually going to bed, a dull ache in her heart.

Isabel lay in bed for hours, but it was no use. Sleep would not come. She threw back the covers and paced her bedroom before leaning against the window, watching clouds pass over the sliver of a moon. She could wait no longer. Putting on a dressing gown against the cold, she picked up a candle and silently made her way through the dark corridor.

Simon was stretched out on his bed, still in the clothes he'd worn to the ball. Isabel walked in, locking the door behind her. She set the candle on his nightstand and whispered his name.

He sat bolt upright as if a loud bell had pealed. "What is it? Is Henry unwell?"

"It's not Henry." She perched on the edge of the bed.

"Where have you been?"

Simon shrugged. "It doesn't matter."

"It matters to me."

He just shrugged again and climbed out of bed.

Isabel frowned. Good gracious. Where *had* he been? A tavern? A brothel?

He crossed the room to the basin and splashed his face with water, then took his jacket off and turned to face her as he removed his cravat. "You're here about what happened the other night."

"Yes."

"I thought—"

"Simon, let me speak."

He nodded. She'd never have believed such a guarded look from those eyes could be directed at her. But no matter. Her next words would change them instantly.

"When you kissed me, I admit I was taken off guard. It was unexpected and yet—" She paused and pushed a strand of hair behind her ear.

"And yet?" He dropped the cravat on the floor and watched her intently as he approached the bed.

She looked down at her lap, her face turning pink. "It felt natural. And…and pleasant."

The bed creaked as he sat beside her.

Isabel's heart pounded as she met his eyes and spoke the words she could never take back. "Simon, I've been considering being your wife in truth."

An elated smile came to his face as hope sprang into his eyes.

"You must understand," she said emphatically. "Robert is the keeper of my heart, my soul, my very existence."

"But Robert is gone." He shook his head. "I don't know why I acted so rashly the other night. I should have spoken to you long before now."

"You've been closer to me than any other man, save Robert. We've lived together for years. I've been with you, in fact, longer than any time I spent with Robert. You and I have raised a child together. Oh, don't you see? Of course we love each other, and are drawn to each other. We're tied together, you and I, for all of our lives. But not in the same way as Robert and I."

"But Robert won't come back. I'm here. I'm ready to love you, always," Simon said earnestly, tentatively reaching for her hand. She entwined her fingers with his.

Isabel weighed her words carefully before she spoke. "Simon, I love Robert. I will always love Robert."

He nodded. "I would be your second choice, but I'd accept that."

"You would be much more than my second choice. I care deeply for you. But I can't help thinking that if I'm your true wife I would be betraying my own soul."

"I'll help heal your soul. Let me try. Please."

He must have seen her resolve waver, for he gave her a questioning look and, when she nodded, took her into his arms. She wrapped her arms around him and leaned against his chest, listening to his unfamiliar heartbeat. He took her face in his hands and kissed her gently. It awakened feelings she'd never thought to have again. She abruptly pulled away and stood up.

Simon looked at her quizzically.

"I'm not ready. Not yet."

"But you will be?" he asked hopefully.

"I would remain as we have been for at least a while longer. I won't come to you with Robert between us. It would mean saying goodbye to him, but perhaps it's time," she said, stumbling over the words as tears came to her eyes. "Oh! I am torn in two."

"But you love me? You do love me?"

"I do." She could not deny this truth.

"As a...as a lover?"

"I believe I could, in time," Isabel said, meeting his eyes. "But I won't hurry into anything."

Simon held her gaze. "I'm patient."

She wrung her hands. "I don't want to get your hopes up. I cannot say for certain—"

He nodded in understanding. "You don't know if you can let Robert go. But you're going to try, and if you do...if you do, we'll be together."

"Yes."

The look in his eyes told her he had no doubt she would one day be his true wife. She kissed him lightly on the cheek before getting up and swiftly leaving the room.

****

Simon didn't press Isabel, but she noticed him watching her speculatively at times over the next few weeks. She was at a crossroads. In one direction, the future; in the other, the past. Letting go of Robert felt like base betrayal, and she felt guilty even contemplating loving Simon. And yet there was something there. Something solid, something real. Simon was no ghost but a real man. Though it grieved her to acknowledge it, Robert was no more than a memory now.

She'd spoken the truth when she told Simon she could love him. She already did, as a friend. But was it enough? Could it ever truly be more? What kind of love could she have with him if she was "choosing" or "trying" to love him? Falling in love with Robert had been gloriously inevitable. A flood, an avalanche, a force of nature that swept her away. They were entwined like clouds and the sky, waves and the sea. Simply a part of each other.

She didn't begin to consider that she could have that with Simon. But what would happen if she allowed herself to be swept away again? Perhaps not so far, not so deep, not so completely. But there was no reason she and Simon couldn't have a steady, loving, happy marriage for years to come.

They set out for the horse fair on a fine spring morning, Henry riding with Simon on Apollo. Simon never seemed to tire of answering Henry's questions about everything he saw, or listening to his thoughts about the pony he'd be getting. As Isabel watched them, she imagined holding another newborn in her arms, perhaps with Simon's hazel eyes. Henry would have brothers and sisters. The idea tugged at her heart.

The afternoon turned into a cool evening, and soon campfires sprang to life up ahead. Tents stretched as far as the eye could see, horses neighed and whinnied from all directions.

They stopped at the Robin's Nest Inn on the edge of the fairgrounds to inquire about rooms.

"Welcome," said the innkeeper when they arrived, "I'm Mr. Biddlecombe."

"We'd like two rooms for the night," Isabel said.

"Two? Let me see…we have a large attic room, and a small chamber just across the hall."

"The small room will be fine for me," Simon said. "My wife and son will take the larger."

"Very well," Mr. Biddlecombe said. He gestured to

a pretty young woman. "Nan, take these people to the attic rooms."

"Yes, Father."

The room for Isabel and Henry overlooked the bustling fairgrounds in a neighboring field. Simon tucked Henry into bed, where he fell asleep at once. He kissed him lightly on the brow and covered him with a blanket.

"I'd like some hot water, please," Isabel told Nan.

"Yes, ma'am," said Nan. She gestured to Simon. "Your room's across the hall, sir."

Simon turned to Isabel. "I'll be back in a few minutes."

A jealous twinge grew in her stomach as Nan led Simon from the room, hips swaying provocatively. They'd only been gone a few moments when, on impulse, Isabel stood and followed them. Nan's lilting voice halted when she appeared in the doorway, and Simon gave Isabel a quizzical look.

"I'd like to see your room," Isabel said with a shrug.

Nan, who'd been standing much closer to Simon than necessary, took a few steps back and bumped into the washstand, knocking over an empty pitcher. She picked it up, her face scarlet.

Isabel said, "Thank you. Now, if you could please bring the water to our other room?"

Nan glanced sideways at Simon, then seemed to deflate slightly. "Yes. Right away." She tromped out of the room and down the stairs.

Isabel walked in and sat on the bed. "You'll be comfortable here."

"I'm sure I will be." He crossed his arms and raised his brows at her, a smile spreading across his face.

She attempted an innocent look, but finally said, "Well, she knows you're married."

"I have a feeling I'll be seeing her again. She left ample hints about warming my bed."

"I doubt she'll try that now."

He laughed. "Now that she knows I have a jealous wife?"

"I'm not—" She broke off, laughing. If she *was* jealous, was it a sign that she could fall in love with Simon one day?

"I have a simple solution. I'll bolt my door."

"I would if I were you. Of course, she might have a key." Isabel rose from the bed. "I'd better check on Henry."

She moved about her room quietly, careful not to wake him. Before long, Nan returned with hot water. Neither woman spoke a word as she set the pitcher on the table and left. Soon after, a light tap came on the door.

"Simon?"

"Who else?" She could hear the smile in his voice.

When he came in, he went immediately to Henry and lightly kissed his forehead. Isabel and Simon stood side by side, watching him sleep.

After a few minutes Simon whispered, "If you need anything I'm right across the hall." He kissed Isabel's cheek and their eyes locked, an unfamiliar racing in her heart. She fought back the urge to take his hand, to draw him in. It wasn't time. Not yet. She wouldn't do anything until she was absolutely certain.

"Good night, Simon."

"Sleep well," he replied, and returned to his room.

Isabel was up before dawn. She stayed in bed, appreciating the last luxurious moments before the busy day began. With a start she realized the date. May Day. Five years ago she'd woken at Verity's house, excited for a day at Thornwood. Little had she known she was about to meet her love, her destiny. She remembered Robert's smiling eyes, his hand on her waist as they danced.

"Good morning, Mama," Henry said, stirring Isabel from her memories. He knelt on a chair beside the window, watching the scene below.

"Good morning. Perhaps we'll find your pony today. Now come and dress."

A little while later, Simon entered. "Who is ready for horses?"

"Me!" Henry shouted.

"After breakfast we'll find the perfect pony," Simon said.

"I want a gray one, like Apollo."

"That's what you'll have, even if it takes all day," Simon assured him.

"If we can find one," Isabel said. "We'll see what's available."

"Papa says we will have a gray, so we'll have gray," Henry said with confidence.

After breakfast, they walked around the fair, Isabel and Simon trailing along behind Henry, who stopped every few feet to look at the booths and marvel at new sights and sounds. They continued on to a field where the horse sellers were located.

"What he really needs is a strong horse," Simon said.

"He's too young for a horse," Isabel protested.

"No, he isn't. He's been riding ponies since he was almost three years old. It's time for him to take the next step."

"Perhaps," Isabel replied, still unsure.

"We'll start him out on a lead. He'll be perfectly safe."

Isabel sighed. Simon was most likely right.

After searching for some time, Henry was drawn to a gray palfrey with a mane and tail the color of straw. Simon helped him mount, took the horse's bridle, and led them in a circle. Isabel kept her eyes on her son, confident and strong in the saddle. Simon was right. Henry was ready for this, even if she wasn't.

"I want to ride her all day," Henry said as he dismounted.

"They'll take her back to the inn and stable her with Apollo. Tonight you can feed her a carrot before you go to bed, and tomorrow you'll ride her home," Isabel told him.

"By myself?"

"With Papa's help."

Henry ran over to see his horse one more time, and then they wandered through the fair, stopping now and again to watch musicians or visit a merchant's stall.

"I want to get these for my horse, Mama," Henry said to Isabel as he stopped to look at some leather saddlebags.

"I'm sure she'd like that. And you'll need to think of a name for her."

"Oh, yes, she must have a name."

She smiled as his brow immediately furrowed the way it did when he was studying his letters.

"Shall we go see that your horse is settled?" Simon asked.

Henry didn't answer and Isabel knew he was still busy thinking up names. She took his hand and held out her other to Simon, who entwined his fingers with hers. By the time they arrived at the stable to visit Stardust, as Henry had named his horse, the boy was exhausted.

Just outside the inn, Simon put a hand on Henry's shoulder and met Isabel's eyes. "I think someone could use some quiet time."

"I think you're right," she said as Henry yawned hugely. "Perhaps after a rest we could go out again. There's an archery range I'd like to try my hand at."

"Why don't you go by yourself, and I'll take Henry back to the room."

"Yes, I'll do that. I may look around the fair some more. I could use a new quiver."

"Take your time. I don't think we'll be going out again today," Simon said, and they both looked at Henry, whose eyelids were drooping.

"I'll most likely be back by suppertime. If not, you should eat without me."

"We'll wait." Simon smiled and turned away, leading Henry by the hand. She sighed. He was a good man.

Isabel meandered through the fair, visiting some booths to buy gifts—for Henry a wooden top decorated with fish, for Simon a green waistcoat that matched the gown she'd worn to the Darlingtons' ball, and for herself a new quiver. After arranging to have them delivered to the inn, she set out for the archery range.

On her way she passed the maypole, ribbons swirling in the breeze. She picked one up and closed her eyes, recalling that other May Day, a lifetime ago.

At the archery range Isabel spent a happy hour hitting every target and afterward struck up a conversation with the other archers. By that time, dusk was falling; it was time to join Simon and Henry for supper.

As she walked back to the inn, her heart gave a sudden lurch, and she tripped, nearly colliding with the person in front of her. In the flickering torchlight a man in the crowd looked so much like Robert he could have been his twin. Well, an identical twin. Goodness knows she didn't want to see another William. The past was indeed with her today.

Halfway to the Robin's Nest, she stopped to buy sweetmeats to bring back as a treat. When she returned, she'd talk to Simon about staying on another day at the fair. Henry was enjoying himself, and leisure time with Simon was easier here than at Ridgefield, where there were so many demands on him.

Isabel looked to her left, where a gibbous moon reflected on the dark lake. She made her way to the shore and sat on a bench close to the water. Folding her hands in her lap, she let out a long, contented sigh. It was a perfect evening. Perhaps after Henry was asleep she'd invite Simon out for a moonlit walk.

The minutes ticked by as she sat listening to the night sounds—birds calling to each other, a minstrel playing his lute somewhere close by, and countless whinnies and neighs coming from the horses in the big field.

Just as she'd decided to make for the inn, Isabel heard light footsteps approaching from behind. Probably a person or couple that wanted the bench. She stood and picked up her parcel.

"Isabel?"

She'd heard of flesh creeping before but had never understood what it meant until now. From head to toe her skin tingled, and she was overcome with an alarming sense of vertigo. The voice had sounded so much like Robert's. She shook her head.

"Isabel?" the voice, cracking, said again.

She fell back onto the bench, her heart hammering. Who here would know her name? She was about to look behind her, but there was no need. The footsteps crept closer until someone stood before her. It was an eternity before her eyes made their way from his feet to his face.

Chapter Twenty

Everything stopped. Her world reeled as she tried to comprehend what she was seeing. What she *couldn't* be seeing. For there, standing before her, was Robert.

"Isabel?"

He stretched out a hand, but she leaped to her feet and backed away. What was this? Had her mind snapped? Had she lost her reason? She put a hand to her forehead.

He took a step closer. Lanterns from a nearby tent illuminated him as he stepped into the light.

"What? How?" She peered into his face, her eyes narrowed. "Robert? *Robert?*"

His voice broke as he spoke. "It's me."

"But...but it can't be you." Her breath came in ragged gasps and she clutched her chest, rooted to the earth as he stepped closer. Now she could see his eyes. His eyes. Henry's eyes. Robert's eyes.

He held out a trembling hand. Isabel reached hesitantly, as if trying to force her hand into a roaring fire. When their fingers finally touched, lightning bolted through her.

"Robert!" she shrieked and flung herself into his arms. She clutched at him, pulling him closer. His strong arms were truly around her, his breath on her hair. Solid. Real. Alive. *Alive.* They clung to one another in disbelief. She pulled away just enough to look at his face. "Robert,

Robert," she whispered shakily. She took a step back, keeping his hands in hers. She searched the beloved face. Changes, yes. The passing of years. A scar that was not there before. But still her Robert. Nobody else had ever looked at her that way.

"Isabel, my heart, my love." His voice was music and sunshine and glorious starry nights. It pierced through to her soul. Her knees failed her and she sank to the ground, her entire body shaking as she fought off encroaching dizziness. He was beside her in an instant. She broke out in spontaneous laughter and sobs, impatiently wiping away the tears that prevented her seeing his face.

"My God. My God. Robert!"

He lifted her onto the bench, sat beside her, and wrapped an arm around her shoulders. She ran her hands over him, reassuring herself that he was real. Her fingers lingered on his face as he smiled through streaming tears.

"How? How are you here?" she finally asked.

"I would ask the same of you. I thought you were dead." He took her hand between his own, brought it to his lips, and kissed it. The look of disbelieving amazement on his face was surely a mirror of her own.

"I thought *you* were dead. All these long years—we could have been together! You must tell me what happened."

"In a moment. Or an hour. Or a day. Right now, I only want to look at you."

She was happy enough to comply. They stared into each other's faces, touching each other constantly to convince themselves they weren't dreaming. It was some time before the tears had dried on their cheeks.

Isabel noticed the fair around them had quieted.

She'd forgotten where they were. What was the time? Supper? Past that? She hoped Simon wasn't worried. Simon. She spared one moment of her bliss to realize that Robert's return would shatter his dreams of her ever becoming his wife. The marriage they went through hadn't been valid, as she had a husband living. *Living.* But that was for later. For now, there was only this miracle. Robert had returned to her.

"Tell me how this happened. Where have you been?" she asked.

A cloud passed over his face. "I don't like thinking about that day. Especially now. If I'd known you lived, I would have found you."

"We can't look back. We're together again, that's all that matters."

Robert took a steadying breath. "That day at the river, I thought I would die. I woke and you were gone. I assumed you were dead, that the river had taken you. I lay unconscious for hours on the riverbank until William found me, far downstream from where we jumped."

"William!" Isabel exclaimed. "It's William who is partially to blame for our misery. If he hadn't been trying to keep us apart, none of this would have happened. We would have been together all this time."

"I know, Isabel. He's felt such remorse. He's been kind to me. He found me a place to live and made certain I was well supported and cared for."

"Forgiveness doesn't come so easily for me. But I'll try, for your sake. Go on with your story. How did he find you?"

"I don't remember any of it. William told me later I was incoherent when he found me in the middle of the night. I was delirious, feverish for days. I had a deep gash in my leg that took weeks to heal. There's still a scar there. I had broken ribs and too many bruises and cuts to count. It's truly a wonder I survived. William, Edmund, and his friend Dr. Nobles nursed me back to health. I spent the first few days in the ruins of the abbey, but then they moved me to Dr. Nobles' home in Salisbury. If not for his prodigious skills, I doubt I would have made it. Edmund and William feared for my life."

"The abbey! It's not an hour's walk from the cottage."

"I know. At the time, I was barely conscious and hardly aware of where I was. It was only later I realized they could have taken me to the cottage instead, if only I'd been alert enough to show them the way."

She didn't bother telling him what he would have found if he'd gone there. "Why didn't you go home?"

Robert laughed harshly. "I had no home. I blamed William for our separation, and I was furious with my father. I wanted no part of either of them. I wanted no life without you. If I'd gone back, they would have insisted I marry Margery. With you—" He closed his eyes as if remembering the pain of Isabel's loss, "…gone…I didn't think I had the strength to resist them anymore, but I could never be with anyone else after what I shared with you. I let everyone in Holton believe I was dead."

Their stories were virtually the same. If only one of them had come out of hiding! Surely they would have been reunited long before now…

Isabel touched the scar on his jaw. "Where have you been all these years?"

"I spent almost a year recovering at Dr. Nobles'. He helped keep my survival a secret. He's a good man.

When I was well enough, I moved to a small house by the sea. I led a solitary life there. It was what I wanted."

"You've been alone, all this time?"

"Yes, though Edmund and William visited me when they could. They pressured me to go home, but I never would."

Isabel wrapped her arms around him. "You won't be alone anymore."

They sat in blissful silence for a time. Finally, Robert asked, "And what of you? What happened that day?"

"I don't like to think of that day. I would have died there by the river, but Simon found me and—"

"Simon? So we both had people watching over us. Strange that William didn't come upon you in his search for me."

"Simon found me the next morning, but William rescued you the night we jumped. Maybe he missed me in the dark, or perhaps I was still in the river or on the opposite bank. Simon came out at dawn to search. He let his men think I was dead and left me by the river, but told me to meet him at the cottage. After he waited for hours, I still hadn't made it there, so he searched the woods for me. I was weak and could barely walk because of my injuries. He carried me to the cottage, and there he tended me until I was well."

His eyes widened. "The cottage. Our cottage? You were there the whole time? And I was but an hour away…"

She nodded. Dwelling on the fact was pointless and could only cause them regret.

Robert must have felt the same way, for instead of saying more about it, he asked, "Why would he tell them you were dead?"

"Everyone assumed we died together in the falls. Simon thought the men of Thornwood would take revenge on me if they'd known I was alive. We knew I'd be safer if nobody was searching for me anymore."

Robert shook his head. "What I owe to him," he said, and kissed her hand. "Why didn't you return home?"

"I was afraid. I knew my stepfather would never stop hunting me if he knew I was alive. If he'd caught me, I would have been married to Marcus. And, honestly, there was nothing in Holton or Salisbury for me. With you gone, my home was gone. I made plans to go overseas."

"But you came back, thankfully. Where did you go?"

"Oh, I changed my plans. It didn't work out." If he noticed the strained look in her eyes, he didn't say so. She had to tell him about Simon and, most importantly, about Henry. But she longed for just a little more time with no complications, only this sweet reunion.

"I'm glad. We may never have found each other if you'd stayed overseas."

"How did you know I was here?" she asked to change the subject.

He smiled. "The archery range. I was watching the archers, and I saw a woman who looked remarkably like you. I thought it was just a coincidence. But when I was walking through the crowd later, I passed you. I still couldn't believe it, but I had to know for sure. I followed you here."

"I saw you! It gave me such a start because you looked so much like, well, yourself. I thought I was imagining the man looked like you, because you've been on my mind all day."

"Have I?" His eyes sparkled as he brushed her hair back from her face. A thrill went through her at his touch.

She lifted her shoulders. "It's May Day."

"The day we met. And the day you came back to me."

They reached for each other at the same moment, and Robert's deep blue eyes swam with tears as he took her face in his hands and slowly, reverently, bent to kiss her. She raised her face to his, heart pounding, head swimming. When their lips met, she came back to life. A warm glow rushed through her and the years apart disappeared as if they had never been. Isabel could have danced, sung, perhaps even flown. *Robert.* Her Robert. She ran her hands over his shoulders, his back, his muscular arms, breathing in his familiar, perfect scent. His hands were on her face, her waist, entwined in her hair. He kissed her until she was breathless, and then kissed her some more. She could have gone on like this for hours if the sudden clanging of a bell hadn't interrupted them.

They broke apart reluctantly, faces flushed, beaming at each other.

Robert sighed. "Midnight."

"Is it? I've lost track of how many times the bells have rung." She'd lost track of everything.

"At any rate, it's late. I never asked…how did you come to be here? Are you here by yourself?"

Isabel's stomach churned. Now was the time to tell him. That she was married. That he had a son. He'd be thrilled about Henry. But what of Simon? If he thought of it as a betrayal, she could lose him all over again. If she could have kept her marriage to Simon a secret, she would have. But it had to come out.

She took a deep breath and met his eyes. "Well, actually, I'm here with Simon."

"Simon!" Robert's face lit up. "Where is he? I can hardly wait to see him. How did you end up traveling together? Weren't you in hiding?"

"For a time, yes. You remember I told you he saved me and took me to the cottage?" Her mouth was suddenly dry.

He nodded.

"I—I've been with him ever since."

"*With* him?" His brow furrowed.

There was no easy way to say it. "We're married. He and I have been raising our son."

All the color drained from Robert's face, except his eyes, which were stormy. When he stood up his sudden absence cut like a knife.

"Married? Your son?" He grimaced and rubbed his forehead.

"Let me explain!" she said as he started backing away.

"It's all right. I understand. You thought I was gone and you…" He swallowed as though about to be sick. "You fell in love with—with Simon. You should have told me sooner. I shouldn't be carrying on so and kissing you. A married woman. I thought I'd found you again, but I've only lost you a second time." His face crumpled as he collapsed on the bench, his face in his hands.

"No, no! It isn't like that. We are married in name only. Robert, look at me."

He did not.

"Robert?" She took his hands, which had gone cold,

and began to speak, though he kept his eyes focused on the ground.

"Simon is my friend, and we have been raising *our* son—yours and mine."

His head jerked up, light flooding back into his eyes. "A son? *We* have a son?"

"His name is Robert Henry, after you, but we call him Henry. He has your eyes, and your smile. He's the sweetest, smartest boy."

"A son," he said under his breath.

"He's here with us. You'll be able to meet him." The meeting she'd never imagined would happen.

Robert's forehead wrinkled. "But what's this about you and Simon? Why are you married? Have you and he… Are you…"

It looked like he couldn't bring himself to say the words, so Isabel continued.

"Please don't be angry. Simon saved my life. When we knew a baby was coming, we moved to Ridgefield. In the beginning, we only pretended to be married, but when Henry was born I did marry him, to give Henry a name. As far as we knew, you were dead, and I could never go back to Holton. Mr. Branwick would surely have found me there. Staying in Ridgefield with Simon, living as his wife, was the best thing I could do for Henry. He's such a strong, happy boy. Simon is known as my husband, but there's nothing between us. I love him as a friend." She didn't tell Robert what had almost happened between her and Simon, and shuddered to think how close she'd come to giving up Robert.

"So Simon's taken my place with our son, but not my place in your heart?" he asked hopefully.

"Nobody could take your place. My heart has been

yours since the day we met, and it always will be. Simon knows that. He's been my dearest friend through the years, and he's devoted to Henry. He's been a wonderful father to him and we couldn't have had a better protector. But now that will be over. You're alive. My marriage to Simon cannot be valid, for I already had another husband living." Isabel savored the words. Living. A husband living.

"I'm not angry, now that you've explained. I will owe Simon for the rest of my life." He paused and said again, wonderingly, "A son."

"I'd stay here with you forever, if I could, but Simon will be wondering where I am. I told him I'd be back in time for supper, which was hours ago."

"And the boy? Henry?"

"I'm sure he's fast asleep. But you will meet him tomorrow. You'll see them both tomorrow. If it weren't so late, I'd take you up now. Simon will be so happy! But also shocked. Even with you sitting beside me, holding me, I have a hard time believing you're really here. I think it's best if I explain to Simon tonight, and you can come to us in the morning. We'll make our plans then." She vaguely wondered if she was insane, willingly separating from Robert when she'd just found him again. But no. There was a certainty deep within her that they'd never be truly parted again. All the same, she threw her arms around him and buried her face in his shoulder.

His arms encircled her, he lifted her off her feet and kissed her deeply. Then he laughed.

She smiled. "What is it?"

"When I woke up this morning the only thing on my mind was if I'd find a decent horse at the fair. And here I am, holding you in my arms. The love of my life, the other half of my soul. My dear, sweet wife. Isabel, are we dreaming? I dreamed of you so many times over the years, only to wake up with empty arms."

Tears started in her eyes. "We aren't dreaming. I'm here. We'll be together for the rest of our lives." She rose on her toes and brought her lips to his in a tender kiss.

As they walked back to the inn, Isabel kept looking sideways at Robert to be certain he was still there. His hand in hers was proof enough, but still too fantastic to be a waking truth. Just outside the Robin's Nest, Isabel stopped and turned to him.

"Henry is your son, but please understand he's spent his entire life believing Simon is his father. I'll tell him the truth, in my way, when the time is right."

He nodded. "I'll do whatever you think best. But I'll be able to see him, talk to him?"

"Yes. He's a bit shy with new people, but he will warm up with time."

"How will I stand the hours away from you?" Robert asked, taking her into his arms.

"I wish I knew. I'm certain I won't sleep a wink tonight." She leaned on him for a few moments before pulling away but kept his hands in hers. "Where are you staying?"

"In the field yonder." He pointed toward the field just outside the inn. "I pitched my tent on the other side, close to the trees. I was worried I'd be recognized by somebody from Holton and only came out when the sun went down."

"I didn't even think of running into anyone from Holton. We're so far away it didn't cross my mind. I must be more cautious while we're here. So you're still hiding?"

"I have been, yes. But now that I have you again, that will change. Everything will change."

"One thing hasn't changed. My love for you," she said, and kissed him.

"Mine has changed," he said, staring into her eyes. "It's deeper and stronger than ever. I love you, Isabel."

She could have wept with joy to hear those words from that voice. "I love you, Robert."

They embraced, and after one last kiss, Robert walked away into the darkness. Just before he disappeared, he turned back. "I'll see you in the morning. You may depend on that."

"Goodnight, my love," she said, reaching her hand out to him, and he was gone.

Isabel stood outside for a long time after he'd gone, putting off the moment when she would tell Simon. He'd be over the moon to find out Robert was alive, but it would be an end to their life together. An end to his hopes of her becoming his wife. She took a deep breath and went inside. Waiting wouldn't make it any easier.

The inn was dark and silent. The only light came from a fire in the common room. What time was it? One o'clock? Two? She picked up a lit candle from the mantel, crept upstairs to her room, and opened the door slowly.

Her heart pattered at the sight that greeted her. Simon lay on top of the bed, Henry curled at his side, both fast asleep. She took her shoes off and crossed the room to the window. A few campfires still glowed in the field below. One of them was Robert's. If only she knew which one. Strange to think she'd overlooked the field this morning and he'd been out there somewhere.

"Isabel?" Simon's sleepy voice said from behind

her.

She jumped. "Oh, you startled me. I thought you were sleeping."

"I was. What time is it?" he whispered, rubbing his eyes and sitting up carefully so as not to disturb Henry.

"I'm not sure. Late."

"Has something happened?" he asked, looking into her face. "You look...different."

"Yes. Yes, something's happened. We need to talk. Right away."

Hope leapt into his eyes. *Oh, no.* He must think she was going to give him an answer about being his wife. She must tell him at once, much as it would break both their hearts for different reasons. "Not here. Let's go to your room."

He nodded, then lifted Henry gently and put him into the bed, tucking the covers around him. Henry rolled over in his sleep, clutching a blanket Simon had given him when he was a baby.

Simon reached for Isabel's hand, and she took it. For the last time? They crossed the hall to his room, where he moved the clothes off his bed so she could sit down, but she settled herself in the chair. He raised a brow but shrugged and sat on the bed in front of her.

"What do you want to tell me?" he asked eagerly, leaning forward.

"You must prepare yourself for a shock."

His face fell at her tone. "What is it?"

In a sober yet trembling voice she said, "Robert is alive. I've just come from him."

He stared blankly at her. Then he drew his head back, his brow furrowed. "What are you talking about?"

She stood, almost bouncing on her heels. "Robert!

He's alive! He's here. I know it's hard to believe."

"It isn't hard. It's impossible. Do you mean to say you've seen someone who looks like Robert? It's clearly unnerved you." He stood and reached for her.

"No. I have *seen* Robert. Met him, spoken to him, touched him!" Her hands flew to her mouth, joyous tears pricked her eyes, but she held them back for his sake.

Simon shook his head like a bear warding off bees. He stumbled back until he bumped up against the bed and collapsed onto it. He didn't speak for a good three minutes. Isabel waited patiently in the strained silence as his expression flashed between amazement, grief, and sheer bewilderment.

Finally he spoke. "It cannot be. It cannot."

She sat in the chair, placed a hand on his knee and said firmly, "Robert is alive." She met his gaze steadily, trying to convey the truth with her eyes. As the seconds ticked by, his countenance changed from one of incredulity to wonder.

"Where is he?" he asked, his voice thick.

"He's sleeping in the field just outside the inn."

Simon leaped to his feet. "I must go to him. I must see him with my own eyes."

"He'll be back in the morning." She glanced at the sky outside the window. Only a matter of a few hours.

"How on earth is this possible? Tell me everything."

Isabel gave him a brief version of what Robert had told her.

When she finished, he said, "But why isn't he with you?"

"I wanted a chance to tell you before you saw him. It was hard enough for me to believe, even when I heard his voice and held his hand. I wanted to spare you the same shock. And there are some things we must discuss."

"Henry."

Isabel nodded. "I told him what you've done for us, and that you're all Henry knows as a father. I told Robert we'll tell Henry the truth someday, but not any time soon. It would be too much for him to understand."

"Did you tell him we're married?"

"Yes. He didn't like that. But I explained that it was in name only."

Simon frowned. "It was a bit more than that. We've been everything to each other. You, me, and Henry."

"Not quite everything."

Simon's face turned red. "No. Not quite." He sighed. "It's unimaginable."

"Like something out of a dream."

"This will change things. Utterly," he said, his voice hard. "You won't need me now. I'll be cast aside."

"Simon, we'll still need you. You won't lose Henry…or me, for that matter."

"How? How will I not? You're Robert's. You've always been Robert's."

"It's true, I have. You knew that, even when we married."

"Our marriage is no longer valid. You've never been my wife," he said sadly.

Isabel stood and took his hand. "These years with you have been wonderful. You gave me a home, and you've been a father to Henry."

"But I'm not his father. Robert is."

"But Henry doesn't know Robert. He knows only you."

Simon looked into her eyes. "I love you, Isabel. I hoped you could love me, but that is not to be. I can't hold that against you. Robert is back, and it's clear you belong together." He turned away. "But what of Henry? I've raised him as my son. You and Robert will take him, and I'll never see him again," he said in a strangled voice.

"You know me better than that. To Henry you *are* his father. He loves you. I'll tell him the truth at some point, but you'll never be gone from his life." Isabel took Simon's arm, forcing him to look at her. "Do you hear me? Never. I wouldn't do that to either of you."

Simon sat on the edge of the bed and wrapped his arms around Isabel's waist, his head resting against her stomach as she stroked his hair. After a few minutes he gave a deep shuddering sigh and released her, wiping his eyes on his sleeve.

"What must you think of me?" he asked.

She sat beside him. "Don't think I won't grieve for what we've had."

Simon looked at her, surprised. "But Robert is home. You have all you've ever dreamed of."

"That's true, but I've loved the life we made together. Our home, our time together with Henry… I'll miss all of that. I'll miss you."

"Isabel, if Robert hadn't come back, would you…would we have…?"

She hesitated, wondering if it would hurt Simon to know this truth. But what good would it be to keep it a secret from him? "Yes. I'd planned on telling you when we got home that I would be your wife. In all ways."

He winced and let out something between a sigh and a groan. "I was too late."

"No. Even if you and I had been….together…up to now, I'd still have gone back to Robert, which would have hurt all of us more."

"Perhaps," Simon said, though he didn't sound convinced.

"I need to tell Robert about what happened between us."

Simon shook his head. "It would only hurt him. And he won't be so forgiving of me."

"I have to," she insisted. Isabel dreaded breaking the sublime happiness their reunion had brought, but a persistent, irritating thought had been breaking into her mind since she'd returned to the inn. How could she start over with Robert when there was this secret between them?

"He won't like it, Isabel. He'll be angry with both of us. It's in the past. And as we both know, nothing came of it." He frowned and looked away.

"I know. Hopefully he'll understand. I think he will." She bit her bottom lip. He had to.

"We can tell him together tomorrow," Simon said, taking her hand.

"I'll find a moment to tell him myself. I think it will be better that way. Perhaps in a few days."

"All right. Let me know when you've told him. He might want to speak to me."

"I will. I'll explain it all." Talking to Robert was one of her favorite things in the world, but just thinking about that particular conversation filled her with dread.

After sitting in silence for a few minutes, Simon asked softly, "What will I do without you?"

"You'll eventually find a wife. Then you'll have no time for me," Isabel said in as cheery a voice she could muster.

"You know that's untrue."

"It's not. You have so much to offer to someone,

Simon. Truthfully, I've always felt guilty keeping you to myself, keeping you from finding your own true love."

"I've had all that I needed."

"What will you do now? Return to Ridgefield?"

"For the time being. Once you and Robert are settled, I'll move close to you, so I can see Henry often."

"Will you? I'm glad." Her life couldn't be complete without Simon close at hand.

"Do you think you'll go back to Holton?"

"I really have no idea. Robert and I haven't discussed any of it."

They sat together on the bed, holding hands. These were their last moments together as the family they'd known. She put her head on Simon's shoulder and talked about Henry's days as a baby, and their adventures since. They spent a happy hour reminiscing about their time together.

After a time, Simon stood. "We'd better try to get some rest."

Isabel knew she couldn't sleep, but she sensed Simon needed time away from her. "Do you want to go in with Henry?"

He nodded. "What time is Robert coming back?"

"He didn't say. But I expect it will be early." Her heart skipped a beat. She would see him soon.

He opened the door, then stopped and looked back. "What will we tell Henry?"

"The truth, as much as we can. I saw an old friend of ours last night, and he's coming to visit."

Simon nodded and left the room.

Isabel undressed and got into bed. She ran a finger over her lips. Robert had just kissed these lips. Was he awake, thinking of her, out there in his tent somewhere?

She smiled and turned on her side to wait out the rest of this incredible night.

Chapter Twenty-One

The next morning Isabel was surprised to find she'd slept a little. Refreshed, she sat up and stretched, her heart picking up its pace. Would Robert be here soon? She could hardly wait to see his face and hear his voice. She wanted to know more about what he'd been doing during their time apart, and her heart broke when she thought of all he'd endured without her by his side. It broke just as much for Simon. Splitting up their family would be devastating for all of them. There was no other choice now that Robert had returned, but if only there were some way to make it easier.

After dressing, she crossed the hall, where she found Henry and Simon ready for the day.

"Good morning," she said.

"Good morning." Simon's eyes were puffy and he sounded as though he had a cold.

Henry came over and took her hand. "Mama, why did you sleep in Papa's room? You would have fit in the bed with us."

"I meant to, but Papa's bed is so cozy I couldn't help falling asleep in it."

"If it's so cozy, perhaps I'll sleep in it tonight," Henry said thoughtfully.

"We may be back at Ridgefield tonight," Simon said. "Mama and I need to discuss our plans."

"I'd stay here another day," Henry said, "but I do

307

think Stardust will like her stall at home. There are kittens in the barn. She can play with them."

Isabel's and Simon's eyes met over his head and they shared a smile.

She turned to Henry. "Did Papa tell you I saw one of our old friends last night?"

Henry nodded. "A man you used to know, and he'll join us for breakfast."

"Speaking of which," Simon said, "Shall we go down?"

Henry rubbed his stomach. "Yes, I'm hungry."

"So am I." Simon took Henry's hand and, after a watery smile at Isabel, led the way downstairs.

Isabel's stomach was a storm of nerves. Robert could be waiting at the very foot of the stairs. She stopped to glance at herself in the mirror. Did she look that much older? This morning she could have been twenty again. Her eyes were bright and a pink flush softened her face. She wiped her suddenly moist hands on her skirt and followed Henry and Simon.

Robert wasn't there. Isabel asked Mr. Biddlecombe if anyone had asked for them, and he said no.

"Don't worry, I'm sure he'll be here soon," Simon said.

"Yes, of course." She craned her neck to see out the windows.

Mr. Biddlecombe directed them to a private dining chamber, where a crackling fire in the grate cast a warm glow over the room. They'd just taken their seats when Nan served fresh bread and butter, platters of sausage, bacon and eggs, and a tureen of porridge. Simon and Henry took their seats and started breakfast, but Isabel's stomach was in knots. She couldn't possibly eat anything.

"Isabel, have some of this bread, at least. You haven't eaten since yesterday," Simon said, a wistful look in his eyes when they fell upon her. She took the piece he offered her and nibbled at it, her ears straining the whole time for sounds of Robert's arrival.

"When will I see Stardust?" Henry asked.

"I'll take you to the stables right after breakfast," Simon said.

"Here, take one of these apples for her." Isabel picked one from the fruit basket and handed it to Henry.

"One for Apollo, too," Henry said, taking another.

A loud rap sounded on the door and Isabel jumped to her feet, overturning her chair.

Simon hurried to her side and whispered, "Remember, we're greeting an old friend. Nothing more." He glanced pointedly at Henry, who was watching them curiously.

Isabel nodded. "Finish your porridge," she said to Henry before facing the door.

Mr. Biddlecombe entered the room. "Someone asking for the Kensington party. Can I show him in?"

Isabel tried to say yes, but all that came out was a little croak. Her head was buzzing, her heart stampeding in her chest.

"Yes, show him in," Simon said to the innkeeper, who nodded and left the room.

Simon put an arm around Isabel's waist and most likely felt her shivering. She took his hand and met his eyes with a nod. She would hold herself together, for Henry's sake.

The door opened, and there he was. Robert looked even more handsome than he had last night, and somehow taller than she'd remembered. His eyes moved from Simon to Isabel, then lingered on Henry, who hadn't noticed that he'd come in. Isabel righted her chair and sat down, for her shaking legs would no longer support her.

****

Robert stepped into the room and closed the door, heart thundering in his chest. Nobody spoke. A low tension thrummed in the air itself. They were staring at him. Isabel, shining with love. Simon, clearly struggling to accept the truth before his own eyes. The boy, Henry—his son—eating a bowl of porridge, hadn't even looked up. He looked like William with that fair hair. Or Simon, who had his arm wrapped protectively around Isabel. She clutched his hand as if for support. Odd to see them so close together. Before the waterfall, they'd been practically strangers.

His eyes were inexorably drawn back to Isabel. It was impossible to believe she was here in the same room with him. Over the years she'd grown even more beautiful. All he wanted to do was take her in his arms and bury his face in her hair. Last night he'd noticed it smelled the same, a sweet mix of lavender and honeysuckle.

It was up to him to break the silence. "Good morning," he said hoarsely. His voice seemed to snap them out of a spell.

"So it's true. My God. *Robert.*" Simon strode across the room. The two friends stood staring at each other before Simon pulled him into such an embrace that his feet were lifted off the ground. They stood in each other's arms for a few moments before breaking apart. Robert wiped away a tear.

"How?" Simon asked with a shake of his head. "How? You were gone."

"Simon, I explained it all last night," Isabel said brightly. She turned to Robert. "Good morning."

Her voice. He'd dreamed for so many years of her voice.

"Isabel," Robert said breathlessly.

"Please, sit down," Simon said. He took his place beside Henry and directed Robert to a seat at the head of the table. He'd rather sit beside Isabel, but followed Simon's suggestion.

They all stared at each other in silence until Henry finished his porridge. "Is this your friend? He looks like the man in the miniature, the one in the parlor right next to yours, Mama."

"Yes. This is our friend, Mr. Robert Claremont," Isabel said, hastily wiping away tears. It sounded so formal, but Robert knew he couldn't possibly be introduced as "your father."

Henry left his chair and went to place a hand on Isabel's knee. "Mama, why are you crying?"

"I'm happy. It's been a long, long time since we've seen Robert. Why don't you say hello?"

"Hello." Henry made a little bow.

"Hello, Henry," Robert said, barely keeping his voice steady. What did one say to a son you never knew you had? "It's a pleasure to meet you."

"I have a new horse. She's gray like my papa's." He didn't wait for a reply but walked over to Simon and took his hand. "Can we go see Stardust now?"

"We had a plan to visit his new horse after breakfast," Simon explained to Robert. "I'll take him out and be back shortly."

As soon as the door closed after them Robert rushed to Isabel's side. "It wasn't a dream."

"No," she said through her tears, and hugged him.

Robert took her face in his hands and kissed her as they clung to each other.

"I love you. I love you," she said.

"I love you," he whispered in her ear. All the tension left his body now that she was beside him.

She pulled away to look at him, smiling as she wiped away her tears.

"Will Simon be long?" Robert asked.

"I don't think so. He wants to talk to you. Have you eaten?"

He shook his head. "I was too nervous."

"So was I. But now you're here, I think you brought my appetite with you. Let's eat."

They filled their plates and had just finished eating when Simon returned, alone.

"Where's Henry?" Isabel asked.

"He didn't want to leave Stardust. One of the stable lads is keeping an eye on him for a while. And I thought we'd need to talk about things he shouldn't hear." He sat in a chair, his hands clasped tightly in front of him on the table.

"We will," Isabel agreed. "We need to decide what to do next. Especially about Henry."

Simon stared at Robert. "I'm sorry, I just—I simply can't fathom this. It's beyond belief. Where have you been?" His tone was more challenging than curious.

He didn't want to tell the story all over again. "Isabel told you last night, didn't she?"

"She told me some. But what I can't understand is why you didn't contact me. Why didn't you tell me you were alive? You've always been as a brother to me. To think how I've missed you all these years. And Isabel—" Simon glanced at her, she was shaking her head vigorously and scowling at him. "You have no idea how much she's suffered. She broke, Robert. She broke when you died. It took her months to fully recover from her injuries after the waterfall, but that was nothing—nothing—to her heart. I've never seen anyone so changed. It was as though a part of her was missing. She tried to hide it, but I always knew how tormented she was, day after day, year after year. I did my best to make her happy. If it hadn't been for Henry I don't know how she would have made it through. It was terrible to see her—"

Robert blocked his ears. "Enough!"

"Simon!" Isabel said, putting her hand on Robert's shoulder.

Simon leaned back in his chair and crossed his arms, his face not in the least apologetic.

Robert raised his red-rimmed eyes to Simon's. "You don't need to tell me what a fool I've been." It was only what he'd been telling himself all night, once the euphoria of finding Isabel had subsided somewhat. He'd given up trying to sleep at daybreak, pangs of regret burning into his soul.

"No, Robert, don't blame yourself," Isabel said soothingly.

"It's true. Simon's right." He looked into her face and took her hand. "You had no choice but to hide. Branwick would have come after you if he'd heard even a whisper that you'd survived. Once I'd healed from my injuries, I could have come home any time I wished, but I was too proud, too furious, too hurt."

"I know you didn't walk away from that fall unscathed," Simon said, his tone softer.

"You must know, Simon, it wasn't a matter of trust. I did consider telling you, but William, Edmund, and I all agreed that if I was to be believed dead, the fewer people who knew otherwise, the better. In hindsight it was the worst mistake I ever made, not telling you."

"I could have helped you," Simon said with a slight shake of his head. "But what's done is done, and we can't change it now."

"No," Robert agreed, looking out the window at Henry, who was grooming his horse. He couldn't change missing the first four years of his son's life, or losing five years of being Isabel's husband. "I can never, never thank you enough for what you've done for Isabel and our son. She told me how you saved her and kept her safe. I'm more grateful than I can say."

"You need not thank me. I look upon Isabel and Henry as my family."

It was clear to Robert that they *were* a family. How would he fit in? Was it even possible?

"We are your family," Isabel said fervently to Simon, "and we'll always be your family."

"Yes, but now that Robert's home, things won't go on as before. We'll need to split up. We're going to tear apart the only family Henry has ever known, and he won't understand why," Simon said, his voice breaking on the last words.

Robert could tell he was trying hard to keep the bitterness out of his voice. The sound of Henry's laughter came in through the open window, and Simon covered his face with his hands. Isabel got up at once and went to him. She put her arms around him, and he leaned his head on her shoulder.

Robert couldn't help feeling like he was intruding. They were so natural together. The way they spoke of Henry, cast glances to each other, were somehow in tune with each other's moods, all indicated they were the couple and he the outsider.

The three of them sat in silence for some minutes. The enormity of what they needed to do hung over them like a cloud. Finally, Simon uncovered his face. Isabel kept her seat next to him, but her eyes were on Robert as she spoke. "We need to do what's best for Henry."

"Yes," Simon said. "We need to make this as easy as possible for him."

"He can't be torn away from you, Simon," Robert said. "I won't be responsible for that. I want him to get to know me. I want to spend time with him. But not at the expense of his happiness."

He caught the relieved glance they shared and had to stifle his jealousy.

"I have an idea that could make this easier," Isabel said. "Why doesn't Robert come to our home? There's plenty of room at Ridgefield. He can live with us. What better way for him and Henry to get to know each other? And then later—much later—we'll tell him the truth."

Robert mulled over her words. *Our* home. Live with *us*. He'd feel like a guest, and he wasn't sure how welcome, based on Simon's expression. But what other choice was there?

"What do you think, Robert?" Simon asked.

"If that's what you think is best for Henry, I'll do it."

Again that shared glance between them.

If only there were another option. Perhaps if he wasn't moving into their home he'd feel less like a stray they were taking in. Isabel clearly loved him as much as ever. After the initial shock last night, the years had melted away as if they'd never parted. He had no doubt of their devotion to each other. Which brought a question to his mind about this plan to move to Ridgefield.

"What about me and Isabel?" he asked. "Are we supposed to act like we're only friends? After all these years apart, I want to be with my wife."

Simon winced at the word but looked like he tried to hide it. "That will be a problem. It's obvious to me and anyone else who sees you that you're in love. You could be friendly to each other, of course, but no more than that."

Isabel glanced at Robert, eyes shining. "I don't think I can hide it."

"And I don't want to," Robert said.

Simon huffed and, crossing his arms, leaned back in his chair. "Then he can't live with us. We need to think of Henry. How will it be for him if his mother is making moon eyes at our new 'friend' and he comes upon them kissing in the garden?"

Isabel flushed.

"We can control ourselves. We aren't young lovers anymore," Robert said.

"The way you controlled yourselves back in Holton all those years ago?" Simon arched his brows.

"Simon, you must trust us to act appropriately. We won't be pawing each other all day like a groom and a kitchen maid."

"I'm not William," Robert said sulkily.

They all laughed, breaking the tension in the room.

Simon cleared his throat. "I have a suggestion. What if I take Henry home with me to Ridgefield and you two have some time by yourselves. Henry won't even know you're together. We could tell him Isabel's visiting Salisbury."

"For how long?" Isabel asked. "I've never been away from him."

"A few weeks? A month? Whatever you need."

Robert would have liked to suggest two or three months, but he could see the idea of parting from Henry distressed her.

"We'll start with a fortnight," Isabel said, "and will send word if we want to stay away longer." She looked at Robert and gave him a dazzling smile.

Simon sighed heavily and turned to Robert. "Where have you been living up to now? Perhaps you and Isabel could go there."

"I'd rather go to the cottage for a time," Robert said. He met Isabel's eyes and knew they were thinking the same thing.

She nodded, her eyes bright. He could hardly wait for the moment when they would be alone.

"As long as you're careful, that would be as good a place as any," Simon said. "I've kept an eye on it over the years, seen that it didn't fall into disrepair. I let the shrubs and trees grow back over the path to keep it hidden. I always thought Isabel might like to take Henry there one day."

Robert noted the hint of sadness in his eyes. If only his reunion with Isabel didn't cause Simon so much pain.

Isabel placed a hand on Simon's arm. "You and Henry will have a wonderful time at home. You can teach him to ride Stardust, and take long walks, and go fishing, and all the other things you love to do together. Before long Robert and I will join you."

Listening to Isabel, it occurred to Robert that it had been years since he'd lived anywhere he could truly call home. A startling idea came to him.

"Perhaps it's time we went back to Holton," he said. "All of us. Finding Isabel has made me realize I should have come out of hiding years ago. Not only because we could have been together, but it's made me see how much my absence has hurt those I love. My mother and father have mourned me. I've been selfish. It's time to go home. And it wouldn't be home without both of you. And Henry."

Isabel and Simon looked at each other.

"What about Ridgefield?" she asked.

"That's easily dealt with," Simon said, "Mr. Wentworth can watch over the estate. I could visit Ridgefield from time to time, and bring Henry. He'd like that. In fact, I think he'd fancy having two homes to call his own. And it would only be temporary."

Isabel's face fell. "You mean you wouldn't stay with us in Holton?"

Simon took her hand. "As much as I'd love to live with Henry for the rest of our lives, that won't be possible. At some point he'll need to know the truth, and I'll move back to Ridgefield. But I don't foresee that happening any time soon. In the meantime, he'll get to know Robert, and when we tell him it won't seem so terrible that I'm not his real father. I'll always be here for him and support him, and he—all of you—will be welcome at Ridgefield any time. I am his godfather, after all."

Isabel wiped her eyes. "My son is the luckiest boy in the world. He has not one but two wonderful men to look up to."

Simon and Robert shared a look, and he knew Simon wouldn't stand in the way of him reclaiming his place at Isabel's side or get in the way of him bonding with Henry.

"Now that's settled," Simon said, "when should we go to Holton?"

"It will be complicated," Robert said. "We can't return to Thornwood immediately. Perhaps in a few months, after we've all had some time together at Ridgefield. I'll need to explain the situation to William first, and he can tell our parents. It would be too much of a shock for them if we all appear unannounced. They believe Isabel and I are dead, and they're not even aware of Henry's existence."

"I hope they'll help us hide the truth from Henry," Isabel said.

"They will," Robert assured her, "if I make it clear that we can only stay if they do. The main thing is to keep gossip from reaching Henry's ears."

Isabel nodded, and it meant the world to him that she had such faith in his words.

"I'll need to find somewhere for us all to live," Robert said.

"Thornwood, of course," Simon said. "Goodness knows they have space for all of us."

"If William agrees. I won't presume to take his place, or even share it with him. And he may not want us intruding on his first years of marriage. I'll know more after I speak with him and my father." The thought of walking into his ancestral home filled Robert with unexpected longing. It would be good to be back.

"Robert," Isabel said, "What about Mr. Branwick and Marcus? They won't make it easy to return."

"Damn them both!" Robert said, banging his fist on the table. "They've taken enough from us. We won't let them drive us from our home again."

"Marcus has been married for years and lives in Plainfield, so he won't be a problem," Simon said. "But Branwick has a house in Holton now and splits his time between there and Salisbury. He'll need to be faced eventually. You'll have my support when the time comes."

Robert met his eyes. "I'm glad to have you back by my side."

Simon was about to answer, but the door opened and Henry came in. He skirted around Robert and hurried over to Simon.

"Are we staying until tomorrow, Papa?"

"No, we'll go home today. I think it's time Stardust was settled, don't you?"

Henry nodded.

"I'll be taking a trip to Salisbury," Isabel said, "so you'll need to look after Papa for me."

"Salisbury? What for?"

"Just to visit some old friends."

Robert was surprised Henry didn't ask more questions. He supposed there was much he needed to learn about children.

"Papa, would you like to see Stardust? She's brushed and washed, and her coat is shining."

"It seems a trip to the stables is in order," Simon said with a smile as he stood and took Henry's hand.

Robert felt yet another stab of jealousy and yearned for the day when Henry would call him Father. When he rose and followed them out of the room, Isabel came up from behind and took his arm. A thrill coursed through him at her touch. It would take some time to grow accustomed to having her with him again.

As soon as he stepped into the stables, Robert heard a familiar, unmistakable whinny. Could it be? He ran through the stables until he reached Apollo, who was kicking his stall, trying to get out. Robert burst in and threw his arms around his neck. "Hello, old friend."

Apollo nickered and nudged him with his nose.

Henry strolled over, hands in his pockets. "You know Papa's horse?"

"We're old friends," Robert said, stroking Apollo's neck lovingly.

"Apollo is Robert's and I've only been looking after him," Simon said. "But now he'll have him back."

"Stardust will need a new friend, then," Henry said. "Perhaps from the merchant who sold her to us, so it's a horse she already knows?"

Simon ruffled Henry's hair. "We'll find her one."

"Come see Stardust." Henry pulled Simon's hand and led him to a stall not far from Apollo's.

Robert kept his eyes on Henry, studying his features while Simon saddled his horse and helped him mount, then led him through the stable.

"You see, Mama? Stardust is the perfect size for me, and she's much stronger than a pony," Henry said as they passed, beaming with pride.

"I'll walk him around the inn," Simon said.

Henry held tightly to the reins as Simon led him out of the stable.

"He's a fine boy," Robert said. "I'm sorry to have missed so much."

"You're here now, and perhaps there will be another," Isabel said, smiling.

"A new chance. Our whole lives." Standing next to Isabel without taking her into his arms was almost impossible. But they must be discreet, as she'd said. As soon as they were alone, he'd make up for every moment they'd spent not touching. He let his eyes wander over her, taking her all in. She was exquisite.

Isabel must have read his face, for she smiled and said, "I know that look, Robert."

"Am I that obvious? And here I told Simon I wouldn't act like a foolish young lover."

"You will act every bit the foolish young lover, I hope, once we're alone." Her cheeks were pink, her eyes daring.

He reached for her hand and entwined his fingers with hers. "Once we're alone, you'll see how much I've missed you. I will take you to bed and not let you out for a week."

Isabel arched a brow and grinned. "Only one? I'd hoped for at least three."

Robert pulled her into an empty stall and crushed his lips to hers, letting his hands roam over her. Curse the fabric between his fingers and her skin. Her arms slid up his back as her mouth opened willingly beneath his. After some minutes they collapsed against each other.

"What was that about a groom and a kitchen maid?" Robert asked, straightening his jacket.

Isabel laughed. "Come, we mustn't be found here."

They left the stable and stood at a respectable, but painful, distance from each other while awaiting Henry and Simon's return.

****

After stabling Stardust, Simon sent Henry to the inn for refreshment. Then he turned to Robert and Isabel.

"I'll get Henry ready to leave as soon as possible. We'll stay in Auburn tonight, at the Kempthorne Inn. I spent a few nights there recently—it's a reputable establishment." He glanced at Isabel, who would know which nights he referred to. "It's not too far for Henry to ride on his first day. But before we can leave I need to find a mount."

"Are you certain?" Robert asked. "Apollo has been with you for years."

"I can't keep what does not belong to me," Simon said, though his eyes rested on Isabel, not Apollo. She looked away.

Robert, who had apparently caught the exchange, said, "Take the horse I bought yesterday. I won't need him now that I have Apollo."

"That is most generous."

"I need to gather my things, but I'd like to speak with you first, Simon, if I may. Alone," Robert said with a glance at Isabel, who looked just as puzzled as Simon felt.

"Certainly. Only, Henry is expecting me inside," Simon said, motioning to the inn.

"I'll go to him," Isabel said with a grin. She stood before them, her eyes flickering between the two men as her eyes glistened with tears. Of joy or sorrow? Simon wondered. Both? In days gone by, he would have taken her hand, or put an arm around her shoulders and asked what was wrong. But it was not his place to do so anymore. His heart lurched when she gave Robert's hand a squeeze and walked back to the inn. Simon watched until she disappeared inside, then turned to find Robert staring at him.

"You love her," Robert stated, but with no anger in

his voice, as Simon would have expected.

He answered without thinking. "Yes." What else could he say? Robert must know already. But perhaps he didn't know how deep it went.

"Let's go somewhere where we can talk."

They strolled to a meadow behind the inn. From the corner of his eye Simon saw, or rather felt, Robert's familiar gait. How many times had they walked thus? Simon shook his head, recalling how hard he'd tried to discourage Robert from courting Isabel. It had been like trying to keep the sun from rising. Back then, Isabel had come between them because Robert was willing to give up everything to be with her. And now? How could she not come between them? They both loved her, but only Robert could have her. Even though he, Simon, had saved her life, lived with her, raised a child with her, helped her, loved her for five perfect years.

Robert came to a stop beside a narrow stream. Sounds of the fair drifted over to them on the breeze, and in the distance horses grazed and frolicked in the sunshine.

Robert sat on the grass. "I never thought I'd see you again. Either of you."

"No. Nobody could have foreseen this," Simon said, sitting down with his legs stretched out in front of him.

After a few moments Robert asked, his eyes on the ground, "Are you sorry I've returned?"

"No!" Simon said. And then more softly, "No. Only…I wish you'd never left, or come back sooner. Isabel wouldn't have suffered, and I—"

"What?" Robert asked, trying to meet his gaze.

But Simon looked away. "I wouldn't have grown to love her."

"But you did."

"Yes, I did." He paused. "But can you believe, Robert, that Isabel wasn't the only one who mourned you? So many times I wished you were with us."

Robert put a hand on his shoulder. "I missed all of you. I should have come home. I could have been with Isabel and Henry all this time."

"You'll be with them now," Simon said, trying to keep the resentment out of his voice. He'd told Robert he wasn't sorry he was back, and he wasn't, not really, but his return destroyed all that Simon held dear.

Robert met his eyes. "They wouldn't even be here if not for you. Isabel would have died by the river. My God! When I think of all you've done… You set aside your own plans to take care of her. You saved her life."

"It was an honor to do so," Simon said, his voice cracking. "She and Henry have been—they have been everything to me." Just the thought of losing them made Simon feel like a ship without its anchor. He couldn't comprehend how he'd walk through Ridgefield without hearing their voices, spend days without talking to Henry, pass the evenings without Isabel by his side. But he said none of this. It wasn't Robert's fault they were in this situation.

"I can never, never thank you enough. You have no idea what it means to me to find her again—happy, whole, complete. And how do I repay you? By taking her away, by breaking your heart. I'm sorry—I'm truly sorry. This is my fault for staying away, and now what should be a wonderful reunion is tainted because I'm breaking up a family. Your family." Robert covered his face with his hands.

Simon remembered Isabel's words that fateful night,

"*Robert is his father.*" Though he'd stood in as a father, he'd never held that precious place in Isabel's heart. Robert had been there, a ghost, the whole time. "They were always your family." He drew up his knees.

"No." Robert shook his head. "I was her…her lover. You were her *husband*. Just looking at the two of you I can see it. For five years you've stood by each other, sharing things I can only dream of. And Henry. I mean nothing to him. It is I who don't belong."

Simon put his hand on Robert's arm. "You do belong. Henry will learn to love you, and Isabel never stopped loving you. I told you earlier how devastated she was when she lost you. But the strength that kept her alive came from the love you'd shared. She swam out of that river for you, survived for you. You're all she's thought about, all these years." Simon wondered if it would help Robert to understand how dedicated Isabel was if he told him what had happened between them. Isabel wanted to tell him herself, but Simon sensed it would be better coming from him. He took a deep breath. "Robert, there's something you don't know, but you need to hear it. You know I love Isabel. But what you don't know is that I asked her to be my wife—a true wife, just last month. And, well, I kissed her."

"But—" Robert's face fell, and he stood. "She told me you're only friends. She said there's nothing between you. At all." He looked around as if seeking an escape route.

Simon jumped to his feet and caught Robert's arm. "We *are* friends. You mustn't be angry. Remember, we thought you were dead. But I wanted to tell you, to help you understand."

He kept an eye on Robert's sword hilt, but the way

he was holding his fists made him think he should be more worried about his own jaw.

"I think I understand everything perfectly well." He started to walk away.

"No, you don't. Stop being so stubborn and listen to me." Robert stopped and didn't turn, but Simon could tell he was listening. "I kissed her, I poured my heart out to her, I begged her to be my wife. And she did consider it. But she told me she's yours. Her heart is yours. Her *soul* is yours. Those are her words."

Robert turned to him, his expression hovering between hope and despair. "But she still considered...being with you."

"Yes, she did. And why not? You were dead. *Dead.* We're close friends and she was lonely. All Isabel wanted was to be loved." He sighed. "But not by just anyone. By you." And as he said it, Simon realized that even if Isabel had come to him, there would always have been a part of her that he'd never reach. They may have shared a bed, and she may have loved him, but Robert would always have stood between them, whether he was alive or dead. "You mustn't hold this against her. She did say she'd consider being with me, but she would never have truly been mine. She's yours. She has always been yours."

Robert looked at him as if for reassurance. "I felt that when I kissed her, when I held her, when we spoke together last night. It was like not a day had passed."

"And remember, except for this one incident, we've been only friends all these years. Try to forget what happened between us. She's planning on telling you about this herself—she insisted that it not be kept a secret. Don't ever doubt her commitment to you."

Robert's eyes met his, and instead of looking angry

327

they were sad, regretful. "If Isabel turned to someone else for love, it's nobody's fault but mine. I'm lucky she still loves me at all. She could have truly married you long ago and you could have had more children and it would be impossible for her to come back to me."

Simon tried not to show that the nightmare scenario he was describing would have been his own dream come true. "We needn't think of that. You're home and you'll be together."

Robert gazed at him for a long minute. "If she had to turn to anyone for comfort, I'm glad it was you. I wish there were something I could do to make this easier for you. For all of us."

"The only thing you can do for me will be easy," Simon said with a sad shrug. "Take care of them."

"I will. You have my word." Robert held out his hand, and Simon shook it.

Just then Simon looked up and saw Isabel walking toward them.

"Here you two are," she said. Her face was drawn and worried. Simon knew she was trying to hide it, but she couldn't, not from him.

"Where's Henry?" Simon asked.

"He's with Stardust. He can't stay away from her," she said, smiling. "Mrs. Biddlecombe is keeping an eye on him."

"We were just talking about Henry," Simon said, "and our plans for the future."

Robert put a hand on Simon's shoulder. "I was thanking him again for keeping you and Henry safe and happy all these years."

"I keep telling you, I need no thanks," Simon said with an exasperated sigh. They acted as if he'd been doing them a favor, not living the happiest life he could imagine. It was like being thanked for breathing. "I had some ideas about Henry. While we're at Ridgefield I'll tell him about Robert and all the adventures we had when we were boys. And I thought perhaps Robert and Henry could exchange letters as a start to getting to know one another. I'll help Henry write his replies, and read him the letters Robert sends."

Robert started to say, "Thank—" but stopped when Simon gave him a good-natured glare. He grinned. "That's a wonderful idea, Simon. I wouldn't have thought of it. Once we're all back in Holton, we can take him out riding and maybe Isabel will teach him archery."

"I already have," she said.

"You should have known," Simon said, and they all laughed.

"I think he should continue calling Simon Papa, and maybe I could be Uncle Robert? For the time being."

"That's an excellent idea," Simon said. "In a year or two, we'll tell him. We'll explain the whole story, and though it might be difficult for him to grasp, he'll understand that you two are his parents and were married before he was born. And we'll make sure he knows that I'll always be close by, and that he'll never lose me."

The three of them stood in silence for a few moments before Robert said, "I'd better go gather my things. What time do we leave?"

"Perhaps we should wait another couple of days," Isabel said. "So the separation isn't so sudden."

Simon shook his head. The last thing he wanted to do was prolong the parting. He was thrilled that Robert was alive, and so happy that Isabel had him back, but he'd be lying if he didn't admit that every touch, every glance they shared bruised his heart. He wanted to get right away with Henry and enjoy the time they had together, just the two of them. They were both looking at him, so he said, "I want to get Henry home. And you two have a long journey if you're going back to Holton."

"I'll meet you outside the inn when I'm packed," Robert said.

"We should get ready to go, too," Isabel said to Simon, and they started back to the inn as Robert walked across the fields to his campsite.

After settling Henry in the private dining room with lunch, Simon trudged up the stairs behind Isabel. Was it only two days ago he'd practically sprinted up these stairs? He'd been so sure Isabel would soon be his wife. He wondered if he'd have come to the fair if he'd known what would happen. He sighed. Of course he would have. Isabel belonged with Robert, and he would have made sure they found each other.

"I have a few things to gather, and then I'll come help you," Simon said.

"All right." She pressed her lips together and went into her room.

When he finished, Simon crossed the hall and found Isabel in a flurry of activity. Everything was already packed, but she was straightening the bedclothes, checking under furniture for lost items, closing the windows, and for some reason taking candles out of their sconces.

"Isabel?"

"Mm?" she replied, fluffing the pillows.

"I think you can stop now. You're making this room look better than when we arrived."

She bent to pick up a fallen blanket.

"Isabel." He crossed the room and touched her elbow.

She seemed to melt at his touch and turned to him, her eyes brimming with tears. "Oh, Simon."

"What is it?" he asked, though he thought he knew. She was ecstatic to be reunited with Robert.

To his surprise, she wrapped her arms around herself and started sobbing, staring at the floor. These didn't look like tears of joy.

"Isabel?"

She looked up at him, her face blotchy, her eyes wet. "Simon, is it—will you—?"

"Anything," he said urgently.

"Would you still…hold me? Or would it be wrong?" she asked through her sobs.

In answer, he pulled her into his arms, holding her tighter than he ever had before. She collapsed against him, her hands clutching his shirt. He rested his chin on top of her head and rubbed her back gently until her sobs turned into soft weeping. After a time she took a shuddering breath and wrapped her arms around his waist. Would this be the last time he ever held her? Already it felt like holding the Isabel of years ago—a beloved friend who needed his help. The knowledge that she definitely wouldn't be his wife dulled the yearning somehow. He still loved her, but it was almost a relief to know they could never be together, because he no longer had to torture himself with impossible dreams.

They clung together until she pulled away, wiping her eyes with the heel of her hand. He gave her a handkerchief, and she dried her face, then looked up at him.

"How I wish my joy were not your sorrow," she said.

"You've been by my side for so long, and I can't imagine life without you."

"You won't be without me."

"But things will change, Simon. Like you said last night."

"The whole world is changed."

"But we won't change. I'll always be here for you."

"And I for you." Suddenly he laughed. "Look at us. Parting for a matter of days, acting as if this is our final farewell."

"It is a farewell, though," she said through a watery smile. "A farewell to what we've had together, what we've been to one another. A farewell to our little family, just the three of us."

"A farewell to heartbreak and loneliness for you. A farewell to the emptiness in your heart that's been there ever since Robert disappeared."

"But what of you? Leaving you alone feels like a betrayal. You stayed with me all those years ago, you—"

"Isabel—" He tried to cut her off, but she stomped her foot. He smiled. She only did that when at the height of vexation.

"Simon, you've said time and time again that you didn't mind staying with me, that it was an honor to watch over us. And I believe you. But what about you? We had a life together, you had hopes, plans. And they're all gone like flower petals on a summer wind. You don't have to protect me from your feelings. I won't leave this room until you know how grateful I am, and until I know how you are. Tell me."

"I'll be all right." He put a hand to his forehead. He wanted to get through this day, this hour, this minute without tarnishing her joy.

"Tell me." She put a hand on his arm and looked into his eyes.

"There's nothing to say." His head ached.

"*Tell me.*"

"Tell you what?" he asked tiredly, putting his hands on her shoulders. "Tell you that I love you, that saying goodbye rips my world in two? Tell you that I'll be missing you for years to come? I don't want to tell you that. I want you to go away with Robert with not a thought of me. I want you to be happy, Isabel. It's all I've ever wanted. You belong with Robert. You and I had a…a brief yet happy marriage. When we lost Robert, we shared a kind of nightmare together, and then we turned it into a dream." He ran his hand softly down her cheek. "But now the dream is over. You woke up. *Your* dream has come true. And mine?" He shrugged.

She put a hand to his cheek and smiled. "Perhaps there is a dream for you, Simon. Your own dream, with your own happy ending."

"You were my happy ending." Finally, after hiding his sorrow all day, after staying strong for Isabel and Henry, he fell onto the bed and wept. The world disappeared as he lay there, wracked with grief. He didn't want Isabel to see him this way, but it was too late. She sat beside him on the bed, patting his back and making the kinds of sounds she did when Henry was hurt or frightened.

She handed him a handkerchief and he wiped his eyes but didn't sit up. He almost laughed. The woman who broke his heart, comforting him. But no. Isabel hadn't done this. Fate had done it. Or the cosmos, or who knew what. He sighed heavily. All he wanted now was to sleep, but Henry was downstairs, and soon it would be time to leave. To go home. A home without Isabel, but home nonetheless. He pulled himself up and leaned back against the pillows.

"I'm sorry," Isabel said. "The last thing I ever wanted was to hurt you."

"I know. And I'm sorry you had to see me this way."

She shook her head. "I'm not sorry. How many times did you hold me, comfort me, over the years? It was the least, the very least, I could do for you right now. I do love you, Simon. And I'll miss you."

"I'll miss you, too. But not for long. You'll go away with Robert, and then we'll all go to Ridgefield and move to Holton in time. We'll see each other often. We'll be living in the same house, so it won't be difficult," he said with a small laugh.

"You're right." Their eyes met, and they both knew that even if they did see each other, it would never be the same. But they would both be all right.

"Come," Simon said, and stood. "Let's go see Henry and have lunch."

She took his hand and they went down to the dining room together.

****

After gathering his things, Robert went back to the inn, where he saw Isabel and Simon just inside the stable, sharing what looked like a heartfelt goodbye as Henry stood by with his horse. She was crying, and it was possible Simon was, too. They shared a long embrace, and Robert had to remind himself that though she clearly loved Simon, she was not in love with him. Whatever they'd gone through together had bonded them for life, and he'd have to get used to that, but he knew Isabel's love for himself was as strong as it was the day they'd said their vows. It could only get stronger now that they were back together. He marveled again at the chance that had brought them together. William and Edmund had practically begged him to go to the fair, and he'd resisted. He'd still be sitting alone in his house by the sea while Isabel lived out a full life with Henry and Simon. But now? She was walking across the yard, practically skipping in her eagerness to reach his side. She didn't take his hand when she reached him but met his eyes with love.

Simon and Henry came out of the stable, leading their horses.

"Keep Henry safe," Isabel said.

Simon smiled. "I always do."

Isabel lifted Henry into her arms. "Be good for Papa."

"I will." Henry threw his arms around her neck, and she buried her face in his hair for a moment before handing him to Simon, who helped him mount Stardust. "Farewell, Mama."

Simon, now mounted on a handsome palomino gelding, turned. "Goodbye, Isabel. We'll see you soon at home." Robert couldn't help noticing the tightness in his voice and the way his eyes lingered on Isabel's face.

"Very soon. Goodbye, Simon," she said, her voice catching.

"Goodbye, Robert, it was good to see you." He shook his head and laughed. "It was *unbelievable* to see you."

"Farewell. And farewell to you, Henry," Robert said. It tore at a deep part of him to say goodbye to his son before he'd even had a chance to know him. But there would be plenty of time for that in the future. For now, it was enough to see his timid smile as he muttered a goodbye. Simon and Henry waved one last time and were soon lost in the crowd of travelers leaving the fair on the main road out of town.

Chapter Twenty-Two

Isabel was quiet as they walked back to the inn, and Robert guessed she was distraught about parting with Henry. He took her hand.

"It's all right," he said. "You'll see Henry again soon."

She stopped walking and looked into his eyes. "It's not about Henry."

"What is it?"

"I need to tell you something. But not here."

He followed her upstairs to her room, which looked bare since she'd already done her packing. She closed the door and leaned against it.

"What's going on, Isabel?" He tried to stop the myriad of worries bombarding his mind. Was she ill? Was she having second thoughts about moving to Thornwood? Did she want to stay with Henry and Simon? *Ah...Simon.* The kiss. He wouldn't tell Isabel that he knew, since Simon said she wanted to tell him herself.

She looked at him. "I need to tell you something. Something about when you were gone."

"Go on."

She stood in front of him as though placing herself on the edge of a yawning chasm. "When you were gone...Simon kissed me, and I kissed him back. And then a few nights later, it happened again. I was lonely.

337

At the time, I thought I'd never see you again, never love again." She took a deep breath. "There's more. I have to tell you because we once promised each other that we would have no secrets. A few weeks ago, Simon asked if I would be his wife in all ways."

He kept his voice even and his expression calm. "But you don't love Simon."

"It isn't that I don't love him. I do—as a friend. I thought perhaps, with time, I could grow to love him romantically." Her brow creased and she put a hand to her head. "Perhaps we would have remained close friends and had some semblance of a true marriage. But as much as I might have hoped to fall in love with him, I somehow knew I never would have." She raised her eyes to his. "I'm already in love. Hopelessly, eternally, desperately. With you."

He took her hands. "It's all right, I understand. I'm not angry."

And he wasn't. How could he be? Who on earth ever heard of someone coming back from the dead? He couldn't deny how jealous the thought of her with someone else made him, but she had in no way betrayed him. And that it had happened so recently proved how long she'd stayed loyal to him, how many years she remained lonely in honor of his memory. She loved him enough to be honest with him, she trusted him enough to know he would still love her after she shared this secret. He was overwhelmed with an even deeper, purer love for her. There were no secrets between them now. Only a binding, strong, true love that had outlasted separation and death itself.

Isabel was watching him as though waiting for him to say more. He grinned sheepishly. "You might be angry with *me* when I tell you that Simon already told me about the kiss, and…and everything else."

Her eyes widened. "He did? When?"

"This afternoon. I should have told you, but Simon said you wanted to tell me about it yourself."

She put her hands on her hips, a smile coming to her lips. "Robert Claremont, I can't believe you let me think I was breaking your heart when you knew all about it already."

He gave her a lopsided grin. "Are you angry?"

"Not in the least. I did want to tell you myself. And now, between Simon and me both explaining it, you know I never loved him that way. You do know that, don't you?"

"Yes. There's no doubt in my mind that you love me."

"Good." Isabel looked away, and he could tell something else was troubling her.

"Isabel?"

She closed her eyes as if bracing herself. "While we were apart, were you ever…with someone? It's all right if you were. You thought I was dead, and—"

He rushed to reassure her. "No. No, I wasn't."

She looked at him and let out a slow breath. "I'm glad. But I would have understood."

"As I told you before, I lived a solitary life. I didn't socialize very much, and when I did I wasn't looking for love. I'd already found it, and nothing could have equaled what I have with you."

"Oh, Robert. I hate to think of how lonely you must have been."

"But I won't be anymore. We're together again, and will be for the rest of our lives. I love you, Isabel."

"Oh, Robert. I love you so much." She wrapped her arms around him and kissed him.

He broke away to look into her deep, loving eyes, then lifted her in his arms and placed her gently on the bed. She was just as beautiful as Robert remembered. No, more beautiful. She was softer, more open somehow. "How many hours I spent dreaming of you. I dreamed of your neck." He trailed light kisses from the hollow of her throat to just below her chin. "I dreamed of your soft skin," he said huskily, feeling her shudder as he eased a hand inside her bodice. "The part of you I most missed were your eyes," he said, lifting himself on top of her and staring into her brown eyes. "Your eyes are where I see you, every part of you. I dreamed of your voice, your thoughts, your feelings, your desires. I dreamed of my Isabel, believing you to be forever a lost dream. How many nights I lay in bed, my arms empty. But here you are, filling them," he said triumphantly. He kissed her as she lay beneath him, her lustrous hair spread out around her, her eyes alight with love.

Robert tugged at her bodice. "How do I get this off?" he said, half laughing. She giggled and, between the two of them, her gown was soon in a pile on the floor.

Isabel gently pushed Robert onto his back and began undressing him. "I dreamed of you, too. Of your voice, your sweet laugh." She slipped his shirt over his head, her lips finding their way to his shoulder, his chest, his neck. "I dreamed of your strong arms holding me," she whispered, caressing his arms, stroking his back. "I dreamed of your love for me." He shivered as she pulled his breeches over his hips. "Kiss me," she said urgently. "Give me all the kisses I longed for, that I thought would never come."

He kissed her with a blinding passion that made him forget everything else. There was nothing—nothing—but Isabel. His heart beat frantically as he ran his hands over her warm, supple body, and a desire beyond anything he'd ever known surged through his veins.

"Robert," she purred, clutching him closer.

They held each other's eyes as they came together—united at last, whole at last. Each kiss, each caress was a promise. A promise to never part again.

****

They set out for Holton the next day. Their days were spent in talk and laughter, the nights in each other's arms. Along the way they described in greater detail what had happened to each of them during their years apart. Isabel gained a deeper understanding of Robert's solitary years and his arduous physical recovery after the fall. Robert asked question after question about Henry. His likes, dislikes, what he'd been like as a baby. Isabel seemed more than happy to answer them all. Robert thought she could have spoken for days about Henry and never tire of it, and he loved the way her eyes glowed when she spoke of their son.

When they finally arrived at the meadow, they turned to each other and shared a smile. The cottage looked almost exactly the same as the night they'd left it five years before. They stabled the horses and walked hand in hand through the yard.

Isabel turned to him with a smile. "We're home."

"I've been home since the moment I saw you at the fair." He swept her into his arms, carried her into the cottage, and stood just inside the doorway.

"It's hardly changed at all," Isabel said.

"No, but we have."

"Yes, on the outside. But not here." She pressed a hand to his heart.

"I have. I love you even more than when we first fell in love."

"Robert," she said, brushing her lips against his, "take me to the bed."

He clumsily kicked the door closed behind them, crossed the room and, instead of gently laying her down, caught his foot on the bedpost and tripped, toppling them both headlong into the musty bed.

"Are you all right?" he asked, face burning.

Isabel only nodded, tears of laughter streaming down her face.

Robert, laughing along with her, brushed the hair off her face as they gazed into each other's eyes. It took only a moment for the laughter to die away and passion to take its place. Their lips met in a fiery, desperate kiss as they began tugging at each other's clothes.

Some glorious time later, Robert rolled onto his side and took Isabel into his arms. With a contented sigh, she rested her head on his chest. He took a lock of her hair and rubbed it between his fingers.

"Have you been happy?" he asked softly, "All these long years?"

"Happy? For the most part I've been happy. But I was never complete after you'd gone."

Robert's grip on her tightened. "I've missed so much. Our son's birth, his first step, his first word. I've missed years with you. Years! I'll spend the rest of my life making up our lost time together."

"We'll have the life we always wanted. But first there is today. What shall we do?"

He lifted a brow. "Do you mean to say you don't

wish to spend the rest of the day in bed?"

"I didn't say that," she said, her hands wandering, "But I'm hungry."

"I see that I must feed you before anything else," he said with a laugh.

When he got out of bed, Isabel caught her breath. Robert turned to see her examining him closely. He was nude, and she stared at the scars he'd acquired that day at the falls. He'd grown so accustomed to them over the years he hardly noticed them anymore. She stood and reached out to touch them gingerly—a gash in one leg, multiple scars on his chest... She ran a finger down the long, jagged scar running the length of his back.

"They didn't look as bad when I saw them by candlelight," she said.

"No, you haven't yet seen them in the full light of day. My clothes cover most of them."

"Except this one," she said, kissing the scar along his jaw.

"You have some, too," he said, bringing her back to bed. He bent to kiss several pale scars on her legs.

"We both have marks upon us from that day."

"None as deep as the ones on our hearts." He gathered her into his arms.

She kissed him softly. "But those are healed now that we're together again."

They lay entwined in each other's arms for most of the day—talking, listening, laughing—before finally getting out of bed to eat food they'd bought in a village they'd passed through the day before.

As they sat side by side at the table, Isabel sighed happily.

"What are you thinking of?" Robert asked.

"Henry. He'll love it here."

"Before long he'll be with us," Robert said. He was anxious to get to know Henry better before they took on the daunting task of moving back to Thornwood.

After eating, they took a long walk through the forest, reminiscing. They did not go near the river. When night fell, they returned to the cottage and, after talking for hours beside the fire, climbed into bed and were soon asleep.

Robert awoke a few hours later. Something was wrong. In his sleepy haze, he didn't understand at first. There was a smell that didn't belong. And…heat. Heat? Fire!

His eyes flew open. Flames were everywhere. He shook Isabel awake.

"Is it morning already?" she asked sleepily.

"Isabel! Wake up! Fire!"

She sat bolt upright. "Fire?"

They clung to each other as rolling flames crept along the ceiling, eating the roof. Fire slithered across the floor and up the walls like some demented, unceasing monster.

Smoke stung Robert's eyes as he sought an escape route. "Make for the door!"

Isabel nodded.

Their eyes met before they sprang from the bed, heat scorching them as they leaped over licking flames. They immediately pressed themselves to the floor, crawling as fast as smoke and flame would allow. In minutes that felt like years, they reached the door. Or where the door should have been. It was now a solid wall of fire.

"We must go out the window!" Robert shouted, helping Isabel to her feet.

He ripped his shirt off, wrapped it around his hand, and smashed the window panes, then draped the shirt over the sill.

"Go!" he said, coughing.

"Together!"

"Go, Isabel. Now!" He shoved her away in his insistence that she escape the inferno.

Isabel looked at him, fear in her eyes.

"I will follow at once!" he said.

"At once!"

Robert lifted her onto the window and she climbed through, lowering herself to the hot earth outside. Once she was clear, he hoisted himself onto the sill. Then came the deafening crash.

After running a few paces to escape the heat, Isabel turned to see Robert halfway out the window. With an ear-splitting roar, the roof collapsed, obscuring him from view.

"Robert!" She rushed forward, then gasped as arms like iron bars grabbed her from behind.

Isabel spun around. "William!" she spat. Thrashing wildly, she clawed at his hands. "Let me go!"

"Take her, for God's sake!" William thrust her roughly into someone else's arms and bolted toward the burning cottage.

Kinder, gentler hands held Isabel back. "Isabel, be still!"

She froze. "*Mother?*"

Jayne Branwick threw her arms around her and they stood crying, staring at the cottage as the flames raged on, unhindered.

"Robert…Robert…" Isabel muttered.

"Shh," her mother soothed, stroking her hair.

At last William emerged, covered in black soot, smoke clinging to his clothes. In his arms he carried a motionless Robert.

"Robert!" Isabel cried and hastened to his side.

"Give him space," William snapped, laying Robert gently on the ground.

Isabel ignored him and knelt beside Robert, softly calling his name. At last his eyelids fluttered, and he coughed violently for some minutes. She patted his back until at last his breathing returned to normal. Relief swept over Isabel, and she threw herself upon him.

"Isabel…" he said hoarsely.

She ran her hands over him, looking for burns. "Are you hurt?"

"Not seriously, thanks to William. A bit singed. And you?"

"Burns only, and none too serious. When I thought you were hurt, or worse, my heart stopped."

"We'll never be parted again." Robert brought his lips to hers with unrestrained passion.

William put his hands on his hips, rolling his eyes. "Can this not *wait*?"

They broke apart and stood up, arms around each other.

Robert looked at William. "What a terrible accident. Thank God we woke in time. But—why are you here?"

"This was no accident," William said darkly.

"What do you know of it?" Isabel asked him. "And why *are* you here?"

William crossed his arms. "I would ask the same of you. You're dead, or so I was told."

"As was I," said her mother. "Oh, Isabel! Where have you been?"

"It's a long story. Too long for now," she said.

"You're alive, that's all that matters," her mother said, embracing her.

Robert clapped William on the back. "I owe you my life. Again."

"Let this be the last time," William said shakily with a half-smile, gripping Robert's shoulder.

Robert nodded and gestured to the inferno. "What happened?"

"We arrived here just as that wretch ran off," William said, pointing toward the forest. "I was too concerned for you to give chase."

Robert scowled and seemed almost at a loss for words. "Do you mean to say this was deliberate? Who would do such a thing?"

"My husband," Isabel's mother said in a cold voice.

"Branwick!" Robert exclaimed.

Isabel looked at her mother. "You're certain?"

She nodded. "Marcus came to the house late last night, and I overheard him talking to Giles. He said he saw Isabel at a fair and followed her back to Holton. I thought there must be some mistake, but he was convinced it was her. Then they discussed their plans and I knew that, impossible as it was, Isabel was alive somewhere and in trouble. Giles said she would burn, as his mother had burned!" She covered her face with her hands.

"So you followed him?" Isabel put an arm around her shoulders.

"Yes, but not before I sought assistance."

"This is how you come into it?" Robert asked, looking at William.

"Yes. Jayne came to Thornwood in some distress.

She said there was a chance Isabel was alive but in grave danger. It sounded like nonsense to me, but I took no chances. I was correct in assuming that if Isabel was alive and in danger, she would be bringing that danger to you," William said, casting her a dark look. "We set out soon after Branwick, but clearly we were not fast enough. It took some time to find this place, and by the time we arrived the cottage was half gone."

"Did you see Marcus?" Isabel asked, looking into the trees with a shudder. To think he'd followed them all the way to the cottage and they'd had no idea.

"No, I sent a message to the magistrate," William said. "By now Marcus should be in his custody. But somehow Branwick slipped through the net and continued here on his own."

"Set upon in our very bed," Robert said. "It's an outrage!" He turned to Mrs. Branwick. "Your husband couldn't seriously think to avenge his mother by killing Isabel, could he?"

"Will someone explain what this is all about?" William cut in, throwing up his hands.

"Giles believes that Isabel's father was to blame for his mother's death years ago. This is his skewed idea of vengeance," Mrs. Branwick said bitterly.

"That is madness!" William exclaimed.

Isabel for once agreed with him. She should have known Branwick would seek revenge if he knew she was alive, but it was all so long ago she'd almost convinced herself he would have forgotten about her. But he never would. This is what he did the moment he discovered she was alive! She felt faint when she realized how close he'd come to exacting his vengeance, and her very soul shook when she considered that Henry could have been with them in the cottage tonight if not for Simon's idea to take him to Ridgefield.

Robert stared at the burning cottage, his face hard. "Where's Branwick now?"

"He ran into the forest," William said.

"I'm going after him." He peered into the trees as if trying to gauge the best direction to search.

"He may already be gone," Isabel said. "We should go to Thornwood for help."

Behind them, the cottage glowed red as flames consumed every inch.

Robert looked her in the eyes. "This ends now. We will not spend our lives looking over our shoulders. I'll capture him, and we'll bring him before the magistrate."

William stepped forward. "I'll come with you."

"No. This is between him and me. I need you to protect Isabel and her mother in case he comes back."

"Be reasonable. You can't run after a madman on your own," William pleaded.

"The time for reason has passed! I must go before he escapes."

"Robert, please," William said.

"Enough! I'm going. Give me your sword."

William reluctantly removed his sword belt and gave it to Robert, who buckled it on at once.

"Robert, let me come with you," Isabel said.

"Absolutely not. He'll kill you if he gets the chance. Go with your mother. Go to Kerensly Hall and wait for me there."

She drew herself up. "I swore never to be parted from you again."

"You never will be. I'll take care of Branwick and we'll be out of his shadow, once and for all." He kissed her and bounded into the forest.

Isabel sprang after him, but William caught her arm.

She struggled against his grasp. "Let me go!"

"No," he said, his lips curling into a smile.

"I must help him. My stepfather will kill him!"

"For *once* do as Robert tells you! If you'd stayed away from him, as *I* told you to, he wouldn't be in danger. It was a dark day when he let you into his life."

"You ever think the worst of me! We're wasting time," Isabel shouted. "Whatever you think of me, set it aside for now. We can't let Robert go against Branwick alone."

"You'll only distract him if you're stumbling through the woods trying to help."

Mrs. Branwick spoke then. "Isabel's right. Giles is only one man, but he's dangerous as a viper. He killed my husband. If you love your brother, you need to go after them. Now!"

William considered her words for only a moment before darting into the woods, Isabel close behind.

All manner of thoughts raced through her mind as she ran. Had she found Robert only to lose him again? How could she have been so foolish at the horse fair? Her failure to disguise herself could cost Robert his life. If only she had her bow! She'd then easily be able to stop Branwick before any harm came to Robert. She tried to keep her panic from rising as she hurtled through the trees after William.

As they neared the river, William put a hand out to stop her. "Listen."

Barely audible above the roar of the waterfall came the sound of clashing swords.

"They're at the falls!" William sprinted through the

trees.

Isabel tried to keep up, but he was gone in an instant. She finally made it to the riverbank, a stitch in her side, her breath coming in heavy gasps. When she stepped out of the trees, her heart jumped into her throat. Before her was a scene from her nightmares.

Swords drawn, Robert and Branwick circled each other on the very cliff she and Robert had leaped from. Branwick held his sword with one hand; the arm she'd wounded years ago hung at an odd angle, apparently useless. She gasped when he lunged with his sword and Robert teetered on the cliff's edge, but Robert pivoted and aimed a blow, missing Branwick by inches.

William crept up silently behind Branwick, who was so focused on Robert he didn't know William was there until it was too late. William pounced, pinning his arms to his sides.

"Unhand me!" Branwick yelled. William twisted his arm until he was forced to drop his sword on the ground.

"This is finished," William snarled.

"It is never finished!"

"We go from here to the magistrate," Robert said, not sheathing his sword.

"I'll yet avenge my mother, killed by that bastard Edward Tate!"

"Edward is dead. Is that not enough?" Robert asked.

"No, it's not enough! His death was quick, easy. The flames will destroy Isabel, as they destroyed my mother!"

Isabel hurried along the riverbank toward the cliff, frantically trying to think of anything she could do to help.

Robert pointed his sword at Branwick's heart. "You

will come to the magistrate. If you don't, you'll pay for your crimes here and now."

"Robert, stop. This is not the way," William warned.

"Listen to your brother. Lay down your arms, release me, and no harm will come to you."

"Your words mean nothing," Robert spat, advancing.

"Robert, no!" William said.

"What he has robbed me of! My wife, my son, almost my life itself!"

Isabel climbed onto the cliff unnoticed by the three men, who had their backs to her. She was about to address Robert, but William spoke first.

"The law will take care of him. Drop your sword."

Robert looked at William and shook his head.

In that split instant, Branwick wrenched free of William's grasp, reached down, and regained his sword, attacking Robert with a fierce cry.

"Robert!" Isabel lunged forward and shoved him to the ground.

The force Branwick would have used to run Robert through propelled him to the edge of the cliff. He let out a wail as he fell, but with a sickening thud his cry was silenced.

Robert, gasping, dropped the sword and buried his face in his hands.

William peered over the falls. "Dead."

Isabel went to look over the side, but William held her back. "It is a grisly sight."

"I must." She pulled free of William's grasp and looked down. Her stomach lurched. Branwick's limbs were askew, blood pooled around his head. He'd landed on a flat boulder far below.

Isabel turned away, hands over her mouth as Robert stood and pulled her into his arms.

"It's over. At last, it's over," he said, rubbing her back. "But you should have stayed with your mother."

"I couldn't leave you. I had to make sure you survived."

"She's quite stubborn, this wife of yours," William said, not without a hint of admiration. "Come, we must get back to Jayne and tell her you're safe." He sheathed his sword and ran into the forest.

Isabel and Robert stood together on the cliff, their backs to the falls. The roar of the water had an almost mesmerizing effect as she tried to clear her mind of the last time they'd been here. That had been an end and, as incredible as it was, they now stood on the brink of a new beginning. Their long, dark years of separation were over.

She took his hand, strong and warm in hers. "Come away."

Walking through the forest, they saw black smoke billowing up from the trees and knew their cottage was gone.

"We'll rebuild it," Robert said confidently.

"It will take some time."

"We have time now, all the time in the world." Robert took her into his arms.

She smiled and reached up to touch his cheek. "The rest of our lives."

Their lips met in a deep, sealing kiss.

Epilogue

Three years later

Robert paced the courtyard of his new home, which he and Isabel had built atop the ruins of the cottage. They still lovingly called it "the cottage" though it was a stately manor built of stone. His father had ceded Robert the meadow and surrounding land and helped him design the house. Once he'd gotten over his fury at being deceived, Mr. Claremont had been overjoyed to learn his son was alive. Robert's mother had been another story. It had taken her months to forgive him, and sometimes he still caught a cold glint in her eyes when they fell on Isabel. Robert's parents doted on Henry, whose very existence did much to reconcile them to Isabel.

The question of who would inherit Thornwood had been answered satisfactorily to all. With Robert's "death," Mr. Claremont had been forced to hand responsibilities over to William. He'd been pleasantly surprised and gratified to see that William was much more capable than he'd previously shown. More surprisingly still, his marriage to Margery was proving a success, and the birth of his daughter the previous year had done much to curb his wild ways. Though Robert now had his own property to look after, he and William worked together to keep both estates thriving.

Isabel's mother—once more Jayne Tate—was now

a widow of substantial fortune, and had moved to Holton to be near Isabel, Robert, and Henry. She lived in a fine mansion with Isabel's half siblings, Victoria and Philip. Henry was much amused about being older than his Uncle Philip and only slightly younger than his Aunt Victoria. Isabel met Jayne and Verity for tea a few times a week, and had regained that close relationship with her mother that they both held so dear.

Robert ceased his pacing when Simon, Henry, and William rode into the yard.

"Hello, Father. Is my brother born yet?" Henry asked as they all dismounted.

A groom came out and took their horses to the stable.

"Not yet," Robert said, smiling on his firstborn.

Henry wrinkled his forehead. "I thought he would be born yesterday. Papa said I'll be able to hold him when he's still very small."

"I'm sure the baby will like that. But you could have a sister," Simon said, ruffling his hair.

Henry shook his head. "No, you already told me you've a feeling it's a boy."

"We won't know until it's all over," Robert said. "How was your ride?"

"Splendid!" Henry said, smiling. "I showed them the trail you took me on last week."

"Fast," William said. "Henry wouldn't slow down the entire time."

Henry shrugged. "Stardust likes to jump. I'm going to the kitchens to see if there are any cakes, and then I'll be in the library with Edmund. Tell me when my brother is born," he said and ran into the house.

Robert turned to Simon and William. "It's been

hours."

"It was like that with Henry," Simon said.

"Birthing is a long and messy business, from what I hear." William tapped his boot with his riding crop. "Don't worry about Isabel. She's strong. She bested me on the archery range just last week and teased me about it, as usual."

Simon laughed. "I told you not to try."

"She said the same thing. But she knows I can never resist a challenge, the little minx." Ever since she'd saved Robert's life, William had been almost as enamored of Isabel as he was of Margery.

Ignoring them completely, Robert looked toward the house. "Oh, why must it take so long?"

"It will be over before you know it," Simon said.

William slapped Simon on the back. "It's your turn next."

"Me?" Simon exclaimed.

"I assume you'll be taking your bride to bed."

Simon flushed. "Rosamond isn't my bride yet."

"Only a fortnight until your wedding," Robert said, "and Isabel insists she'll attend, newborn or no."

"She takes credit for my marrying Rosamond."

"Why?" Robert asked, curious but not in the least surprised.

Simon grinned. "She found so many excuses to bring us together."

"Not that she needed to," William said. "To hear Margery tell it, Rosamond's been pining for you for years."

"Pining?" Robert asked.

William smirked. "Four years ago she named one of her puppies Simon."

"Well, whatever the reason, I'm glad I found her," Simon said. A year after they moved back to Holton, Simon had noticed that Rosamond seemed to appear any time he was alone. And he was alone often. He saw Henry every day but knew it was important for him to spend more time with Robert, so he took solitary rides or walks most afternoons. Or tried to. Rosamond always happened to be walking or riding on the same trails. They began talking every day, and soon laughing together every day. One morning, a whirlwind started in Simon's chest when Rosamond said his name. The little whirlwind soon became a maelstrom, and he spent every moment he could with her. She was everything he'd ever wanted. Kind, funny, supportive, sweet, and beautiful. He couldn't understand why anyone considered Margery the beauty of the family when Rosamond, with her wavy red hair, warm green eyes, and easy laugh stood beside her. Simon felt like a tree that had finally found its roots, and six months ago had proposed without even planning to. They were sitting beside the library fire playing with her dogs, and when she looked up and smiled he knew his heart was gone. He proposed that instant, and she accepted almost before he finished asking. The deep, loving bond he shared with Rosamond made him feel cherished in a way he'd never imagined. The joy of his life was to see her happy, which was easy, for all she wanted was to be at his side. Rosamond adored Henry and was eager to begin a new life with Simon, splitting their time between Ridgefield and a house her father had gifted them on the Penhollow grounds. So now Henry would have three loving homes to call his own. Four, if he counted Thornwood—which he did.

All of the men looked up as the door to the house

swung shut and Margery strolled into the yard. After a warm look at William she hurried to Robert's side. "Congratulations, Robert."

Relief flooded through him now that it was over. "What is it? How's Isabel? What is it?"

"A boy."

William clapped Robert on the back. "Another son!"

"And…" Margery said with a grin, getting the attention of all three men, "a daughter."

"Two?" Robert spluttered.

"Yes, two," Margery said, and laughed. William sidled up to her and put an arm around her shoulders. She smiled and presented her lips for a kiss, which William granted enthusiastically. A bit too enthusiastically, under the circumstances.

Simon coughed loudly, and they stepped apart.

Robert noticed nothing but stared at the house as though trying to see through the walls and catch a glimpse of Isabel and their babies.

"Congratulations, Robert," Simon said.

"And Isabel?" Robert asked, looking at a flushed Margery.

"Exhausted. She's asleep right now."

"May I see her?"

"Come up. I'll ask the midwife."

Halfway up the stairs, Margery stopped, and when Robert made to move past her she shifted so he couldn't.

He raised his hands. "Margery, *Please.*"

"I wanted a word with you alone."

"Now?" She truly was William's other half.

She shrugged. "Yes."

"I need to get to Isabel," he said urgently.

"I told you, she's sleeping. This will only take a

moment."

He put a hand on his hip and looked up at her. "Well?"

"I want to congratulate you again, and to say I'm happy things worked out for you and Isabel." She paused. "All those years ago, when I was acting like a cow, it wasn't about you. I'd have been like that with any man my father tried to marry me off to. William has always been the one for me." Margery gave him one of those radiant smiles she rarely bestowed on anyone but her husband.

Robert smiled. "I'm glad you two have been happy. But why are you telling me this *now*? I'm ready to leap over you to get to Isabel."

"I suppose because, now that your babies are born, it reminded me of beginnings. And as mad as it all was, my beginning with William was the same as yours and Isabel's. That May Day. But come, I won't keep you any longer."

"Thank you, Margery. All these years I thought it was because you'd never forgiven me about the fish pond."

She laughed and moved aside so they could walk upstairs together. He paced the hall outside Isabel's chamber while Margery checked on her.

After a few moments she, Jayne, Peg, Maria, and Mrs. Claremont streamed out of the room, each congratulating him in turn. He vaguely wondered just how many women were needed to deliver a baby, but put it out of his mind when Nell held the door open for him to enter.

"Congratulations," she said, grinning as she passed him on her way out.

He gave her a nod and a smile and practically ran into the room.

Verity placed a baby in the cradle, then looked up and gave Robert a wide smile. She came over and took his hand. "Here they are, finally," she said, tears in her eyes. "Congratulations."

"Thank you," he said, his eyes on Isabel.

"You must bring the whole family to Kerensly as soon as Isabel can travel."

"We will. Henry always enjoys seeing his cousins. John's been taking him fishing, and they sometimes allow little Emma to watch. Henry told me holding Miranda was good practice for when his brother comes," Robert said, laughing.

Verity grinned. "Now he'll have a brother *and* a sister to hold, and in a few months another cousin to play with." She ran a hand over her round stomach. She gestured toward the bed. "Isabel is having a well-deserved rest. She's exhausted after the births, but everything went smoothly. She and the babies are all perfectly healthy. I'll be back up in a while, but ring for Nell if you need anything sooner." After another peek at Isabel, she left the room.

Robert made his way to the bed, where Isabel lay propped up on pillows.

"Isabel," he whispered.

Her eyes fluttered open and she beamed at him. "Two babies. Our two. Have you seen them?"

"Not yet."

"There they are." She pointed to the cradle beside the bed.

Robert peeked inside. There they lay. His children. One with a shock of dark hair, the other delicate and fair.

His heart flew away from him in that moment and unexpected tears came to his eyes.

"May I hold them?"

"Yes, of course," Isabel said. "The dark-haired one is our son, the other our daughter."

Robert picked up the boy and gazed into his face, sure he saw shadows of himself there. He kissed his son's soft round cheek. After a few minutes, he handed him to Isabel and lifted his daughter out of the cradle. She was fair, and heavier than her brother. As Robert looked into her perfect face, she opened her deep blue eyes. She made sweet cooing sounds as her hands moved inside her blanket.

He took his daughter to the bed and sat beside Isabel. They sat in silence, each gazing at the baby in their arms.

"What will we call them?" Isabel asked.

"I haven't thought of it yet. I thought we had weeks before we needed names."

"I thought so, too. Your mother told me you and William were early. Peg said twins are rare and she's only delivered a few in her life. She did say they're often born earlier than expected."

"Perhaps we could name the boy for your father."

Isabel smiled softly. "He would have liked that. His middle name was Arthur. We'll name the girl after your mother."

"That will please her. Her middle name is Margaret."

"Arthur and Margaret Claremont."

"They're perfect," Isabel said, grinning. "Where's Henry?"

"He's with Edmund."

Isabel glowed as she gazed at the babies. "He'll

meet his brother and sister later."

"I have all I ever dreamed of," Robert said, bursting with pride as he looked at Isabel and their twins.

"How glad I am that I came to your house that day, all those years ago," Isabel said, taking his hand.

"May Day. A day for beginnings, and the beginning of our life together."

They shared a soft kiss, basking in the promise of the future.

Isabel yawned. "Oh, how tired I am. I must sleep."

Robert placed the babies in their cradle, where they went to sleep at once. He lay down in bed with Isabel and took her into his arms.

They had fought hard and come close to losing everything, but now, impossibly, they were together. The lost dreams had come true, the family they'd always wanted was theirs, and a life of love, unity, and joy stretched before them. At long last their interrupted journey began anew, promising to be more wonderful than they'd ever imagined. Here, safe in their cottage, they were finally home.

A word about the author...

Kate Ellington grew up in a small, woodsy town not far from the New England seacoast. She read her first historical romance at age eleven when a teacher challenged her to find a book in the library written by an author she'd never heard of. Thus began a lifelong love of love stories.

She currently resides in the Pacific Northwest with her delightful family and three cats. When not writing she can be found reading, baking, traveling, and spending time outdoors.

Thank you for purchasing
this publication of The Wild Rose Press, Inc.

For questions or more information
contact us at
info@thewildrosepress.com.

The Wild Rose Press, Inc.